CW01376660

The Best Intentions of Toller Burstock

By the same author

The Exile of Nicholas Misterton
The Reawakening of Edgar Porlock

The Best Intentions of Toller Burstock

Vance Wood

For Pam

Best wishes,

Vance Wood

21 July 2016

CONJUROR

First published in the UK 2016 by Vance Wood
www.vancewoodnovelist.co.uk

ISBN 978-0-9929613-4-3

Copyright © Vance Wood 2016

The right of Vance Wood to be identified as the author of this work has been asserted by him in accordance with the Copyright, Designs and Patents Act 1988.

All rights reserved. No part of this publication may be reproduced, stored in or introduced into a retrieval system, or transmitted, in any form, or by any means (electronic, mechanical, photocopying, recording or otherwise) without the prior written permission of the publisher. Any person who does any unauthorized act in relation to this publication may be liable to criminal prosecution and civil claims for damages.

This novel is entirely a work of fiction. The names, characters, with the exception of a few historical figures, and incidents portrayed in it are the work of the author's imagination.

1 3 5 7 9 8 6 4 2

Typeset by Ellipsis Digital Limited, Glasgow
Jacket design by Ian Cardwell
Printed and bound in Great Britain by Clays Ltd, St Ives plc

This book is sold subject to the condition that it shall not, by way of trade or otherwise, be lent, re-sold, hired out, or otherwise circulated without the publisher's prior consent in any form of binding or cover other than that in which it is published and without a similar condition including this condition being imposed on the subsequent purchaser.

For all those I love.

I would like to thank Debi and Ian at Ellipsis for their support in the production of this book, and I am eternally grateful to those who inspired me, in different ways, to write the story.

The Best Intentions of Toller Burstock

Chapter one.

It was not the best time of year for it, Toller knew, but it had to be done. Outside his cottage, snow spat at the windows, intimidating him, pushing him into what felt like an eviction. Furious wind intruded under the door where the wood had been rotting for months. The faggots by the hearth, piled in case circumstances had been different, would not now be burnt, and the heat shared. He had left things tidy, did not want folk thinking the worst of him when they broke in and discovered him gone. Taking with him dashed hopes, unborn memories, his leaving Pilsdon was necessary, and not the flight he had first thought it.

I must let her know, do things proper, he had said to himself. Time be when she might think better of me for the honesty.

The only two sheep he had not sold had disappeared. Even the red marbling of blood, seeping from their slit necks into the snow, was now covered with fresh flakes, his accomplices; he should leave no trace of himself, he had decided.

Pilsdon was beguiling. He guessed the road to Shave Cross, relying on his remembering certain trees, the curvature of the hedgerows. In his pocket was his key, a cold tool he would never use again. He put on a hat, tied a scarf round it to keep it in place, lifted one foot in front of the other, and sank up to his knees.

"That you, Toller Burstock?" he heard.

The voice was faint, had no owner in the blizzard.

“’Tis certain. Be you a ghost? Show yourself, and detain me not with your tricks.”

“’Tis only I,” said Forston Sampford. “Gone to clear the traps. Look ’ee ’ere.”

Sampford, a neighbour at the top of the hill, dangled two rabbits, knocked them together to illustrate how frozen they were.

“Then make haste, old man, before your knees lock, and you die a similar death.”

“You going somewhere, a day like this?”

“Everybody on their way some place,” muttered Toller, continuing his journey.

“Then God be with ’ee, Toller. We argued enough beout fussing over what be Providence.”

Toller kept close to the hedgerow to protect himself. In it, he saw a robin, a single flame.

“’Tas taken you to warm me, little redbreast, and to give me the strength to get to Shave Cross, which be a grey smudge on the horizon, yonder, if my eyes be true.” Toller’s beard was stiff with ice, and his coat was lost in the landscape. “’Tis as well my legs be young as my heart, as Shave Cross hab a-wandered off a spickle, be my reckoning.”

Soon, the farmhouse for which he had been looking came into view.

I will knock and give up what has been between us and is no more. Hepsy has made me a tramper, and she must know that she can now walk to the top of Pilsdon Pen beout fear of meeting me. She loves the vale from up there, and so must I put myself out of her sight.

With these thoughts justifying his last visit to Dugdale Farm, he knocked on the door with raw knuckles. One final word with Hepsy, he thought, and then ’tis done.

Hepsy Valence peeped at him through the window, and recognised his shape and size. It has to be father, she had first thought when she had heard the knocking. She always locked the door when her father was out in the fields. "Best to keep it shut," he had told her, "on account of gypsies. Hears stories about 'em." She guessed it was Toller. Now what be he a-doing here, this weather? she wondered, wrapping her red shawl around her shoulders, and touching her thick, black hair to make sure she was presentable.

"'Tis Toller?" she asked. His green eyes were just visible between his scarf and hat. "Will you come in? Father is out, bringing the sheep into the barn before they get trapped."

The icy blast made her withdraw a little behind the door. Toller looked at her red cheeks and black eyes.

"I won't, Hepsy, though 'tis kind."

"But the snow!" she protested. "Step just inside or we will perish."

Even now, with the pain she had inflicted still feeling like the kick of a horse, he wanted to protect her from the storm, so went in, and she shut the door behind him. The snow fell onto the flagstones, and disappeared. He wanted to knock the flakes off his coat, but the sooner he said his piece, the sooner he could leave. He did not show more of his face; she did not invite him closer to the fire.

"I have come to tell 'ee that I am leaving, that you will be free to walk up Pilsdon Pen, and look upon Marshwood Vale without fear of seeing me. 'Tis a dreadful day, as bad as there's ever been, these parts, but go I must, on account of the strong likelihood of us meeting by chance, and me being reminded of what might have been between us. There. Now I've said it, I'll be on my way."

He turned, and opened the door.

"You don't have to leave because of me. Pilsdon be your home," she cried.

Out in the blizzard, he took one last look at her, and, stepping into the horizontal, white blast, began to trudge towards Bridport.

She shut the door. On the floor was the puddle where he had

stood. The realisation that it was all that was left of him sent her to the window, but he had gone.

He's a good man, and though father thinks him beneath me, he told me of his parting with courtesy, and without a spickle of anger in his voice. 'Twasn't exactly the mellow tone of forgiveness, but 'twas sweet enough. And now I am alone biv only father for company, and perhaps two more months of winter's spite before he will take me to Lyme for a new dress, as he promised.

She fed the fire, sat as close to it as the heat would allow, thinking how Toller need not have come to tell her, how it had all gone as stale as bread left too long, till the silences were no longer signs of contentment but different visions of the future.

Toller rested, from time to time, and ate a morsel from his bag. There was some relief in the downward stretches, but uphill was a trial, especially in the exposed, wide bends, where snow had drifted and snuggled up, in smooth, high banks, to the hedgerows. Then he stumbled, could not easily stand again, and wondered how long it would take to be buried in it. Somehow, he found the will to continue, as he knew from his progress that, within an hour, he would be touching Bridport.

Trees gave him some protection, and it was in a lull of the wind's roar that he heard the cry for help. The voice expressed pain, desperation so great that Toller called back to give its owner some hope, reassurance that someone else knew he was there, and would seek help.

"Where are you?" called Toller.

He thought the reply came from the field to his left.

"My ankle be broken. Fetch help or I am finished."

"Raise your hand."

The injured man was in the middle of the field, the last before the sharp rise to Dottery, and the descent into Bridport. I cannot carry a grown man in this deep snow, judged Toller. Only a horse can save him. I must to Bridport, where I can get help.

"You must bide a while," Toller called. "You will need lifting onto a horse. Keep still, and be patient, and if the Lord be willing, you will be saved."

As much as he was able, Toller increased his pace, intent on saving the man whose relief at being found did not immediately become hope of surviving when the wind found fresh energy, and began to sculpt the snow into a barrow around him. With a massive effort, the man tied his handkerchief to his crook, which he had been using to prod the snow to find buried sheep. It had become obvious that he would lose many of his flock, but he had persevered, until he had twisted his ankle. Even above the growling of the wind, he had heard the crack of the bone.

If only I had listened to Hepsy! he lamented. And yet of all men 'tis Toller Burstock on whom my life depends, and now I must wait to see if he is a man of his word, for he would be justified in leaving me to die, 'tis certain. I have given him reason to hate me, yet he says he will save me.

So surprised had Toller been to hear a cry for help, and such were the direction and strength of the wind, that he had not, at first, recognised the gruffness of Ebenezer Valence, the man who had poisoned his daughter's ear with the notion that she deserved a richer, better man than a common hillside shepherd.

On the fringe of Bridport, the two lines of cottages huddled together, as if trying to keep themselves warm. The road was deserted. No child was playing in the snow. The coaching inn, Toller knew, would have a horse available. He himself was too exhausted to return to the field. What man, he wondered, would turn out on such a day to save another's life and risk his own?

In Bucky Doo, only the ghosts of long-gone soldiers run through by Boney's men, and now insensible to cold, braved the storm.

Toller entered the inn. Men smoking pipes had decided that being trapped there was preferable to being confined to their own homes, and looked up when they saw him.

"Come by this fire," called one, seeing that Toller had not the strength to shake himself down, "though take care not to get the hot aches, which tingle like a thousand pins a-pricking."

"A horse," gasped Toller. "A man has need of one, just past Dottery. He be stuck in the field on the right, towards Broadoak. He be like a rabbit snapped in a trap. Be there a man who will save him? A cart will not do, as the snow be deep. A man strong enough to lift another onto a horse be wanted. I fear the man might be dead already."

"Then no use for us to put ourselves at risk," said Barnabus Dibberford. "A dead man can't be helped no way."

The room went silent. The inn-keeper felt the tension. Some lowered their heads, a gesture of indifference, or fear that they, too, might become entombed if they volunteered.

"How long you been coming 'ere?" asked the inn-keeper of Barnabus.

"Why, all the years you been serving me, which be too many for my fingers to count, especially since one got scythed off five harvests ago, when young Cutty Stubbs, as he be now known, had too much cider, and mistook my finger for an ear of barley."

Barnabus laughed, but the mood had changed at Toller's news, his bedraggled appearance, and urgent tone.

"Who'll go? There be a horse in your yard?" asked Toller. "Every second be important. Seen two rabbits frozen in their traps. Don't take long to stiffen up, this weather."

"Then why don't *you* go?" said Jude Broadwindsor.

"There be a horse, all right, but 'taint right to send this man" – here, the inn-keeper looked at Toller for a name, and Toller gave it – "Toller, out again. Come, sit down. Miles Yondover, you be strong, and not so piddled as the others. You go rescue the poor soul, and there shall be one free pot of cider every day, for a month!"

Miles' blond hair reached his shoulders, and his muscles bulged like windfall apples in a sack. The inn-keeper had chosen well, for

Miles loved a challenge, to lift stooks, and sculpt mounds with them.

"Then if there be a cape and a hat fit to keep out the snow, I shall go," offered Miles, coming forward. "Prepare this man some soup and a bowl for the one I brings back, and some bacon and tatties for me, for I shall need spadefuls when I return."

"The man be called Ebenezer Valence," said Toller, "and 'tis quicker to take him to Dugdale Farm where he lives. His ankle be hurt bad, and his daughter will worry if he don't return today."

"Then show me your horse, and I shall be gone."

Toller nodded his gratitude, and fell to the floor like a tree hacked and pushed over.

When he awoke, he did not recognise the room in which he was lying in bed. His mouth was dry, and as he tried to get up, he fell back, too weak to do anything. Downstairs, Biddy, the inn-keeper's wife, heard the noise of the bed moving on the floorboards, and went to see what had happened.

"Why, you alive after all!" she cried.

Toller quickly covered himself with his blanket.

"I been dead?" he asked, not fully awake enough to understand his circumstances.

"You been at the signpost, scratching your head, 'tis certain. Two days you been a-argumenting biv the angel who came for you. Seems she now gone, and you here to stay. Well, as long as 'tis judged so by the Lord, who himself seems confused betimes."

Slowly, Toller retraced his last steps: goodbye to Hepsy, Ebenezer, alive yet waiting in a white coffin, and Miles riding to rescue him.

"What happened?"

"The feber. You had a feber as hot as a furze fire, but 'tis now doused enough for breakfast."

"But Ebenezer. Be he saved? Miles is returned safely?"

"No one knows. The snow just beginning to melt, and 'tis

running off the hills biv so much mud that the cows and sheep, if any be left, bill be stuck up to their udders."

So, thought Toller, Miles has not returned, and if he has died on account of my wanting to save the life of a man who hates me, then 'tis a shame the angel did not drag me with her. Nay, I would have gone willingly, such was my foolishness. I should have left Ebenezer there.

"Will I get to Dorchester?"

The inn-keeper's wife peered out of the window.

"Hard to say, what biv all the hills a-rising and a-falling, and a-twisting and a-turning like a giant adder squeezing the life out of the land. Anyway, why you so keen to get to Dorchester?"

"Work. I be starting again. Perhaps, I'll get me a job on the train. Shepherding's all I know, but Pilsdon I must leave behind."

The inn-keeper's wife left him with the news that there would be a curling or two of bacon if he wanted to come down.

His legs trembled, at first, and he felt light-headed, as if someone had stolen into the room and emptied his skull, so that it felt almost detached from his body.

Downstairs, the inn had the air of a place enlivened by comradeship and then subdued by the reluctant departure of the protagonists.

"How long will it take me to get to Dorchester?" asked Toller.

The inn-keeper replied, "You get there on foot, 'twill be a miracle. Coach due mid-day. Seen nothing of it while you been upstairs. Might come, might not. 'Tis the way of things when winter be all grumpety."

Toller ate, slowly, at first, his appetite tricked by the bacon's smell, then more quickly, till he felt almost recovered.

"Then the coach it'll be or no."

When it arrived, it was late, but Toller climbed into it, and soon fell asleep.

At Dorchester, he woke to a rough shaking of his arm. The coachman was saying, "Wake 'ee, young man, or you'll be soon at

Weymouth, when 'twould be a pretty penny more. Dorchester, you said, and that's where we be," when Toller's eyes opened.

Dorchester, too, had been smothered in snow, which was now melting. What few people were in the street were placing their feet carefully, knowing from experience the treachery of ice hidden under water.

Toller looked about him. Only once had he been there before: when his parents had taken him to see a sick grandparent. Grandfer Burstock had been just a faint, pale face, lying in the dark. Deaf, he had looked up at the ceiling, wailing to go. All that way, we've come, Toller remembered thinking, and he can't even hear us. Toller's father had sent him outside so he would not hear the death rattle, and Toller had just stood in the street, leaning against the wall, throwing stones at pigeons strutting in front of him.

In his bag, his shepherd's smock was tightly rolled up. He had left his crook in Pilsdon, but it would have helped him to stagger through the drifts. He was hungry. Where was an inn to feed him? Ahead was the church, and there the door was sure to be open.

As he made his way, he saw a woman coming towards him. She was stooping, her bonnet hiding her face. She wanted to hurry, but there was caution in her step.

"Begging your pardon, but be there an inn nearby?" Toller asked. "I am newly come and be a stranger, these parts."

The woman looked up. In her face were lines of anxiety etched so deeply that Toller feared his question had alarmed her. Her lips made to speak, but no answer came, so Toller repeated his question, and reassured her that he meant her no harm.

"I know no one, these parts, either," she said, at last.

"Pray, don't upset yourself," said Toller, seeing her tears. "'Tis passing strange, this place, to a newcomer, but soon the snow and ice will be gone, and the cold air will become warm breath upon our cheeks, which be numb."

"I am sorry. I have slipped and slided all the way from Tolpuddle, and am weary. I fear that I shall not survive tonight when the slush becomes ice again."

"You have nowhere to go? A Dorset winter should lock us all indoors."

"I could not bide in Tolpuddle, nor anywhere folk knows what happened. And now I cannot look upon any knoll where we sat for fear of sweet remembrance of what was and cannot never be more."

You talk in riddles, girl, thought Toller.

"Whatever 'twas that sent you here will pass, though all our hearts weigh heavier with pain."

"Do a man know what 'tis like? You cannot feel what I endure, for I have been made a fool of at the altar by a man who had said he would love no other. And so I must find a place to hide from the world, as Tolpuddle will whisper whenever they see me. I have fled for fear I shall bump into him in the fields, at harvest-time."

"Then you and I be matched, for I, too, know the sour taste of a refusal, which be the tartest of gooseberries. Come, let us find an inn, and swap our tales in earnest, and there, in the telling, be the honey to take away the bitter."

"'Tis kind," said the young woman, "and I accept, for I can suffer no greater shame than my loss, and you, too, know the cut of it. I be Mattie Venn."

"And I be Toller Burstock."

Together, Mattie and Toller looked for an inn, and when The King's Arms came into view, Toller said, "Be my sister, and 'twill prevent the staring."

"Come, then, brother Toller, for though the sun smiles, the air be still the morning's scowl, and my body feels like 'tas been lying in the grave."

Chapter two.

Miles set off and quickly realised how treacherous the snow was. His horse began to falter on the long slope up to Dottery, and Miles' words of encouragement acquired a note of desperation before he reached the top. He turned left, and was briefly protected from the ferocious wind by the towering banks and hedges. There, the snow was not so deep, but when the road began to fall again, the horse hesitated, so Miles dismounted, and led it by its reins, in the hope that it would be able to maintain its balance.

He is in the field on the right, near Broadoak, he remembered the man saying. At the bottom of the hill, the wind once again began to whip him so viciously that he had to cover his face with his gloved hands, and peep through his fingers. All he could see, however, was a sea of white with no horizon. Even if he had been able to open the gate held fast by the snow near its top, he would have sunk so far into it that he would have perished.

"If Ebenezer Valence be here, then death will have frozen him till the thaw, when worms will be hungry. No, I must on to his daughter at Pilsdon. She will be a-fretting, and 'tis best to let her know that I, at least, tried to save her father. 'Tis a cruel winter, this. Besides, he might yet have called one last time upon his strength to save himself, and only by going to his cottage will I know the truth," he said to his horse. "'Tis a deathly day, and hard enough for a man like me with two good legs, let alone one with a broke."

He looked again for a sign – a raised hand, perhaps, or a footprint or two not quite smothered – that Ebenezer might still be alive, but saw none, and made his slow way to Dugdale Farm.

The farmhouse wore a thick, white bonnet. Miles sniffed. Even in a wind moaning and screeching like a thousand tormented ghosts, the sweet smell of blazing oak could be discerned. If 'tis not Dugdale Farm, then 'tis one where I must stay anyway, as my legs be as stiff as fence-posts, and my fingers so numb I know not if they still belong to my hand.

Indeed, he felt nothing as he knocked on the door. He had left his horse in the barn, where the wind could not lash it, and it had lain on the straw Miles had raked into a hasty bed.

"Father!" cried Hepsy, as she opened the door.

"Forgive me, Miss," gasped Miles, stumbling inside and shutting the door, "but my rudeness bill prevent my death, which bill have come about on account of your father's bad leg. That is, if you be the unfortunate daughter of Ebenezer Valence."

The word *unfortunate* was a warning that he brought no good news of her father's whereabouts.

"Why say you *unfortunate*? Bad leg? You have seen my father? Pray, let me know how 'tis that you are one with such a doom-laden message."

"I have seen only oceans of snow paddled in by no fox or human."

"But how came you to know of his bad leg?"

"Miss. Valence, may I sit by your fire a moment, before I explain my presence here? I am but a frail spectre, though once a strong, and fear I shall not have breath sufficient unless I thaw. Have you a morsel and a cup to save me?"

Hepsy looked at him. He need not have come, she realised, so took pity.

"Remove your coat and boots, and come warm them and yourself by the fire, which has been blazing since the storm started, and

I will fetch you bread and cheese, and tatty and onion soup, which be all I have. The sooner comforted, the sooner you will give me the telling of your journey, which will serve me not a spickle of comfort, I fear, but news as sharp as the bitter blast besieging this battered house."

While Hepsy went upstairs to find some of her father's clothes – he and Miles were the same height, Ebenezer heavier – Miles tried to control his chattering teeth, hoped that he had found shelter in time to prevent his premature death. A man I know not lies in a field, my place of work, too, and I die by his fireside. 'Tis enough to set a labourer a-thinking of the queerness of how things turn out, when normally there baint time.

Hepsy watched him eat, saw in his shaking hand the spoon wobbling, heard it rattling on the bowl. His numb lips did not feel the soup's heat peel their skin off, and around his feet was a widening puddle of water.

"When you've done, you must dry yourself, and put on these. Though they be father's, they will fit, I think. You will catch a fever if you stay in those. I will go upstairs. Call me when you're done. Then you must tell me the tale of your journey: why you came, father's lot."

When she had gone, Miles put down his bowl, and removed his sodden clothes. Closer to the fire, he dried himself. Upstairs, despite her anxiety, Hepsy imagined the restless light from the flames on the stranger's naked body.

He wrung the water out of the clothes, draped them on a chair, which he placed near the fire. Soon, steam arose from them. Dry, he knew then that he was safe, but in a dead man's clothes. Ebenezer was gone, surely, if the stranger at the inn had been right about the broken leg. Only when the snow had melted more would he know for sure.

"Thank you," Miles called. "They fit."

Hepsy came down slowly, as if wanting to delay his story. In those clothes, 'tis as if father lives yet. The snow blocks all paths, swaps landmarks. But father has gone, 'tis certain. He would have been back by now.

Trembling, she said, "Tell me how you came to look for him, and give me your worst, as you see it."

"A man – I know not his name – came to the inn, and said someone needed help and a horse, the fellow having snapped his leg like a dried twig. The bringer of the bad news had not the strength to carry him as well as himself; only a horse would do, the snow being too deep. He told me to take the man to you, that you would be a-fretting for him, but as I gets to the field, which looks as wide as Chesil Beach, there be no sign of him, on account of all living things being smothered. Miss. Valence, 'taint certain, but no man can survive for long in that. Only when the thaw comes will we know."

Hepsy burst into tears of frustration, clung to the hope that somehow her father might have found shelter, and decided to wait till it was safe to return to the field. Was he not hardy? Had he not slept out, during lambing, endured rain on exposed hillsides, gone without food so that he could help the ewes deliver their lambs?

Miles said, "'Tis once in a lifetime, this snow, though Dorset takes its share, I know, and 'taint for us to ask why, but for God to say who lives and dies in it. Thank 'ee for these clothes, though I hopes they don't cause 'ee distress, them being your father's."

Hepsy dried her eyes, took a deep breath. Her weeping in front of a man who had risked his own life for her father was no reward, scant gratitude.

"You can stay till 'tis safe. There be a fire made up in his room. 'Twill last till morning. What be your name?"

"Miles Yondover."

Hepsy had heard of the Yondovers. Her father had, once or twice, mentioned them, but she could not remember what he had said about them.

"Yondover been on father's tongue, a time or two."

"You sure about me staying?"

"I am. No one near to go a-looking through these windows. Besides, when the thaw comes, I'll need you to search the field with me."

Miles repaid her kindness by chopping wood in the barn, where he fed his horse. The morning after his arrival, the storm exhausted itself, so he was able to wade through the drifts without being bullied by the wind, the axe heavy enough in his hand to help him keep his balance. A good night's sleep had revived him, and Hepsy, mindful that bright sunlight hides not the ravages of a troubled sleep, had brushed and arranged her hair, applied a caress of rouge to her lips and cheeks, and put on a clean dress and boots, which she was reluctant to cover with a coat. Miles noticed her effort, smiled, and said, "Look, the snow has stopped, though the thaw yet tarries."

His face had begun to glow with the first swings and thuds of the axe. Hepsy noticed the faggots, which had been trimmed neatly, in the hearth. He had risen early, was someone used to hard work, and unafraid of danger. Toller had not been such a man; he would have sought permission, asked her how she wanted them stacking.

"Too soon to find father?" she asked.

"See," he said, showing her the snow-line on his trousers.

"I fear he has gone," she said. "He would have returned by now."

"Let us wait. There be one thing: me, here. 'Tis what you want?"

She nodded. He had come to help, one way or another. No one else was there.

"Stay till we know."

Miles felt the power her reliance on him gave him. In bed, he had pictured her, on the other side of the wall. So close to a woman he had never been, save the time he had attempted futile fumblings with a Bridport girl, who had beckoned him close, because she knew she could, and then had pushed him away. "Don't you dare!"

she had warned him, when he had tried to kiss her. "These lips be saved for the man who will marry me, and he be one father has said must not be a labourer or a journeyman."

Miles had found himself momentarily tempted to knock on Hepsy's door, and ask if he could slip into her bed, but the pronouncement of Ebenezer came between them, warned him not to be so stupid. What could such a man not do if he could wield power from under three feet of snow?

During the next two days, the snow began to melt, and Miles felt he could not justify remaining at Dugdale Farm without attempting to find Ebenezer.

"I will come with you," Hepsy declared.

"Stay here. I must take the horse. 'Tis too much for a woman."

But Hepsy would be kept from her father no longer.

"I, too, have a horse, and not all women are as feeble as you think."

A scowl accompanied her barbed tone.

"As you wish."

The snow felt and sounded different. There was no wind, just the gushing of water into ditches from higher ground.

"Here on the right be where the man said he was."

Miles remembered clearly Toller saying Ebenezer was in the field, on the right.

"'Tis covered biv snow."

"Side by side, we shall walk, and then we shall find him. The snow gives way to the sun. We can see the soil at the top. Come, let us begin."

They walked from hedge to hedge, using hoof-prints to make sure they did not miss a patch. Once, Hepsy's horse trod on something, and lurched, and Miles dismounted. Hepsy's heart pounded at the prospect of finding her father. Miles bent, felt the obstacle, the familiar shape, with both hands. Looking away, Hepsy asked, "'Tis him?"

"A sheep."

Hepsy gasped. If the field was empty bar dead sheep, then there was still a chance he might be alive.

"Then he must be elsewhere. Maybe someone rescued him, gave him shelter, is nursing him, this very minute."

"But his leg. The man said your father's leg was bad."

Miles did not want to shoot down her soaring hopes, but the man had been clear: Ebenezer had been in agony in the snow, and could not move.

"A day or two more. Give it a bit longer. It's possible we have missed him."

Miles hung his head.

"Folks'll worry about me."

"I want you to stay with me till we find him."

"I must go now but will return when the fields are nearly clear, and the thaw has put things back in their place. Those who know I came will search for me, and it must not seem to certain others that I have stayed for the wrong reasons. 'Twill protect *your* reputation, too, for folks, these parts, chaunt what they do not understand, and their notes be flat or sharp, to give their song an unfamiliar story."

Hepsy looked at the field. Father is not there, she reflected. Miles and I have punctured together the snow. Till I find a corpse, I will believe him alive.

"Go then, Miles, and thank 'ee for your help. You are expected back; let them not think the worst."

Miles began his journey, and Hepsy watched him till he left her sight.

When Miles entered the inn, Barnabus was just finishing his first drink of the day. Jude was snoring, head on the table, lips quivering. The inn-keeper had allowed them to sleep there, though thought the weather now kind enough to allow them to go home.

"Why 'tis Miles Yondover!" exclaimed the inn-keeper. "You

found the unfortunate soul? We thought you'd done yourself a mischief, and had gone. Three days we aint seen you. You just back?"

"A plate, sir, if you please, though I don't rightly recollect whether 'twas soup I was promised, or tatties and bacon, or even all three, but 'tis certain that I be starving and have had a wasted journey, on account of the man with the broken leg not being in the field on the right," said Miles.

"I baint one to break my word, so I say 'twas all three 'ee were promised, but 'twas definite the man be in the field, his leg a-hanging by a thread of muscle. The man who told us, and who hab gone on to Dorchester, was adamant. We all recalls how he came in all a-desperate, and how you volunteered to take the injured fellow to his daughter, who would have been pulling her hair out biv worry, at Dugdale Farm."

"I don't rightly remember the volunteering, but 'tis true that his daughter was all a lather, and that she remained so when we searched the field and found nought but a frozen sheep."

Jude woke up with a start, as if he had heard a gun-shot, and rubbed his eyes.

"Why, if 'taint Miles Yondover. We'd given you up for dead. Where you been?" he asked.

"Dugdale Farm."

Barnabus winked to the inn-keeper.

"You been on your own with the daughter of the fellow you been trying to rescue?"

"She invited me to stay, the weather being so harsh. The storm was all a-whistling and a-whirling. I would have died, too, if I hadn't taken shelter there," explained Miles.

"'E dead? But you hab not found his body," pointed out Barnabus.

"No, but in the field on the right was where the man said Ebenezer Valence was. We walked the length and breadth of it, Hepsy and I, and he was not there. 'Tis certain."

"Then he been carried off by some eagle," said Jude, now fully awake. “They say there be one, in particular, with wings as wide as Chesil, a beak as keen as a cutthroat razor, and talons strong enough to lift a full-grown sheep.”

Miles withdrew into a corner, to wait for the promised food. When it was possible, he would return to Dugdale Farm, to help Hepsy look again. Then he would win her favour. So close he had been to her, and she had made an effort with her appearance, trusted him in her father’s clothes and bed.

Meanwhile, she had returned to the farmhouse, having neither hope nor grief in her heart. She went to her father’s bedroom. Miles had left his impression on the covers. In the air, she smelt his dampness, the fire now white ashes. I must make everything as it was, for when father returns. Me being idle will make his death seem a fact rather than a suspicion, she thought. So she made up the fires; the house had cooled while she had been searching with Miles.

Further up Pilsdon Pen, Forston Sampford was talking to himself while tying up his boots. Loneliness had bred this habit. He had shaken his fist at the storm, had hung some frozen rabbits retrieved from his traps, that very morning, in front of his fire, and soon he had been able to rip off their skin, and drop them into a pot with a turnip. His sparse, white hair stood up at all angles, giving him the appearance of someone who lived somewhere between madness and antagonism.

He had to find comfort, and his spirits lifted when he stepped outside.

“’Why, ’taint no more than a spickle, this snow, and Old Sojer needs a stretch. I will to Bridport, where I hab my usual business to attend!” His hoarse chuckle revealed rotting stumps. He jangled the coins in his pocket, spat on the palm of his hand, and tried to flatten his unruly hair. “’Tas been a while now, and Forston Sampford is ready. ’Tis certain.”

His horse bore him grudgingly along the Bridport Road. Sampford shielded his eyes. At the foot of the climb to Dottery, he glanced to his left. A sheep's head poked above the snow. Motionless, upright, it stared straight ahead, and Sampford waded over to it.

"'Tis a sculpture," he muttered, "and there'll be others. Keep me through winter, it will, as there be no raddling mark or branding on it."

Sampford stumbled on another sheep, walked in a circle, and discovered several more, huddled together, all statues. Then he saw it, the hand reaching up. He blinked, cried out, and stepped back, almost fell into the snow. The fingers seemed to want to clutch something, wave to someone who might help. With his bare hands, Sampford burrowed for the rest of the corpse.

"'Tis Toller, for sure," he said. "Went out into it like the fool he be. And now he's gone." But soon, Sampford saw that it was Ebenezer Valence. "Why, 'taint Toller, after all!"

Sheep had gathered around Ebenezer, as if trying to keep him warm, till he could be found. His eyes had rolled upwards, till only their whites could be seen, and his mouth was stopped with snow. So still, thought Sampford. Like church marble.

Sampford said, "Ebenezer, 'tis I, Forston Sampford, your neighbour. Be you alive? Speak or make a sign."

When there was no reply, Sampford searched Ebenezer's pockets. There was no money, but Sampford took the gold pocketwatch, and chuckled.

"No use, no more, for it, Ebenezer. You won't begrudge me this for all your years of cursing and argumenting. 'Tis a just repayment. Worth a lot, this. But I aint heartless enough to not tell your daughter you be found."

Excited by his discovery, he turned back to Dugdale Farm.

Hepsy cried, "And 'tis certain it be father?"

"Knowed him all my life. He be in the last field, on the left, before the sweat to Dottery."

"The left? Not the right?"

“Well, ’twould be the right if I be coming *down* the hill.”

Hepsy bit her lip, remembered what the man had told Miles at the inn: the field on the right. But did he mean going to or coming back from Bridport? Oh, Miles! she cried within. Right be on the left, coming back from going. We might have saved him.

Inside Sampford’s pocket, the watch, too, had stopped, not having been wound recently.

Old Sojer stirred.

“Let me show you, Miss. Now Toller hab left, you only got me to help. Up onto the horse now, and you’ll be safe in my arms.”

“Thank ’ee, sir, but I shall take my horse, and trust to Providence, which be my way of doing things, now I aint got father to make my decisions for me.”

“Just like your father, you be.”

She put on her coat, locked the door, brushed past Sampford, and set off for the field on the left.

“’Twas kind of ’ee, Miles, but a man need to know his left from his right. Come, Delilah. Take me to father. The sooner found, the sooner laid to rest.”

“Yes, you ride, girl, though I shall call again soon, and save me a trip to Bridport, and keep pennies in my pocket.”

Chapter three.

In The King's Arms, a man crouched in front of the fire, feeding it small faggots he had fetched from an outside store. From behind, he appeared to be warming himself, so Toller coughed, to alert him to their presence. Mattie hung back, preferring to trust her newly discovered brother to manage the formalities of their arrival. The squatting man looked over his shoulder, nearly lost his balance, and leaned to one side to gain a better view of Mattie, but she moved behind Toller.

"The day is raw, despite the sun," opened the man.

"'Tis certain," replied Toller, "and such a raw whets the appetite of two travellers in need of hot food and a table near a fire."

The man stood up, shuffled towards the grandfather clock in the corner of the room, and squinted at it.

"'Tis time Cook were doing in the kitchen, I believe. Pie? Tatties? An oyster or two?"

"Enough to save our lives," smiled Toller, taking out a coin, and offering it.

The man leaned to one side again, inviting an introduction of Mattie, as he pocketed the money.

"This be my sister. Come, dear, and warm yourself by the fire, though not too close, so you don't get hot aches."

She took his hand, realising that she must play her part if they were to be served. The man lit a straw spill, and held it, with a trembling hand, to the candle on the table, and Toller and Mattie looked at each other through its feeble light.

When the man brought them cups of hot chocolate, he declined the offer of another coin, saying that such generosity was unwarranted, that good service was in his nature, and that he was never one to take advantage of his customers.

Toller and Mattie sipped from their cups, and felt awkward, each waiting for the other to tell their story of unrequited love.

"Do 'ee think the man suspects we aint kin, on account of us looking so different?" Mattie asked. "I do wonder."

"'Tis Nature's way, betimes. All trees have leaves. Some are wide and strong, as be the oak, while others be pale and thin, like the birch," reassured Toller. "Don't make either less or more a tree."

"'Tis so, I know, but I am nervous. We are unknown to each other, one minute, yet are become brother and sister, the next. 'Tis passing strange."

"Here come our plates. Smile if you can, and 'twill quell his suspicion and curiosity, which have caused him to look at you oddly."

When it came, the smile was unconvincing; Toller thought it warned more of the onset of biliousness than joy at the prospect of nourishment.

Cook had excelled herself: steak and kidney and oyster pie shared the plate with tatties and turnips coated in a thick gravy, in which onions had found a home.

When the first pangs of hunger had been subdued, Toller said, "Come, Mattie. Tell your story, and then I shall tell mine, and let us see if the listening to another's woes puts our suffering so far into the distance that we gain the strength to live as happily as we once did."

Mattie hesitated, as if she thought that revisiting scenes in which she had sung with joy, then cried with sorrow, might be a trial so severe that she must ask to be released from their pact. Then, realising that no one else was offering to help, she brightened again, and said, "Let us finish eating, first, for the pie be excellent, and 'twill spoil."

So they ate, till the last spot of gravy had been scraped from the plate.

Feeling stronger, Mattie began her history, which she embellished not a jot, for fear that a colourful description of the man who had spurned her on her wedding day might invoke her wrath again.

During the course of her account, Toller nodded when he recognised how she must have felt, and wanted to ask her questions, to try to understand more fully her plight. At first, Mattie answered, but became uncomfortable when she felt a question too intrusive. Then Toller apologised, and let her continue.

"So you see how cruelly I have been used," Mattie concluded. "But I baint the first, and 'tis certain I won't be the last. 'Tis ever thus, though it hurt like a horse's kick."

"You have been wronged almost beyond endurance. And he has not spoken to you since?"

"Not spoken, nor even sent a word. 'Tis certain he a-upped and gone off all draped in his excuses and cowardice. But, Toller, dear brother, the sharing with you has been a balm to my wound. Let me now listen to how you came to be in Dorchester, so that you, too, will be soothed."

So Toller began, and, during the telling, Mattie began to cry. Her tears hung from her eyelashes, and splashed onto the table, as she leaned forward to squeeze his hand.

"Brother of mine, she is not worthy of your love and goodness. In time, when others have wooed and used her, she will realise that her father was wrong, that rich don't necessarily mean honest and loyal."

Ebenezer. Was he dead? Toller wondered. Had Miles Yondover rescued him before the cold had encased him in ice and snow? Toller knew that he himself had done what any man would have done: tried to help. And if Ebenezer be dead, then Hepsy will be free to choose her own husband.

The waiter collected the plates, and said, "Then you be still hungry, judging by these plates. Will 'ee take a slab of blue vinney?"

"We will, indeed," said Toller.

They ate silently, aware that, though they had much in common, they would go their separate ways, shortly.

"Thank 'ee," said Mattie. "I was hungry, but have not much money, and will need to find a room, which will cost me a pretty penny. I need to leave these parts, and go where they don't know me, where I can start again."

Toller put his hand into his pocket, and took out a key.

"Here, sister. Take this. 'Twill open my cottage door at Pilsdon. There you may live, free of rent, as long as you wish. I cannot return till I have gained my self-respect again, and turned myself into a better man. Go on, girl. 'Tis yours."

Mattie looked at the key, and was sorely tempted, but acceptance of his offer would mean some obligation to him, in the future, and she was not sure she could trust a man again, for a long time.

"But I'd feel all of a cuckoo in your nest, and folk'd talk," argued Mattie. "'Tis kind, but I cannot accept."

Toller thrust the key towards her, and nearly knocked over the candle.

"Baint a sister allowed to live in her brother's house? That be all you need to say: that you be a long-lost sister. I will write you a note of permission, which will cut out the tongues of any who besmirch your good nature. Now, take it. Farms always need milkmaids. You milked before?"

Mattie laughed, showed her hands, and Toller saw the calluses, the broken nails.

"Cows been known to jostle for these!"

"Bridport baint far from my house, on a horse, and there be

maids' work in Marshwood Vale. Take the coach to Bridport. There you can ride a cart to Pilsdon."

"Never rode a horse in my life!"

"Time for everything, sister. The cottage be yours, and I shall not return till this day, one year's hence. I shall not take no, girl, as I don't want mice and spiders to take over. Keep it neat and tidy. Get a cat. I shall send you a bit of money, every month."

"But –"

"'Twon't be a fortune, but enough for a shard of blue vinney, Sundays."

"And when you returns? What will become of me?"

"That be for you to decide."

"And if I wish to leave before next winter makes us white statues? And the key, then?"

"There is a tree behind the cottage. Leave it in the knotted hole, and cover it with leaves or moss."

Mattie looked at the key, a token of friendship from a man known only for the duration of little longer than a meal. There was nothing else implied; she was free to leave whenever she wanted. And Pilsdon: a safe haven, hers for a year. There she would heal herself; not forget, but not recall the shame, the sense of abandonment, with such pain.

"Then I will accept your offer, and, in a year, each of us will feel better about the world. But what will you do?"

"I will make something of myself. Been a shepherd too long. I sold my sheep, and have a spickle of money. I will stay here tonight, but 'tis a few hours to Pilsdon, so you must go soon, as, though the snow be melting, it hardens and upends us, in the evening."

The waiter provided a pen, ink, and paper, and Toller wrote the note of permission. Blowing on the letters formed by his unsteady hand, Toller winked and smiled.

"In a year, sister," he said.

"In a year, brother, shall I see you again."

"'Tis certain."

And then Toller was alone with his thoughts again. Today I will rest, and tomorrow I begin to make myself the sort of man Ebenezer would have wanted as a son-in-law.

Later, when he returned to The King's Arms to secure a room for the night, he found the waiter gone, and was greeted instead by a man in more formal attire. Though the man's collar was not clean, and had not been put on properly, he bore himself upright, as one befitting a figure of authority. He looked disdainfully at Toller, and then at the trail of puddles on the floor, unaware that the establishment had already fed him. Toller felt conspicuous on his own, and wished Mattie had still been with him.

"You have a room for the night, sir?"

The man looked him up and down. Toller's coat, though not the one he wore when working in the fields of Marshwood Vale, had a button missing, and his shepherd's hat betokened a class of man not usually served in such a place. A day labourer or a journeyman, probably, with a penny or two saved for when work in the field was impossible. Toller knew what that look meant, though he had never been cut by it before. This was the first time he had wanted to stay in an inn, and he was about to be disappointed.

"No rooms here," answered the man dismissively, turning his back on him.

"I have eaten here within this last hour," added Toller, in the hope that this might make him more acceptable.

The man stopped and, without turning, said, "All the rooms are taken."

"Then can you recommend another inn?"

Still without turning, the man said, "The Raddleman."

"And 'tis for men like me who smell of sheep?"

The man turned; Toller had surprised him. Usually, there were no raised voices, only polite conversation, maybe the odd guffaw by a corn merchant, his tongue loosened by too much drink.

"I've no idea what you mean. The Raddleman may have a room. You asked a question, and that was my answer; no more, no less."

As he left, Toller said, "I won't always stink of the fields, I won't, and when I returns here, one day, I'll see you and your airs off. Let me have just one last look at your face." The man took a step back at this escalation of the tension between them. "O'er-plump in your cheeks, which be two dumplings; collar not white or starched enough to belong to a gentleman; and a manner as welcoming as a Dorset blast. 'Tis nearly Christmas, and there will come a day when our places will switch, and you will beg for shelter from me."

The man was visibly shaken by Toller's eloquence, which was at odds with his attire. Toller's ire was unexpected, and his assumption that people like him were welcome was one not normally made. As he left, Toller slammed the door. The Raddleman, he thought. I'm not too proud when needs must. I'll have slept in worse places.

Meanwhile, in Bridport, the darkness discouraged Mattie from finding someone to take her to Pilsdon. In the coach, she had decided to find a room at an inn, and enquired of a man if he knew a suitable place.

"I'll take you there, myself. 'Tis mainly a good, honest inn, with plain fare and a tolerable bed. 'Taint often you sees a lady in there, but take no notice of there being only men, a-supping. Inn-keeper got a wife, though she stays in the kitchen when the pipes are a-flourish, or a belly needs filling," said her travelling companion.

She thanked him for his trouble, and though she was nervous about entering alone, she kindly refused his offer of privately introducing her to the inn-keeper. Strengthened by the knowledge that, the next day, she would have her own cottage, and that her daily needs would be met by her guardian angel, she entered. All eyes turned to her, as they would have, had it been one of the regulars. She made her way to the counter, holding her breath as she cut through the fug.

The inn-keeper smiled, leaned forward to hear her request for a room; in the background, the men had resumed their conversation, and her voice was quiet. He invited her to step through to meet his wife, who would show her to her room, and bring her a plate of stew.

"You in trouble, girl?" asked the inn-keeper's wife. "Late for a lone woman to be looking for a bed."

"No, I baint. Tomorrow I must go to Pilsdon, to live in my brother's house. I shall need a ride there, but the snow baint so bad, now winter's tantrums be over. 'Tis almost a shame to see the snow die and drip, so all the ground be muddy and glimmy."

"'Tis certain. Who be your brother, if you don't mind me asking?"

Mattie flinched. Telling lies did not come naturally to her.

"Toller Burstock."

"'Taint a man who come in 'ere. Know all who live, these parts, I do."

"Not a drinking man," made up Mattie.

In the morning, Mattie rose early, wanting to arrive at her cottage as soon as possible. She ate the fried potatoes and eggs with relish, and the landlady told her that she had arranged for a man called Jude to take her.

"A sleepy head, 'tis certain, but he has a cart and horse, and as he could not pay for his drink, last night, I says he must pay by taking you. Lanes will be clotty, and if these be all the clothes you have, then I suggests you buy more. He will be here at nine, and 'twill be only a sore head which bill rob him of a civil tongue."

"How much will he want? I have a spickle but must pay you, and 'twill be January afore my brother sends me more."

"The ride be free, as Pilsdon be where cows, sheep and birds go, and not wide coaches."

"Then you are kind, and, one day, Mattie Venn will repay you."

"Go, girl, and get ready, for Jude will not be late, on account of him knowing that if he lets me down, he shall not set one foot over the threshold again!"

Instinctively, Mattie leaned forward and hugged her.

"Thank 'ee so much."

"Go on, girl, and no tears, mind!"

When he came, Jude touched his hat, the brim of which he had tilted to avoid the glare of the slush, and to prevent Mattie seeing the red whites of his eyes.

"Pilsdon?" he croaked.

"'Tis an empty cottage I must find, the one just after Dugdale Farm, but no higher, though there be one there."

"Empty?"

"Bar my brother's furniture and personal possessions."

"And what be your name?" continued Jude, clicking his horse into motion.

He had wedged a bale of straw in the cart for Mattie, who lurched at the horse's first pull and snort.

"Mattie Venn."

"Don't know a man by the name of Venn, these parts."

Mattie hesitated, had answered too quickly, and not thought it through.

"Venn be my married name, Burstock my maiden, and Toller be my brother, who has asked me to live here while he be away."

In the circumstances, she felt Jude's questions to be natural enough. His curiosity was kindling to make small talk, but she was unsettled. I must be careful, she thought, and tread carefully, mind I don't disturb the adder sleeping in my lies, by chance. Folk must not be drawn to my woes by my own clumsy slips.

Fortunately, the effort Jude had so far made had worn him out, and Mattie was relieved when the questions stopped. At the sign-post for Dottery, she heard what sounded like snoring, and she saw Jude lean to the side, his head swaying like a lantern on a pole in the wind.

"Sir!" she cried. "Wake up if you be asleep, for both our sakes."

Jude sat upright, grunted, and said, "A bad night. 'Twas something I ate kept me awake, so's my eyes won't prop themselves open. Left, Daisy, left! Broadoak be next, then Shave Cross, then Pilsdon. 'Taint far now."

At the bottom of the hill, Jude pulled on the reins. In the field, on his right, was a man on a horse, shielding his eyes, and scanning the field.

"Why, if it aint Miles Yondover!" said Jude.

Miles was too far away to hear a cry, but acknowledged Jude's wave with one of his own.

"You know him?"

"One of us, at the inn. Finishing off a job he started, the other day, when the storm stopped him."

"He a farmer?"

"Works on a farm off West Bay Road."

"Be that far?"

"The other side of Bridport. Smell the sea air where he works. His master's lamb be the saltiest in Dorset."

Mattie looked at Miles spurring his horse into all corners, could see that he was frantically examining every tuft that poked its head up.

"Looks to me like he lost something," she said.

"He has."

"What?"

"A dead body."

Mattie gave a cry, and held her hand to her mouth.

"Don't rightly matter, as it looks as if the corpse hab come alive again and gone home in time for Christmas!"

Mattie shuddered, horrified that Jude could speak so lightly of such a matter.

Jude laughed and shook the reins, and soon they had left Miles behind. They passed Dugdale Farm, where the curtains were closed, and began the slow climb up Pilsdon Pen.

"This be it," said Jude.

Mattie made sure she still had the key.

"'Taint much," observed Jude.

"'Tis more than I had. Thank 'ee for the ride."

Mattie jumped down, clutching her bag to her body, and made straight for the cottage. Jude watched her, but she waited, smiled, and only put the key in the door when he had turned the horse and cart round and set off. From the eave fell drops of water from melting icicles. 'Twould kill me if one of them stabbed me in the head, she calculated. Best to knock 'em off through that there window.

She opened the door, and stepped inside. A *man*'s home, she thought, as she noticed the absence of a tablecloth, cushions, an ornament or two. In the grate were the ashes of Toller's last fire. On the shelf above, a stopped clock. The cottage was cold, and she would need to light a fire. She spotted an oil lamp and candle Toller himself had made, but she had nothing with which to light one or the other. She went upstairs, tried the straw mattress, had to push hard on the window to open it, and leaned out to break off the icicles. From that spot, she could see to the top of Pilsdon Pen, which looked near yet was a breathless sweat away.

In her bag, bread and bacon the landlady had given her tempted her. And tomorrow I shall make this my own: clean it, put away Toller's bits till he returns. Water. The pump may yet be frozen. To melt ice, I need fire. If there be no tinder-box, I must go to Dugdale Farm, explain, ask to milk, clean, earn.

She went downstairs, intent on discovering what she could put to good use. Then she screamed when she saw him sitting in a chair, his feet crossed on the table, and smelt his filthy clothes, the reek of old flesh. His fingers were interlocked behind his head, completing a picture of amused and relaxed curiosity.

"Well, you aint Toller Burstock, for sure," he said, "but you be prettier, 'tis certain. What you doing 'ere?"

Her heart pounding, she took a deep breath, and said, "'Tis my house now. This note be the proof. He be my brother. I do nothing wrong."

"Then I be your good neighbour: Forston Sampford. Toller and I are the best of friends. Said he wanted me to take care of his cottage while he was away. So what you want me to do for you, eh? Don't be shy, girl. What you need the most?"

He chuckled lasciviously, revealing rotting stumps.

"I'd be grateful if you would leave, Mr. Sampford. I've things to do."

She eyed the poker in the hearth, and took a side-step towards it.

He said, "Door was left open. Thought Toller come home," and departed.

Mattie locked the door, and leaned against it.

You never said about him, Toller, she said to herself. You should have told me there was such a one would come a-nosing.

Outside, Sampford called, "I could do something for 'ee, dear. Make an old man happy," but his words were swallowed by the quarking of a skein of geese flapping wildly overhead.

Mattie went over to the clock, its key on a nearby hook. The sun was not yet overhead. She would check her shadow later; when it was but a smudge, she would wind the clock, keep it going.

Suddenly the room turned, and she sat down, took a deep breath. Here it was again, the nausea, which had disorientated her, the last two days. She put it down to fatigue, anxiety, lack of food.

"'Taint surprising, after all I've been through," she said aloud. "'Twill pass on just as 'tas before, and 'tis nearly the time when I am cursed, as are all women, when there be blood, and though it tarries, it will come."

Chapter four.

The Raddleman looked as if it had been shooed down the hill and told to mind its manners, be not so impudent as to assume it had a right to be in the centre of town. It had turned its back on the main street, looked as if it had been sulking after being scolded. Yet it welcomed Toller, that night, and his spirits were lifted when the fiddler arrived and played merry tunes. Men and women who, like Toller, would not have been allowed to stay in The King's Arms were at home in The Raddleman, and sang and danced when the tables and chairs had been shoved to the walls, and a space made.

But melancholy thoughts quietened him, late in the evening, when the tune became slower, and the words sadder. The dancers sat, and sang in hushed tones, as if they had just succeeded in persuading a young child to go to sleep upstairs, and did not want to wake him.

"Come 'ee not to my door
and ask for my kisses;
as another I love,
and 'tis *his* lips I misses."

Try as he might, he could not stop the image of Hepsy, her dark hair loose on her shoulders, returning, haunting him.

"Come, friend, and take off thy gloomy mask, which be more at home on a marble tomb in church. Never seen 'ee before, but, all night, you have sung and danced as if you been in gaol, and hab forgotten the taste of freedom. The ditty be sad, 'tis certain, and though a man must feel it as much as a woman, 'taint nothing but a made-up song to pace the night."

The man who had tried to cheer him up offered his hand, which Toller took.

"Toller Burstock I be."

"And I be John Trevelyan, Cornish born but Dorset bred, which hab suited me well, these years. Come, Toller, and mind not the song's slowness, for 'tis but a passing moment to catch our breath."

"Thank 'ee, John," said Toller, shaking his hand. "'Ee have set me to right, and 'twas nothing but a memory returned, and which is now banished. Come, and let me fill your tankard, for today I rest, and tomorrow I seek work."

John willingly passed him his pot.

"'Tis kind, though know that it seem the rest of the world be 'ere, looking for work. Hiring fair be in spring, and the railway be for engineers and important-looking folk in uniforms. Been a labourer, all my life, myself, and hab worked on the Misterton estate. Miss. Miranda be a fine employer, even though she be but a woman. You could try there. What be your trade?"

"Shepherd. Had my own flock and a bit of land, Bridport way."

"Then why comes you to Dorchester?"

"Done with shepherding."

"What will you do?"

"I want to better myself, be somebody."

John smiled.

"A fine sentiment, Toller, if you don't mind me saying, but that be the curse of the time, it seem to me. All this getting to places faster puts ideas into a young man's head. Take it from me: we never knows what we got till it baint there no more."

"Thank 'ee, John. There be much wisdom in your words. Just

can't be Pilsdon all my life. But tonight, I shall put away solemn thoughts, which be mere trifles, now the fiddler be resting, and drink your good health."

"And I shall join 'ee, but now you must get that tankard filled, case the landlord runs out, which be likely tonight. The spirit of Christmas hab walked in unnoticed, and relieved us of our woes."

The streets of Dorchester were awash, the next morning. By the time Toller had awoken – he could not face any breakfast; even the usually enticing smell of a rasher or two of bacon exacerbated his nausea – the snow had almost gone, but there was mud everywhere, and a brown stream ran down the hill and out of the town, as if it had to escape and flood the already sodden fields surrounding Stinsford.

Toller dithered outside The Raddleman. Whither shall I go? he wondered. Mattie, he remembered, would be in his cottage by now. Sister? His head hurt, and his stomach burned, and though the landlord had allowed him extra time in bed, Toller felt he needed several more hours of sleep before he could plead for a job. So he made his slow way back into town where others were going about their business.

He sat on a bench, and closed his eyes, which stayed shut until the mid-day chimes woke him. His lips had cracked, and he licked them. He felt in his pocket, but the money he had brought in a purse had been stolen.

"I deserve this," he said, leaning forward, and holding his head in his hands. "I shall never drink again, 'tis certain."

He stayed in that position for some time, till he became aware of a group of people close to him.

"You sick?" asked one, looking like an undertaker on his way to the chapel of rest.

Toller noticed the silver knob on the man's cane, the intense blackness of his top hat and tails, and wondered whether the Lord had sent him to fetch yet another poor, unfortunate soul.

"'Twill pass. Go, do. I am the author of my own sad tale, which hab no place in decent folk's ears, on such a sunny day."

"As you wish. If you be destitute, then go to the Mission up the hill, yonder. There waits a bed and a welcome, though no alcohol be allowed."

Toller gave a weak salute in acknowledgement of the man's help. 'Taint my time yet, thought Toller, though his appearance be a warning I must heed, as life be as slippery as this mud beneath my feet.

The group dispersed, but the man hesitated.

"Grateful to 'ee, sir," said Toller, indicating that the man could go, too.

"Do you have a name?"

"So hab we all, and mine be Toller Burstock, from Pilsdon."

"And mine is Henry Swanage. You heard of me?" Toller shook his head. "I tarry for fear that you suffer too much, and I seen too much of it, these parts. Often, 'tas been the drink, and sometimes 'tas been a woman, and a woman's scorn is as potent as a pot of the strongest cider. Your eyes say 'tis more a woman than drink you must forget, though there be a red marbling which suggests a pot too many."

Toller looked up. The man had hazel eyes, which complemented his black attire. Even his moustache, waxed and twirled at its ends, had not a single grey hair.

"Then you have lived and must know of these things. Tell me what I must do."

"I cannot decide for you, but I know that men who lose their worth in their own eyes do rash things they live to regret."

"'Tis certain. But what manner of man are you to know all this? Are you a parson? Undertaker? I think you a man to bury folk."

The man shook his head, took a step to show he was about to leave.

"Neither, though close to both."

"Why disturbs 'ee me with all your talk?"

"Because I have heard the final words of such as 'ee, time after time. I be the town's hangman, and 'tis to be hoped I don't become acquainted with the thickness of your neck and your futile cry for mercy. Good day, sir."

With that, the man left, swinging his cane, as only one with the confidence to end a life can.

Toller shuddered. The stranger, black in deed and attire, be a warning. He sees what I am come down to, has breathed upon criminals so degraded that he must take their life with a rope, in the name of justice. I must act, make today the first without drink, which be a noose, too.

But Toller had no money, no immediate prospect of earning any. Shepherding would not improve him, he knew. Yet what to do?

Then he heard ferocious barking, followed by a scream. Round the corner, he saw a black dog snarling and snapping at a horse pulling a trap, in which rode a distressed woman. The dog was frothing at the mouth, and the horse reared and suddenly bolted.

"Whoa!" cried the woman, but the horse did not obey.

The trap rocked from side to side, and the woman dropped the reins, and clung on to the back of her seat. She slid to the left, and nearly fell out. Seeing the danger, Toller shook off his lethargy, and, ignoring his headache and nausea, ran alongside the horse, and grabbed the reins. He pulled the horse's head to the side, and it bared its teeth in protest. Calling to it, Toller dug in his heels, slid in the mud, nearly lost his footing. The horse pranced, then submitted when Toller's soothing voice had reassured it.

Suddenly, there was a loud gunshot, which scared the horse again, forcing Toller to pull with all his might. The woman looked round at a man standing over the dog.

"Do not shoot again!" she pleaded. "The horse."

The man nudged the dog with his foot, careful not to get blood on his shoe, and saw that there was no need for a second bullet.

"Mad. Been prowling for a few days. Should have shot him yesterday."

Toller stroked and patted the horse, spoke to it quietly, and did not look at the dog.

"Thank you," said the woman.

Toller ignored her. The horse needed more physical contact, and she watched Toller's hands rove over its flanks, haunches, neck, nose. He caressed gently, finding the places that pleased the most.

He has special hands, she thought. Must work with horses.

"You have a way," she said.

"There," he said, satisfied the horse was under control again.

Then he looked up at her. Her cheeks were ruddy, and her breathing had not yet returned to its normal rhythm.

"I would have been thrown from the trap had it not been for you."

"And your clothes would have been covered in mud."

She was not sure if he was mocking her immaculate presentation: expensive, clean, velvet-collared coat, and hat, shoes looking new.

"I was thinking that I might have broken a bone or two."

"Possible."

His eyes returned to the horse, and the woman felt he either lacked basic manners or was unused to gratitude. She reached for her bag, and rummaged in it.

"Let me give you something for your troubles," she said, offering him a palm full of coins.

"'Twasn't any trouble, so there be no need."

She looked at his clothes, him. Not much money. Proud, too. Yet strong, agile, confident. Five and twenty years he has, and no more, she guessed.

"My name is Misterton. You looking for work?"

He hesitated enough to suggest he was lying when he said, "No. Just visiting when the snow captured me. Been a prisoner in Dorchester, a day or two."

"I can think of worse places," she said, smiling.

He lowered his eyes, only just managing to stop himself reciprocating. I've been before in the snare of women's smiles, bait few men can resist, he reminded himself.

"So you will not take it?"

"I have no need."

He stepped backwards, as if inviting her to continue her journey.

"As you say. However, if you change your mind, come to Misterton Manor and ask for me: Miranda. The estate always needs strong, quick-thinking people. Christmas creeps up on us, and there is much to do: fences to mend, livestock to manage. These streets are cold and uninviting in winter, even dangerous underfoot and in shadows. I am not blind. I see you might need help. There would be warm accommodation for you, cheerful company. Think about it, and put nothing in the way of singing Christmas carols at Stinsford church. If you stay on this road, you will see a milestone for it. The manor is signposted at Stinsford. If you get lost, ask the way, and soon you will find us, as almost all know and work for me. Now, good cheer to you, sir, and if you be less than the man for whom I take you, I thank you and wish you well in your attempted escape from Dorchester!"

Can't control a frightened horse, but she weaves words into wreaths as pretty and tight as any I seen on the front doors of some big houses in Bridport.

Toller watched her go down the hill, then turned to walk up it. The man had already picked up the dog, and taken it away. The trail of blood dripping from the hole in the dog's head led into an alley, which Toller passed with a cursory glance.

Then he saw an object on the floor, picked it up, examined it, and put it in his bag. He felt now much more awake; he had exerted himself when controlling the horse, shaken off his weariness a little. But he had no money or work, despite the offer of both.

There was the Mission, recommended by a man who earned

money by dropping a trapdoor and watching faces turn red, as, hands tied behind their back, they convulse once, maybe twice, before going blue.

'Tis charity, which I've never begged before, and won't now, though nothing jangles in my pocket. Something will turn up, and a night in an alleyway will keep rain off me, though draughts will whip down it with a ghostly groan.

He meandered slowly through Dorchester, and noticed that no one looked at him. Those whom he thought might be employers he tried to engage, but there were no jobs. At the railway station, they asked him a few questions, but when he could not supply an address in Dorchester, the interview ended.

"We gets a lot of journeymen like you," said the Station Master. "They comes in from all over, but we only sets on Dorchester folk who can be vouched for. Engineers be different. Dorset baint known for its engineers, but other jobs – tickets and signalmen, for example – be for local men, on account that they can be spoken up for, so we knows the type of man we got working for us."

Toller could see it was no use trying to persuade him to change his policy, so left. I'll just have to get me an address. 'Tis all a tangle. No money, no address, no job. Can't get any one of 'em beout any of the others. And hunger tightens me, sets me on an edge so sharp that my next words might slash anyone who speaks to me.

Darkness slid into Dorchester. On the edge of the light from a street gas lamp, more wrapped up than lonely men usually prefer, stood a woman. As Toller passed, he stopped to look at his pocket-watch, which he was considering selling. What be the use of knowing the time if there be no food in your belly?

It had been his father's till Mr. Burstock died of pneumonia. "Take it, son," he had said, knowing he would soon not need it, and Toller had done so, believing that while he had it, a bit of his father would always be with him.

"You got the time?" asked the woman, stepping more into the light.

"It wants a minute to the bells, be my reckoning," answered Toller, looking intently at his pocket-watch.

"You want to go down 'ere with me? A shilling first for whatever you want, as long as you don't hit or strangle me, as some try. You won't get cheaper, even if you goes up Maumbury Rings, what biv Christmas a-coming."

"No money."

"That's what bey all say, but 'tis a shilling even so."

"No money be true, and if you don't believe me, you listen to my belly, which gurgles like a brook."

The church bells rang, the notes bouncing off high walls and echoing in the crisp air.

"Tanner for my hand? Threepence, then?" the woman called, as Toller moved on.

He saw men standing outside the Mission, drinking from bottles. No alcohol inside, he remembered. I cannot sleep next to such, listen to their cursing and farting, smell their pissy clothes. I baint dropped down that far yet, though it seems bottomless, the well of shame and humiliation, and I be looking down into it beout anyone pulling me back from jumping.

So he walked till he came to the ruins of a Roman villa, where he stretched out on a wide, low wall.

"Guard me, centurions and slaves alike, biv your spears and swords, for I am tired, but will face the new day with Rome's ambition and valour in my body and soul," he said.

And then he fell asleep.

"What be the date?" he asked a man who had come to sketch the villa, and had set up his easel before Toller had awoken.

The man said, "Why, it's Christmas Eve! Know you not, sir?"

But Toller moved away, and walked and walked, stopping only to drink water from a stream. Though weak, he managed to find the door on which he wanted to knock. A man opened it, and Toller explained his reason for calling.

The person he wanted arrived, not recognising him, at first. On the door hung a wreath of holly. Toller stepped forward so that his face could be seen.

He delved into his bag, and took out what he wanted to return, and said, "I found it. It must have fallen off while you were holding on for dear life. It was just down from the dog. The wrapping be ripped, though the rest baint damaged. Least, no blood on it. I checked. Thought you'd want it back, being it Christmas. There be words written on the inside of the front cover. Had to look, on account of trying to find out whose it was. I remembered where you said you lived, and your name."

She took it from him, looked at him, and said, "You've come all this way to bring it?"

"Looks so. I don't mean anything by it, but I read a bit, and 'twill occupy you many an hour, as 'tis long and full of a man who hab done wrong, but I will say no more as 'twill spoil. You know, with it being a present for you, or so it seem, though I don't wish to pry."

She removed the paper, and lovingly stroked the spine of the book. Carefully, she opened it and said, "Twice you have helped me, but will you not now let me help you? Take you to the others, who will soon make their way to Stinsford church with their lamps? Give you something to eat? Like a wise man from afar, you have brought me a gift."

"'Tis not from me but another, a woman."

Having fretted since she had become aware that she had lost the present given to her, earlier, that day, Miranda read the words to herself: *To my dear friend, who has done more to help me than she can ever know. Christmas 1886. From Emma Lavinia.*

"Her husband wrote it."

"And what be it called?"

"The Mayor of Casterbridge, a new." After a moment or two,

during which she seemed to sigh silently, swallow a little sadness, she said, "But come, grant me this one wish: that you will join the choir, this Christmas Eve, for if your heart be empty, it will fill, or, if already full, will overflow."

"'Tis certain," said Toller.

Chapter five.

The undertaker recommended burying Ebenezer without delay. Though the snow had slowed the rate of decomposition of the corpse, there had been significant deterioration, and there was little the undertaker could do to mask the ravages of death.

"A powder scented with lavender here, a cream to hide the blemishes of advanced years there, invisible stitching of the lips to prevent the mouth accentuating his agony – all would do little to alleviate your distress. It would be better, to prevent noxious smells, if nothing else, to have the grave-diggers set to work immediately, though it is highly likely they will charge more than usual, on account of the soil remaining hard below the surface."

Hepsy sighed and said, "Do what you must. Just let me know the time. Whitchurch Canonicorum be best, you advise? The roads are clear?"

"From Bridport to here be passable, and there will be the coffin and two. You wish to ride with us?"

"I will follow on my horse. There is no time to inform his acquaintances; friends he had none, to the best of my knowledge, on account of him being like a sprouting of nettles, betimes."

"As you wish. Again, Miss. Valence, be assured that Messrs. Cobb and Cap, Bespoke Funeral Directors of Bridport, extend their sincere condolences to you, and will come upon you, with your father, tomorrow at eleven."

With an obsequiously low bow, Cobb took his leave, remarking, when he conveyed her requirements to the vicar, that Miss. Valence was in such shock that she appeared almost indifferent to her loss.

The funeral took place, and the vicar said all the usual words, most of which were, to Hepsy, mere sounds devoid of meaning and truth. She reflected instead on how it was possible to have one's achievements, body, significance to others, nailed into a box destined to be covered by soil, for eternity. All for a few sheep, she mouthed; all because he was a farmer. He might be alive today if he had been a vicar. What should I put in the newspaper? What words match his deeds? Pointless, she concluded. For paper, and words assembled in their finest order, be kindling's grate-fellows.

It was not until Christmas Eve that she saw yellow smoke coming from Toller's chimney. Earlier, she had ignored Forston Sampford's knocking; finding her father would not buy her long-term friendship or gratitude. Toller back? she wondered. After what he had said? He had feared a chance encounter, wanted Pilsdon to be all hers. If it is him, she thought, his departure, a grand gesture, was almost a fanfare to his return, so quickly has he come.

She did not know what to say to him, except that her father had died. But when her curiosity had overwhelmed her caution, she went to investigate. That was how she had always known if Toller was in: the slow pulsing of smoke rising and leaning backwards into a mustard plume, appearing in the same place in the sky, in line with Pilsdon's peak.

The curtains were open. Toller often left them closed, to protect his eyes from the sun, till it rolled out of direct sight. Hepsy approached, unsure whether to go and knock or observe for a while. Soon, however, she saw someone step outside and cut a few small branches of holly from a nearby bush.

A woman. Pretty, too. And preparing for the season. Why, 'tis Christmas Eve, and while I wear weeds and a sorrowful face, as befits a daughter who has only just buried her father, another gathers berries, maybe intending to drape them above the door or fireplace. Perhaps, she has returned with Toller. If so, he hab married in haste, and there be a mystery to solve, and 'twon't unfurl beout my making myself known.

Hepsy called, "Hello. Be Toller back? 'Tis Hepsy Valence, a neighbour who saw the smoke. Thought him gone for good."

Mattie looked up, startled, pricked her finger on the holly, and a berry of blood bloomed and burst.

"Come hither if you wish. 'Tis for the holly and not the cold I show my face. I be Mattie Venn."

Hepsy went to her. Mattie's hand shielded her eyes from the sun, and Hepsy moved, making it easier to be seen.

"I am pleased to know you. Indeed, 'tis good to talk to another, as my father has died, and my heart be a stone."

Hepsy bit her bottom lip. Mattie noticed her misery, and said, "The day be cold. Let us sit by the fire, where our new acquaintance will be warmed by the flames."

Hepsy followed Mattie, had known the cottage's owner, but had never ventured inside, or been invited to. Trespass of a furtive kind, it felt. This was how he had lived, and all the time he had sought her hand in marriage, he had waited patiently there, amid the objects sustaining him. The oak settle by the hearth had been rubbed to a sheen where he had sat. No smell of him was in the air, but he was invisibly present. On the table was his lamp, the wick nibbled brown by a flame in whose light he had read the few books he possessed. There they were, on a dresser, their spines facing outwards, his collection of four acquired at Bridport market. How strange that he had gone, left his life there so impulsively that its obvious signs had frozen in that moment, and been left for others to discover!

Mattie indicated the settle, and drew up a chair for herself. Hepsy sat down, glad of the blaze, and sought the words for the question to which she must have an answer. Mattie saw the struggle in her face, and spoke before Hepsy could ask.

"I be Toller's sister, Mattie, as I hab said, come to look after here while he be gone to make his name."

"Sister? He never said he had one, though 'taint a crime not to say. A *name* he seeks? Why, he has one, a good one, too, and don't need another, be my opinion. He was a good shepherd. Where's he gone? I ask as a neighbour who was sad to see him go."

"Dorchester way. For one year will he be away, to make something of himself, as 'twas his lowly shepherd's smock which shamed him and lost him a wife on account of it, he said. But all be Providence."

Mattie sighed.

Hepsy knew that very woman was herself. A whole year must I wait for him before I tell him, face to face, that father watched o'er me as closely as he did his sheep, that 'twas hard to go against his word.

There settled a silence, cut up into Hepsy's speculations, and Mattie was afraid that she herself might say something Toller might want to remain private. Then Hepsy remarked, "You caught rabbits already?" Mattie followed the line of her nod. On the table, they were lying on their side, eyes staring aimlessly, legs stretched as if reposing on grass, in the sunshine.

"Not me, no, though I knows how to skin and cook 'em. No, 'twas strange. I found 'em tied together and hanging on the nail by the door. They weren't there when I arrived. Somebody must have been thinking of me, and 'tis fortunate, as there be not a crumb in the house, though there be a bottle or two of strong stuff, which I don't touch, on account of its taste, which be too bitter."

Forston Sampford, thought Hepsy. He, too, must have noticed and come skulking, sniffing at the door.

"The holly be a decoration?"

"'Tis my first Christmas in such loneliness, so the berries on the bough bill cheer me. And there be mistletoe, too. 'Twas under such that my fiancé first stole a kiss."

Hepsy noticed a tear on Mattie's cheek.

"Now don't you go upsetting yourself. And you are engaged? Your name be Venn, you say?"

"No, I be married," stuttered Mattie. "The kiss was when we were first engaged."

"And now?" pressed Hepsy. "He minds not you coming here?"

"Not at all, as he has left me, to go I know not where. I must start again, and my brother and I hab swapped places, hoping that we will both be happier for doing so."

Hepsy looked around Toller's cottage. Next to the fire she knew he had sat. When he had been there, she had not thought of him, of what his life must be like indoors, and now that he had gone, she missed him, regretted her indifference. And she liked his sister, a pretty, young woman. Mattie's arrival was a sign of hope that, one day, Hepsy could make amends, even if his plan to become wealthier failed, and he returned a shepherd.

"'Tis Christmas Eve, and 'twon't do for either of us to sit and cry over missing loved ones, so will you come over to the farmhouse tonight? There be a bit of bacon and cheese and bread. I can make some stew, too. Hot it bill be, all a-steaming with tatties and wild garlic. I will light a fire in your room."

Mattie went over to the table, and picked up the rabbits, one in each hand, by their back legs.

"And I shall skin these, so you can roast them in a pot over the flames. They shall be my Christmas present to 'ee, just as your invitation, which I accept, be mine from 'ee."

"'Tis settled, and tonight I bill tell you all about Bridport, and Lyme Regis, which be my favourite, on account of its air, and the pretty dresses which glide along the Cobb."

"And in the hours before I come, I will deck this cottage with the season's boughs, for its spirits, like ours, must be uplifted, and remain so into the New Year, which we hope bill be better than this, which gutters like a candle whose wick and wax be all but spent."

"Then I shall go, and take with me these rabbits, which shall feed us, this Christmas Eve and tomorrow, 'tis certain."

When Hepsy had gone, Mattie trimmed the holly and mistletoe, and placed it round the lamp, and in the hearth, in the hope that the flames would light up the berries.

She looked down at her dress, the hem of which was muddy. One other dress she had brought with her, a blue one bought to please her husband-to-be, who had said it would suit her, and that she should always wear it whenever his spirits were low. Its associations were yet painful to her, but she took a practical view of her misfortune, and decided to wear it to Dugdale Farm. She had not had time to consider her appearance since meeting Toller in Dorchester, and decided to wash her hair in warm water.

"'That be better," she said, as she teased out the strands of her hair, in front of the fire. "He be out of my hair now."

With an hour or two to fill before she was due to go to Hepsy, she could not resist the temptation to look in all the places Toller might have wished to remain private. She chided herself that she should want to go where she had no right, but he had not explicitly forbidden her access to any particular drawer or box.

The dresser, firstly. In the left drawer, a pipe or two, a pen, ink, and a pistol. In the right, a letter addressed to a Mr. Hugo Lockington, and another to Miss. Hepsibah Valence. She wondered whether Toller had forgotten to send them, or had changed his mind, thought better of it, or even postponed their delivery until he returned. Hugo Lockington of Lyme Regis; Hepsibah Valence of Pilsdon. As mistress of the cottage for a year, Mattie felt somehow responsible for its maintenance, but not Toller's affairs. She did not know Hugo Lockington, but had met Hepsy. With the letter in her hand, she felt powerful. It probably contained instructions in case he did not return, she speculated.

But Mattie decided to return the letter to the drawer whence she had taken it. 'Taint for me to meddle with Providence, she decided.

The few hours Mattie had to wait to go to Hepsy became a mixture of barely contained hunger and excitement that Christmas Eve would not be spent alone. Occasionally, the letters drew her back to the dresser, and she touched the one addressed to Hepsy, only to warn herself that Toller would, one day, return and hold her to account for her actions.

It was with great anticipation of a good meal that Mattie left for Dugdale Farm, and the smell from the pot, when she entered, whetted her hunger.

"The rabbits, your gift, be nearly done," remarked Hepsy, stirring the pot above the fire.

"'Tis certain."

Mattie watched her hostess, noticed how she bent like a willow to the pot. 'Tis a wonder Toller habn't set his sights on her. She be pretty, and her dress be best quality, which makes mine seem like a corn merchant's sackcloth.

Hepsy noticed the uncomfortable restraint Mattie showed when eating. Whenever Mattie felt herself relishing the stew, she made herself put down her knife and fork, and ask a question about Bridport or Lyme, so that she did not seem ill-mannered, desperate. Over Hepsy's shoulder, she saw a shepherd's crook by the door. Remember, she is like me, Mattie told herself: lost a loved one. This sharing be a blessing.

"And he spoke not of his neighbours? 'Tas been many a year since he last saw you. 'Tis a wonder he hab not told you all about us: the farmers, Bridport, Forston Sampford," probed Hepsy.

"Our time together recently was brief. 'Twas planned before he left here. He sent me a letter."

Hepsy frowned, felt in the midst of a conspiracy.

"He never spoke of you. 'Twas as if he kept you a secret."

Mattie became wary of making Toller's plan more complicated.

Her additions to the facts made their conversation more dangerous, the path through the evening so uneven that she might stumble. Then she would be no reliable sister of Toller.

"The stew is good. 'Tas been a while since I last tasted rabbit. The hedges rustle biv them, spring, Tolpuddle way."

Hepsy backed off, acknowledged Mattie's praise for her cooking.

"'Twas Forston Sampford bill have brought them."

They ate slowly, eyes on the plate, feeling the steam on their faces, not opening up to personal questions. Mattie thought about telling her that her brother had proposed marriage to a local woman, that she had turned him down on her father's promise of a richer, better catch, but she held back, not wanting to stray too far away from ordinary matters.

"A grotesque man, hair all tangled, Forston Sampford?"

"The same. Let him not over your threshold for he is a vile, old man biv the reek of the farmyard on his clothes."

"He has visited me, but I sent him away."

"You want an apple been hiding in a box in the barn?"

Mattie nodded and smiled.

"'Tis a Christmas to remember!"

"And there be a trickling of honey to soothe the tang of the flesh."

"You like it whole or peeled?"

"Peeled and cut, and I dips the pieces in the honey, which father told me off for."

"And rightly so!"

When they had finished, they sat by the fire.

"No singers, this year. 'Tis a peaceful night, and a clear, biv moonlight all over."

Then a firm but not aggressive knock at the door made them start. The visitor had seen the light through the window, had stood there, rehearsing his words, trying to find the courage to explain his choice of time to visit.

"Forston Sampford be our only neighbour?"

"If 'tis him, I shall not open the door but send him home. He baint welcome here."

Hepsy tip-toed to the door. Again there was a knocking, louder, this time, though still without offence. Then came a voice, a man's, less unctuous than Sampford's, younger, more sensitive.

"Miss. Valence, forgive my coming here, this night, but not a day more will pass beout me apologising to you." The man sighed, and continued with, "'Tis true that my left and right be muddled, but you know me well enough – you were kind to let me stay here when the snow been high as a hayloft – to say I tried my best, and though 'twasn't good enough, there wasn't no other man would have stepped out into that blizzard."

Miles Yondover, the man who had slept in the bedroom next to hers.

Hepsy looked at Mattie.

"'Tis the man who helped me look for father, I think."

Mattie said, "I will leave if you wish."

"No, stay. You are my guest. I will ask him in. He has come a long way, from West Bay Road. 'Tas weighed on his mind, his error. He is a good man, and is without blame."

"If you are sure."

"'Tis Miles Yondover?" called Hepsy, touching her hair.

"The very same, though I would gladly change it, ashamed as I am to wear it."

Hepsy opened the door. Behind Miles stood his horse. Mattie felt the intrusion of the cold air, and shivered.

"Come in. 'Tis cold without," invited Hepsy.

Miles tied his horse to the paling, and entered.

Mattie looked up at him, and he took off his hat.

"I did not know you had company, Miss. Valence. I come to pay my respects to your father, who be buried now, I hear, and to ask forgiveness for my mistake, which bill be a cow's bell to me for the rest of my life."

Mattie looked away, did not wish to hear their private words.

"His death was none of your making, Miles, and there be nothing to forgive. This 'ere be Mattie Venn, who hab moved into the cottage further up Pilsdon. She be the sister of Toller Burstock, a shepherd who used to live there, but who hab gone to make his fortune."

Miles looked at Mattie, who smiled too sweetly, thought Hepsy.

"Then I am pleased to make your acquaintance, Miss. Venn, though I did not know you were here, or I would not have called."

"And I am glad to meet you, too, Mr. Yondover."

Miles smiled broadly.

"Will you take a plate of stew for your trouble, Miles? After all, 'tis Christmas Eve, and we should part, this evening, as good friends," invited Hepsy.

"I will, indeed, Miss. Valence, and then I shall not keep you from your guest a moment longer."

But before Hepsy could protest, Mattie had gone to the pan, and ladled some stew onto a plate.

Toller Burstock? thought Miles. Now where hab I come across that name before?

"There," said Mattie, putting the plate before him.

And Hepsy looked on, feeling almost a stranger in her own home.

Conversation between Hepsy and Mattie ceased. Both women watched him eating, and he raised his blue eyes to first one, then the other. He felt conspicuous, chewed noisily, wished he had not accepted the offer of food, though was glad of it. Mattie smiled whenever he looked at her, though Hepsy frowned when he tilted his plate to drink the gravy.

"Begging both your pardons. I baint used to eating in the company of two ladies," he said, licking his lips, and leaning back with the air of satisfaction of one at home, to indicate he was more than full.

"There be apple," said Mattie.

Hepsy shot her a look of disapproval. Miles shook his head, and said, "'Tis kind, but I must be getting back to Briddy. Miss. Valence, you have treated me fairly, for, as you know –" Hepsy raised her hand, and moved to the door. His stay was over. "Yes, well, I should go now." He went through the door, hesitated, and asked, "Bill you show a light to the road, and point me?"

Hepsy fetched the lamp, though there was bright moonlight, and guided him and his horse into the lane. It was a minute or two before she returned. Mattie had been looking into the flames, thinking Miles handsome, flirtatious: he hab an open face, though I see from Hepsy's that there be more to his visit than to seek forgiveness.

Hepsy took her time to make eye contact with Mattie again. There are some things that can never be hidden by the masks we wear, Mattie had discovered, in her recent experience, and 'tis certain that Miles hab taken a shine to me. But when, at last, they were ready to talk again, Hepsy cursed that, not only did Miles not know his left from his right, but that he was seemingly unaware that it was ungentlemanly to try to kiss a woman whose father was barely cold in his grave. Though Mattie did not see what had happened in the lane, Hepsy suspected that she knew, as even in the half-light of the fire and lamp, Hepsy felt her own eyes sparkling like flinty stars in the night sky.

"Forgive me, but I must go," said Mattie. "Thank 'ee for the stew. 'Twas passing good."

And Hepsy let her go without a word.

Chapter six.

Toller sat at the back of Stinsford church. There was a hum of animated conversation as the congregation awaited the vicar, much good-natured jostling in the pews, to accommodate all the lanterns on poles, and furtive sips of brandy. Miranda had asked Michael Salisbury and Charlotte Mapperton to look after Toller, and they had complied with her request. On their way there, they had stood either side of him, and fed him questions, the taste of some of which he had not liked. He had, of course, anticipated them, and had prepared a fascinating personal history, which, apart from his name, was a work of fiction as imaginative as any composed by Mr. Dickens or Mr. Collins. Determined not to lose Toller in the merry throng, the guardians had marched him to the very last pew, Michael in front, and Charlotte behind, so that he could not slip away. Their desire to please their mistress oppressed Toller, and he was on the verge of requesting leave to take a breath of fresh air when the vicar arrived, and the door was shut, dashing any hope of escape.

The orchestra had hitherto been tuning their instruments in a most discordant manner, and a loud cheer, swiftly accompanied by applause, arose. The vicar did not usually receive such a warm welcome, and acknowledged it with a generous wave, first to one side of the aisle, then the other. Perhaps, they like me, after all, he thought. Maybe they do appreciate my sermons, do understand why I mildly castigate them, from time to time. The Bishop ought to witness this. Then he would see that I am worthy of promotion. Ah well! A vain hope. But my present living is not the trial it was when I first arrived. This flock of mine I have come to know, every one of them, and it would be hard to leave.

The vicar stood behind his lectern, and allowed the high spirits to subside. More folk here than usual, he noticed, even for Christmas Eve. Anxious to begin the service, he led an opening prayer, and they all sang a carol.

Toller listened. This was a rare experience for him. Church had always been a place in which he had heard solemn words about men being cut down before their time, and had said goodbye to loved ones, but now he found himself in a jolly crowd, whose voices soared to the rafters. How persuasively had Miss. Misterton cast her spell! I would not be here, thought Toller, if I had closed my ears to her. I returned her book, and she charmed me with the promise of work and lodgings. There be a price to pay for everything, but I should not complain, as this be a small one for a roof over my head, on Christmas Eve.

Toller sniffed. Michael had been drinking – Toller had suspected this on the way when the sweet fumes of cider could be smelt, every time Michael spoke – and was leaning heavily on him. Charlotte looked at Michael, and whispered to Toller, "'Tis the cider which pushes him over, and soon he bill snore, and I hope the vicar be all said and prayed by then, as 'twill sound like thunder or God's grumbling, and all eyes bill turn."

The vicar seemed determined to extract further adulation from his congregation when he announced that they would sing the first carol all over again, but he had misjudged their mood, and a groan rippled through the pews. Michael was about to snore, but the cry of protest woke him, and he cried, "The rams have all tupped their ewes, Mistress!"

The two rows of parishioners in front of him looked over their shoulder, and laughed. Some looked at Toller, who was pushing Michael away; Toller did not want them to think he was Michael's friend.

"You silly man, Michael, to think of sheep on Christmas Eve, 'less they belong to the shepherds, who did watch, sitting down, their flocks by night, when the angel came a-fluttering down," said Charlotte.

The orchestra spared Toller further embarrassment when they began to play, but his attention was drawn towards a woman who had turned at Michael's outburst. She wore a black bonnet, and her brown eyes were soft and liquid, and a smile began to play at the corners of her full lips.

She knows me not, seems to ask me a question beyond my name. Turn at the end of the music so that I may see those eyes again, he silently told her. He sang more loudly, wanted to remind her that he was still behind her, to let her know he had noticed her smile.

A sigh of relief rippled through the congregation when the last word had been sung, and was followed by laughter when Peter Portland deliberately started a fresh carol with the wrong notes. The vicar wished everyone a merry Christmas, and people began to leave.

Outside, the lanterns gathered into a ghostly circle amidst the headstones in the graveyard. Toller watched the woman pass, and their eyes met, he sure that she had inclined her head slightly, as an acknowledgement that they had already done so, a few minutes before.

"Come, Toller. 'Tis time to go round the houses, a-singing Christmas songs, to cheer those who hab not come to church. And biv a spickle of luck and many a right note, we shall be watered with a cup of seasonal strong stuff," said Michael, guiding him out of the pew.

At the door, the vicar was shaking the hand of a man with a moustache. The man's wife stood back, watching, her smile clearly for the occasion. The people behind them wanted to pass, and began to press, but the vicar seemed intent on retaining the man's hand, as if it were worth ten times any other at the service.

"Come, Tom," urged the woman, seeing the queue. "We must let these good people pass."

"Goodnight," said the vicar.

Outside, Mr. and Mrs. Hardy fell silent.

Toller looked for the woman with brown eyes, but she was nowhere to be seen. In his hand he held a lantern, and moved, unknown, invisible, among the crowd. Gone already? he wondered.

Then, as if prompted by some unspoken cue, people began to sing, their red faces now yellow in the eerie light. Others joined the knot, which then unravelled on the way through the churchyard gate, and to the few cottages, just beyond the rectory, on the left.

"Old Jonas be not a-bed. I see his light, and though his knees be bent like a snapped twig, and his hips creak like a cart's wheels, they bill carry him to his window. I'd hate to think we would pass him by without a note, since his wife died not two harbests ago, and 'tis a time for friendship and company, baint it, all and one?" said Toby Wanderwell.

It took some time for Jonas, crowned with a nightcap, and holding a candlestick, to open his window. As the choir sang, Jonas trembled, and when they had finished, he called down, "Thank 'ee, one and all, for your sweet singing, which has broken the gloom of old Jonas' house. 'Tis passing kind, but all and one must know that I cannot share your happiness. 'Tis certain that, by this Christmas Eve, next year, I bill have gone to join my dear wife, who gets ready for me. I will not offer 'ee anything, as is the ancient custom, these parts, as the well be dry. I bid 'ee goodnight."

With that, he withdrew, and shut the window, leaving his visitors disappointed. Some thought him mean-spirited, but Toller said, "Be not too harsh on him, for 'less a man let you into his body and mind, we cannot truly know his joy or hurt. Judge him not so."

A stranger in their midst had contradicted some of them, but Michael, remembering that he had been charged with the supervision of Toller, lightened the mood with, "'Tis true, Toller. Let not Jonas' misfortune steal our mirth. Come, all and one, for the night runs ahead, and we must catch her up, and sing our hearts out, for the infant Jesus be born soon, and 'twill be daylight in a spickle if we tarry longer, chewing on morbid thoughts. So on to Widow Brownsea, who might be more cheerful and generous."

As they walked and sang, Toller contemplated his journey to Stinsford. Desperate for food and shelter, he had been rewarded for his good deed with the companionship of strangers – jolly ones, the like of which he had come across in The Raddleman – and the promise of a bed for the night. Charlotte thought he cut an ungrateful figure: his shoulders be slumped, as he can't get what he wants, and he hangs back, as if ashamed to be seen, even in lamplight, when beauty and ugliness be twins. She had relinquished her hold on him, knowing that he would not be supervised any longer.

When they had run out of cottages to visit, it was time to return to Misterton Manor, where it was the tradition to sing a final song, before eating pies and pickles, provided by Miranda, in the big barn. There, the musicians played something reviving, more vigorous, till all began to dance, and only when sleep had dragged them onto the straw, and the fiddler had begun to select the wrong notes, did they cease their merriment.

Toller climbed a ladder into the loft. Something scurried through the straw: a mouse, come in from the cold, was making room for the newcomer.

In the quiet of the loft, Toller made a decision. Tomorrow, I will see Miss. Misterton. There baint nothing for me here but field and hill work, which will keep me as lowly as all the other country folk. 'Twill seem I be ungrateful in her eyes, but I baint a shepherd any more, he reasoned. What I am I know not, but things will be better, one day, I vow.

Drowsy from the drink, he closed his eyes and fell asleep.

In the morning, the barn was a painting. As Toller moved quietly between the snoring bodies draped over the bales, he decided he would return to the house, to see Miranda. He did not want to appear ungrateful. Let her not think me a worthless tramper. Besides, she may give me advice others cannot, may know someone who can help.

She saw him, looked him up and down, recognised that his night had been long.

"You are leaving us already?" she asked.

"I have to, though you have been kind."

Miranda screwed up her nose, and said, "Is it because I am a woman? You cannot take money from a woman?"

Piqued, Toller stood more upright.

"'Taint that. I just want to try something different."

After a pause, Miranda said, "I understand, but I had high hopes for you here. The horses: you have a way with them. We breed heavy ones for the brewery as well as our fields. I need a good man for the matching."

This was different, and he hesitated. It will seem I pick and choose, but I am too proud to do labouring. I want, *need*, something to raise me up more.

"'Tis kind, but do you know of anything going, Dorchester way? I baint a man of the sea, which all there is likely to be, Weymouth way. Not got the stomach for the waves," he confessed.

She smiled. His ambition, desire for independence, impressed her. Few would turn down work in the stables.

"Wait here," she instructed.

When she returned, she handed him a letter.

"What is it?"

"An introduction. After this, it is up to you."

The letter burned in his hand as he read the address.

"Why go to this trouble for me?"

She knew that he had stopped the horse, and returned the book, that he had been properly rewarded. Yet she could not tell him that he reminded her of her father, not in appearance and years, but in his aloofness, his shifting facial expression. "You have a past from which you are running," she wanted to say, "and you must find what you are looking for. The prize must be great." But she held back.

"Because you are different."

Toller nodded, fought back the tears.

"And so be you, too."

She watched him walk away, knew he was aware that she lingered. The cold air had made her cross her arms for warmth, exhale trumpets of grey breath.

"Good luck!" she called.

Toller felt the letter in his pocket, and turned and smiled, at last.

"A man must leave before he can return for ever." These words she remembered her father telling her when he had explained everything, years ago. "And some things can only be sorted by tens of new moons and the gathering of harvests," he had added. "'Taint no use a-rushing. Providence hab its own stride."

She waved back, and thought: in due course will Toller return, and when he does, he will have his own tale to tell, and I will listen to it, just as I did to father's, which made me love him more than ever.

Christmas Day. The sharp, cold air bit Toller into a quick pace, but he had to moderate it when he became tired. The ground was too wet with frost to rest on, so he continued, determined to reach Dorchester, and see the place to which Miranda had sent him, while it was still light.

He shook his aching head. This baint a destination of my choosing, but it baint lambing either, or out on the hills on a sodden night, or checking the raddling on the ewes, or packing wool into sacks for barely a penny. Besides, Miss. Misterton would not have taken the trouble to write if she had thought it was a path leading nowhere.

She had given him the confidence to see it through, though they had only recently met. The way she had waved him off and not taken offence at his refusal to work on her estate were signs of solidarity. She was on his side. At last, someone cared what happened to him, just as he had looked out for Hepsy, and the remotest lamb in trouble.

Soon he came to Dorchester. The Durnovaria Brewery was his destination. Nobody worked on such a holy day, and the streets were empty. Only when he came to The King's Arms did he see anyone. He nodded to a man coming towards him, his own tongue too timid, too fearful, to give him the season's greetings.

"Good day, sir," acknowledged the man, lifting his hat.

Toller wanted to speak, but merely nodded again. The man wore fine clothes, a sign of wealth, and passed by. They had nothing in common, thought Toller. Then he remembered the letter; he had to find the brewery. Perhaps, the man could help.

"And there you will find it," he finished, after much pointing up the hill, and subsequent twisting of the wrist to denote necessary turns.

"'Tis kind of 'ee. I am a stranger, these parts, and seek work there."

"Then I wish you good luck, sir. These are improving times, and many come to the town to seek their fortune. If respected, the brewery is a friend, yet an enemy if not: the source of work yet misery. Much it can do to dash or raise us. But you look as if you have spent an uncomfortable night. Know you the Mission? On this, of all days, no man should pace the streets."

"I know of it but cannot bring myself to go there. My purse was stolen, but I hope to gain work when Christmas has passed. I have seen the men outside, and their faces, all red and dead, are a reminder that I must not become one of them."

The man stood silent a moment or two, then, putting his hand in his pocket, and taking out some money, said, "If I try to give you this, you will, no doubt, rebuff me, so accept it as a loan. All men face unexpected misfortune, at some time or other."

The man offered the money, and Toller hesitated.

"No, sir," said Toller. "'Tis charity."

"Then you are not the man I thought you. A loan, sir, payable when you have earned some wages."

A further extension of the man's hand, a direct look, persuaded Toller to take it.

"I will pay you back, sir. Every penny. I will work hard, and you will have your money before spring pushes winter to one side."

"I believe you."

"But where will I find you? I know not your name or address."

The man took Toller's hand, placed the coins in it, and tightened Toller's fingers around it.

"My name is Langton Godmanstone, and you shall find me, God willing, when you report to the Durnovaria Brewery, the day after tomorrow. If I am not present, ask for my sister, Zenobia. I shall tell her to expect you. Now, I must go, for it is a special day, and I must visit someone. Good day."

"Burstock. I be Toller Burstock."

"Till the day after tomorrow, Toller."

Langton Godmanstone left him. Toller looked at the name on Miranda's letter. The very same! he noticed. My luck changes. I shall not let her down. Or him. These coins will buy me a bed and food, both of which will present me in a new light. Within these next twelve months, I will be reborn.

Chapter seven.

Toller followed Langton Godmanstone's directions, and found himself in front of Durnovaria Brewery. He again took out the letter, the key he hoped would unlock the door to a job worth having, to greater self-worth, which had been, in Pilsdon, trampled into the sheep-dung by Ebenezer and Hepsy Valence. He thought Durnovaria a long, strange word, foreign, signifying something important, mysterious. Inquisitive, he looked through the bars of the gate like a prisoner feeling insecure after release, and into his nose drifted the unmistakable whiff of fermenting ale. The Raddleman. Of course. That was where he had smelt it before.

The money he had borrowed would buy him a bed for a couple of nights, a drink, but not like before, when he had had too much. A good impression is what I must make when I present myself for a job. Yet I must get to know the ale, its fumes, what makes it potent, if I am to work at the brewery. But Durnovaria: a puzzle I must solve. A scholar would know, but where to find one, on Christmas Day?

"Yes, yes, I'm coming!" called the landlord. "Can't a man get a decent lie-in, these days?"

Toller's knock had become insistent, desperate, even.

The grey, worn nightshirt dangled just above the landlord's ankles.

"Why, you be shrinking!" his wife exclaimed, when she noticed how long it seemed. "You been a-wearing your legs away!"

“’Tis on account of all the running about I have to do in this place!” he explained.

Toller called, “I be Toller Burstock, looking for a room for two nights. ’Tis Christmas Day, and I beg you to take pity on a man who once supped right through the night here with John Trevelyan and others.”

The door opened. The landlord’s thin, white legs glowed in the dim interior. On his head he wore a woollen hat, on which moths had been clearly dining for some time.

“What be you wanting a room for?” he asked.

“Why, to sleep in. ’Tis a day of good will to all men. I hab money, and expect nothing but a bone to chew on, a tankard of ale, though just the one, on account of how it argues with reason and good judgement, in all daily matters.”

“Who be that?” shrieked the man’s wife.

“Toller Burstock, one who has stayed before, and now begs your hospitality again.”

The landlady put on her wig and dressing gown, and went to look at her visitor. Her bodiless face was a moon, its craters like the blotches of a drunkard.

“Why, I knows this man. You got money?” she asked.

Toller jangled the coins in his pocket.

“Wants a bone to chew,” the landlord informed his wife.

“Got a bone or two,” she said, “but they be extra.”

“Even a dog gets a free bone!” protested Toller.

The landlord was just about to slam the door in his face when his wife stopped him and said, “Money now, bones later.”

So the deal was struck, and Toller slept off Christmas Eve in a cold, hard bed, having decided that the bones could wait till the morning.

“Durnovaria,” wondered Toller before he went to sleep. “What does it mean?”

When he awoke, grey light, signifying the butt of the day,

slouched through the small window misted by condensation. He felt better now, and the small knot of hunger tightening in his stomach made him think of eating. Bones, he remembered. Surely, there was something better to be had.

He went out – there was no movement, no sound in the rest of the house – for some exercise. In the air hung a faint smell of overcooked meat and vegetables. One or two people were walking as aimlessly as Toller. The Mission had stayed open all day. Suddenly, panicking, he thrust his hand into his pocket. The money was still there. He had paid, in advance, the innkeeper's wife for two nights, trimmed bones, and a cup of ale. A few coins remained, too little to buy new attire, but enough to treat himself if the chance came.

As he passed an alley, he heard wanton voices.

"You know of a chop-house open, nearby?" he called to them.

The man and woman were a tableau of debauchery.

"You want to wait your turn five minutes?" asked the woman. "He be nearly done, and 'twould have been your go already if you hadn't put him off his stroke."

The man started his thrusting and grunting again, and Toller, realising what they were doing, said, "Sorry."

As he walked away, he heard the inevitable groan of relief. In this cold, too! he marvelled.

Soon, he heard behind him the panting of the woman trying to catch him up.

"You want anything?" she wheezed.

Down the hill, her client was walking away, whistling, as if he had just emerged from his own house and was going to church.

"You know what Durnovaria be?" Toller asked.

"Never done that before, 'less it be the latest name for something they do down Weymouth way. You know what sailors be like after they been at sea a few months."

"No. It's the name of the brewery."

"Then you should ask them at the brewery, and not try to show a poor girl up with fancy words."

Toller turned away. Christmas Day. Keep your money in your pocket. I habn't paid for a woman in my life, and don't intend to start now.

The soles on his boots were thinning, and a stone pulled him up. A quick examination revealed they would have a hole in a few days. As night fell, he did not want to return to his room at The Raddleman. Where are all the places that usually light up? A chop house maybe, or an inn. Not The King's Arms, but a less grand one, its feet up, down some back-street, open for casual business. There be nowhere better to visit when folk want to be quiet, till the need to return to normal living overcomes them, and they shuffle again into the town's open spaces, for human contact, sharp words, soft touches, relief.

The streets were silent. Nobody solicited his company, except the woman who wanted payment. No house hinted it might offer sanctuary for an hour or two. He passed the time by walking quickly, then slowly, to keep warm, to preserve the soles of his boots. Somewhere in Dorchester he had to find cheap accommodation, a room bereft of even minimal signs that it had been meant for a human being. He had no money to pay rent in advance, or to buy food, after his loan had gone. I cannot ask Mr. Godmanstone for more; he will think me wasteful, will assume that I have spent it on expensive pleasures, and won't be easily persuaded. This was now Toller's main preoccupation, but it was not the day to be helped. The whole world seemed intent on staying indoors, surviving.

At The Raddleman, the bed was damp, and there was no wood or coal in the grate. Only when he was really tired would he return.

Then, from out of the shadows, on the other side of the road, he saw a man in a uniform. In the amber glow of the gas lamp, a soldier was lighting up a cigarette. Toller thought the stranger nodded, so called back, "Evening."

"Quiet round here. Must be Christmas," said the soldier.

Toller hesitated, took a step to cross, but the soldier beat him to it. The man's moustache was black, hung like a yard brush over his top lip.

"Nowhere open."

"Want a smoke?"

The soldier took out from his pocket his tobacco tin, and held it up.

"'Tis kind, but no. It be five lambings since I smoked, and then 'twas a pipe."

"Never used one."

Toller became inquisitive, wanted to engage him, had never seen a uniform close up, how it changed a man, marked him out with a certain colour, rank, destiny.

"You live Dorchester?"

"On leave. Back tomorrow, though. This time tomorrow: Southampton, to await orders."

"Your family live here?"

The soldier studied his feet. How best to describe his wasted journey? To capture that hollow feeling that comes with the news that a fiancée has taken up with a man with a bit of money and a house of his own?

"You don't want to know my troubles. Women: they're all the same," he declared authoritatively. "But we're out of each other's hair now. Better we part now than when I've lost an eye and a leg somewhere for Her Majesty."

"I see."

"Do you? Do you really?"

After a moment or two, Toller said, "Yes, I do. That's why I'm here: to start again."

The soldier drew deeply on his cigarette, looked up at the freckled sky, and apologised.

"That's how it gets you. We get picked up and dropped just as soon. But I'm wed to the army, and though she's a bitch, she always wants me, welcomes me with open arms, and I've sworn to lay down my life for her."

"I understand."

"Some don't, though."

Toller could not convey his empathy any more convincingly, so said, "Good luck, wherever you're posted."

"Luck don't come into it. Fancy a quick pint before I turn in?"

Here it was: the moment when he had to admit he had no money to stand his round. His shame smelt of stale sweat, tasted of cold, unseasoned tripe.

"No money. After tomorrow, I may have a job at the brewery, but no money to rent a room till my first wages."

"You poor bugger. Worse off than me! Ever thought of joining up? Here, take this. I shan't need it where I'm going." Not a Dorset accent any more; his sounds had been roughened by billeting with soldiers from all over England. The man saw that Toller was about to protest, and insisted. "Take it. You're more than welcome. Accept it as a loan. Meet me here, same time, same place, next year, and you can pay me back, and buy me a pint. That'll get me through, that will: knowing you owe me. I'm a great believer in people paying their dues."

The soldier smiled, and Toller took the money. The companionship of men had armoured the soldier with selflessness. They shook hands, and the soldier swallowed hard.

"I shall be waiting for you here," said Toller. "But what be your name?"

"Titus Chettle, it be."

The soldier smiled again, turned, and was gone.

Alone once again, Toller resumed his walk.

At the top of the hill, he stopped when he heard the sound of brass instruments. He strained his eyes, and saw a group of people in uniform, arriving at the church. Following them were others, who gathered loosely into an audience.

Toller made his way towards them, anxious to find out what had drawn them there. As the musicians played, some of the onlookers began to sing. Close to them, Toller asked a man, between hymns, what nature of players they were, and the man replied, "Why, know you not the Lord's Army? Have you never seen their dark uniforms as they go into battle against want and neglect?"

"No, sir, I have not, me being a stranger, these parts. What sing they?"

"Hymns, in praise of the Lord. Do you not recognise these clarion calls? Where have you come from that you have not heard them before?"

"Pilsdon, and hab never heard of such an army. 'Tis a lonely place, but nearer to Heaven than some."

The man shook his head, and joined again in the singing.

Though glad that his solitude had ended, Toller felt ashamed that he had rarely attended church, except for funerals. The man in the crowd had spoken to him disdainfully. Why, if that is how they encourage folk into the Church, thought Toller, then I shall never enter. 'Twas a trial, last night, in Stinsford church, and I felt like a hand that don't fit snug into a glove.

After several more hymns, the band ceased playing, and the soldiers dispersed into the streets. Toller followed a man and a woman, saw them bend to a body huddled in a doorway. In soft, friendly voices, they invited him to the Mission, but the man turned them away. "Steal my boots, they will!" he cried. "All be thieves and trouble-makers."

People with such goodness in their hearts put others before themselves! Toller marvelled. And their uniform marks them out. How little I have done to help my fellow human beings! How cut off I have been in that cottage, insulting Forston Sampford, when I could have been doing better things than shepherding!

The woman noticed Toller observing them.

"Need you help on this night?" she asked.

"No, not I, who be inquisitive, and hab never seen your like before, but will know you by your uniform, in future. Forgive me."

Her fellow soldier stood up and asked, "Will you join us, then, and learn our works? Then you will truly know us. Your curiosity be a first step to joining."

Toller hesitated, could think of no good reason for refusing the man's invitation.

"I . . ."

The man saw Toller's confusion, and said, "Don't 'ee feel obliged. Come when your heart tells 'ee. Just listen to it."

They said goodnight, and went to look for others in need. For a while, Toller could not wash the sound of the instruments and singing from his head. He had known none of the words, yet their beauty had mesmerised him, petrified him with their other-worldliness. Much have I learned, he acknowledged. I never knew anyone cared for my salvation.

Reluctantly, he began to make his way back to The Raddleman. Images, questions, ideas, plans jostled in his head. The day had ended with a reminder that the world was not just the one in which he had been living. Some people had made personal sacrifices to help others, while he had been rounding up stray sheep with a dog he had had to shoot when he had decided to leave. 'Tis the soldier's calling, though not mine. There are many ways to contribute, but a uniform would puff me out too much. A brewery man I shall be, a humble to start, but I shall learn my trade so well that my shepherding will have been but a dream. I shall add up to more than that.

And that's when he heard it, in the cold night air, which had made the chimes from the church shiver against the facades of the buildings. Toller recognised it, had heard it many times in Marshwood Vale, when a farmer had shot a pheasant or two. Then the noise had echoed, rolled through the winter woods, scattering whole flocks of flapping crows into the sky. Now the crack bounced off the walls, though originating from some distant street, near the Roman ruins.

On Christmas Day? Toller wondered. His natural reaction had been to flinch, to avoid whatever danger might accompany it, and the back of his neck bristled, as a dog's when sensing danger. He looked around, but saw no one, though a curtain, high up at a window, twitched, and a woman's face half-appeared, looking for what had disturbed her. Then, when Toller heard the second and final shot, he ran to a doorway, and pressed himself against the door. That noise was louder, more conclusive, as if declaring that the second bullet had, indeed, made sure that its target was dead. This baint a farmer after crows, Toller thought. Someone angry.

Chapter eight.

Toller sat on a grassy knoll overlooking Marshwood Vale, and bit into the sweet apple, his only nourishment, so far, of the hot day. The heat haze broke up the outlines of the trees at the bottom of the field, where his sheep, like sacks the colour of clotted cream, were lying in the shade. His dog, Pickle, was panting next to him. It was a relaxing day, one for looking at scenes they ignored when working, for contemplating finer, sometimes abstract, notions.

Pickle's long, frothing tongue hung out, in his eyes sparkling diamonds of anticipation of a small offering from his master. Flies irritated, drawn by the apple's perfume, and Toller wafted at them half-heartedly. This was another day without his father and mother, who would have enjoyed sitting outside the cottage, he on an upturned box, she on a wooden chair he had made, her sleeves rolled up to her elbows, her hands red-raw from washing clothes. The memory was as sweet as the apple, as perfect as the peace.

Now there was just Toller and his dog, in the warmth. Two hills in the far distance cupped the grey sea, held it up like an offering to the Gods. How near it looks on such a day! Even the heat's gauze does not obscure it, remarked Toller. All that water held in the horizon's cleavage!

Yet for all his inner peace, Toller fidgeted. He could die in his cottage, and no one would know, for he had no friends, save the bustling, fussing birds, feeding, at the end of the day.

And what of Forston Sampford, older and just as solitary? Toller remembered that his own father, chopping or digging in the garden, had never looked up when Sampford was passing. There had been more than the spiteful hawthorn between them: something vulgar, an event buried in silence but surviving in taut expressions. Toller's father's and Sampford's enduring refusal to look at each other had always been a loaded gun.

"Do not speak to him," Toller had once been instructed by his father.

"Why?" Toller had asked.

"Never you mind. Best if you don't, that's all."

So Toller never asked again, knew that his father would never tell him. That was how the tension had remained: by Toller turning away when he saw Sampford coming, by copying the indifference of his father. Anything else would have been a betrayal.

From his vantage point, Toller could see a horse being led by a young woman. Something in the horse's agitated movement of its head suggested all was not well. By its side, the woman stroked it, to soothe it as it limped. Pickle stood up and barked.

"'Tis Hepsy Valence if I baint mistaken, and her horse be a-dragging itself like an old man. Maybe she needs a hand, though she hab never noticed me, to speak of. She be as beautiful as Marshwood Vale, 'tis certain, though haughty with it."

Hepsy, hearing Pickle, looked up the field to see Toller striding towards her. She stopped, and called, "My horse is lame, I fear. A stone, back there. Will you help? I tremble too much."

Toller's strides became leaps, but the hedge separated them, so he made for the corner, where there was a gate. Toller climbed first, and Pickle jumped onto the top bar.

"Away, Pick!" ordered Toller.

Ignoring Hepsy, he murmured to the horse, gently stroked its neck, and glanced down at its leg.

"It must have been a sharp stone, I think, spilled from the soil," said Hepsy.

Toller continued to ignore her, assessing instead how badly the front right hoof was injured.

"There, there, my fine fellow."

His voice was like the distant hum of a bee, barely audible to Hepsy, who moved into his line of vision. It was not out of spite that he avoided making eye-contact; the horse was his priority. She had called for help, had she not?

"Will he have to be shot?" she asked, exasperated.

"Let me have a look, boy. Gently does it."

Hepsy watched his hand slip over the horse's flank as smoothly as a piece of silk, downwards, building the horse's confidence in him.

Why does he address the horse and not me? she asked herself.

In Toller's pocket was the remaining half of his apple, which he had stuffed into it as he had upped and rushed down to see Hepsy. Slowly, he took it out, and let the horse see and smell it, so that it would recognise him as a friend, and not as someone who would add to his pain. As he held the apple in the palm of his right hand, he continued his downward stroking, his soothing words a balm. The horse took the offering, and allowed Toller to examine the hoof.

Meanwhile, Hepsy had crossed her arms, hoping perversely that the horse would kick him, as a punishment. Yet she was fascinated by his confident handling, when he crouched to verify what she had suggested was the problem. She knew this man, with whom her father was on nodding terms, by sight, by trade. Once, Ebenezer had enlisted his help – reluctantly, when his own dog had broken its leg, and had had to be put down – and had sworn he would never be put in such a position again. He hated asking for help from anyone. Toller had merely nodded, but had been disappointed that he had seen Hepsy only briefly, as Ebenezer had sent her indoors. There was something about Toller of which Ebenezer had been wary. Strange, he had thought, that such a young man took no pleasure in Bridport, but was content to breed and sell sheep.

"No sign 'twas a stone," concluded Toller. "He'll be all right. Just don't ride him for a day or two."

"Could've sworn it was a stone," she insisted.

Toller shrugged, but had no longer a reason for avoiding eye contact. Hepsy unfolded her arms, and took the reins he was offering. He could bear the embarrassment no more, and turned. Yet she knew it was not a rejection, more an acknowledgement that there were other things that might be said, as any two young people in a remote place might consider saying.

Not wanting him to go but to learn more about him, she said, "You want paying? I mean, I have no money with me, but if you call at Dugdale Farm . . . 'Tis Mr. Burstock, baint it?"

When he turned, Toller noticed she had taken a pace forward, was anxious to keep him there.

"Toller be my first name. For the horse there be no charge, 'cept for the apple I was eating."

Hepsy saw through his straight face, and laughed.

"Come take your pick in the orchard. The boughs bend with their weight. The skins be yet green."

Toller accepted her invitation, this time overcoming his embarrassment. Not ten yards away, Pickle whined.

"Away, Pick!" ordered Toller.

"Sour green, they be, 'less cooked in a pie with sweet plums."

"They be hazel, not green."

"The apples?"

"Your eyes."

"A jest? Brown, they be. Your sight be as weak as father's."

"He sees well enough?"

"When he wants to, when things baint going his way. Then he be a hawk, spots a wrong as soon as a right begins to spoil." She hung her head at the awful truth of it. "His eyes be my gaolers when it suits him."

"You are not free to come and go as you please?"

Hepsy shook her head. They were less than a broom apart.

"My wings have been clipped by the loss of my mother," she sighed. "But I keep you from your work."

"May I pick an apple tomorrow? See how your horse is?"

Hepsy's face was like Marshwood Vale when a cloud passes, and the sun peels away its shadow.

"You may have the ripest for today's trouble," she promised, "but come early in the afternoon, when he is away at the hunt, Crewkerne way."

"Come, Pick," called Toller, and returned to the field.

Before the sun set, painting blushing haloes behind the hill-tops, Toller took out from a drawer clean clothes: not the suit he had bought for his mother's funeral, but working attire. It is best, he decided, if Hepsibah sees me as I really am: an ordinary labourer with a few sheep and a cottage left by his father. All Hepsibah ever known be such, and will find in my appearance a few marks of her own father.

In the morning, Toller dipped his head into the barrel of water outside his cottage, not bothering to skim off the dead insects trapped by its surface tension. He pressed off the water with his palms, and brushed his hair, leaving it to dry naturally. His beard, untrimmed for months, had tightened into tiny springs. In the mirror, he smiled. 'Taint often I looks at myself, but today I see that, if I add up to anything, in the future, a wife might not be too annoyed to see me when she a-wakes, mornings.

He arrived just when the butterflies began to flap and hop from flower to flower. Hepsy was outside. Round her head she had wrapped a veil, and was scraping honey from a comb she had carefully drawn from one of the hives. The bees showed little interest in her, in the rising warmth.

She wanted Toller to catch her in her pale blue dress, in which, one day, she would draw rich men's eyes, as her father had predicted, when she had been trying it on in Lyme Regis, after it had been made especially for her. Toller decided to stand there, at a distance, and watch her moving gracefully about the garden, nipping, with her long nails, the reddest, juiciest strawberries from the plants, and gathering wild flowers for the table, so that it felt, in the evening's eerie, feeble lamplight, that she was still in the garden.

And he did. She sensed him waiting, blending into the background of dense hawthorn, long-limbed brambles grown wild, and trees bent by galaxies of ripening apples.

"The bees have been kind to you, this morning?" he called.

She lifted her veil, as a bride preparing to receive a solemn kiss from her groom.

"They rarely sting me. 'Tis father they like," she replied.

He went towards her, in the air the sweet scent of roses.

"Your father?"

"He is at the hunt, and won't return till the hounds have savaged every fox between Crewkerne and Chard."

She said it matter-of-factly, having never witnessed a kill, but she had been thrilled to watch the huntsmen in their bright red jackets, trotting down the lane, to see them doff their black hats to her, the hounds, ready for the call to chase, just ahead of them.

"Your horse walks well, this morning?"

Toller was now within touching distance.

"I have waited for you," she said.

Toller was not sure whether her words were an expression of anticipation or a castigation.

Taking his arm, she led him to the stable. Toller had not been expecting the contact, wondered what it meant. Her hand rested almost weightlessly, like a sleeve, and he feared to respond lest she withdraw it.

Toller looked at the horse, knew from the way it was holding itself that the worst was over.

"He stands well. There is nothing to fear. Have you been near him?"

She shook her head, and said, "I have watched him from this side of his box's door."

"Walk him tomorrow, but don't ride him yet. I will come again in a few days, try him on a long rein, to see if he falters."

She wondered whether he had taken advantage of the horse to obtain another meeting; that is what men do, her father had warned her, when he had seen their eyes turn towards her: manufacture occasions to impress women further, sometimes for dishonourable purposes. Somehow, though, she did not suspect Toller of being such a man. Too awkward under her gentle hold, he had, she felt, petrified.

"You are too kind. Will you take a drink of elderflower cordial? I made it myself."

"'Tis kind on such a day. Thank 'ee."

"Will you come inside the farmhouse, where 'tis cooler? The heat wilts me."

"But there is shade under one of your trees?"

Toller felt uneasy at her suggestion. Ebenezer might return, all a-froth in blood-lust, from the hunt. To cross his threshold would be a step too far, to invite his disapprobation, when Toller really wanted to win his neighbour's respect.

"As you wish," said Hepsy, clearly offended by Toller's caution. "The oak behind the house is a favourite of mine. The sun is a stranger underneath it; the branches are a parasol."

She led him to it, and he sat on the grass.

"God's throne," he explained, when she gave him a wry look.

"My dress," she pointed out. "The grass will stain it. Will you carry the chairs from the house?"

"As you wish."

He placed the chairs facing each other, but thought that too contrived. Side by side meant their eyes would not meet, so he chose an oblique angle, to allow stray looks to be noticed and responded to.

She carried a silver tray bearing two glasses of cordial, pointing her toes towards him, avoiding sudden movement, as she made her way to the chairs.

"Here be all right?" Toller asked.

"Yes, 'tis perfect in the shade."

Toller sipped.

"You made this, you say?"

She nodded and said, "I baint just a farmer's daughter, you know. Ten a penny they be, these parts. Any maid do cordial: pluck the flowers in the hedgerows, crush them in a barrel of water, and leave them a tolerable time before straining."

"And what else do you do, besides being a farmer's daughter?"

"Sing tolerable."

"Do you have a tune to go with this cordial?"

He presumes much, thought Hepsy.

The veil was still round her neck and shoulders.

"'Tis too hot for this!" she complained.

Tetchily, she removed it, hoping that he would not ask her again to sing. Toller saw her discomfort, guessed her reluctance, and watched the veil fall to the floor.

"And too hot for a song?"

Hepsy picked up her veil, folded it carefully, and began to fan herself with it.

"*Far* too hot."

There settled a silence in which Toller allowed her space to become less flustered, and, slowly, her agitation became the kiss of a zephyr. The sips of her cordial had helped, had prolonged, as intended, Toller's visit. He himself had taken two swallows to empty his glass, and she had wrongly seen this as a sign that he was keen to leave. Therefore, she took tiny sips in the hope that he would entertain her, and not she him.

Suddenly, she dropped her veil, and screamed. Her chair fell backwards, and Toller jumped up, alarmed.

"I am stung!" she cried. "It must have been in my scarf. Oh, how it hurts!"

Toller seized her hand, and said, "Best let me see to it afore 'tis inflamed."

Seeing no sting in the back of her hand, but noticing where it had penetrated, he stretched her skin, and sucked hard, before spitting out, away from her.

"It's not quite gone, the pain," Hepsy complained, her heart pounding at the sensation of his lips on her skin.

Toller again brought her hand, with both of his own, close to his lips, but, this time, they did not meet. The cry of "Hepsibah!" had prevented their union.

"Father!" gasped Hepsy, withdrawing her hand.

Ebenezer had returned prematurely from the hunt, his arm in a sling, following his fall at the entrance to a copse which was impenetrable to all but hounds, his face contorted with pain and questions yet unformed but gathering shape, ready for utterance.

Chapter nine.

Toller made himself as presentable as possible by flattening down his long, unruly hair with his palm pasted with saliva, after a troubled night of constantly turning his head on the pillow. Dragging his fingernails downwards, through his beard, like a labourer raking hay, he wanted to make sure that he himself, and not just the letter, secured the job at the brewery. "Thank 'ee, Miss. Misterton," said Toller to himself. "'Twas Providence nearly tumbled you out of the trap, and flipped the book for me to find. That mad dog paid with his life for bringing me this chance."

The brewery was already at work when he arrived. He was heralded by the banging and rumbling of barrels being rolled onto and off carts. Two horses had their noses in bags, oblivious to the activity around them. Toller asked one of the men where Mr. Godmanstone's office was, and the man glanced at his mate. It was a meaningful yet inscrutable look. He's mocking me, felt Toller. The face is still as marble, but not the fidgeting eyes, a tell-tale sign.

"Over there," said the man. Neither a nod of the head nor a pointing finger clarified where he meant. Again, Toller asked. This time, the man replied, "Yonder." His mate smiled, continued pushing his barrel towards the boards up which it had to go.

Toller clenched his fists, stiffly stood his ground, intent on confronting this lack of respect. Both men, however, became wary when they saw his eyes fixed unblinkingly on them, stalking them.

"That way, in the corner, be the door," said the first, sensing trouble.

"My name be Burstock," Toller told them. "Toller Burstock."

"And so?"

"Just so's you know."

"Why would I want to know?" asked the second.

"So you can tell the police who broke your friend's neck."

Calmly, when Toller had stayed just long enough to let them know he would leave when *he* decided to, he went to the corner of the building.

"Those men bother you?" asked Godmanstone, greeting him on the stairs, having watched the encounter through the office window.

"No. Just pointing me in the right direction."

Godmanstone led him back upstairs, and Toller slipped his hand into his pocket, opened his clenched fist, insecurely felt the letter he would soon hand over.

"This is my sister. She'll be interviewing you. I have to be elsewhere soon."

Toller recognised the woman who had turned and looked at him in Stinsford church: brown eyes flecked with gold, and full lips, two segments of pink grapefruit. She was wearing no bonnet, and her black hair, swept up and held in place by two ivory combs, looked silver in the light from the window behind her.

"Pleased to meet you, Miss. Godmanstone."

"My brother has told me about your chance meeting in Dorchester."

The loan. Of course. Was that just a polite way of letting him know that she knew he owed money? Money be supposed to set you free, not make a slave of you, thought Toller.

"He was kind enough to lend me some money, which I will pay back as soon as I can. I have a letter from Miss. Miranda Misterton, over at the manor, Stinsford way."

He handed it to her, and she read it, then passed it to her brother.

"*You* deal with it. I need to catch those two before they leave," said Godmanstone.

He left, taking the steps two at a time. In the yard, the men watched him striding towards them. This time, there was no ironic smile on their face; his urgency had banished it.

"You are highly thought of," opened Zenobia, perusing the reference.

"'Twas nothing, the incident."

"Then why should she go to such lengths to write a glowing reference?"

"I returned the book to her, that's all."

"Book? There is no mention here of a book."

"I have not read the letter."

Zenobia touched a seat, and he sat down. On the written word of a woman, I have handed myself over to another, he thought. Between them, they have the power to make or break me. Have I been foolish? There could be anything in the letter. Perhaps, I am too trusting of women.

"Do you drink?"

"No, Miss. At least, not any more."

"Then if all our customers were like you, we would soon be out of business!"

Zenobia laughed heartily.

"Not to excess, I mean. There was one time –"

"You need not apologise, Mr. Burstock. How much you drink is a matter for you alone, unless, of course, it prevents you doing your job. But tell me, what did you do in your last employment? Many come and find that it is too much like hard work."

Toller's lips tightened, and his tone was defensive.

"I baint afraid of getting my hands dirty, 'tis certain. Been a shepherd, Pilsdon way, near Bridport. Out on the hills, all weathers. Never missed a day, 'cept to bury my mother and father."

Zenobia gave the impression she might sit or remain standing; Toller sensed that he had yet to convince her of his suitability.

"Might you not miss the open spaces of the fields and hills? The sunlight? There is not much natural light in the brewery."

"I can lift barrels onto and off carts as well as the next man."

Zenobia exhaled, sat down, and referred to the letter again.

"It says that you are ambitious, that you felt compelled to turn down Miss. Misterton's offer to take charge of her horses. We buy ours from her. I am not sure that the work here matches your ambition. Most people who come to us are labourers, happy just to deliver casks to inns. We already have managers overseeing the brewing. Tell me, honestly, why you have come all this way to ask for work here, when there is a perfectly good brewery, to which you could have applied, in Bridport. You have heard of Palmer's?"

He knew of it, had passed it on his way to West Bay. This leaving of Pilsdon, must it always follow me, like a shadow, so that I have to explain that I cannot bear to see Hepsy Valence? I might have saved her father's life, but 'tis clear he wants his daughter to marry a man of means, and she herself has had her head filled with notions of a world much bigger than Marshwood Vale. Why, she be more interested in Lyme Regis than Bridport. But I am as good and honest a man as any of them, and I shall return and claim her, once I've made something of myself.

While these thoughts, churned a thousand times since he had left Dugdale Farm with Hepsy's "No, Toller" echoing in his ears, were contorting his eyebrows and lips this way and that, Zenobia realised she had asked too personal a question, and so said, "Forgive me, Mr. Burstock. I was not prying. I merely wished to know what brought you here. Many come to Dorchester to work, but few with such ambition."

"There be a time in everyone's life to move on," he replied. "Got my reason, but 'tis time to start again."

A woman, guessed Zenobia. He is, as I suspected, a man of

feeling. Miranda would not have written to me unless she had seen something promising in him.

Again, Zenobia read the letter to herself, stopped at *Like I imagine my father to have been when he was that age*. Miranda had been touched by Toller, she could see.

Decisively, Zenobia said, "There is a vacancy here, on the carts. You are used to horses, and are physically strong. Will you take it? I cannot promise you advancement at the moment. Indeed, you will be on a week's trial, to see if the work suits you. But you will find us fair employers, and we have been known to promote workers when they have shown desire and an aptitude for the job."

"I be more than grateful to accept. 'Ee'll find me a willing and a sober, and I shall pay off Mr. Godmanstone's money as soon as I can."

"On the subject of money . . . " Zenobia went to a drawer, rummaged among its contents, and placed a bag of coins on the desk. Toller looked at it. Too far out of reach to be meant for me, he thought. "Take it."

"I cannot. I have not lifted a finger here yet. I shall not touch a penny till my back aches."

"Then Miss. Misterton will be disappointed that you have spurned her help." Zenobia picked up the letter, and read: "'It is a token of my gratitude for his help. He will, no doubt, refuse it. His pride is made of Portland stone, but do press it into his hand. If he deems it too much, tell him he might return, one day, and repay some of it.'"

Toller hung his head.

"Thank 'ee."

Zenobia did, indeed, press it into his hand.

"Come," she said briskly. "There is work to do."

She led him into the yard, where a man was waiting next to a horse and cart.

"Ezra, this is your new drayman, Toller Burstock. Starts right now. I know it's a bit soon after what happened to Arthur, but sometimes keeping busy takes your mind off things. You got your job-sheet?"

Ezra nodded.

"I'm all right, Miss. Godmanstone. 'Twas the shock of it. Hearing about it's one thing, but him not here's another."

"I'll leave Toller in your capable hands, then. And, Toller, do drop into the office, at the end of your round. There's a bit of paperwork for you to do."

With alacrity, she returned to her office.

Toller found Ezra cold and indifferent.

"Let's load the cart. The sooner we get done, the sooner we can be away," said Ezra.

"Where first?" asked Toller.

"The King's Arms. Daily order. Our best customer."

"And the furthest away?"

"Tolpuddle: The Martyrs' Arms."

Looking down on the streets from such a high position, Toller felt important. People could see he was working, that he had come to Dorchester, and had begun to make his mark. Yes, he had been lucky to have met someone who had taken an interest in him, that a vacancy had arisen, but he had not begged for money. He desperately wanted to work.

The first delivery was just down the hill.

"Go and tell the landlord we're here, and to open his cellar trapdoor. I'll make a start on the barrels. When I pass one to you, let it roll down your chest, bend at the knees, and put it on the floor. Pass me the first, and I'll show 'ee."

Ezra demonstrated, and Toller had a go.

"'Tis all in the timing," remarked Toller.

"'Tis certain."

And I be sure that be where Mattie and I sat with our food,

telling the worst to each other, he said to himself, as he followed a man through the inn to the cellar stairs.

"Mind the steps. They be steep enough to break the strongest neck if you slip."

The cellar was damp and cold, smelt of ale and rat droppings, an odour not even the strongest of Dorset winds, roaring in from the sea like a hostile marauder, could remove. Toller gagged, was glad of the light tumbling through the trapdoor when the cellarman hooked back the bolts with a pole.

"Always smell like this?" asked Toller.

"Mice and rats. Other man left?"

"Don't know."

Toller saw Ezra's legs, hands, and the barrel.

"You reach up?" asked Ezra.

"Good job you tall. Did for one man when he missed his hold, and the barrel broke his skull. Brains all spilled out. Barrel all right, though," informed the cellarman.

"Steady," advised Ezra. "You got?"

"Got."

"Take it on your chest, but catch the weight on your knees by bending 'em."

The barrel felt heavy, coming from above. The cellarman stood back, and when it was safely on the floor, said, "'Twas well done. Over there now with it."

The cellarman's lamp illuminated a dark corner, scattering a huddle of rats.

Ezra passed three more barrels to Toller, who, anxious to be out of the foul atmosphere, turned to go.

"Don't be forgetting the empties," said the cellarman, and Toller offered them up to Ezra.

"All right?" asked Ezra, when Toller was back on the cart.

"Tolerable."

"Tolerable be passing good in this job."

When the last delivery of the day had been made, Toller asked impulsively, “What means Durnovaria?”

“Don’t know. I be just a drayman, not a scholar. That be one for Master Godmanstone. ’Tis *his* brewery. Ask him. He be sure to know.”

Without inviting Toller, Ezra led his horse to its box, where a groom was waiting to feed and water it.

Toller remembered Zenobia’s request to return and complete some paper-work, but he did not wish to end the day without saying goodnight to Ezra, so he waited.

“First day over,” said Toller.

Ezra noticed Toller’s weak smile, surprised by this hint of good spirits.

“Just as well. See ’ee in the morning,” said Ezra straightening his cap, and striding towards the gates, as if afraid they might clang shut and incarcerate him.

’Tis me, thought Toller. I have taken the place of his mate, and we have nothing in common except lifting barrels of ale. But my silences can be just as loud as his. Nay, can even deafen him if he invites ’em.

Zenobia kept him waiting a while outside her door. She had observed him standing in the yard, till he had begun to make his way towards the entrance of the building. The ledgers on which she had been working were in front of her, and she feigned attention to their messages, so that, when Toller obeyed her summons, she was the verisimilitude of absolute concentration.

“Ah, Toller. Numbers! They haunt my dreams, and are like naughty boys: disobedient, and difficult to keep still long enough to increase their worth.”

She looked up at him, her brown eyes ringed with tiredness, and he replied with, “Boys be a handful, ’less they be given a firm hand.”

So you have a sense of humour, after all, she remarked to herself. “And how would you treat figures that defy my will?”

"I would hire a man who, by hook or by shepherd's crook, would make them do as they're told."

Zenobia sighed, put down her pen, and said, "A possible solution. Unfortunately, debtors match in number our reliable customers."

"Yet you still supply them with your ale?"

This implied criticism stung Zenobia, and she sat up straight.

"We do. They pay eventually. But our accounts aren't what I called you back for. I need some basic details about you for our records."

"You stop 'em their ale, they soon pay up," persisted Toller.

Zenobia slid the paper and pen across her desk.

"You read?"

"Tolerable."

During the awkward silence in which Toller wrote down personal details, Zenobia fought the anger she would have unleashed on any other worker who had had the audacity to advise her. She wanted to increase the number of customers, not reduce it. Yet what argument did she have against his suggestion? She had never tried it.

"You a question?" she asked when she saw him hesitate.

"Can't say where I reside, on account of me having nowhere to live, at the minute. Now that I have Miss. Misterton's kind loan, I shall find a room just as soon as possible."

"But you must do so at once! The ice is already forming. The sky is so clear that anyone under the stars tonight will perish."

"*I* could get the customers to pay their debts."

Toller handed back the pen and paper.

"You? You have only just joined us as a drayman!"

"Let me try. No harm in it."

Zenobia's jaw dropped. When she spoke, it was with a mixture of incredulity and interest.

"And how will you persuade them to pay, pray? Durnovaria

Brewery will countenance no violence, no matter how tempting the invitation."

"No matter. I'm not a fighting man, if that's what you mean."

She shook her head, then bit her lip, as if giving his suggestion serious consideration.

"I should talk to my brother. Now you must go, to find accommodation."

"Before I go, there be two things I must ask. What do Durnovaria mean? And what happened to Ezra's mate?"

"Why, Durnovaria is the Latin name for Dorchester. As for your second question, you must be the only person, these parts, not to know."

"Know what?"

"That he was shot dead not a brief stroll from here! That is what has become of us in these modern times: cold, heartless murderers. This century baint what it was, and some say the sooner it expires, the better."

Chapter ten.

During January, Hepsy avoided her father's bedroom, which she knew was untidy and illustrated his habits, lest it feel as if he had not died at all. She feared, mostly, the odour of him, remembered it from when he used to bring her closer to him, and kissed her goodnight. But when she began to smell his unemptied chamber pot, she felt she could delay no longer confronting his last moments in the room.

She felt as if she risked waking him when she slowly opened the door. There came a whiff of him, then the reek of the chamber pot, which she decided had to go immediately. She threw it out of the window, and watched it smash and splash on the ground. It mattered little: it had no handle, had only been kept by Ebenezer through lack of desire to replace it.

When she turned to look at the room, it felt more a place for storing things than a personal space. Only an open Bible, the corner of a page turned over, on the bed suggested a personality.

"I did not know he read this," said Hepsy aloud.

She opened the drawers in which dusty, brown moths had disintegrated on his clothes. And nowhere could she find his silver pocket watch, for which she had searched in vain, downstairs.

In the grate remained white ashes; on the shelf above it was a box, in which he kept a black curl, cut, as a keepsake, from his dead wife's head the moment after he had closed her eyes and weighed down the lids with two penny coins. Otherwise, all Ebenezer's energy had drained from the room.

"'Twas the expectation of finding him there that put me on edge, and now his possessions are as dead as him. They say nought but that he, whose life was *beyond* the walls, had slept in the room," she said.

She gathered his clothes and hugged them.

I will burn these, she decided, case the giving of them to another soul in Bridport leads to me coming across them, on another occasion.

So she made a fire, watched it consume all she had removed from the bedroom, and, not stopping there, searched for other belongings. All were thrown onto the fire, save some papers spread out on his desk. They had to be kept. When she had time to look, she might discover that bills had to be paid; money might be owed to the farm. No farmer herself, she had to think about the future, shape it to her liking, as far as possible.

She read everything, even the letter her mother had sent her father before they were married.

Aloud, Hepsy muttered, "'How happy you have made me – hope every minute will pass quickly – till I am your bride – Sidmouth.' Sidmouth? She a Sidmouth girl? Never said a spickle about that."

Then she picked up a letter from Hugo Lockington, of Lyme Regis. Twice she read it, hoping that the second reading would make more sense.

"Codicil – heretofore – revoke – Redvers Holditch of Crewkerne."

She looked at the date at the top.

"I must to Lyme, without delay!" she cried. "I fear this serves me ill."

Urgently, she sifted through all the documents again, in case there was another from the same man, but there was none.

"All these years with father, and not a whisper of Hugo

Lockington. Tomorrow, I shall take the coach to Lyme, to meet him, and only when his explanation has calmed my palpitating heart will I be satisfied. And Mattie will come with me. I shall not leave her at the mercy of Forston Sampford, who will sniff at her cottage, the moment I am gone."

It was some time before Mattie came to the door, and the reason was soon apparent: Mattie's face was as pale as white marble sculptures on horizontal tombstones. No money had yet arrived from Toller, and she feared that his plan had failed, that he had not yet found the job to elevate him to a high enough level, and that the little money she had would not go far. She had lived, since the meal she had shared with Hepsy, in the hope that, till Toller kept his promise, the wild mushrooms he had dried, a few months ago, would sustain her. But, after she had cooked them, their smell nauseated her, and she was obliged to leave them in the pan.

"But your face be a snowfall!" exclaimed Hepsy. "What ails you that all your blood has drained from your head?" Without answering, Mattie stood back to allow her in. "I must go to Lyme, and am come to ask you to go with me, but I fear you are sick. One or two in Marshwood Vale have been snatched by the 'sumption, and, though 'taint particular who it takes, I had thought you at least its equal, on account of how you can't be more than one and twenty years old," said Hepsy.

"'Taint the 'sumption, though that would be no worse than what I suffer in this cottage. No money hab yet come from my brother, but 'tis to be hoped he will not let me down."

"The delay be but temporary, I am sure. Toller is such a man of his word that his goodness ties him up in knots impossible to unravel, betimes. Come with me, and I will pay. Know that I owe Toller money from last lambing, when he took a bit of cake and some cordial for tending my horse when I thought father might have to shoot it, so lame it limped in the lane. 'Tis what I owe him, so prepare your valise, and tomorrow we shall take the cart to

Bridport, and there catch the coach to Lyme. This way will I repay my debt to him, as an apple be but a spickle of what he did for me."

"But the jolting of the cart won't help me none, as much as I would like to go see the ladies' finery."

"The air on the Cobb will blow away your illness, 'tis certain. Come. What say you?"

Just then, Hepsy's eyes strayed to the table. There sat a tin of snuff, which she recognised. Mattie saw her looking, and turned to it.

"'Tis a tin box belonging to my brother. I found it in a drawer," said Mattie.

"I never knowed him one for snuff."

Anxious to revert to Hepsy's invitation to Lyme, Mattie said, "Then I will come with 'ee, though I be at your mercy, and 'tis to be hoped that a stroll in a new place bill return me to health."

"Then I shall call for you at first light. The coach stops at Bucky Doo, at eleven by the dome's clock, and 'tis a fair distance to Briddy."

Before she left, she took the liberty of picking up the snuff box and looking at it. The show she made of her examination unnerved Mattie.

"Why, 'tis passing strange, as this be similar to Mr. Yondover's. He nearly left his at the farmhouse during the bad snow, till I ran after him, calling, 'Your box, sir. Don't want to get all that way and be beout it!'"

Hepsy left.

Mattie thought: she suspects 'tis Mr. Yondover's, though I know better than to admit it, as 'twill cause her to make up a story in her head, one as winding as the road we shall take in the morning.

The journey to Lyme increased Mattie's persistent nausea. Fortunately, the other passengers were sympathetic, when, on another day, they might have demanded she leave the coach. As they began the descent into Lyme, Hepsy, having installed Mattie by the window, seized the chance to point out the sea, to distract her. Indeed, it did so. Never had Mattie seen it from such a high angle, and her own insignificance was brought home by its silver-plated vastness, curvature, and textures made various by its currents, the few clouds that broke up the cerulean sky, and the breeze.

"See how the sky melts into the sea!" marvelled Hepsy. "'Tis as if it be all one curtain."

"And Lyme be far?"

"Down the hill, a-twisting and a-turning, which might be uncomfortable for you, but, oh, Mattie, how beautiful and pleasant you will find it! We shall take rooms in a hotel where father" – here the memories of the few times Ebenezer had brought her surprised her, made her dab her eyes – "had me measured up. Then I shall take you to a doctor, father's very own, while I pay a visit to the office of Mr. Hugo Lockington, notary, who wrote to him, in early December."

"But, Hepsy, this sickness will pass as surely as the grass grows, in time. I have no need of a doctor."

"Let us not argue, dear. *I* shall meet the doctor's cost, and though he be not cheap, he be the best in Lyme, and maybe in Dorset."

Mattie, fearful that the coach might tip over, held her breath as it gathered pace; no further objection could be uttered.

But soon, the coach began to climb again, slowly, affording Mattie time to feast her eyes on a few shops. Hepsy began to point out her favourites, and, for a brief while, was able to rid herself of the anxiety caused by Hugo Lockington's letter.

The coach stopped at the top of Broad Street, and all passengers alighted.

"I'm afraid we must walk back down the hill a little. The hotel is on the left, half-way down. 'Tis infuriating, but coaches have their official places for picking up and dropping off, and will only stop if there be a highwayman, and there hasn't been such a one pulled his pistol in Dorset for fifty years. Come, Mattie. There will be a time for seeing the town's charms, this afternoon. Let us find our rooms, rest a while, and then let me take you to see the doctor, whose premises are not too far away."

In the privacy of her own room, Mattie wept. She had never been examined by a doctor, had never even seen one. Why do I weep, all the time? she wondered. How do I come to be here, when, only a few weeks ago – three, four? – I was in my bridal gown? Ah well, such be Providence, which I must accept.

The doctor would see her, once the consultation with a woman who paid him handsomely was over. He usually sent this patient home with a bottle of medicine he claimed would be effective, and this satisfied her.

So Hepsy left Mattie in a cheerless room into which flitted, occasionally, a haughty uniformed nurse. Mattie bit her lower lip, summoning up the courage to explain to the doctor why she was there.

Meanwhile, Mr. Hugo Lockington, a man with a bushy, brown beard, round spectacles, and an air of inscrutability reinforced by shelves of tomes, sat in his chair, and prepared himself to be addressed by Hepsy. He fiddled with the chain of his pocket-watch, and checked the time regularly, calculating how much money he might make if all his business, that day, were conducted as smoothly as he anticipated.

"I think it best if you could explain this letter you sent to my father," began Hepsy, placing it on the table.

"He is well?"

"He is dead, sir."

"Dead?"

Lockington gasped, and peeped over the rim of his spectacles, to emphasise the shock of this news, and Mattie thought his eyes unsympathetic.

"Very much so, sir, and has been buried, these last two weeks."

"He seemed in rude health when he came to amend his will and last testament, in early December."

"He died buried in snow. I found this amongst his papers. It clearly relates to his will. Father, you must know, did not confide in me its contents. I expect he himself thought it a subject he would raise with me nearer the age of three score years and ten. But I like not my ignorance in this matter. What means your letter?"

Lockington fidgeted, made a gothic window with his fingertips, thinking how to explain the letter's implications.

"Miss. Valence, your father was fortunate enough to have owned Dugdale Farm. In my safe reside the deeds to it. A small annual fee guarantees they are not lost or destroyed. Many years ago, your father made a will, and left the farm and some money deposited in a bank to your mother. He told me, on his last visit, that your mother had died, a few years ago, and that he wished to change his will. In legal parlance, the will has a codicil. The letter I sent, and which you have brought today, confirms that I have carried out his wish."

It seemed to Hepsy that Lockington was holding something back, so she said, "And how does this codicil affect me? Dugdale Farm is my home."

"Now that your father is dead, it affects you greatly. I am afraid it no longer belongs to you."

"Then whose is it?" she asked, alarmed.

"It has now passed to Redvers Holditch."

"Sir, you play games. Who is Redvers Holditch?"

"His son, Miss. Valence. His son."

Hepsy wanted to understand how she came to have a brother, but her lips were numb. In front of this stranger, who had had to reveal her father's secret, she was embarrassed, confused. A son named Holditch?

Lockington let her grapple with the implications of his revelation. Soon, he would have to clarify them for her, and this would distress her. All those unanswerable questions would keep her awake, at night, for the rest of her life.

"He never said anything. I had no idea."

"In these circumstances, men rarely do. It is more common than you think."

"Is there anything else I should know?"

"Now that I know your father is dead – I presume you can furnish a death certificate – I must contact Redvers Holditch. I have no idea, of course, of his circumstances, or whether it will be as much a surprise to him as you."

"But what if he wishes to sell the farm?"

Lockington sat up straight, had seen that particular look of terror many times. "Hard truths," had once said a fellow notary, "are what we deal in. Not emotion, speculation or fabrication. Hard truths alone," and he had accepted that as an immovable point on the legal compass.

"If so, he has a right to. At the moment, you are living in his house, I believe."

"And what if *he* wishes to live in it?"

"Then he has a perfect right to."

Hepsy shook her head. Losing her father was hard enough. But why, she asked herself, has father left the farm to a son he has said nothing about? He has left me, his own daughter, nothing!

"And do *I* have any rights?"

"I'm afraid not, Miss. Valence. If I may offer some advice – free of charge, I hasten to add – I would wait to see what Mr. Holditch's response to his windfall is. He may not want his bequest. Indeed, it is entirely possible that he does not even know that he is your father's son."

Hepsy asked, "And are you obliged to let him know of my father's change of mind? There is no hope for me?"

Lockington stood up, ending the conversation, emphasising its closure by removing and folding his spectacles.

"Now that you have informed me of your father's death, I am afraid I must. As for hope, I cannot say. I am sure, in time, the issue of your tenancy will resolve itself."

Hepsy, too, stood up; it was time to go.

As arranged, she met Mattie at the bottom of Broad Street. Mattie was waiting on the fringe of the beach, her back to the town. The sky was grimacing. What does she stare at, wondered Hepsy, that fixes her so? For a minute, Hepsy watched the forlorn statue, not daring to disturb her.

"He has given you something?" called Hepsy, eventually. Mattie turned. Her tears had dried, though their pathway down her cheeks remained. On the horizon was a white sail, though it was not the object of her focus. She stared instead into an uncertain future. "I have finished, and I wish with all my heart I had burned Mr. Hugo Lockington's letter. Dugdale Farm now belongs to another, apparently, and I may have to leave. Will you take pity on a poor neighbour?" It was clear, however, that Mattie was too preoccupied with her own thoughts to empathise with Hepsy. "Will you stroll with me? There is much I have to tell you." Hepsy took Mattie's arm, and led her onto the promenade. "Do speak, dear. What did the doctor say?"

"He is almost certain it is a temporary condition."

When Mattie had finished telling her, gulls flocked, screaming dementedly. A dark cloud then shut out the sun, and, in the distance, a slanting band of rain was moving from west to east. Hepsy squeezed Mattie's arm.

"I, too, said it would pass, did I not? Come. I am hungry. Let us eat."

But, within a few paces, Mattie stopped.

"Oh, Hepsy!" she cried. "I cannot deceive you. 'Tis not a passing illness, at all, but a sign that I shall be scorned by every wagging tongue in Dorset. I shall be pointed at, shunned. And when my brother finds out, as he must, one day, he bill turn me out of his house. What am I to do, Hepsy? What am I to do?"

Chapter eleven.

Mattie's hands were sore, their skin puckered. All morning, she had been washing pots from breakfast, which had been a grand affair, there being lots of guests for the weekend. Lord Hector and Lady Intrinseca Dewlish had thrown a splendid dinner, the night before, and had been surprised so many had come down to eat from the hot and cold dishes lined up on the long table.

Mattie tried to stifle yawns that came in waves, at regular intervals. After the dinner, the kitchen staff had not been released from their duties till the last knife had been put away, and Mattie had not opened her bedroom door till the clock had struck one. Still, she reminded herself: that is the price I must pay for working at Maidenhampton. "We are all here," she remembered Mrs. Canford, the cook, telling her, the day she had been set on, "to do the bidding of Lord and Lady Dewlish. There are plenty who would take our place!"

Though Mattie understood this, she felt there had to be more to life than scurrying around the busy kitchen and draughty corridors. Where now was the chance to meet friends, as she used to? All those dances in the hot sun, when she was draped in ribbons and crowned with flowers, and the fluttering eyes she used to make at all the youths in Tolpuddle, were ever-receding memories.

"You may go now, Mattie," said Mrs. Canford. "Once I've put the cold fare in the baskets for the shooting party, I can put my feet up for an hour or two, but I want you back by four. 'Twill be another late night for us all!"

Mattie dried her hands, and said, "Thank 'ee, Mrs. Canford. 'Tis kind."

"Oh, go along, girl, and mind you don't go mixing with the wrong kind in Dorchester. Here, Roddy, you start taking the baskets up to the hall. His Lordship won't be tarrying when there are all those pheasants to shoot."

Despite the considerable weight of the basket, Roddy Cattistock, who had recently been taken on to serve under Mr. Milborne, the butler, caught up with Mattie, and said, as he was overtaking her, "You do me the honour of taking a stroll with me in Dorchester? Mr. Milborne says 'tis on account of our hard work that we have the afternoon off."

Mattie lowered her head, had not yet made up her mind to go. Mrs. Canford's warning was still in her ears. Roddy's voice is too confident, thought Mattie. 'Tis as if he's polished it up on other girls, but how it gleams today! And he a proper young man, too, not a sapling that bows in the wind, but a strong and upright.

"Perhaps, though I don't rightly know, because of all the others," she replied.

"I be a stranger to Dorchester, being a Cerne Abbas man, but they say 'tis a pleasant place, 'specially on market day, and when the sun sets on the golden stone. I should like to see it. You know Cerne Abbas?"

He put down the basket, stood in her way, but not too obviously.

"No. Don't know many places. Tolpuddle, mostly, on account of me being born there. But I don't want to die there, as 'tis small, and I bill soon be forgotten in the mossy churchyard, when the wind hab rubbed my name away, and there be no one to sit by me, and talk."

"Cerne Abbas be not much better, but though it feels bigger in size, 'tis too small in other ways. Still see the same faces, feel the folk staring."

"They stare at *you*?"

Just then, they heard Mrs. Canford calling, "That my first basket not there yet?"

"Just going now!"

Mattie trembled at the possibility that Mrs. Canford might blame her for the delay.

"A tongue on her," whispered Cattistock. "Do stroll with me, Mattie, for I have taken a liking to you and your morbid thoughts."

"Oh no, Mr. Cattistock. The churchyard baint a sad place at all. 'Tis a quiet, yes, but no one hurts you there. The headstones be all green and leaning, like they're listening to you. And my parents be there, side by side, and though 'twas the 'sumption took 'em, leaving me to fend for myself, they be at peace now. A neighbour paid for a grave, on account of him knowing the stonemason as a friend, and 'tis father who squashes mother."

"You are a funny creature, Mattie, but I like you all the more for that."

He picked up the basket, and Mattie went to her room to rest. Why, I have talked like my true self again, and 'tas been many a ploughing since I did so, she thought. I shall wait till Dorchester, and see what happens, as men, Cath Leweston said – and she should know, as she hab known more than any girl I've met – fly away like winnowed straw when any kind of a wind gets up. I barely know Roddy Cattistock, and though he seems a proper in his honesty to me, I know nothing about him, 'cept he blowed in from Cerne Abbas, which baint to his liking.

Before she took a nap, she recalled that he thought her a funny creature, but had laughed as he had said it. I'm glad I be different, thought Mattie, for I am all that be left of the Venns – at least, these parts – and though I wish for a brother who can look after me, it seem I must make my own way in life, and 'tis better folk notice me than not.

In the afternoon, a cold wind blew in their faces from the minute they stepped down from the cart. Cattistock had winked to Mattie, on the way, and she had blushed, had dreaded the time when he would separate her from the rest. The two other kitchen maids, Dulcie and Dora, linked arms, and Dulcie offered her free one to Mattie.

"Come biv us, girl. Let's find a teashop to warm us up a bit."

Mattie hesitated. Dora saw Cattistock waiting, recognised the ill-disguised expectation in his eyes, the tacit agreement he and Mattie had come to.

"'Tis kind, though I want a stroll first, so you two run along now."

Giggling, Dulcie said, "Then mind you don't get yourself in any bother." Then they left Cattistock and Mattie alone.

When the girls were out of earshot, Cattistock said, "Hussies."

"They mean well."

Mattie was waiting for him to resurrect his offer to stroll with her, and he said, "Shall we?" She looked at the arm he was offering, blushed at the thought she would be touching a man in a grown-up way, for the first time. And what will it signify to him if I take it? she asked herself. Will I be his from that moment on? "Come, girl. I won't bite 'ee," he said. Dulcie and Dora were soon out of sight. But, oh, if they saw her, arm in arm with him, she would die of embarrassment!

To end her indecision, Cattistock took her arm, and locked it tightly against him. And now you're mine, his squeeze said.

"The wind is up," she remarked.

"You would be inside?"

"Only if you would."

"We have come to Dorchester, so let us walk to Maumbury Rings, and return for tea later."

From time to time, he asked her a question, which she answered frankly, but when she asked one of him, he was evasive, changed the subject, answered so vaguely it gave the impression that he had not heard her properly, that the wind had blown away her words.

"And this be Maumbury Rings?" she said.

"Yes. Been here for hundreds of years."

"'Tis a horse shoe."

"Come. Let us enter the space. The high sides might protect us from the wind."

Mattie still clung to his arm. In the middle of the amphitheatre, she felt exposed, as if all the eyes of those who had sat on the grassy banks, down the centuries, were watching her, expecting something momentous to happen. Dorchester had vanished from sight. Only a great, semi-circular hill was visible.

"'Tis mysterious. What is it for?" asked Mattie, her head turning to assess its size.

"Who knows? Fights, displays, executions. Maybe a play."

"And what is it used for now?"

It was Cattistock's turn to look around him, use his imagination.

"People like us."

"And folk gather? 'Twould be ideal for May Day, or showing rams."

Cattistock laughed.

"Maybe. I don't know everything. I been a Cerne Abbas lad till recently, remember."

Mattie shivered.

"Come, dear," he said. "Let me warm you."

He pulled her to him, and she stiffened. All those ghosts watching us! And is that why he's brought us here? she wondered To make me his?

Feeling her doubt, he said, "Tell me, and I shall let go, and we shall not mark this spot, this time, with a kiss. Let me know, and we shall go and take tea, and find awkward words that will collide as soon as uttered. Is that what you want, Mattie?"

Had it been anywhere else – the street, the kitchen, an alley – she would have withdrawn, but the possibility of a first kiss in that great arena, before the eyes of history, was too romantic a prospect to abandon.

"No," she whispered.

He felt her shake her head against his chest.

"Come, dear. Look at me."

He pressed his lips against hers, held her more tightly, and she knew her life could never be the same again.

When he slackened his hold, he saw the change in her eyes. Now they were liquid, unfocused, and submissive.

"I don't know what you must think of me," she said.

"I think your lips be the softest silk pillows."

She smiled, flattered, but thought the praise slid too easily from his.

"Shall we take tea? 'Tis cold here."

"You are not warmed by our kiss?"

"Remember the others. It must not seem . . ."

"Your reputation is safe, dear Mattie. Let us leave this spot, and return one year hence, when we are married, and then we shall play out this little scene, and every twelve months afterwards, till we are buried, in Tolpuddle's churchyard, if you so wish."

So quickly, thought Mattie, on their way back to Dorchester. I am gone from kitchen girl to bride-to-be in one short day, without a say of my own, yet with the strong beat of my heart, which yearns for that first commemoration of such a holy day. Mattie Cattistock: there is much in that name, yet so little substance. But to be a spickle of Maumbury Rings' history be something a Tolpuddle maid only dreams of!

In the tearoom, facing each other, when it was impossible not to read the excitement mixed with doubt in Mattie's face, and the message that one kiss alone would not suffice in Cattistock's, the couple looked a picture of expectation. Spoons clattering on cups and saucers replaced words, and no matter how many times Mattie looked out of the window to try and spot Dulcie and Dora, the memory of what had happened in Maumbury Rings drew her eyes back to Cattistock.

"And shall we be married?" he eventually asked. "I have watched and admired you from the day I first saw you in the kitchen at Maidenhampton."

Is it true that I have noticed his fine head, dark eyes, and that I have today kissed him, which is an encouragement I had not planned? Yet I cannot say whether I love him. His lips kindled mine, 'tis certain, but what happens when the faggots, having blazed, die? Must there always be grey ashes, as mother used to tell me?

"I cannot say today that we shall be married, though I will not tell another that I am his, either," she replied.

"You love someone else?"

Cattistock's slightly raised voice alarmed Mattie.

"People will hear, Roddy, and you have misunderstood me. I meant that your offer be the only one I shall consider, and, to put an end to your suffering, shall give you my answer when the moon is full swollen, which baint an eternity away, on account of it being, last night, but a sliver of the moon under your fingernail away from its wholeness."

Roddy, being a man who suspected that her procrastination was a matter of social convention rather than a genuine desire to give serious consideration to his offer, replied, "Then so be it, dear Mattie, for 'tis a blink of an eyelid till then, so I will be satisfied. All that I ask is that you will say nothing of this to anyone, particularly Dulcie and Dora, who will peck at you for a taste of what has passed between us, this afternoon."

"Of course. I would not drop them one grain of what is solemn and private, but I have something to say: I will pay my share of the bill for this pot of tea, for I would not wish you to see any agreement on my part to *you* paying as a sign that I shall be your bride."

During this speech, Mattie grew in confidence, which irritated Cattistock.

"But if your husband-to-be cannot buy you some tea, then it is a shame."

Mattie heard the hurt in his voice, and relented a little.

"So sore that I should respect you in this way? Come, Roddy. Drink your tea. Let us make the most of our time, for soon we shall be with Dulcie and Dora again, when we both must act as if 'tas been an ordinary day."

Cattistock looked at her, and smiled.

"Dear Mattie, you are so sweet, and so practical. I shall have the best of wives, one day. And will there be another kiss before we return to Maidenhampton? I could not bear to wait for the moon to wax fully before another. Come, dear, and promise me. After this tea, will you kiss me again?"

Mattie was amused by his eagerness, the way he smiled, believing it helped his case, and she giggled.

"Enough for one day, Roddy, for I fear that any more bill be like too much cider, and go to your head!"

On the cart, as expected, Dulcie asked what they had been doing, where they had gone, and no mention was made of Maumbury Rings. Dora made up a story about she and Dulcie being approached by two young men, of excellent breeding and appearance, who insisted on escorting them. When she turned to Dulcie, at regular intervals, to confirm what had happened, Dulcie replied, "Yes, Dora. 'Twas exactly so, and much more so in the telling than before!" Once, Dulcie had winked to Mattie, who knew what that meant.

"Who shall give us a song? 'Tis a shame to sit and wane with the light," said Dora.

"Come, Roddy," urged Dulcie. "I have heard 'ee in the kitchen, and you know full many a song to pass the time. What say 'ee, Mattie? Is he to sing?"

Mattie replied, "'Tis true you have a voice as good as any, and 'twould impress us all to hear a song now."

Cattistock, at first, refused to sing, but soon agreed when he calculated what might be at stake, though the women must understand that he had not practised recently, and that they must forgive him if the notes sounded as if they came from rusty hinges on a gate. The women assured him that they would do so, for their own voices were much worse, like the crowing of a cock when the sun first yawns in the morning, exaggerated Dulcie.

Roddy cleared his throat, which made them all laugh, and then began.

"There once was a maid,
who lived lonely and sad,
who milked all the cows
in good times and bad,
and what she missed most
was her love, the dead lad,
who'd drowned in the river,
and now was a ghost."

"Oh, no, Roddy! 'Tis a sad. Sing another full of happiness, for we are young and should not be weighed down by the millstone of death and lost love."

Roddy looked at Mattie, who said, "She be right. A merry, please, and one we might join in the chorus of, if 'tis possible, for we be a jolly cart, and should set our mood strong afore tonight's dinner, when Lady Intrinseca bill have us run our legs off for her guests."

Backed into a corner, he rolled his eyes up to the sky, as if trying to recall such a ditty. Mattie laughed, and he did it again before beginning.

> “We shall dance round the maypole,
> weave ribbons, and sing,
> and the sun will shine strong
> as we skip round the ring,
> singing, ‘Come choose your sweetheart,
> and one of us pick,
> and you shall be loved
> till the end of life’s wick.’”

The three kitchen maids applauded him, but said it would be something rare to meet a man who maintained his interest that long.

Back at Maidenhampton, their merriment faded, and soon, in their working attire, they began to prepare for that evening’s dinner. Whenever he caught her eye, Cattistock winked at Mattie, and she smiled shyly.

The next night, the clouds obscured the moon, and Cattistock cursed. He crept to her room, and knocked, but she pretended to be asleep. To hear her name whispered through the keyhole thrilled her, and more than once was she tempted to open the door.

The night after that, the moon, now as full as a wheel of blue vinney, was clearly visible, and Cattistock stopped her, as she made for her room.

“The waiting be over now, Mattie. If my eyes don’t deceive me, the moon be close to bursting. What say you to my offer?”

Mattie said, “Roddy, I have thought long and hard about your proposal, and though our acquaintance be only a spickle of what be normal in these matters, I accept, on account of me liking you as much as is necessary to go to the altar. But there be but one thing: let us marry in Tolpuddle and not at the chapel here. Tolpuddle be where I was born, and ’tis where I shall be buried. Mark this last wish, and promise that, if I die before you, you will bury me next to my parents.”

Roddy took her hands, but she snatched them away.

"I promise to do all you ask. And now will you let me kiss you?"

"In time, Roddy. We are but engaged, though I hope we shall be wed 'ere the next full moon, when I shall be freer with my lips."

Lord and Lady Dewlish were disappointed that the wedding would not take place on the estate.

"And I suppose they must have married quarters," grumbled his Lordship. "Ah well! I suppose people will get married."

Lady Dewlish added, "It won't cost us much, if that's what you're worried about. The apartment on the top floor will take little furnishing."

The verger put snowdrops on the altar, and Dulcie and Dora wore their best dresses. The Dewlishes were engaged elsewhere, on the wedding day, but Mrs. Canford came, and Mr. Milborne took Mattie down the aisle – prematurely. There was a cold sting in the air, and Mattie would not wear a coat, wishing instead to show off her wedding dress, but Mr. Milborne insisted she wait inside.

"Come, Mattie. This should not be a day for shivering!" he had said, before taking her arm.

No one had thought it unusual that Cattistock had not been seen that morning. Mr. Milborne had given him the day off, and it had been assumed that he would make his way on the cart, which he had asked permission to use. The Dewlishes had insisted that Mattie take the coach, she having no other means of transport, and it being considered bad luck for the bride and groom to see each other before the ceremony.

When half an hour after the agreed time had passed, Mattie went cold inside, as she realised that Cattistock was not going to come. No speculation that an accident might have befallen him on the way passed through her mind. It was what she had feared.

"He baint coming, is he?" she said, turning to Dulcie and Dora, her bridesmaids. "Has anyone seen him today?"

Mr. Milborne said, "Only when I gave him the letter, which

came first thing. He opened the door a little – I assumed he was in a state of undress – and I passed it to him. I made some light comment about it being a special day, and that I hoped his letter brought good wishes."

"Oh, say that he agreed it was so!" begged Mattie.

But Mr. Milborne hung his head.

The vicar coughed and said, "In view of these circumstances, I think we should postpone the wedding."

But Mattie had already taken the decision to cancel it, and was halfway down the aisle before he had time to say that these things happened more often than she might imagine.

Chapter twelve.

Hugo Lockington, never slow to implement the wishes of his clients, decided that he would go immediately to Crewkerne to search for Redvers Holditch. I will need a few days, he calculated. I know only that Ebenezer Valence said Holditch used to live at Crewkerne but might have sought his fortune elsewhere. Few men, however, leave no trace of where they have been. He has had, more than likely, a forsaken sweetheart, poorly paid employment, maybe a criminal record. In some inn of ill repute, he might have removed the stained petticoat of a starving whore, even fathered a child in the way that he himself had been. But how old would Holditch be? Ebenezer Valence left only his name and the place to find him.

The streets of Crewkerne were emptying when Lockington alighted from the coach. On the journey, a man of means had advised him to stay at The Fox and Hounds, one of the more reputable hostelries.

"There you will be satisfied entirely, sir," said the travelling companion.

"They serve food?"

"The finest in Somerset."

"And there is a pleasant atmosphere to be had?"

"The jolliest, and the establishment is without ruffians and pickpockets. I myself have been there, and can vouch for its welcome."

The man's wife, surprised, turned to him, and said, "Pray, Mr.

Turnworth, tell me at once when I let you out of my sight. On what occasion did you go there, leaving me all alone, at the mercy of my solitude?"

"I don't recall, Mrs. Turnworth, though I vouch it was a grave error, on my part, to leave you on your own, there being no more agreeable a time than that spent by your side, in front of a roaring fire!"

Not wishing his simple enquiry to be the cause of unexpected, marital strife, Lockington said, "I shall call there, and many thanks for your recommendation."

For a minute or two, after this expression of gratitude, Mr. Turnworth suffered further examination, till it ended when his good wife ran out of ways to press him on his foray to The Fox and Hounds.

"Births, deaths, and marriages," muttered Lockington. "Tomorrow: births, deaths, and marriages, and it is to be hoped that Holditch was born, died, or was married here, or my search will be difficult."

It was always at night when he felt the absence of a wife. During tedious working days, spent poring over a mound of legal documents, only intermittently did images of voluptuous women intrude upon his consciousness. But when he had tied the last scarlet ribbon round a will, or sealed with wax a bill to be settled, he often frequented the inns of Lyme Regis. Then, like gulls diving to a net bulging with silver mackerel, women would converge on him from dark doorways, and he would go with them, sometimes behind upturned boats on the shingle, if the weather were kind, or if the women worked for themselves. Then he could smell only the brine in the air, and not the odour of skin unwashed for days. But, alone again in his bed, he could not remember any one of them, not even those who hired a room at an inn, or what they did to him, or charged.

"Know anyone by the name of Holditch?" he asked, as he paid the bill, the following morning.

The man who had taken the money scratched his head.

"Holditch? The name baint heard much, these parts, though I baint saying no one owns it. 'Tis a name as common and rare as the next."

"Redvers is his first name and more rare than his last. He would be youngish, in his early twenties, though I cannot be sure, as I have only his name."

The man slowly polished the counter, giving the impression that he was doing all he could to keep it shining.

"Then that is a shame. Money comes and goes through this door, but not every man gives his real name. It suits some to keep it a secret, and, as a gentleman of the male sort yourself, you will know what I mean, though I don't suggest you baint called" – and here he looked at the register – "Mr. Heath Salwayash."

Lockington slid an additional coin across the counter.

"Well, if you should come across him, please ask him to present himself at this address."

Lockington printed it on a piece of paper, and handed it over.

"And if he baint of a mind to heed this request?"

"Tell him that there awaits good news for him."

The man's eyes flashed.

"Good news be worth more than a shilling, then."

Lockington let the man know immediately that he had misjudged his guest. The man began to choke as Lockington gripped his neck with one hand, the other crushing the nib of the pen on the counter.

"Damn your impudence!" Lockington hissed. "Take care, or you may find that your life won't be worth half that amount."

He let go, and, picking up his bag, left.

The man rubbed his neck, the red marks, where he had been choked, visible.

"You hab a temper, Mr. Salwayash, and 'tis to be hoped that Redvers Holditch can look after himself, and is not likely to upset you, if you ever do meet."

By the end of that day, Lockington had discovered that no Redvers Holditch had been born, married, or died in Crewkerne.

"Then he has come to live here. Ebenezer Valence states clearly that Crewkerne is where he lives. Someone here must know him, and if he is a man, then he must know a woman."

The number of people who initially thought they knew him, but then changed their mind, equalled the unashamedly ignorant of him and his whereabouts.

Lockington found another inn, in the north of the town, and there considered the potential comfort of the woman who served him his evening meal. The flame of the candle lit her eyes, and she smiled as she placed the plate in front of him.

"Will there be anything else, sir?" she asked, wiping a drop of gravy from her hand with her apron.

Lockington hesitated, then said, "Know you Redvers Holditch and where I might find him?"

"No, sir," said the woman. "Don't think I do."

"Are you sure? I'm told he lives in Crewkerne, but it seems no one knows him."

"Then perhaps he's gone for a sojer, or moved Chard way, as some do when work dries up."

"Then my time here is wasted, unless you would come to my room, later."

He jingled the coins in his purse, but the woman said, "I be just a serving girl and no more, and though I shan't say no to a husband with a kind face and a house, I'm not what you think."

Lockington reverted to his professional persona.

"Of course. Forgive me. It has been a long day. I'm charged with the task of bringing good news to the man I mentioned earlier, but it seems he refuses to be found."

The woman said, "I understand, but I must return to the kitchen now."

Lockington had left an instruction with his assistant to place a notice in the Western Chronicle, and this, he hoped, would result in early contact. But, oh, if he could find him, in person, it would save valuable time! Ebenezer had paid Lockington in advance of his death, and Lockington's reputation was at stake.

The beef and oyster pie and Claret alleviated Lockington's frustration. So, he mused, we hate the French enough to buy their wine, do we? Still, this red has washed away my irritation, and I feel more sociable.

At that moment, the door opened, and in stepped a man, his coat collar high. He nodded to Lockington, who wondered if they might converse. The man had impressive, bushy whiskers on the sides of his face, but his chin and upper lip were cleanly shaven, suggesting that, when he spoke, he would not disguise his meaning.

"The night grows colder," he observed.

"I scarcely remember the world without, so well have I dined."

The newcomer glanced at the now empty bottle.

"Then take my word for it."

Lockington thought he said it in a way that suggested he would countenance nothing but the truth, and that now Lockington had been apprised of it, he should never doubt it.

"I do, sir, and count myself fortunate that I have no need to venture out again. Will you join me? I am a stranger to Crewkerne, and would be glad of your company, if it does not encumber you."

"I will – for a moment only, as I expect someone, and have business of a private nature with him. Your bottle is empty, I see. Do you still thirst?"

Anticipating a short meeting only, and anxious to make progress, the following day, in his search for Redvers Holditch, Lockington said he had had enough to drink.

"Hugo Lockington, of Lyme Regis."

The man looked at the offered hand as if weighing up how such a brief association might benefit him.

"Walter Chickerell."

He shook hands, lightly, at first, and then, by degrees, firmly, once he had convinced himself that such a public gesture would not harm his reputation.

"By way of profession, I am a notary," said Lockington.

He had expected Chickerell to be impressed, but was disappointed; the man's face did not alter.

"And you come to Crewkerne on professional business?"

"I do. I come in search of a man for whom I have information on an important matter, but it seems no one knows him. I shall knock on every door, if necessary, but it would help me enormously if I could find him by less exhausting means."

Chickerell listened, and not a muscle on his face twitched.

"It is, indeed, a difficult task," he stated matter-of-factly.

"If I am, by the end of the week, unable to find him, I shall place notices around the town, in the hope that he will see one of them, and contact me in Lyme Regis."

"Notices in public? Then you will need my permission."

Chickerell's voice had stiffened, taken Lockington by surprise.

"Why so, sir? I offend no one, I hope, by bringing good news to one of Crewkerne's citizens?"

"I am the Mayor of Crewkerne, and have the final word on civic matters, but fear not, Mr. Lockington. You have my permission, and I wish you good luck in your search. The end of the week you say? Why, that is ample time to sniff him out. Crewkerne knows itself better than most places, and will yield him before your deadline. 'Tis good news you have for him?"

"It is. I am bound to confidentiality by my professional oath, but suffice it to say that he will be the recipient of substantial wealth. But come, will you allow me to buy you a drink? It is not every day I find myself in such august company."

"I am afraid I must decline your kind offer, having business to attend to. I am here to find my factory manager, whose ear I must have before the morning. It is, perhaps, a little early for him, though it is his favourite haunt. He lives not far from here, so I will make my way to his house. Good evening."

Strange, thought Lockington, that he should leave so soon. Still, he is a man of some importance, and, as a factory owner, must be one of the busiest men in Somerset.

The serving woman returned, and remarked, "I'm sure I heard voices."

"You did, indeed. It was Mayor Chickerell come looking for his manager, and has gone to find him. You know the Mayor?"

The woman felt uneasy at the directness of the question. In what way know him? she wondered.

"He be known to most, as they work for him, one way or another."

"In his factory?" She nodded. "And what does he do?" Lockington took out a coin from his pocket, and showed it to her. "You and I are but strangers. What does it matter if you say?"

He wove the coin between his fingers, and she knew it was for her.

"Sails be what he makes. 'Tis what his father and grandfather done, too. For the navy, once upon a time."

Lockington ceased his manipulation of the coin, and offered it to her.

"Won't buy me, you won't, sir," she said.

"Everyone has a price. What will buy *you*?"

Clean, she noticed. Smartly dressed. Rich, too. She had had worse: malodorous drunkards, violent husbands of frigid wives. In times of acute need, she had taken men behind a big headstone in the graveyard, in the hope that the ghosts might force them to get it over with quickly.

"More than that."

She crossed her arms, feigning hurt pride, felt she was worth more than the price of a loaf of bread and a scraping of jam.

"Come to my room."

"Only if you ask nicely. I likes a man with manners as well as money."

"Well, perhaps this will persuade you."

He waved the note at her, and she went to grab it, smiled at his little game, enjoying the tease.

"'Tas, though you not got the pox, have you? Don't want that. Clara had it, and her husband beat her all the way to Weymouth when he got it, too."

"*I* should be asking that question of *you*. I'm not the first to tempt you, and I expect I won't be the last. Go," he commanded, returning the note to his wallet. "I'm not desperate."

She huffed, angry with herself that she had wounded him, insinuated something about his dark predilections he resented, and left.

The wine had made Lockington drowsy, and he closed his eyes. One or two customers came in, muttered something about the snoring stranger, and settled down by the fire.

Half an hour passed before he was awoken by someone prodding his shoulder. It was almost too light a push to bring him to full consciousness, and only the realisation that he was being addressed by his own name roused him to focus on the young man's face before him.

"What? I have been asleep?"

Tall, the young man had the straggly beginnings, like thin threads of tobacco, of a moustache.

"You have, and it is I who have woken you."

"You? Then I look forward to an acceptable explanation. The inn appears not to be on fire."

"No, sir, it is not, and I do not disturb you lightly."

"There is a matter on which you would speak with me?"

"No, but there is one on which you would speak with me."

"Enough of your impudence. Word games won't do. Speak plainly. I am tired. Your face is friendly enough, so let us conclude this mystery. My bed beckons, and I start early, in the morning."

"My father says he has spoken to you, and that you have some business with me. I myself have had a long day."

"Your father is Mayor Chickerell?"

"The same. Your name, sir?"

"I am Hugo Lockington."

"And I am Redvers Holditch."

"Really?

"Really."

"Then I am about to make your day even longer, though I vouch you will feel neither fatigue nor displeasure at the end of it. The opposite, in fact, is true, for if you are, indeed, Redvers Holditch, then your life is become irrevocably altered."

Chapter thirteen.

The day was fine, faintly warm, like a woman's hand, on the back of Toller's head. In the distance, green hills rose, hewn into their sides narrow terraces on which ancient people had cultivated crops, and grazed animals. Something in the hills' remoteness, in time and space, allowed him to breathe more easily. They were not stone walls, barriers to him, but more like vast gates to another life, a less oppressive consciousness of his limitations. He could walk through them, and they would not castigate him, remind him that he was a mere mortal who was lost, and needed to admit it before he could find himself.

"You want a ride?" asked a man on a cart, slowing to Toller's pace.

Toller looked up at him, tried to match to the face and voice a name. Months earlier, the man had sung out of tune in Stinsford Church. On the other side of Toller had been Charlotte Mapperton, also assigned to look after him, on Christmas Eve.

The brim of Michael Salisbury's hat cast a shadow over his face, and in the back of the cart were items he had bought for Miranda.

"I be going to Misterton Manor," replied Toller.

"I know you?"

"You might. I be Toller Burstock."

The cart stopped, and Michael stared hard at him.

"Why, your face is familiar, though your name be hiding from me. You been to Misterton Manor before?"

"Christmas Eve, for the carol-singing. The cider and the dancing in the barn left everyone on the floor, as I remember, though a lot has happened since then. Miss. Misterton offered me a job, but I was a fool and turned her down. 'Twas the wrong way to repay her kindness. I sometimes need a harness to hold me back, stop me thinking I can be someone I'm not."

"'Twas a grand Christmas Eve, as I remember. We all went round the cottages, and our faces were all ghostly in the lanternlight. I knows you now: the stranger Miss. Misteron took a fancy to. She told us to keep an eye on you, that you might be working with us soon, but you went, on account of it all not being the life for you. Sad she was, as if she had hopes for 'ee. 'Twas as if you'd been friends for a long time, and you hadn't just turned up like a day-labourer. So, you want a ride or not?"

"I will, once you've told me your name."

"I be Michael Salisbury."

The smile was on Toller's face before he could fend it off. It had been a long time since one had been there. He climbed onto the cart, aware that his clothes were different now.

"'Tis certain."

"And 'ee a gentleman, by the looks on 'ee. Miss. Misterton won't recognise 'ee!"

"Let us hope she does, as if she blows a gale in my face, which she be entitled to, the ungrateful I was, then westward must I go, back to Pilsdon. The year be only half gone, and my time here be not done."

Michael was in no hurry, and pointed out special places. That way he took to see Grandfer Salisbury, who rocked in his chair, smoked a pipe, and told himself stories, in the hope that in his solitary retelling of them, he would never forget them. The other way, he went to see his aunt, his dead mother's sister, who told him tales of the heath, of itinerant grinders and journeymen, who stumbled across her secluded cottage, and chopped wood in exchange for a cup of elderflower cordial.

"You love this place," said Toller.

"As much as I do Charlotte."

"You are now married?"

"Yes, we have been wed not long. 'When the crocuses shoot in the wood, then shall we be wed,' she said, and so we were, and there be no secrets between us. And 'twas only a penny or two, as well as her wish for spring, that was keeping us apart. So when the Mistress asked me to breed her horses, after a word or two from a man Abbotsbury way – Geoffrey Burton-Bradstock he be named, and his name hab so many parts that I be surprised I remember it – I was the happiest man in Dorset!"

Toller hung his head, his hope of a second chance gone, a will o' the wisp.

On arrival, Michael enquired if Miss. Miranda would see a visitor. While he waited, Toller looked at the house, wished he had had a hand in the making of it, perhaps had simply carried blocks of stone up a ladder, or, even better, had lovingly carved the leaves and beads into them. Instead, he had produced nothing of beauty. Oh, I recognise it when I see it, but I have never done anything amounting to it, he lamented. The house was as he remembered it: overpowering, towering, as if it had been meant, in its design, to remind human beings that it would outlive them.

"She be over at Max Gate, and won't be back till late. Perhaps, you'd like to come down to the kitchen door, have a bite to eat. 'Twill be a surprise for Charlotte to see 'ee. A pair of gaolers we were, though not fit for it, on account of how you escaped us as easily as if you had the key to your cell door!"

Toller was hungry, had hoped to pick up work with horses, but Michael had beaten him to it. Miranda had offered Toller a chance, and he had refused it. He would not beg for work beneath him, yet he knew that there was a vale between dreaming of the life he would like to live and actually earning it. Had Miss. Misterton been there, I would have asked, but there is desperation in a man who waits for charity at a kitchen door, he told himself.

Yet Michael's pleasure at seeing him again made Toller hesitate. Was it too late? Had he the humility to recognise that he had to start yet again, that his time at the Durnovaria Brewery had had to come to an end?

Then he decided: he would go.

"Thank 'ee, Michael. 'Tis passing kind of 'ee, and I be glad that you and Charlotte be wed, but this house be a happy one, and don't deserve the shadow of my situation."

Just then, from round the corner of the house, came an old man, walking stick in hand, and with the gait of one who had worn out his hips.

"Evening, Master Nicholas. The evening be warm. Them bats behaving themselves?" said Michael.

"Sweet and quiet, Michael. 'Tis the spell of the night I like, but 'tis still late afternoon. My daughter back yet?"

"Not yet. This 'ere be Toller Burstock, come to see her, but about to go."

Nicholas Misterton looked at him, knew him already. Bits Miranda had told him, time after time.

"She been expecting 'ee," he said.

"How so?" asked Toller.

Nicholas smiled as one who often does: eyes nearly closed, face wide, teeth showing.

"In her blood. It's dying out, but she hab it."

Nicholas passed Toller, and then turned to look at him.

"I must go," explained Toller.

"I understand. *All* of us must go, one time or another. Jobs come like geese, but then you don't see them for months. There's a flapping of wings, followed by an empty sky. But we all must come back."

"Why so? What if we don't fit?"

"Time be when we *all* don't fit, but we have to push and wriggle till we do. Never give up a-jiggling till you be snug in your own hearth."

"Thank 'ee," called Toller.

Nicholas carried on walking, raised his hand in a vague acknowledgement.

"You should listen to him," advised Michael, when Nicholas had gone inside.

"I have done. Tell Miss. Miranda I came, that I'll write when the hour suits."

"Well, goodbye, Toller."

"Goodbye, Michael."

"Watch out for bats!"

"I will."

Toller set off. Maybe someone will give me a ride, though 'tis late for any soul to be setting off for Bridport. The Raddleman it be, then! He laughed, then felt his pocket for his purse, and squeezed it. The coins ground together, a fistful of wasted time, of vain aspirations, of self-betrayal.

Then he heard a voice, exhortations to pull harder. The fading sunlight dripped through the green sieve of the trees' leaves, and Toller stood to one side to let the horse and cart pass. The man nodded to him, but Toller's hat was pulled low over his eyes.

"Fine day it be," called the man, when the cart had passed.

But Toller took the track again, and did not see Miranda, or hear her say, "He comes from the direction of the house. I wonder what he wants."

"Clothes too good for a tramper or labourer."

Miranda turned and looked at Toller, and sighed.

"Ah well. If 'twas me he wanted, he'll come back."

"And how was Mrs. Hardy?" asked Alton Pancras, the driver of the cart.

"Bearing up. I have some ideas that her husband might use in one of his stories. Not that he needs any help, mind, what with him being famous throughout the land."

"'Tis kind of 'ee, Miss. Miranda, and I hopes you don't think I talk out of place when I say he must pay you some of his money if he uses what you gid him!"

Miranda laughed, a torrent that usually came when the day was done, and the prospect of nearing home fermented a generous spirit.

"Then you must keep an eye on his future books, Alton."

"Not I, Miss."

"And why not?"

"I can't read, Miss. No one ever showed me my letters. Only time I ever touched a book was when I placed my hand on the Bible when I wed Mrs. Pancras, God rest her soul."

"Well, then I shall teach you!"

"'Tis kind, but I be past all that. Me and letters don't rub along, I know. No, 'tis certain you'd be wasting your time. Alton Pancras be born to drive a cart, and do what please God."

Back at the house, Nicholas was sharpening a stick.

"Mind you don't cut yourself!" warned Miranda.

"Cut hundreds of these. Pigs be stubborn beout a prod. Man came to see you."

"Thought so."

"He'll be back, one day."

"He say so?"

Nicholas blew on the point, and tested it with the end of a finger.

"All we need now is pigs," he said. "Aint had a pig since we left the cottage."

Miranda left him alone. At the age of sixteen, following the unexpected death of Florence Palfreyman, she had inherited Palfreyman Manor, but Florence's will stipulated that her assets must be entrusted to Nicholas until she was twenty-one. The leaving of the cottage, when it came, was a severance he did not want, but, as Emily, Nicholas' sister, pointed out, at the time, he had to make sure Miranda received her due.

Maisie had given him a son, to go with Miranda, whom Ruth Abbas had left him, after he had deserted her, not knowing that she was expecting Miranda. A better father I have been than my own, he was now able to believe.

Nicholas' longing to be back at the cottage often took him on long walks into the woods, to smell the wild garlic, and wait for the bats to cut up the sky. He used to stand, in years past, overlooking the cottage's paling, and listen to the silence of the evening, when his awareness of the landscape was as sharp as his whittling blade.

Miranda took a chair outside. This balmy air always led her into the garden. It was only a germ of an idea, but Toller's ambition, the way he had torn himself away from her offer for it, had gripped her. Might it be of use to Mr. Hardy? she had thought. Could he tell Toller's story, give Toller the hope she could not to complete it? Does a man who finds a book and returns it not deserve the chance to have his own story chronicled?

Emma Hardy had not invited her to Max Gate, but Miranda had turned up, unannounced, having read The Mayor of Casterbridge. This itch to share her idea had taken her there on impulse. But what did Toller's return signify? she kept wondering.

"Thomas is upstairs," Emma had said, as a greeting.

"But I have come to see *you*."

They had sat facing each other, and Miranda had explained her purpose.

"Then it *is* Thomas you need to see."

"I thought if I told you . . ."

"It is better it comes from you. My judgement is not as good as his!"

Though she had laughed, there had been a degree of restraint.

Tom had listened to why Miranda thought Toller's desire to better himself might make a good story.

"You are kind, and Toller Burstock's history would be interesting if he were to stumble over obstacles, were ill-fated in love and vocation," he had politely said.

"I believe he wants to prove something."

Emma had turned away, not part of the conversation.

"But we all do, at some time or another."

Discouraged, Miranda had proceeded no further.

When Tom had gone back to his study, Miranda had said to Emma, "My idea was well meant. Your husband, however, sees no merit in it."

Emma had shrugged, was no longer taken into his confidence in these matters.

Upstairs, Tom had picked up his pen, and written: *man – prove himself – university – wife? – children? – a bit obscure.*

Toller, a few hours after this, decided that he would make straight to Bridport. On such a clear night, the moonlight would make his journey less difficult. He walked at a slow pace, thinking he would sleep, like a sheep, huddled against a hedgerow or tree. To knock on a door, at that time of night, would invite rejection, a taste he wanted to wash from his mouth.

So when a cart slowed to offer him a lift, he chose the easier option.

"You going somewhere?" the man asked him.

"Bridport."

"Then you're lucky. That be where I a-going."

"Thank 'ee. I have money."

"'Tis company I seek, not money."

Toller was tired, and yawned visibly.

"Forgive me. As company goes, you will find I talk less than your horse, so tired am I."

"No matter, friend."

After a few minutes of silence, during which both men expected Toller to fall asleep, Toller said, "Good job you passing. You live there?"

"West Bay, which be a spickle further on than Bucky Doo. I works on Canonicorum Farm."

"'Tis a strange name."

"The farmer of that name be long since dead, and Master wanted to keep Canonicorum, as otherwise the name will join the rest of his family in the graveyard. I be a stock manager."

"Then you are a lucky man."

What would I not give now to be such a man! thought Toller. 'Tis an honest labour, hard and natural.

The man stopped his cart, and lit the lamp.

"Hop in the back if you want sleep. Pull the sheet over, though. Sheep been in there, and don't want your fine clothes to smell of their muck!"

For a few minutes more, they talked in the warm glow of the lamp. Above, the moon was the third and silent face of the group. Then Toller climbed into the back, and fell asleep.

When the cart arrived in Bridport, the man called, "Bridport! I turn left here."

It had been the loss of the cart's vibration that had woken Toller, who fumbled for his purse with one hand, and rubbed his eyes with the other.

"Bridport, you say? I never asked your name. Forgive me."

"'Tis Miles Yondover, friend, and here I must leave you, on account of me about to have a good sleep."

And Miles waved away what Toller was offering.

Chapter fourteen.

Barnabus Dibberford finished his cider, and licked his lips. The one hour he had told his wife – a philosophical woman, who had long since come to terms with her husband's inability to tell the time – he would be gone had stretched well into three, and looked like becoming four. Jude Broadwindsor had, that evening, lured his usual drinking companions into a snare from which none could extricate himself. When he was not proposing to women looking for richer and more sober husbands, he was wont to tell stories, and was rarely without an audience.

"And that be the tale of old Bradwell Peverell, whose ghost, they say, still haunts Bucky Doo, to this very day," he concluded.

The innkeeper shook his head, and said, "'Tis true Peverell was hit over the head, and robbed, and died, that same night, and I don't blame a man for wanting to catch his own murderer, fiend that he must have been, but that were a very long time ago, and if he was a-going to happrehend him, he would have done so by now. And come, brothers, say which of you has actually seen old Bradwell Peverell, all gaunt and pale, as death paints you when you're a-gone? Which? None, I'll wager. Though I must say, Jude, you had us all a-twitching on the edge of our seats, and all it would have taken was that very inn door to open slowly, and a murderer to walk through it, for us to scream our fuddled heads off!"

The inn-keeper's wife had been listening, and added, "And 'tis a door with the sort of croak to set anyone a-wondering who be on the other side. Sometimes, when I be on my own, and the hinges start, I looks up, and it takes me all my nerves to stand my ground and not cry out to my husband."

"And I'd know what 'twas that made you scream, as that door hab the creak of a coffin lid when a corpse be lifting it."

All this talk of ghosts and squeaking doors did nothing to prepare them for the inn door to actually start slowly opening.

Barnabus nearly fell off his chair when Jude grabbed his arm. They all froze, eyes bulging, as they looked across the room. Whoever was opening the door did not, at first, reveal himself. He paused, as if listening for a sign that the inn was still open, then stepped forward.

"Time for a bite, and a bed for the night?" he asked. "Baint too late?"

Barnabus said, "Come over here by the fire so's we can see the colour of 'ee."

"You got blood in them veins o' yours? Or be you just another shade that haunts Bucky Doo?" asked Jude.

"For if you baint human, then I ask you to quit the warmth of this good inn, and take your torment to the graveyard, which be more suited to your wailings," added the inn-keeper.

Toller shut the door, and walked towards the hearth.

"See, in this fire's glow I be all flesh and bone, though why there be a fire on such a warm evening, the Lord alone knows," he said, extending his arms so that the others could feel them. He had not intruded upon their society, by dropping in unannounced, as is the habit of supernatural beings, to frighten any one of them.

Satisfied, that he was, indeed, more human than ghost, the inn-keeper said, "Forgive us our hesitation. 'Twas just a moment before your arrival that we were a-swapping tales of such things, and then the door yonder opens, as if –"

"I understand," interrupted Toller, "but bring yourself to my question because if there be no room here, then I must find a pleasant enough field to lay my head."

The inn-keeper looked at his wife, who said, "Yes, there be a bed for 'ee, as soft as a bale of straw."

"Then I will take it, for I have slept here before, and know the comfort of your mattresses. Remember when the snow came so hard and fast that it kept us all within for several days? You recall me not?"

Jude said, "Your face be familiar."

"Why, yes. Now you come back to me," said the inn-keeper. "You staggers in here, all a-shivering, after you been trapped in snow, Pilsdon way."

"That's right," confirmed Toller. "I found Ebenezer Valence in it, and someone took a horse to bring him back. Ebenezer was too heavy for me to carry, or we should have perished in the trying. But tell me, anyone, of the fortunes of both men, for since the day I left for Dorchester, where I had hoped to have better times, I have wondered if they survived."

Jude said, "Miles Yondover be right, and if memory serves me correctly, the man perished, on account of Miles not learning his left from his right. You said the man was in the field on your right – or was it the left? – near Broadoak, and Miles gets it all muddled up, mistaking whether you meant on the right going or coming to Briddy, and can't find him. He holes up with the daughter, and, when the snow shrinks enough, the man be found, and hab been buried in Whitchurch graveyard ever since."

Toller quickly deduced that the fault could have been his own and not Miles'. Perhaps, he himself had not been clear enough to Miles about which field to search. How easy it would have been to have marked it with a bright rag on a gate-post!

"Then 'tis a shame that between us a man has died," said Toller.

Barnabus shrugged, wondered why Toller had lowered his head in shame, had seemed to crumble at the news of Ebenezer's death.

But Barnabus knew nothing of what Toller's attempt to save Ebenezer might have meant to Hepsy.

"Don't 'ee go a-fretting over left and right. Any man who be out in such bad weather be asking for trouble. I'm no church-goer, and do not believe in the word of God, but I do know that sometimes it baint the wish of God when we go, but 'tis our own stupidity which determines the hour. Get the man a drink and a few tatties. Come, sit down among us and be merry. There's time will be for sorrow later."

The inn-keeper's wife huffed at Barnabus' disregard for God and the Church, and said, "A plate of tatties and a slice of lamb will do him nicely, but this inn be a place where there be no bad words said against the Lord. Why, 'tis *Him* who rules over everything."

Toller saw that any protraction of this altercation would delay the satisfaction of his hunger and a good night's rest, so he intervened.

"This inn be broad-shouldered enough to bear the weight of all opinions, but tell me what news there be of Bridport and West Bay. I have been away, these last six – or be it seven? – months, and 'twould change the subject to know how these parts have fared since that terrible snow-storm."

The inn-keeper viewed this tack as a chance to shoo his wife into the kitchen. A man of simple tastes and views, he wanted a quiet end to the day.

"Briddy be the same as always, s'far as I know," opined Jude. "This hot spell done the fields good. Folk come and go, but 'tas always been so. No, Briddy be as slow as ever, and long may it remain so, be my judgement, for change for its own sake be bound to be for the worse."

"'Taint the fashion to change, these parts, 'tis certain," agreed the inn-keeper, "but 'tis creeping upon us, like the fog do, and just as the fog come and won't be stopped, so change tiptoes up to us, till it be there in our work and in our heads. What say you?"

Toller said, "I agree. Stay with what you know works, be my

view. Something grows up in our flesh and bones that binds us to our land and work, and no matter how hard we pretend we be someone else, we're pulled back to what and who we know. Trying to escape be vain. There. 'Tis a melancholy thought to some, I admit, but 'tis based on what I done and learned as I have lived."

Though in the grip of an alcoholic near-paralysis, Barnabus said, "Well said, stranger, yet newly returned. There be wisdom in what you say, and I knowed it for a long time but had not the words to describe it. What more could a man want but to sit around this fire, even though the night be warm, and to talk about the ways of the world?" Here he paused to allow others to mutter agreement. "Nothing, my fine Briddy friends, for this hearth be a sort of womb, protecting us from a hostile world, betimes, out there."

And so this train of thought sparkled in their conversation like a vein of quartz unexpectedly exposed in the sandstone cliffs at West Bay.

Toller ate his tatties, and the inn-keeper's wife brought him a dish of rhubarb pie and cream, which drew envious looks from the others. When the dish and plates had been scraped clean, Toller excused himself.

"'Tas been a pleasant, but I am weary from my journey, so I will to my bed. I never was a man to come to Bridport except to buy provisions, but I shall make an effort to join 'ee, from time to time. I've kept myself from your company for too long."

When Toller had gone, Jude said, "And such a man as he be welcome here. He has a story which gives him a sad air, but he seems a good and true, which will do for us, will it not, friends?"

"It will!" they all cried in unison, raising their glasses.

"One last?" asked the inn-keeper, and they all agreed that it was a splendid idea.

In the morning, after paying his dues, and feeling refreshed, Toller stepped out into the white light of a Bridport morning. Already, market stall-holders had set out their wares on the ground and tables. People wanting to secure a bargain were there early, examining kettles, oil lamps, tools, rope, kindling.

Toller shielded his eyes. They have their own lives and concerns, he mused. And I have mine, my time wasted like a field of wheat stunted by blight and bad weather. A few months sooner am I returned, but to what? Will I retrieve the key I told Mattie to leave in the tree's hollow knot? Or will she be happy, at last, soothed by the peace of Marshwood Vale? And Hepsy, fatherless Hepsy, will curse me, when we meet again, for my bungling, my lack of clarity about the field in which her father had hoped to be rescued.

Toller would meet both women again, but he had nothing to show them for those recent months: no position of worth, no fulfillment. It was pointless to try and mask his failure. He would recant his ambition and vanity, settle in the place Providence chose.

The last time he had been on the hill between Bridport and Dottery, he had trudged through snow, which had slipped over the top of his boots, and numbed his toes. All around him, nothing had looked the same as he knew it to be. Now, however, in a light so bright the air seemed to sparkle, long, shooting galaxies of white elderflower frothed at the foot of the hedgerows. The fields, some green, others golden with ripe corn, were sewn together by brambles threaded through the dense, prickly branches of hawthorn. Above, the pale blue sky, in which a stiff buzzard glided, and crows flapped and clapped in raucous gangs, reminded Toller what had made his shepherd's life so pleasant: sitting down, in summer, on a hillside, with his dog, and watching his sheep lying in the shade of trees and hedges.

He walked self-consciously through Broadoak. There was the church, all compact and neat. The few cottages watched him shyly, and he looked in vain for a familiar face in their gardens. All at Denhay Farm, they must be, he thought. Milking, 'tis certain.

Beyond that hamlet, he thought of what he would say if Mattie were still in his house. He had given her the key to his door, as a temporary measure, to help her, but he was back before the year was up. Of course, he would not evict her. Who evicts his own sister, after all? That was what they agreed she would say, that they were brother and sister, and she seemed such an honest soul that he doubted not that she had followed their plan. But the pretence could not last. Both could not live in the house indefinitely.

And what if she had not gone there, after all, had thought better of it, had judged the idea unworkable? Or had gone to Pilsdon, had been shrivelled by its isolation, and had sought the tree? Forston Sampford. Toller shuddered.

His pace now quickened, then slowed, and it was with embarrassment that he slunk past Dugdale Farm. He hugged the hedge, to be inconspicuous. Hepsy must not know of his return until he had had time to consider a proper explanation for it, but just when he thought he had safely passed her house, he heard whistling, an air competently delivered by a man, if he was not mistaken. The hedgerow was so dense that only by peering into the garden from higher up the lane did Toller confirm to himself that the tune belonged to one who looked at ease with his situation. Indeed, so at home did he appear that Toller interpreted the man's leisurely stride, and hands in his pockets, as signs that he had been there before, maybe now lived there.

Toller's heartbeat quickened. So, she has wasted no time in finding a husband, he concluded. The brim of the man's hat masked his face, but Toller guessed him to be of a similar age to himself. The posture, the confident movement, the suppleness as he crouched to pluck a weed. Then I must bear it. She was never mine from the start. I wish them well. A man can rarely choose his neighbours, but must make himself a worthy one.

On Toller strode, quickly now, to put some distance between himself and Hepsy and her new husband. The landscape seemed different from when he had last seen it. He thought the lane twisted right there instead of left, was sure that the field at the beginning of the ascent, in earnest, to Pilsdon had a gate. And there it was, as it had ever been: the thatch of his cottage, sitting on a hedgerow. The sun had turned the green, mossy patches brown. Whether Mattie had gone or stayed mattered little now. It had once been his home, and would be again.

He looked for signs that Mattie had stayed, and there they were, hanging limply on a line of string stretching from a tree to a hook on the door-frame. Women's attire, undergarments, the sort he had seen his mother scrubbing when he had been a young boy. So, Mattie had stayed. And how Sampford must have feasted his yellowing eyes on her clothes! Like an adder he would have slithered down the lane to watch her reach up, accentuating her shape, and peg them onto the line. They must be hung at the back of the cottage, from now on. Toller would put up a new line, out of the gaze of passers-by. This solitude and remoteness are no protectors of privacy or virtue. He had heard his parents talking, in low voices, about the liberties young men took with milkmaids. Farms brought men and women together, provided lofts, quiet nooks, where they could go.

Toller looked around his garden. No vegetables had been planted, and the grass was long. He knocked, but no one came. He tried again, and called, "Mattie, 'tis I, Toller, your brother, come home, early."

He heard movement, a key turning in the lock, and the door opened.

"Toller? 'Tis truly you, come home? A sister never wished to see a brother more than at this moment!"

Toller thought her face plumper than the last time he had seen it.

"And this brother be glad to be home, 'tis certain."

Mattie stood aside to let him in. It felt strange, but all looked as he had left it. What few possessions Mattie had added had not changed the atmosphere of the house.

She stood uneasily, as if waiting for him to announce that her tenancy was formally over. His offer had been to help her cope with rejection. He had empathised because he himself had suffered it, but she prepared herself for the worst news.

"I must leave now you are back."

"Why so? This is your home, too."

"But you do not know everything. You would not keep me if you did."

"You talk in riddles. Tell me what I must know."

In a single movement, to describe her change of circumstances, she unbuttoned the black, loose-fitting coat she habitually wore in public, and her eyes drew his to her swollen abdomen.

"Judge me not, Toller, afore I have told you all. Sit down, and let me satisfy you."

Toller made for the settle, and Mattie eased herself into a chair, facing him. The faggots in the hearth still pulsed; she had kept the fire lit, having discovered that the cottage's thick walls kept the room cool, even on hot days.

"A forsaken bride you found me, in a cold Dorchester street, and when you and I swapped places, a mother-to-be I discovered I was. No wedding ring, brother, but a fat belly."

Toller did not know what to say. She had given herself to a man before their wedding day. What else did she expect would happen? But he could not turn her out, not abandon her, as her fiancé had done.

Then they heard a knocking at the door.

"Stay," urged Toller. "Let me answer it. You must rest."

"'Tis only Hepsy. That be her knock: three short raps. It be our code."

"Hepsy? Code?"

"Yes, she be my friend."

"Mattie, 'tis only I," called Hepsy. "The traps be sprung. Two rabbits I bring." Toller opened the door. Hepsy swung the rabbits, one in each hand, in a show of joy that there would be meat to eat, that night. "Toller!"

"Don't leave the girl a-standing there, brother."

Toller stood aside, looked from one woman to the other, and Hepsy put the rabbits on the table.

"I never thought I would ever see you in this house," said Toller to Hepsy.

"But see here, brother. Just as you took me in when I needed a home, so did I Hepsy when she lost hers. Pour the girl some cordial, which be in the cupboard. 'Tis thirsty work, trapping, this weather."

Toller looked at Hepsy, who was in clothes she would once have scorned to wear in such a bad condition. Her hair was unpinned, and her hands were smeared with rabbit hair and blood. She smelt of the undergrowth, feared his wrath, how he might repay her.

"Then set about these, and in the skinning and the stewing, you will tell me how Providence brought you here, when the solemnest promise from me could not tempt you."

"Then the pot must heat slowly, as my story be as long as the cooking."

"'Tis certain," agreed Mattie.

"Fear not impatience on my part, as my appetite for the knowing be as great as for the rabbit."

With that, he went to pour the cordial, reflecting on how, one minute, he had no woman under his roof, and, the next, two.

Chapter fifteen.

Zenobia Godmanstone strode to the middle of the yard, avoiding that morning's horse droppings, stopped, and, with her right hand, saluted the sun out of her eyes. Toller was loading barrels onto his cart. Since the funeral of Arthur, Ezra's previous partner, no one had seen Ezra. Langton Godmanstone had called round at his squashed, dirty room to see what had happened, but his landlady, a wizened, toothless, old woman, who collected the rent by banging on her tenant's door at the same time – seven in the morning, by the chimes of the town's clock – every week, had cackled, "He hab left. Paid up, mind. I'll say that for him. Always paid, and never stained his bed sheets."

Langton had thanked her but, at the point of departure, asked, "I don't suppose he said where he was going, did he?"

"Don't rightly recollect. Could have been Weymouth. Or was it Cerne Abbas? My mind be a sieve, these days."

"Don't play games with me, old hag, or you'll regret it!"

"'Tis true, sir, that a coin or two help the memory, and 'twon't hurt a man of your standing, judging by your fine habiliments, to help an old soul remember such a thing."

Ezra had been at Durnovaria Brewery a year or two, had reliably turned up for work, and made sure the ale was delivered safely. There is a lot to say for such a worker, Langton knew. But Ezra had sent no word of his intention to leave, and, therefore, was not worth spending a sou on.

So Toller had reassured Zenobia that he was quite capable of doing two men's work, and, in return, had been paid extra. This demonstration that the rounds could be done by one man alone had caused resentment among the other draymen, who had ostracised Toller. He made them nervous, gave the impression that he did not want to get to know them.

Zenobia waited in the middle of the yard, expected Toller to come to her, and not she to him. His back ached, his stride was measured; he could not rush but did not want to show her a weakness.

"Good morning, Toller. There is something I wish to discuss with you. Would you come up to the office?" she asked.

Toller was anxious to begin the deliveries, and replied, "Won't here do? I'm off to Abbotsbury first, which be a pretty climb and drop or two, and takes an age."

Zenobia noticed one or two others looking at them, from other parts of the yard.

"The office," she repeated.

Toller followed her at a respectful distance, thought he heard someone call, "Godmanstone's lapdog!" but did not turn; a fight was not a good way to start the day.

In the privacy of the office, she said, "I've spoken with my brother about your suggestion to stop deliveries till the debts are settled, and he thinks we may as well try. Maybe the word will then spread that we are not prepared to give extended credit. However, he believes that it is best if we don't personally get involved but appoint a debt collector."

Toller restrained a smile, and said, "Neither a lender nor a borrower be is what my father used to say."

"In principle, I agree, but few businesses manage, these days, without some degree of borrowing. It is the way of the world, it seems. But we do need to give a strong message that we won't tolerate refusal to pay. Stiff letters have little effect on some, and court action can be expensive. Therefore, we shall, as you suggest, stop deliveries until you have recovered what is owing."

"Me?"

"Yes, you. Go on your round till lunchtime, and then report to me. This afternoon, I'll take you to my brother's tailor, who will measure you to make up a suit. It is important that, as our representative, you exude gravitas, as befits such a role. This sits well with you?"

Toller scratched his head. *Exude gravitas*? It was, indeed, flattering that the Godmanstones had accepted his idea, but he checked his excitement, not wishing to suggest that he had, in any way, manipulated them, which he had not. He had merely wanted to show that he had initiative

"Well, thank 'ee, Miss. Godmanstone, but who will do my deliveries?"

"We will set on another drayman, as well as Ezra's replacement. There are other jobs we would like you to do. My brother and I are thinking of expanding, maybe setting up another brewery, in Taunton. That is, of course, confidential. We need someone to manage our draymen, and the deliveries. We are too much taken up with the day-to-day tasks to think about our grander schemes. When you are not liaising with our clients, you will be managing the draymen, horses, schedules. There will be paperwork, meetings with Melcombe Bingham, our accountant, whose office is down the corridor. Think you are up to it? There will be an increase in pay as well as responsibility." Toller freed the smile that had been straining at the mouth, and Zenobia offered her hand, which he took. "I take that as a yes."

At last, thought Toller, I have a chance of a better future. This is what I was hoping for: prospects.

"I will do my best."

"I know you will, Toller. I know you will. We have watched you closely, and everything your reference said about you is true.

Though you do similar work to the men, you are not one of them, but distant enough to deter them from taking advantage."

In his hand rested Zenobia's, a soft tulip, a reminder that she was a woman as well as a hard-nosed brewer. She left it there just long enough to let him know that she trusted him. Why, he thought, 'tas been ages since I touched such a soft.

All that morning, his right hand felt different. His imagination had endowed it with such a pleasurable sensation that he almost forgot that he must prepare himself for a visit to Langton Godmanstone's tailor. And preparation meant changing out of his leather chaps and donning more respectable attire.

"But other clothes I have baint any more suitable than what I stand in," he informed Zenobia.

"Then I shall see if Langton has anything to fit you."

"But I'd feel awkward in another man's clothes, though 'tis kind you taking me to be measured. Fact is, a man has pride, and can't abide another knowing he's poorer."

"I understand perfectly, but won't you wear Langton's, just for me?"

Toller surprised her by shaking his head; he would not be lured into her power by her smile and pout.

"'Tis the awkwardness. I be who I am."

"But you want advancement, do you not?"

"I do, but I baint begging."

Zenobia sighed.

"This won't do, Toller."

"But I *cannot* borrow another man's clothes. 'Taint a question of won't."

Zenobia went to the window, thinking what she should do.

"On this occasion, I shall have to be humiliated, but when you put on your new suit, there's to be no complaining that you aren't a shepherd any more. Independence is all very well, even good in moderation. However, a debt collector is what you'll be, and a suit is what you'll wear. Understood?"

For a moment, Toller hesitated. This working for someone else did not sit easily with him. That she was an attractive woman made it worse. Alone on the cart, he was happy, because he was outdoors, was his own master, knew what he had to do, but taking orders was a new and disagreeable experience.

"Yes. I won't let you down."

That afternoon, Zenobia watched him squirm. She chose the cloth, the cut, the shoes, the hat. If anything, thought Toller, the clothes will weaken me, rob me of my true spirit.

After their visit, Zenobia went through the debtors, and put them in an order of urgency.

"Do you have any questions?" she asked.

"Do I have a horse? Some of these places be a few miles away."

"Go to Misterton Manor. I shall write a note to Miss. Miranda. They have a large stable. We shall hire one. Tell her I'll settle with her when I see her."

Miranda was surprised to see him. She enquired after his welfare, but he did not tell her about his new role. Somehow, being a debt collector felt demeaning. Why had he indirectly put the idea in her head?

He was aware of the activity behind him: tools being sharpened, saddles being polished in the warmth. In the distance, there was the incessant chattering of a threshing machine. In the air full of smells familiar to him, playful swifts arced and disappeared. I have missed fields, sheep, country folk, he admitted, and now I am as uncomfortable in a starched collar as a man with his head in a hangman's noose.

"You are happy at Durnovaria Brewery?" Miranda asked, seeing his sad mien.

"'Tis what I wanted."

"But are you happy?" she persisted.

"Miss. Godmanstone has promoted me."

"And you are glad?"

Why tell her the truth when she sees it in my face? She knows me well, can read my thoughts. But she is a friend of Miss. Godmanstone, and I must not risk losing my new job before it has really begun, he reasoned.

"Tolerable."

"There is a horse for you, but you must listen to your heart as well as your head, Toller."

"'Twas my heart which banished me from Pilsdon," he confessed.

Miranda said, "One day you will go back."

"How do you know? What special power do you have to know what will be?"

Miranda smiled, and replied, "I am my father's daughter. I be Conjuror Misterton."

Toller hesitated. Her words did not have the acrid smell of a jest at his expense.

"A conjuror?"

"We all, using actions as words, write our own story of ambition, or lack of it, but at what cost? What you seek might be nearer than you think. But enough of my prattle. Zenobia shall have Molly-Mae, a gentle yet strong, and she is free of charge."

Miranda watched Toller introduce himself to his new horse by stroking her flanks and nose, soothing her with murmured endearments. That day in Dorchester, when he had controlled her frightened horse, returned.

Michael said, "This horse be sweeter of temper than my Charlotte, so look after her. The slightest squeeze of the knees be all she needs."

Just then, Nicholas appeared, shirt open at the neck, hand wobbling on his stick, his mother's, the one he had made for her, years ago. He turned his back on them, made his way to a place where he could stand, and look, and remember.

No one wore formal dress on the Misterton Estate, or felt constrained. Toller wondered why Nicholas and Miranda put no distance between themselves and others. They had no stiffness of bearing, did not maintain an air of social superiority. The house suggested a family with at least a crest, a connection with events of historical significance, but though the Mistertons had their own lineage and traditions, the house, unlike the suit for which Toller had been measured, did not seem to constrict their movements, their view of themselves. Where have they come from? he wondered. Somehow the Manor had adjusted itself to the Mistertons, and not the other way round.

Really feeling the contrast between the brewery and the estate, Toller sighed, and said, "Everyone makes a bed, and I'll just have to lie on mine. Can't find the words."

Miranda said, "It's good a man wants to find out how far he can go, but bad when he gets lost on the road. Pilsdon lost to you?"

"I must go, see this through, one way or another."

"Come back and see us."

Toller eased Molly-Mae into the opposite direction, and said, "Go on, girl. Let's see if you as sweet as they make out. Not all pretty women are, as I know to my cost."

When he rode into the brewery's yard, a stable groom came over to see Molly-Mae. Proudly, Toller introduced her, recalled the first horse his father had bought him, that feeling that life will never be the same again. His father's smile, when he heard his son's first words of admiration, had flowered irresistibly.

"She baint a working horse, not a heavy," the groom said.

"Help me get about for Miss. Godmanstone, anyway."

"You not delivering any more?"

"Do whatever I'm asked. Look after her, and I'll let Miss. Godmanstone know she be here."

Zenobia had seen them from her office window, and was making her way towards them. The groom led Molly-Mae to the stables, where he should have been cleaning out the soiled boxes.

"She has a pretty face," said Zenobia. "She costing me much?"

"Nothing. Miss. Miranda said she'd see you."

"Good."

Zenobia turned and walked away.

"What you want me to do now?"

"Come see me later, to go over the accounts I want you to visit."

Toller also had to go to the tailor, to try on the new suit. Zenobia went with him, on the pretext of having to pay.

"Pinch anywhere?" asked the tailor

Toller looked at himself in the mirror. Where had he gone? The hat was too tall, like a steamboat's funnel. His shoes shone, altered his gait, were not the hardy boots he was used to wearing.

"You've changed," remarked Zenobia.

Toller said nothing.

"I don't think we need any alterations," concluded the tailor. "Do you have a bag for your old attire?"

Toller looked again in the mirror, gathered his clothes, and clutched them to him.

Back at Durnovaria Brewery, Zenobia said, "The Raddleman. They're on a month's leeway, but it's been two. It's a small place. *She* wears the trousers. He –"

"I know of it."

"Here's what they owe. Remember, though, that we want their trade afterwards."

The Raddleman: songs, laughter, John Trevelyan. Was that his name? But that gloomy bedroom: how uninviting it had been! The inn had not turned him away. There must always be such places for labourers, folk who have just enough money for a morsel of mutton and a tankard of ale, he believed. And now he was going to have to tell the inn-keeper and his wife that there would be no further deliveries unless they paid what they owed. So where would they go, all those care-worn souls who went to forget, for an hour or two, their aches and pain, the trials the following day would bring? Why should he care? But he did. The Raddleman, of all places.

It was closed when he got there. Try as he might, he could not rouse them from their sleep, if, indeed, they were actually in. Late nights. That was their work, in lamplight, among shadows that flitted across the walls and ceiling stained brown by tobacco smoke.

He called back later, mid-evening, and his suit drew eyes. Was John Trevelyan, a friendly face, there? The room became quieter as he strode purposefully to the bar.

"Who this blown in?" said the inn-keeper's wife to her husband. "Face familiar."

"Came earlier today, but you were out. I'm from the brewery. Come about the money owing," began Toller.

"You been before? You baint the usual chap comes delivering. I usually pays *him*. How we know you really from the brewery?" said the inn-keeper.

"I work for Mr. Langton and Miss. Zenobia Godmanstone, proprietors."

The inn-keeper's wife was suspicious: "We only got your word for it. You got a letter saying who you be?"

There was a vein of defensiveness in her voice. Toller had not expected it, fumbled in his pocket, and drew out the piece of paper on which was written how many casks they had had, and what they owed.

"Tell them that we will take back any unused barrels, and that they must cease selling our ale immediately if they do not settle their account," Zenobia had instructed him.

"We talk in the back?" Toller asked the inn-keeper.

"Come through," said his wife.

When his wife and Toller had gone into the back room, the inn-keeper called to his customers, "Come, put away those faces, for 'tis yet summer, not winter!"

"They want it settling full?" asked his wife.

"You pay in full or we fetch what barrels there be left in the morning."

"Don't I know 'ee?"

Toller blinked, and said sheepishly, "Stayed a night or two."

"Then you must know how 'tis a strain. This inn be all we got, and though 'tis ours, 'less we pay in full, we close. That what you want? You want all these good folk out?"

"You must pay in full or with goods – tables, chairs, beds – to the value owing."

"Even the bed you slept on when you habn't one of your own?"

Toller saw her face shatter. It had been his idea. In theory, a good one, logical, tough, fair, even. He could carve himself a niche in Durnovaria Brewery; a problem the Godmanstones had would be solved. But it was also this couple's livelihood, a place to gather, talk, eat, make sense of the world, too.

"Yes."

"Then close it now, though it rest on your head. In part I can pay, though not in full."

She went out to her customers, and banged a tankard on a table.

"What 'ee say to him?" asked her husband.

Ignoring him, she said, "Drink up, and home to your beds, for this inn be finished."

"What's up? Ale run out?" called someone.

"Go now," advised the inn-keeper. "'Tis a sorry day, and the telling would only make it worse."

"Go, as my husband says," echoed his wife.

Toller left, tried to convince himself that he had nothing to do with the closure. It was the fault of the Godmanstones. Yet such a man was he that the full weight of the shame fell upon his shoulders, and bowed him, and the others finished their drinks, muttering incoherently. In the corner, however, one man remained.

“You, too, when you’re done,” called the inn-keeper. “Go, and remember us as we once were.”

So Ezra got up, and followed Toller. In his head, he brewed a case for his pursuit. Why, he took my partner’s job, and now he took my comfort in The Raddleman. Seem he set himself up to be something he baint, be my judgement. He come a long way hab Toller Burstock, but he baint a Dorchester man, and don’t know of our ways. And ’taint the ale talking when I say there be a price to pay for more things than a few casks of ale. Look to your wits, Toller Burstock, as you bill have great need of them soon.

Ezra cut through an alley, intent on heading Toller off, listened for the sound of his footsteps, judged his pace. Then he stepped out, blocking his progress.

Face to face they stood, and Toller tasted the ale on Ezra’s breath.

“Ezra?” said Toller.

“’Tis certain.”

“Thought you’d flitted.”

“Gone nowhere, me.”

That is all Toller could remember of that particular encounter: three words said in an over-familiar way, and the reek of pickled eggs and ale.

Chapter sixteen.

Mattie listened sympathetically to Hepsy, who explained how she had come to discover that the family to which she thought she belonged now had an additional member: a sort of brother she never knew she had. Hepsy related the events at least three times, in the hope that her repetition might reveal some flaw in the legal process, which decreed she had not inherited Dugdale Farm.

"So you see, dear Mattie, that despite the fact that the law says he is my brother, and that he said in his letter that I am welcome to continue living there – 'at least until I am married,' he added – I *must* leave. It would be impossible for me to live under the same roof as a stranger who cannot love me as a normal brother would. Nor can I love him as would a sister."

Mattie suddenly felt her baby kick. Where are they leading, this news of hers, this child of mine? she asked herself. At least, I have this cottage till Toller, *my* brother, returns. Brothers! Mine gives me a roof over my head, and Hepsy's all but evicts her.

"Though much have you chewed on your circumstances, do you not think you should accept his offer? Folk will talk, yes. 'Tis the way of the world. But you must be practical. It be kind of him to let you stay, and he may turn out to be a good and an honest."

Practical. How readily had Mattie grasped the cottage key Toller had given her! She trusted him, and he gave her hope, just when the chance of it had all but gone.

Hepsy threw back her head, and laughed derisively.

"Good? Honest? Why, there be not a one I would trust any more. And there bin father, tethering me to him till a rich farmer or landowner undoes me and ties his own knot. No small wonder, now I think about it. Father gets me off his hands, first, then he lets me know about my secret brother. 'Tis as well that mother did not know, as 'twould have driven her into an earlier grave!"

Hepsy shut out the thought that her mother just might have known, that their whole life as a family had survived because her mother had managed to forgive her husband, had refused to let his weak moment destroy her.

There it went again, that definite movement inside Mattie, who looked downwards to see it. And your father, faint-hearted Roddy, hab not an idea that you be all I hab, she said to her baby.

"What will you do?" she asked abstractedly, conscious that her preoccupation with the fluttering inside her might give the impression that she was not fully attentive.

Hepsy swallowed, leaned forward, placed her hands purposefully on the table, and said, "I should like it very much if I could come here and live with you. We are kindred spirits, you and I, and are thrown together to give each other support."

"But the cottage belongs to my brother, Toller, and 'tis him you should ask."

Hepsy slumped back in her chair. Mattie was the right companion in the wrong house. Toller would never agree to Hepsy living there after the way she had refused him. Besides, he himself would be returning, one day, but, at least, a month or two would buy her a little time to plan her future.

"I shall be gone before his year be up. Dear Mattie, I am desperate. Father has betrayed me, and do you yourself not know the pain of betrayal? 'Tis the sting of the sharpest knife, the sudden drop into a bottomless well."

Mattie saw the hopelessness of Hepsy's position. Toller had come to her own rescue, shown compassion, and offered her practical help. Should she not treat Hepsy similarly? The baby kicked again, and Mattie's hand cupped the movement. She wondered whether it could feel the warmth from her gentle touch. Lately, she had taken to talking to it, so that it would know her voice before coming into the world. Her loving murmurings broke the silence of the cottage, reassured her that she was not alone, especially at nights, when the door was locked and bolted, when the lamp threw shadows, and the owls screeched suddenly, startling her.

"There be a question that been dripping wax for some time now, though the candle seems as long as ever."

"Ask it, then, and whatever it is, I shall answer truthfully, for there is not a question I fear."

Mattie said, "Though it baint none of my business, I must ask it if you are to come."

"Then ask."

Mattie sighed; there was no easy, comfortable way.

"Be Miles Yondover your lover?"

Hepsy sought words, but they would not come, as she herself was not sure what Miles was to her. She had been flattered by his attention, had found him attractive, was excited by his kisses, but he was no more likely to measure up to the kind of man of whom her father had thought her worthy than Toller. But the question, so unexpected, pinched her, made her squirm.

"He's a good man. Helped me with father, and comes back to me beout me asking. No harm in a man tempting a girl a little. We all need friends."

Mattie smiled, but not in a way which showed satisfaction with the answer; it was more a visage of acceptance that Hepsy would do as she pleased. Can't be like that when you expecting a tiddy one, knew Mattie.

"Just wondered."

"I would tell him not to come if I lived here with you. Three don't fit here. Two be a squeeze."

"And does he know you will leave Dugdale Farm?"

If three don't fit, thought Mattie, then my baby will come before her, no matter what the weight of her desperation.

Mattie wondered whether Miles had got his eyes on becoming a farmer himself. A labourer might well covet all those fields and barns. It would be his quickest way to a good living and a warm bed. For that be how men work, she reflected. Take what they want from a sweetheart, then leave her when they have enough. That be men. They picks all the cherries till the branches are bare.

But Toller. A woman in such difficulty he would not turn away, surely. Vicious tongues will always waft, but Toller would not see a woman out into the lane if she begged to stay under his thatch.

"Then let us not stroll around Pilsdon Pen to find ourselves back where we started," decided Mattie. "And though the cottage be small, 'tis a manor to us in our situation."

Hepsy burst into tears, and leapt to hug her.

"Steady, girl. Mind my tiddy one, who be as lively as a spring lamb today!"

Mattie felt Hepsy's hug slacken, the kiss made salty by Hepsy's tears of relief and gratitude.

"And when shall I come?"

"That be down to you, or when he comes to live there. Though bring nothing but what is to wear or of sentimental value, as Toller left all but a few things, and drawers and cupboards be almost full."

"I won't. And, oh, Mattie, the loss of the farm be like a new beginning. The gloom there weighed me down, and no matter how much the sun shone, it could not reach all those dark corners, in which my father used to sit and mope. I shall come, this very day."

"Then come, and I shall light a fire in your room, as though 'tis summer, and the nights be light, there is a coldness in there from want of heat."

So, thought Hepsy, as she made her way back to the farmhouse to fetch a bag, he has me in his bed, after all. She smiled. He would never have guessed that I would slip under his sheets without the slightest coaxing!

Hepsy returned to Mattie with possessions enough to sustain her, and to ensure that she occupied a space small enough to keep Mattie in a sweet temper. She is Toller's sister, and I rely on her, perhaps to plead my case when Toller returns, Hepsy reasoned. I am a guest, and though I would sooner have her as *my* sister, she now has someone dearer, and I must fit in where I can, wash the floor and pots, chop the wood, and build the fire when autumn's mists unfurl from Pilsdon Pen.

"And you will let me earn my keep?" asked Hepsy, in one of the awkward silences lack of familiarity with each other engendered.

"You may help, and I would be grateful, though I wish to remain busy myself. I cannot sit in this chair, waiting for my baby to come. Those ticks of the clock stretch when there is nothing to do but brood on the unfairness of life."

"Then I shall blow in and out. There are still the animals on the farm to feed till the new owner comes."

"And are you sure there is nothing for you in your father's will?"

"Nothing. 'Tis as if I never knitted or mended his socks, never cooked his lamb stew and dumplings. A servant girl I been, that's all."

Mattie shook her head.

"Nothing means less to worry about. 'Tas been a yoke on your shoulders since your father gone."

"'Tis different for you as you have a brother. Tell me, Mattie, of Toller's childhood. Seem he was born growed up. Has he always been so serious? I must admit that he always paid me his respects, called to see if I would stroll with him."

But Mattie did not want to hear about such things. Already, she felt that Hepsy's problems were bigger than the leather bag she had brought. Mattie would not allow those issues to sit at the same table as her.

“I shall go to bed now. I am tired. Let us not talk about what has been but of what will be. The past has been a poor harvest blighted by disappointment. Our hopes have burnt like ricks struck by sudden lightning. ’Tis too much to hang those pictures on the wall.”

Slowly, she plodded up the stairs, and Hepsy heard the bedroom door close. Strange, Hepsy thought, that she should slide the bolt across. She knows I hear it, wants me to hear it. It keeps me away from her.

Hepsy looked around the room. Where was Toller in all this? Somewhere near she felt his presence. Objects had been chosen and handled by him. And Mattie had not been there long enough to gain the confidence to change things. That clock in the corner had been wound by him. Not once had he mentioned a sister, and Hepsy noticed that, strangely, Mattie had not wanted to talk of their growing up together.

The dresser, on which Mattie had placed a white flower resembling three butterflies in close discussion, drew Hepsy to it. Maybe he made it with his own hands, in this very room, she speculated. Her arms tried to span its width, reach to its top, and when she took her rough measurements to the door, arms outstretched like a ballerina, she realised that a completed dresser would not have gone through it. And it has the look of him about it: solid, strong, practical, and without ostentatious adornment.

Quietly, she looked in the two lower cupboards. There was a box with a brass lock, but she could find no key. Such a strong box must surely contain important things, maybe a document. He’s not a man of poetry, she suspected. Just one verse, dedicated to her, left in the hand that had spurned him, would have given him a better chance, but his words had been simple, put together unfussily, like the dresser.

Then one of the drawers. She had seen Mattie go into it, take out a big spoon. The heat had made the drawer expand, and Hepsy had to pull hard, careful not to alert Mattie. There were the two letters Toller had written and not posted. Her hand trembled. The first was addressed to Hugo Lockington. Why had Toller not sent it, she wondered, to the harbinger of the news that her father had left her nothing in his will? Tempted to open it, she imagined a connection, the nature of which she had no idea, between Toller and Lockington. She eventually satisfied herself that it contained an expression of his wishes concerning some legal matter, and picked up the second.

"Why, 'tis meant for me! There be my name, and there *Dugdale Farm, Pilsdon*."

She quickly dropped the first letter, and rummaged in the drawers to see what else she could find that night pertaining to her, but there was nothing.

She returned to the chair with the missive intended for her. When did he write it? she wondered. Was it before or after he had sought her hand? Most probly afterwards, she concluded, and, therefore, 'tis an unkind message, one intended to wound me for turning him down.

Then her thoughts returned to Mattie, who must have been aware of it. No doubt she would say that it belongs to Toller, that she had no right to bring it into the light of day. But now that Hepsy had it in her hand, she knew she would open it. She carefully slid a sharp knife under the wax, and, taking a deep breath, read. In her head, she could hear Toller earnestly reading the words, when he had finished writing, and she had to read them again to be clear about their meaning.

When she was sure that she understood, she thought of Mattie, of whom there was no mention. How strange, Hepsy thought, that her name should be missing from such a letter! Hepsy returned it to the drawer. Though one letter had been on top of the other, she could not remember which. She hesitated, not wanting Mattie to know that she had opened it, then, resigned to the fact that its contents would soon be revealed, put the one addressed to her on top of the other, closed the drawer, and tip-toed to bed.

She looked out of the window at the bats to-ing and fro-ing between the fruit trees. The best of the light had gone, but there was still enough to discern objects below: a broken wheelbarrow, a water-pump, an agitated badger. The blue tit looked at her indifferently as it clung to the thatch, then flew away.

Hepsy let her mind wander. I have never seen the landscape from this position. 'Tis as if I am in some strange land. And over there I can make out Dugdale Farm, black and silent. This room, Toller's room, looks towards where I lived. From here, he might have spied me riding in the lane, kindled his dream of our being wed.

She turned to the bed. The fire Mattie had made to take the chill out of the air pulsed silently, contentedly. In her nightdress, on the edge of her bed, she brushed her hair in the gossamer candlelight, her back to the fire.

She slipped into bed, and was soon too warm, so she opened the window, letting in the sounds of the night: the javelin of an owl's screech, the enchanting operetta of blackbirds, and then, occasionally, the bleating of her own sheep.

Tiredness came quickly, but she got up and bolted the door. In summer, she usually slept with the window open, so that the dawn chorus would wake her at first light.

As she began to think of the letter again, she swore she could hear someone singing. She held her breath, concentrating, and the voice came nearer. There was just enough light from the fire to let her see her way safely to the window. She did not lean out to look; the light had all but dissolved. The voice was male and merry. In it, she detected a monologue. It was hard for her to understand its gist, but, after a few seconds, she identified the voice as Forston Sampford's.

"Old Sojer's had his leave tonight, by Gad!" he laughed.

"It be Forston Sampford," cursed Hepsy.

Downstairs, the clock chimed, seemingly as loudly as church bells. The sound must have escaped through her window, as she heard him say, "And that be eleven, if my counting baint fuddled by cider and apple brandy!"

Invisibly, he fumbled in his jacket, and took out the pocket watch he had stolen from Ebenezer Valence.

"Hasten home, you old sot!" hissed Hepsy. "I cannot sleep while I hear your ranting."

"Why, 'tis too dark to see, but eleven be a fair guess, judging by those stars which hab guided me from Briddy, as they hab done for many a year."

He resumed his singing, and where the real words escaped him, he substituted others, which amused him more than the original ones. His performance ended with, "Damn these boots, which swell my feet till they be pinched. Briddy get further away, the older I get, but Old Sojer still turn up for duty. Stands to, like a good."

The last few words crumbled into muttering.

Hepsy returned to her bed, satisfied that he was nearer his house than the cottage.

"One day, he bill fall in a ditch, and break his neck!"

With that more a wish than a prediction, she went to sleep.

In the morning, Hepsy rose early, before Mattie, built a fire, and cooked a pan of oats. Mattie could smell them, and the sweetness of the honey pushed off a spoon into the two bowls tempted her, where before it would have made her retch.

"You hungry? Got a pan nearly ready," said Hepsy.

"Hungry, and so be my daughter, judging by her antics."

They ate at the table, each trying to make small talk. Nothing important was said till Hepsy asked, "Where you keep that big spoon? Better stir so's it don't stick."

"Right drawer."

Hepsy was up like a shot, and opened the drawer. Mattie watched her take out the letter, stare at it.

"This be for me?" she asked.

Mattie looked up, never thought that Hepsy had planned the discovery.

"Unless there be another Hepsy, Dorset way."

"Why didn't you tell me it was there?"

"Toller wanted you to have it, he would have sent it. Still belongs to him, be my reckoning."

Clearly disagreeing, Hepsy fetched a knife and deftly reopened the letter. She read it silently, then gave it to Mattie, who also read it.

"So you the one he's left here for? The one who turned him down?"

"He's a good man, Mattie, but 'twas father poisoned my ear with talk of a better. Now I know what I really meant to Toller."

"And what if he don't come back when the year be done?"

Hepsy smiled inappropriately.

"Then this cottage be mine, dear: every bluebottle that bludgeons the windows to escape, every stick of furniture – all be mine. 'Tis here in this letter, written in his hand."

Chapter seventeen.

Toller regained consciousness to the sensation of an inquisitive rat running up his leg. He jerked himself into an upright position, and, so doing, caused himself to vomit. As he flailed dizzily, an unbearable pain in his jaw made him cry out. There was nothing to grasp to steady himself. Legs passed but were out of reach.

"Help me!" he begged.

He put his hand to his face, and felt the swelling, a plump cushion of agony. How long he had been unconscious he had no idea. Buildings spun, he retched again, and the elbow on which he had been leaning gave way. He closed his eyes. Someone had to help him; his jaw was broken.

When he opened his eyes again, he saw a face above him, looking down.

"You're in a right state," said the policeman.

Toller remembered the lightning in his jaw when he had last spoken, and merely pointed to the spot where it had struck. That gesture, and a meaningful grunt, began his story.

"Been there a while," observed a man, who had passed, fifteen minutes earlier.

"You been drinking?" asked the policeman, raising his voice in the belief that Toller's hearing, as well as his jaw, might have been damaged.

Slowly, the need to explain why he was lying on the pavement forced Toller to think more clearly. The Raddleman. Ezra, confronting him unexpectedly. Then nothing. Till the throbbing, excruciating pain.

Again, Toller tried to sit up. The policeman placed his hands under his armpits, from behind, and tried to lift him up. Toller's attempt to steady himself was like that of a drunk trying to appear sober. Feebly, and exasperated that he might appear to be inebriated, he flung a punch at himself, to show what he believed had happened.

"Someone hit you?" Toller nodded. "You know him?" This time, a slighter movement, the first too painful. "You make a statement when you're ready. You been robbed?" Toller felt in his pocket, and shook his head slightly. "You make your way home?" Toller looked at all the buildings around him. Though they were in a straight line, they appeared to form a circle, disorienting him. The officer saw his confusion. "Take your time. No rush. I'll see you home. Just you get your bearings, first. No rush."

Gradually, Toller made his way, carefully putting one foot in front of the other, till he established a rhythm, which persuaded the policeman, who could smell no alcohol on Toller's breath, that he was no longer needed.

As Toller passed The Raddleman, he reflected on the justice Ezra had meted out. It was not supposed to be like this. As Ezra must have seen it, Durnovaria Brewery, of which Toller was a representative, had stolen his comfort, his smoke-filled refuge. Ezra would have said more: that Toller was nothing like his predecessor, had wanted to do more than deliver barrels of ale, and had wanted to put a distance as wide as Chesil Beach between them. Toller saw that now. And he had only himself to blame. Collecting debts, delivering harsh messages of closure as well as barrels, was always bound to lead to resentment, even danger.

That night, he could not sleep. The pain intensified. The slightest movement exacerbated it. He spluttered as he tried to drink water, and relief came only at first light, when, exhausted, sleep eventually claimed him.

Zenobia was anxious to speak to him, to see how his visits had gone, and enquired after him down in the yard, but no one had seen him. Indeed, the workers' body language made plain their dislike of him, his promotion, his aloofness.

"This won't do, Langton. He's made me a laughing-stock among the men. Where is he?"

"Your pacing up and down and peering through the window won't make him come sooner. Something must have happened. If he's not here within the hour, I'll go and visit him at his lodgings."

"At the outset, too."

Her lips tightened, and she folded her arms defensively.

"I do hope Miranda was right about him," said Langton, standing up irritably, and stretching his collar, which had been over-starched.

"She is rarely wrong. Her instincts about people are remarkable. Oh, I'll admit that she had some romantic notion about him. She thought it was rare in a man, these parts, that he should want to better himself, and would have kept him on the Misterton Estate, but he would not have it."

"Too much ambition is also dangerous. Headstrong men are often reluctant to take orders, and, like a horse that won't come quietly, must be broken in. If we don't hear from him by this time tomorrow, he goes."

Zenobia went over to her brother, and gently placed her hand on his shoulder.

"Are you well, Langton? Your view is extreme. Usually, you give the benefit of doubt to people."

"I'm sorry, dear, but sometimes being let down by those we have helped puts me in a dark mood."

"Then let a little sunshine into it. Let's go to Weymouth for the day, and leave today's troubles till tomorrow."

"You are right. Let's not prejudge him. The light is fine. We can be there by lunchtime."

Meanwhile, Toller remained on his back, on his bed, and felt ashamed that, on his first day as a debt collector, he had been assaulted, that he had not turned up for work, the next day. He had no inclination to go to the brewery, and tell them what had happened. The men would see his distorted face, the sort seen in a freaks' booth in a travelling fair, and believe that he had it coming. And Ezra, once one of those men, had done it on behalf of all those with whom Toller had been loath to pass the time of day. It was all up with Toller. He could never face a debtor again. His ambition sat oddly with him now.

For three days, he stayed in his room, managing only sips of water, and lying as still as possible. The slightest movement of his head hurt him, but when he heard knocking on his door, he swung his stiff legs off the bed, and listened.

"Toller?" he heard.

He remained silent, had not expected a visitor. The ringing in his ears, caused by Ezra's blow, distorted the sounds, and he could not recognise the voice. Perhaps, if he sat there long enough, his legs bare, his shirt creased, whoever wanted him would return down the wooden stairs. Then Toller heard the voice again. Zenobia, he guessed. Ah well! She must know sooner or later, and I will be dismissed.

He would welcome this release, and said, "One moment."

Somehow, the need to be presentable increased his ability to bear the pain, and he put on his trousers.

He opened the door slowly.

"Horse breeding not nearly so dangerous as brewery work, judging by the looks of you."

He tried to smile, but he winced instead.

"Let's just say it was not what I was expecting."

"Invite me in, Toller. Your reputation is safe. Stand not upon moral scruples. I have come to help."

He stood back, and allowed her in. The legs of the wooden chair scraped on the floorboards as he pulled it towards her.

"How did you know?" She smiled. "Miss. Godmanstone send you?"

Miranda Misterton shook her head.

"Let's just say that not much escapes my notice, when it's important to me."

Toller looked up at her. She cares, he saw. In all this, when I hab forgotten who and what I am, someone tries to stop me falling off the cliff-top.

"Then they think I just upped and offed?"

"No idea. Could you not have sent a message?"

"Thought I was dying. Wanted to, at first."

"You can't stay here, on your own, not in this state."

The year was not yet up. It would be unfair to Mattie if he returned. Barely six months had passed. He had been late to send her money, but had eventually kept his word. That was one good thing he had done: helped a woman in need of a fresh start.

"I will return to Pilsdon and, in time, build up a flock."

"In time, yes, but come back to the estate, where there will be food and friendship, till you are well again. I will explain to Zenobia what has happened. Do not prolong the agony of your association with the brewery. Remember Michael and Charlotte? They looked after you, once, and will do so again. Come. Gather your belongings."

Toller seemed to physically shrink at what he knew to be a defeat, an abandonment of his plan to become someone important. And what compounded his woe, made him put his head in his hands, was that his defeat was so ignominious, not born of his own will but of his lack of judgement. He had known as soon as he had put on clothes, at the behest of Zenobia, which changed his image. What must she be thinking of me? he wondered.

Yet he was relieved, at the same time, that he had someone who would extricate him from this episode, and take responsibility for his immediate welfare. I shall go with her, let her put me in the hands of Michael and Charlotte, once again. Why, already I cannot wait to go to church at Stinsford on Christmas Eve, and hold my lamp aloft, and sing with them. There shall I be rested, till my heart and head speak as one.

"Give me a minute, would you?" he asked.

Miranda smiled, and stepped onto the landing.

Toller put on the clothes he used to wear at Pilsdon, and left his debt-collector's attire there. Over his shoulder, he hung his bag, careful not to catch his face. His felt hat was tipped over his eyes; he thought that if he could not see others' expressions of curiosity or condemnation, then they would not see him or the swollen price he had paid for closing The Raddleman.

Back at Misterton Manor, Miranda led him to the kitchen, where Charlotte, now elevated to the position of Housekeeper, greeted him with strict instructions to sit down, while she applied a layer of butter to the offended jaw.

"'Twill bring out the bruising, 'twill, and a thin rainbow it will be: first black, then green, then yellow, till you look like yourself again," she said.

Michael had come in to give his wife a peck on the cheek, as he had been wont to do since their wedding in Stinsford church, and, when he saw that Toller had returned injured, kept not to tradition but said, "Why, look what blowed in, Charlotte! I knew you'd come back to us, Toller. Looks like you been kicked in the face by a horse, which be a pity, as you was a handsome sort of man, last time we clap eyes on you. But don't you a-fret. My Charlotte be an artist biv the butter, as I saw for myself when I walks into the door-frame, last Harbest, when the cider moved it from its usual place. My eye was a moonball in no time. On she slaps the butter, and soon I could see again."

"Better, in fact, you said," interrupted Charlotte. "There be nothing like a smearing of well churned butter to take pain and swelling away."

Such remedies Toller knew to be popular in those days, and was prepared for his treatment, though he doubted its efficacy, not being superstitious.

"There you go!" exclaimed Charlotte, when she had finished.

"Why, 'ee look like a buttercup, your face be so yellow!" pointed out Michael.

Toller laughed, causing more pain.

"Michael Salisbury, put away your joking! Can't you see poor Toller be injured?" scolded Charlotte.

"Then I apologise, Toller," said Michael, "though they say that laughter be the best medicine."

"No need for an apology, Michael," said Toller, "for what with the butter and your good humour, I am bound to recover soon."

Toller slept in the hayloft. Blue vinney and bread, broken into small pieces so that he did not have to chew much, had made him feel better. He had climbed the ladder carefully, his lamp in his right hand. Underneath him, the warm straw was soft and supportive. In the morning, there would be questions to answer, he knew, and he would confess his mistake, so that his self-respect, as well as his jaw, would begin to heal.

He awoke to voices below, and became fully conscious quickly.

"You awake?" called Michael. "'Tis mid-day, and Miss. Miranda sent me. She wants to see you when you've had a bite to eat. My Charlotte be boiling soup full of tatties and onions. 'Easy for him to eat,' she said. You a-coming? 'Tis a fine day. Master Nicholas gone for his usual stroll. All be well with the world."

Michael's reassurances were like the butter – balm.

"Coming now," called Toller.

Outside the barn, the sunlight blinded him, and he put on his hat to shield his eyes. In the distance, Nicholas turned and waved to him. Does he recognise me? wondered Toller. Does he really remember me? Toller waved back, and smiled, and there was no pain. He thought: 'taint the butter, though I would not say so to Charlotte. 'Tis the friendship, the land. Today, when my legs take me there, I shall slip and slide in the pews in Stinsford church, for I have some prayers to say, and though they never soared from my heart before, this day shall they spread their wings and hasten to Heaven.

When Toller had recovered enough to give a full account of what had happened, he gave his permission to Miranda to explain to Zenobia his disappearance.

"And what did she say? Did she say why neither of them came to see me?"

Three days after his rescue, he had begun to pity himself, felt that somehow their neglect of him was a sign that he was worth no more than any other worker at the brewery.

"She was sorry that you were attacked, doing your job, which is still open if you want it. Will you go to see her? She has your wages."

"No. I will never set foot in the brewery again. It was all a mistake, a step too far for me. I dreamed I could have a better life, but now I know, in my heart, I be a shepherd, and people must take me as I am. I have my cottage in Pilsdon, where I must go, and must build me up a flock again."

Miranda looked at him. Only once before had she seen a man broken, and that was her father, Nicholas, who had lain on his bed for days when Maisie, his wife, had died. Miranda had heard him blame himself: "Should have saved her. No straw could help, this time."

"You won't stay? There is work here. Help Michael in the stables, plough the fields. There is as much or as little company as you like."

Toller said, "'Tis kind, but I must go. I hab things to see to."

"But you will return, one day, when the time is right?"

Mattie remained a secret. He could not wait to see her again. It was a comfort, in these days of failure, to know that he had offered a sanctuary to one in need, as Miranda had done.

Toller made himself useful: polished saddles for Michael, changed the straw in the stables, groomed the horses. Miranda left him alone, but asked Michael how he was progressing.

"Talks more to the horses than me, and they understand him. One of us, 'tis certain, yet part of him be elsewhere."

One day, when he was preparing himself to leave, saying his goodbyes, Miranda thought better of telling him that when she had passed The Raddleman, she had noticed its doors were open to customers again. She had seen the horse and cart delivering its barrels, but had no idea that the man who had doffed his cap to her was Ezra, who had had his way, in the end.

Chapter eighteen.

Redvers Holditch listened to what Hugo Lockington had to say, and stroked his downy moustache, a habit which helped him to concentrate on what most would view as good fortune. He had always known that the man he called father had a different name, and that his own name – Holditch – was his mother's. When Walter Chickerell married her, against the advice of his family, who warned him about the social and political stigma which would attach itself to him if he proceeded with his plan, she saw no reason why Redvers would need any other name than the one recorded on his birth certificate. That stance was questioned by Walter, but he was satisfied by her explanation: that he was marrying *her*, and that she herself was content to adopt his surname, a clear expression of her commitment. Walter, of course, had never known that if Redvers had taken Chickerell also, the name Holditch would have been lost for ever, there being no one else in the family bearing it.

Hugo Lockington looked for a sign of joy or dismay in the young man's face, but Redvers remained inscrutable. He was happy with life as it was, and enjoyed a salary big enough to lead a comfortable one. What need had he of another house, and land? Yet he was not too young to respond to what others of his age would view as exceptional luck; he would not walk away from his inheritance. There was, of course, the need to come to terms with discovering the identity of his true father. That subject cast shadows from his brow and chin in the orange lamplight.

"You cannot find the words to express yourself, at the moment, I see, but I assure you that I require none. My business with you is now at an end," said Lockington.

"This is, indeed, a surprise. I expect my father, Mayor Chickerell, will find it as puzzling as I do. I know not if this gesture of Mr. Valence's is an act of conscience to right a wrong – my mother always steadfastly refused to speak of the circumstances in which she found herself an unmarried woman – but I would be a fool to turn my back on what would, I imagine, have been mine sooner had he not abandoned my mother in her hour of need."

Lockington warmed to Redvers, whose words belied his age. He has about him, thought Lockington, a practical, rational mind. I see something of myself in him. Indeed, had I a son myself, it is to such a man as this that I would be happy to leave all my worldly goods.

"I shall write to Miss. Valence, and inform her that I have found you, and acquainted you with the gist of the will. In a matter of days, Dugdale Farm and all of Ebenezer Valence's other assets will be legally yours. It is not my responsibility to do anything else. How you deal with his daughter living there is a matter for you entirely."

Redvers brought the meeting to an end with, "Thank you for informing me of the will, the contents of which are a great surprise to me. However, the issues arising from it I shall address when I have had time to contemplate them at greater length."

They shook hands.

"Oh, and one more thing: do tell your mother that he left no item or message for her," added Lockington.

Redvers replied, "That will be impossible."

"Why so?"

"Because she is dead, sir."

Mayor Chickerell received news of Redvers' unexpected inheritance with equanimity. He had always known that Ebenezer – his wife had been truthful about her circumstances from the first time she had met Walter, had told him everything, so that he could walk away if he wanted – had existed, that he might return, one day, for the son he had never seen. That Ebenezer had acknowledged the existence of Redvers was no particular surprise to Walter. Yet to leave his daughter homeless . . . now that puzzled him.

"You will visit Miss. Valence?" asked Walter, who had not referred to Hepsy as a half-sister; a sister of any kind, he felt, was more than a stranger, and a stranger was what Hepsy was to Redvers.

"I shall write. She cannot be evicted. This must have come as somewhat of a shock to her, too. She has lived on the farm all her life, and yet Ebenezer Valence must have had what he saw as a just reason to leave her penniless. I will give her time."

"Are you not curious to meet her?" asked Walter. "You need not spare my feelings. This does not change what you have been, and are still, to me."

"A little, though I am no farmer. Sails are what we make. Perhaps, one day, I may sell the farm, invest the capital in –"

But Walter interrupted with, "Take your time, Redvers. Write, as you must, and be honest in your thoughts. Do not rush your decision."

So Redvers wrote, indicating a date on which he would visit Dugdale Farm, and reassuring her that there was no need to fear imminent eviction, that she could stay there, at least until he was married, an event not scheduled for the immediate future.

When Hepsy opened his letter, she was sitting at the table, slicing a handful of chives into tiny pieces, and releasing their pungency. Their lilac heads she scooped into a pile, to make a pretty posy, to hang outside the door, to ward off bats. She read what Redvers had intended to be comforting words, but her resentment at what she felt was the injustice of the will made her insensitive to his aim, and she prejudged him.

Her thoughts ran unchecked: father bin heartless, and though this man delays my departure, he intends to bring a bride here soon. How can I live here, when my hours burn away like candle wax? No, 'tis charity he offers, and he will remind me of father's mistake. I will to Mattie to see if she will have me there. Two women made homeless by men! And the goodness of Toller seems like honey with blue vinney now, and how I wish I had given him hope, my hand in marriage, even, instead of listening to father's wishes: seemingly fluttering butterflies but really adders lying in the heath.

Her letter of reply to Redvers was as terse as she could make it. She made no mention of their shared father, and let him know that she intended vacating Dugdale Farm as soon as possible, it being better to face up to the fact that she must start a new life. She would leave the keys in the barn, and promised to feed the animals for a week or two, but stressed that it was now his responsibility, and that she was sure he would not wish to see them suffer by neglect. Her last sentence asked him not to seek her out, as a meeting would inevitably refer to matters she would find distressing. Yet when she had finished signing her name, she could not help feeling a little curious about his appearance, his manner. To control that curiosity, she knew, would be a huge challenge.

Walter Chickerell tied the final knot in the rope securing the tarpaulin protecting the sails destined for Bridport harbour. The wagon was ready to go, so Redvers climbed onto it, and picked up the reins.

"My trunk on board?" he asked.

"It is. Mind you take care with the money in those lanes, on your way back. Keep your wits about you. You never know who's about," warned Walter, offering his hand.

"I shall be gone for two weeks, to see how the land lies. You can do without me that long?" Walter nodded. "As for highwaymen . . ." Redvers tapped the gun lying next to him on the seat.

"Goodbye, Redvers."

"Goodbye, father."

The weather was pleasant, made Redvers feel as if he had somehow been freed to begin a new adventure. He tried to picture Hepsy, painted her now with fair hair, now with dark, and by the time he arrived at the harbour, no other thought than of her occupied him. He had written to let her know when he was coming, but had received no reply. All I know is that she welcomes me not, and with justification. She has lost, and I have gained, everything, Redvers reflected.

Once the sails had been inspected by the owner of *Sea Nymph*, and the money handed over, Redvers made for an inn. The ostler fed and watered his horse, and the future seemed a more certain, achievable destination. There were only the directions to Pilsdon to obtain. No doubt, one of the men sitting by the window would point him thither.

Redvers sat on his own, at a distance maintaining the regulars' privacy, but he had not anticipated their interest in him; it was always thus when a stranger entered their home from home. It was not that they were bored with their own company – quite the opposite; they were more than content to hear the same stories, time and time again – but they had a natural inclination to be sociable.

It was Barnabus Dibberford who firstly spoke to Redvers. Barnabus had just related excitingly an episode in which he had fought off four men intent on robbing him, as he went down a dark alley off South Street, and was in a mood to repeat it to anyone else who would listen, so encouraging had been the reception of his first telling of it.

"'Less you expecting company of your own, or you got the 'sumption, you more than welcome to join us round this table, which seats as many as see fit to pass the time of day at it."

Redvers needed not only the route to Pilsdon but human company after a journey made in silence, bar a few words exchanged to conclude his transaction in the harbour. Pulling up his chair, he sat in the space created by Jude Broadwindsor.

"Thank you, all. The reputation of a Bridport welcome as being without equal is, indeed, justified, and, in exchange for the directions to Pilsdon, I am happy to buy you all a drink," offered Redvers.

"'Tis kind," said Barnabus, "and there baint a one of us who will refuse, though 'twould sit better, like a hen upon her eggs, if you will tell us your name, so's we can hatch us a true Briddy conversation."

Introductions over, Miles Yondover, who had gone to the inn after a long day spent pitch-forking manure into a cart, and then out of it, into a field, agreed to show him the way. He had laboured mechanically, and consoled himself that it would soon be time to visit Hepsy Valence again. He smiled at the thrilling prospect of holding her waist, and kissing her again, in the twilight. One day, he vowed, when her lips, still sweet after a first juicy bite of a ripe plum, do not stiffen but give way softly, he would ask her to marry him.

"Why, I be going to Pilsdon myself, after this gathering goes home, and if you give me a ride, then there can be no mistaking the road. Those lanes be a treachery, what with goblins a-swivelling the sign-posts, so that Shave Cross become Denhay, and Broadoak swaps place with Dottery. A treachery they be, Redvers, when the goblins hab been abroad."

"Then we shall go together. You live in Pilsdon, Miles?"

The others smiled, and Miles blushed.

"No – at least, not yet."

Redvers saw the amusement of the others in their suppressed laughter.

"What he means," explained Jude, "be that he hab a sweetheart, and that he would take her for a wife if she wasn't too good for him, him being a lowly farm-worker, and she –"

"Now, men," called the inn-keeper. "Leave the lad alone. He don't deserve all this teasing, and he be worthy of any woman, these parts, him being such a handsome, though the first thing I recommends any wife of him to do is to cut his long, blond hair, which make him half angel, half girl."

They all laughed, but Barnabus ended their mockery, which he saw was in danger of inflaming Miles, with, "We none of us is perfect. Miles here hab the smell of the field; I, as you all know, won't settle till I hab the last word in an argument; Jude here hab been known not to pay his way, on the day – and don't you protest, Jude, as you know your pockets be sewn up, some days – and the inn-keeper here been known to keep ale like vinegar, betimes. So, I suppose a bit of extra fair hair be nought in the scale of things."

They all nodded, puffed on their pipes, settled into a silence broken only when Jude, who had not quite exhausted his mirth, said to Redvers, "And now you know all about our little faults, what be yours? Best not be too small, mind, as we'll all feel bad, but throw us a spickle, just to give us a peep. You look a gentleman, and a young, but there must be something to leave with us, so's we remember you by it."

Redvers saw all eyes on him. They must not be disappointed, he knew. He feigned difficulty in coming up with something, but eventually revealed his worst trait.

"I am afraid my fault will eclipse all yours. I have carried this on my back for years, and it weighs me down, leaving me exhausted."

"Why, your tone and face betoken something you need not tell us if 'tis so big. 'Tis a sport of ours, but not a trial, so be silent if pain to you be the end of it."

Redvers' acting had fooled at least Jude, and his audience must know the truth.

"The noise wakes my father, and a wife would run a mile if I had one. No, gentlemen, the truth is that I snore like thunder, like God was scraping his bedstead across the oaken floorboards of Heaven!"

The listeners then recognised the jest, and their laughter rocked their chairs and tables on the flagstones.

"I like your sense of humour," said Barnabus, "and this chair be always here at this table, should you ever wish to fill it again!"

"I thank you all, and will, indeed, come again, I assure you. Now, let me buy you all a pot of ale, after which I must continue my journey, before it gets dark. Does that suit you, Miles?"

"It does, sir, and 'tis to be hoped the moon be abroad on my way back, or I will lose myself, as I hab done, a time or two before."

They all toasted Redvers, and Miles and he set off in the cart to merry calls from their friends, who had taken a breath of air to wave them off, and were raising their pots, which, they said, ought to be filled just one more time. So much had they drunk and talked, that conversation, a torrent in the inn, soon dried to a trickle in the cart. They swapped details of their occupations, shared tales young men traditionally store in their imagination, for they were of a similar age.

"Pilsdon be not far now," remarked Miles. "'Tis but a sprinkling of cottages and a farm."

The moon was out, and they lowered their voices instinctively.

"There's a big house there, on the left," pointed out Redvers.

"And so there be, and there must I leave 'ee. Dugdale Farm be where I'll drop. And where must be your stop?"

The moonlight shone down onto Miles' hair, crowned him with a halo.

"Did you say Dugdale Farm?"

"I did, indeed."

"Then be you coming to see me?"

"No. The mistress of the house: Miss. Hepsy Valence."

Redvers laughed good-naturedly, then firmly said, "Then you have had a wasted journey, I fear."

"And why be that?" asked Miles.

"Because unless I'm mistaken, Miss. Valence has left, and Dugdale Farm now belongs to me."

And they were the last words they exchanged, that night.

Chapter nineteen.

Hepsy told her story with a measured pace, and Toller listened, looking down at the floor, as if praying. Mattie watched the pot, sprinkled wild garlic leaves into it, her back to the other two. If she did not listen to them, she could concentrate on her task, so she moved to the table, and chopped precisely more potatoes and onions; she thought that taking care with the slicing would remove the two voices from her head, suspecting that what was being said might affect her.

"And that be how I come to be living here now with Mattie, who be expecting a tiddy one, so we help each other, which be the way of things, now the vale be so different from how it was afore you left," finished Hepsy, who looked at Toller throughout her explanation, saw in his sad eyes the memory of his leave-taking on that stormy day, when he had told her he wanted to avoid chance meetings.

"Bit of bread, Toller?" asked Mattie. "Baked it, this morning, in this very oven."

"'Tis kind. Never used the oven myself. What I means is, 'tis the woman who normally cooks and bakes. Smells good and sweet. Give me a piece, Mattie, and 'twill break up the waiting for the pot."

"You want to rip it, or shall I cut?"

"Cut."

"Chunk of blue vinney?"

"A rindy bit, which be the best, as I recall, though 'tis a cheese I hab not tasted since we sat down in The King's Arms, in Dorchester, when we –"

"Were hungry. When the trudging in the snow gave us an appetite," interrupted Mattie, fearful of him revealing that they were not brother and sister, as they had professed, that they had not known each other long, just time to tell each other their story.

"'Twas so," realised Toller. "And 'twas a day I shall never forget."

"'Twas so, indeed," echoed Mattie.

Hepsy saw this history between them, and felt like an intruder. Once, it could have been her here, stirring a steaming pot, but now she was at their mercy.

Soon, Toller saw her eyes flash, look for a sign that he still liked her, that his emotional attachment to her – he had never used the word *love*, she was sure – survived yet. He had run out of objects to stare at, and his eyes rested on her.

"So you live in my house," he said, to start.

"'Tis certain, though I will leave if it be not to your liking."

Mattie turned and said, "But where would you go? Stay yet. You will not mind, will you, dear brother?"

Her reference to him as a brother was calculated to persuade him to agree to Hepsy staying, at least for a while.

Suddenly, he thought of Michael, Charlotte, and Miranda. Why had he not stayed with them, helped Michael with the horses, stared over the paling at the woods and fields, welcomed the bats, in the evening, with Nicholas, as the sky turned dark blue? He smiled at their unconditional acceptance of him, their attention to his well-being.

"Stay, then," said Toller, "and see to the pot with Mattie, who must rest, betimes. And mind I get a big piece of rabbit, as I be hungry."

They ate the rabbit and potatoes self-consciously. When he lived alone, he used his fingers, tore meat off the bone with his teeth, having no one to heed, no table manners to show, with only himself to please. Now he had two women to mind, one he once would have married gladly, the other he himself had all but installed. So he used the knife and fork Mattie had put before him.

Ebenezer had been a man of few words at the table, had reserved them for giving further instructions about his needs – more pie, stewed plums and yellow cream – than for conversing, so Hepsy was used to long silences punctuated by the clinking of cutlery on plates. Mattie, however, had taken her meals with others – maids, servants, cooks – and tried to strike up conversation, careful, however, not to ask questions about Toller's absence, how he had filled it, and whether he had become the man he had wanted to be.

"We will talk tomorrow about when the baby comes," said Mattie.

"People will gossip," warned Hepsy. "The news will wing to Bridport faster than a pigeon."

"Forston Sampford. He still going? Still alive?" asked Toller.

"He hab introduced himself to me," said Mattie, "though not overly. Comes and goes down the lane, but he aint no fox."

"Then you done well, girl. The loneliness does it. Talks to himself, which we all done, betimes."

"Father spoke to him when he had to. Time of day they passed, though father never said what their words were."

"There bill be a time when Sampford will go too far. You kept the door locked, Mattie?"

"I baint a prisoner, Toller. Can't be a prisoner in my own home."

"Toller's," reminded Hepsy. "Toller's home."

Toller scowled at her.

"What be mine be also my sister's."

Hepsy flushed, could have bitten off her tongue at her loose words.

"Of course. Didn't mean anything by it. You know that, don't you, Mattie, dear?"

"Words send men and women to the gallows, and start wars," pointed out Toller.

"Can forgive, too," reminded Mattie.

Toller stood up, wiped his mouth with the back of his hand. Clean nails, noticed Hepsy. Not handled a sheep since he went.

"Thank 'ee. And now I will go and walk my fields, see where I must graze my first ewes again."

He escaped in silence. The women had shrunk the cottage, it seemed, and they watched silently as he left. Then the place filled with sighs, tension as threatening as the seconds before lightning stabs the ground.

Smiles wreathed his face as he strode through the fields. This I have missed, he said to himself, and I will tend sheep again, find a dog to hem and drive them, till they are fattened for market. 'Tis a living I should never have turned against. And 'twas she drove me out, in a manner of speaking, made me a stranger to my own home.

He resented her audacity at moving into his cottage. Toller recognised, however, that she could not have known he would return. Yet she cannot stay, he decided. What I felt for her has disappeared. My life should be a cloudless sky, but 'tis now a granite tombstone at the sight of her.

He increased his pace, hoping that a climb up Pilsdon Pen would put things into perspective. The view from the top had always filled him with peace. The vale below was a patchwork quilt of light and dark green. He liked to be alone with the birds and breeze, but heard whistling, and saw a tall, lean man striding towards him. He is happy, thought Toller, and young enough not to know the pain a woman can inflict. Youth and this landscape seem his friends. I remember myself like him, though it seems like a century ago. There must be, at the most, five harvests between us.

"Good day," opened the young man, when he, at last, saw Toller. "The prospect is worth the breathlessness."

"Good day to 'ee, too. 'Tis the finest in Dorset, if not in England, though I know no other land but these parts, so my judgement be open to challenge."

"You will receive none from me, for I agree that Dorset is beyond compare. The hills have the curves of a voluptuous woman, and secret places men stumble across that so delight that no inducement to leave is persuasive."

"You speak well enough. Your words become you, have the mark of an educated man, not a humble shepherd like me."

"It is the feeling the landscape inspires and not the words describing it which matters. An education of sorts I have had, acquired at the feet of my father, a good man and the Mayor of Crewkerne, to boot. Let me shake your hand, and introduce myself as Redvers Holditch. I have the good fortune to inherit property in this heavenly vale."

"And I be Toller Burstock, a shepherd that once was, and will be again. This view, this air, has today mended me – though I shall not trouble you with my woeful tale – and I am pleased to meet you. Such an encounter I have never had with a stranger, up here."

"Count me not a stranger, Toller, for it seems we have much in common: an agreement that Marshwood Vale be God's finest work."

The handshake was heartfelt; each man was glad of it.

There was something in their ease with each other that made it difficult to end their chance meeting. Toller had sought solitude to acquaint himself with what he used to think of as his domain, but was glad to have met someone with whom conversation flowed as easily as the water down the hills after heavy rain. And Redvers had set out to explore the landscape, and was delighted to have come across someone so agreeable. His father had warned him that country folk were different from those in Crewkerne, and that it would take persistence to win over neighbours, as strangers were nearly always a sign of imminent change, which must be resisted, at all costs.

Reluctant to end the conversation, Toller asked, "And be your new home far? Pilsdon? Broadoak, perhaps, or Shave Cross, where old Stoker been a-clinging on to life for a year or two. He gone?"

Redvers shook his head, and said, "Pilsdon itself. Dugdale Farm be mine now."

For the first time, Redvers felt the shame of that part of his history tying him to the present, to Marshwood Vale.

"Then you and I be neighbours, as I live but a short amble from you."

But Toller could not disguise the shock of discovering that he had met the man whose inheritance had compelled Hepsy to move into his own cottage.

Redvers noticed Toller's sudden and shocking pallor, and asked, "Then you knew Miss. Valence? It is likely you did, as you must have passed the farm, most days. Your expression suggests a change of mood."

"Our paths crossed. That is all. Her father was a man who liked me not, and nor I him. But that is in the past, and he is with the Lord."

Yet Redvers, for all his inexperience in the ways of the world, sensed discomfort in Toller, and decided that he must not let their exchange end in sadness or worse.

"Let us not talk of death, as it walks, in general, alongside older men and women than us. And it is enough to know that Ebenezer Valence contrived his daughter's difficulty, and not I."

Toller was tempted to reveal that she had played some part in his own recent misfortune, though he was cautious, mindful that their acquaintance was yet insubstantial.

"Then Marshwood Vale will be your doctor, and will prescribe air so fresh that any ailment you hab suffered from such a discovery bill vanish soon, I swear."

"You speak wisely, Toller, and let us end this theme when you have told me if you know of Miss. Valence's whereabouts. I wish to be satisfied that her immediate circumstances are not detrimental to her well-being."

Not wishing to reveal just how far his own life was now connected with Redvers', Toller said he knew not where she had gone, he being the last person she would tell.

"And that be the top and the bottom of the matter."

"Then I must give some thought to my future. Marshwood Vale is heavenly, but I am no farmer, and am more adept at the manufacture of sails. I have but temporary leave from the factory at Crewkerne, though this hillside's pleasant air lures me from it like a siren, till I feel I will have to be bound to it, like a sail to a mast."

"So what will happen to all the animals? Farmer Valence had a large flock of sheep. His rubies are well known throughout Dorset. 'Twould be a shame to lose them."

"Then a farm manager I will need. Do you know of such a one, these parts?"

Toller nodded.

"Indeed, I know one, and, if it pleases you, I bill talk to him, see if he be a-willing to come. I know that he will do a good job. Come spring, your fields will be full of gambolling lambs to fatten. He be your man, 'tis certain."

"Then do so, and I will await his answer."

There came a moment when they would continue their walk together or part, and it was Redvers who ended the conversation with, "But I detain you. Let us speak again of this and other matters. Dugdale Farm, remember. Till the next time."

Again they shook hands, and Redvers moved off.

Toller had much to consider. I must prepare to explain to him that his half-sister lives under my roof. Why, had she accepted me, this newcomer and I would be distantly related! The only way I can save face is to ask Hepsy to leave, as is proper. Go she must, as I once had to.

The decision made, he knew that he risked upsetting Mattie, and she would need a woman when the baby came. Then there was Mattie's future to think about. When he had handed over the key in Dorchester, he had not known that she was with child, and would certainly not have done so if she had told him. In fact, he knew that though she had a roof over her head, she still had no means of supporting herself – he would, of course, continue to provide for her, in the short term – and then there was the possibility that he might be thought of as the father. Sampford, he was sure, would have told the whole of Marshwood Vale about the mysterious sister who had turned up after Toller had left.

The land he owned he now remembered, their slopes, their shapes. Five acres of good grazing. It would be hard to neglect them further, no matter what the attraction of managing Dugdale Farm. He would have to live there if Redvers returned to the factory in Crewkerne. And what would Hepsy say? She could have had everything, but would be left with nothing.

Slowly, though, Toller continued to assess his situation. I've been acquainted with this young man barely twenty minutes. A good and an honest, he seems, I'll admit, but I know him not. And have I returned only to acquire again the lust for advancement, which becomes an itch? I must beware, for it will lead to scratching and misery.

A feather of wind brushed his face.

'Tis a friend I forsook but will not again, he vowed. If there be a woman who Providence hab chosen for me, she will knock on my door and let it be known, and if I have a child, it will not be Mattie's but the other's.

On his way down to the cottage, he rehearsed the words to evict

Hepsy, but no matter how he phrased them, they did not sound right.

"Hepsy, you must leave. I need hardly remind you . . . " sounded too much like the anthem of revenge. "Hepsy, the cottage be too small, and what with Mattie . . . " felt too apologetic. I must trust my instinct, hold firm.

In his ear, the wind seemed to whisper encouragement. It was a feminine voice, one urging him to be confident.

At Misterton Manor, Miranda stared westward.

"All must go before they return. 'Tis a lesson father teaches, and a true," she said.

He was tempted to knock on his own door and wait, but opened it without warning. Women inside or not, he was master in his own house. In a chair, at the table, Mattie was carefully sewing up the hem of the blue dress she had ripped on briars.

Mattie turned.

"Where is she?" Toller asked.

"You cannot bear to name her?"

"It is vinegar on my tongue."

"Then your mouth will be no longer offended."

"I must speak to her."

"Oh, but you cannot, brother. 'Tis impossible."

"Impossible?"

Mattie put down her sewing, and turned to him.

"Yes. She said to tell you she was sorry, that you have been more than kind, in the circumstances."

"She has left?"

"Yes, indeed. 'Time to go,' she said. 'And I shall be in my coffin afore the snow reminds me of father's fate.'"

Toller shrugged.

"Then I have no need of words."

"Yes, you do, Toller, though save them till we speak again,

for we cannot continue to live under the same roof beout 'em."

Toller slunk outside the cottage, which he knew was his, but now felt someone else's.

Chapter twenty.

In the days after Hepsy's sudden departure, Toller gradually reclaimed his cottage. At first, he had felt awkward about coming and going as he pleased, and told Mattie when he was going out to check the traps, but, used to being accountable to nobody but himself, he lapsed into his former bad habits: broke wind loudly in the house, and cleared his throat, first thing in the morning, when he had risen before her. She tutted to herself. Brothers: all foul smells and summoning up phlegm.

Then he looked in his dresser drawer, and saw the two letters he had left. The one to Hugo Lockington was still sealed; the other, to Hepsy, had been opened, and the wax ineptly repaired. Toller was relieved that he had gone without posting them, but became agitated at the possibility that one might have been read.

"You been in this drawer?" he snapped at Mattie.

"In the course of things, and at *your* invitation, I hab."

"You been at this letter?"

He brandished the one for Hepsy, and Mattie calmly replied, "I hab read it, though 'twasn't me who broke the seal. 'Twas Hepsy who discovered it, and showed me. Your business baint mine, Toller Burstock, though it be strange how your snapping at her, since you back, hab sent her packing, when you left her everything, as fits a man who cannot shake off the love he has for his woman."

"So she went a-snooping, did she? A ferret! Been through all my possessions, did she?"

"I know not, Toller, except what I have told you, and it baint my business to know. I be a guest here, and behave as one."

"She tittle-tattle about me, as women do to each other?"

Mattie had put up with enough, and said, "And what do you know about what women do, Toller Burstock?"

Toller lit a candle, and fed the letter to the flame. Mattie watched it disappear, till, after Toller had dropped it on the table, there was only a yellow coin of melted wax left.

"All what I felt be smoke and tallow."

"You must have loved her to have left all this."

"More like, I had no one else to leave it to. But all's but a bad whiff of memory now, so we won't hear no more of it. She say where she going?"

"No. She's a free woman, and owes no explanation."

This independence of Hepsy's bill scar another man, one day, he suspected. Why, who would not put it past her to change her mind, and return to Dugdale Farm, take up Redvers' offer? Not me. I should be back to where I was afore I fled – for flee be what I did – if I became Redvers' Farm Manager. My eyes would forever scour every knoll and secluded spot till I caught a glimpse of her or her ghost, and then I would lose count of my sheep. Lost too many, in the past; never again.

"True, Mattie, true."

"And go, too, must I, as I never expected all this, this early return of yours. And a baby's cry will shake the rafters. And the smell, too, baint pleasant, even though you used to tip-toeing round sheep, all day."

"No, stay. I will not see you go on my account. 'Tis your house now as much as mine."

"'Tis kind o' 'ee, but you done more than enough for me. Both our loved ones gone now, like birds bound for warmer air. Can't you see, Toller, that you and I are but landlord and tenant, and nothing more? We swapped our tales, and you gave me a key, but now I must return it."

"Then, let me not be here when you flit, as to be robbed of a sister be worse for the seeing of it," he said.

Out in the lane, he walked quickly; he needed work, and Redvers Holditch was offering it.

Toller picked flowers from the hedgerow, fat berries from prickly tendrils that flopped into the lanes. Tender were the flimsy, translucent, pink petals splotched against the dusty and tangled growth. I will give them to her with a smile. They will be a present, unashamedly a bribe, even. There will be no letting her down; I gave her the key in good faith, with no idea how things would turn out, and she must not feel that my return changes the promise. For what sort of a man would I be to see a woman, so far gone in her time, out in the lane? She would never make it to Bridport, where there would be rasping whispers, and yellow, bent fingers a-crooking at her.

"These be for you, Mattie."

Not till she spoke did he dare to raise his eyes from the flowers clumped clumsily, the stems crushed in his now callus-free hands. The other gift was a full bucket.

"Why, they be breathing!" cried Mattie, peering into it.

The clotted blackberries tempted her, and she chose one swollen till the skin of the beads was stretched to near bursting, and offered it to Toller.

"You first, girl. They be for you."

"That be what the serpent said to Eve in the Garden of Eden, and we all been suffering since!"

Mattie's cheeks were rounder now, polished by imminent motherhood. Crab apples, Toller thought. Then: Eve?

"Who be Eve?"

"You not read your scriptures? 'Tis how we all come to be: from Adam and Eve. Where you been if you not heard of them?"

This gentle mocking was not the laceration it would once have been. There was a time it would have left him bleeding for days, but Mattie's was more a nudge in the ribs than a cut.

"I heard on 'em."

Again, Mattie slowly lifted her offering to Toller's lips. His empty hands, blackened by clumsy plucking, trembled. He felt the merest touch of her fingers on his lips as he accepted, and the tingle jolted him into crushing the fruit in his mouth.

"They be sweet?"

"Sweet, then tart on the side of my tongue."

"Find some cream, Toller, and we have a feast fit for royalty."

She wiped her hand on her dress, felt her baby, and Toller stole another berry.

"Come. Your turn."

She took it, her teeth catching his finger.

"You done well, Toller. These be the season's best."

"Will you stay?"

She heard the plea of her baby, and knew that she must not let her daughter – she was convinced it was a girl – slip out into a ditch.

"I will," she said, "but we must both think about afterwards. Baint a normal way of going on, these or any other parts."

"When be your time?"

Mattie shrugged. As a child, the gossiping of the girls in Tolpuddle had filled her with too many superstitions and misleading tales.

"When the baby be ready. What month be we?"

Toller thought hard. The passing of time was a series of pictures to him: snow drifts, skittish lambs, scything, golden leaves disintegrating into dust when his fingertips rubbed them. And not always marching forward. Sometimes, Hepsy shoved in, and their times together would jostle for the here and now, seem more now than the actual present. He had always found it hard to remember to wind the clock, and he had no idea if the hands were in the correct place. The position of the sun was the best indication, he had always thought. So the month had always been an irrelevance to him. The days seemed to join together seamlessly to form a never-ending tapestry of constantly changing scenes. He had never even seen a calendar, let alone possessed one.

"'Tas the warmth of August."

"Then the baby, my poor, fatherless baby, won't be long now."

"Then you must stay. 'Tis settled."

"'Tis certain."

The day Toller went to Redvers to let him know the name of the man who would make a fine farm manager, Mattie noticed his change of attire. Gone were his labourer's clothes. Now he wore his own best, having left behind the suit Zenobia had had made for him in Dorchester. He had half-expected the moths to have gorged on the clothes in his wardrobe, but they were still in good condition.

"Don't stare so."

"You going some place?"

Toller recalled how Forston Sampford had asked the same question; saying goodbye to Hepsy was not to be shared with such a man. Why did everyone want to know his destination?

"We all be going somewhere," he said, more to tease than to be secretive.

"You almost look like a gentleman."

"Almost?"

"Well, you look like a gentleman, but a gentleman gives a civil answer to a simple question from a lady."

"Then forgive me. I shall reveal all on my return, when there'll be a rabbit or two."

"Can't be many rabbits left, these parts. 'Taint that I baint grateful, but my ears becoming long and floppy, and my two front teeth stick out more."

"Then a chicken it will be."

"You walking?"

Toller left on foot; Mattie guessed he was not going far. Dugdale Farm? Toller had wanted his best clothes to be taken as a sign of respect for the new owner. And what of Hepsy's sudden departure? To tell Redvers of it might complicate matters, set him thinking all over again, and require too much to be told at one go.

Redvers was in the garden, close to making the decision to go into Bridport and enquire after a farm manager, when Toller presented himself.

"Ah, Toller! Just in time. You have come, surely, to let me know if this man you told me about wants to come. If not, then I must to Bridport, for if I am honest, my inheritance feels more like a millstone round my neck than some kind of recompense I have not sought, and to which I am indifferent, bar recognising that I ought to have what is legally mine."

Toller understood the gist of this, but not how Ebenezer's bequest was a recompense.

"I have, indeed, though I have taken a spickle of time, as the man wanted to think about it. He has, however, decided to accept your kind offer, and is able to start immediately. The animals be his special interest, see, and what with you being a manufacturer of sails –"

"Quite," interrupted Redvers. "An immediate start is desirable. I'm afraid it would all go to ruin if it were left to me. Come, Toller, his name. I must, before long, return to Crewkerne. Is this man good with figures? With money?"

Toller gulped, recalling his misadventure as debt collector for the Godmanstones.

"He keeps an excellent inventory, and always gets a good price at market for his lambs, which he fattens without the slightest extra cost."

"He can provide references? I do not doubt your recommendation, Toller, but a sound testimonial from his last employer would secure him the job."

"I believe he worked on the Misterton Estate, Dorchester way. Miss. Miranda had a high opinion of him. It might take a day or two to write. Why not take him on temporary until the letter comes?"

"All right, I will. His name now. Can he start today? He is not in work, at the moment?"

There could be no more procrastination, so Toller said, "The man can start, this very minute, as 'tis I who offer to take the burden of the farm from your neck. I won't let you down. Farming – more shepherding, I say – be in my blood, and I hab returned from Dorchester to start all over again. Will you say yes or no, Redvers? I mean, Mr. Holditch."

"Come inside, and let us discuss in a more considered way. I am a man of business, you understand. My hospitality may extend to a glass of brandy; I found a bottle in a cupboard."

"'Tis kind, but I don't touch the strong."

"A wise man, and a good answer. It is best to keep a clear head."

Redvers led him indoors, offered him his real father's chair, and began a discussion that would last a full hour. Toller was interrogated on all matters agricultural, was found wanting in some answers, but convincing in others. At the end of the interview, Toller felt less sure of his suitability for the position than at the beginning. And he thought: this is a reminder that I am made for shepherding alone. Twice I have let my ambition run away with good judgement. I need to return to what I know best, as to try further will trip me up again, leaving me in despair.

After they had shaken hands, Toller left. Somehow the formal clothes he was wearing felt constricting, ludicrous. I will burn them, for they remind me of false hope, of a life I am not fit to lead. He breathed deeply, and looked up at Pilsdon Pen, with Redvers' words still damning him with faint praise: "Tomorrow, Toller, I will have an answer for you. Take not this delay to heart. It is my usual way. My father – Mayor Chickerell – taught me that hasty decisions hide in your shadow, and step into the light when you least expect to see their unwanted visage."

Toller did not want Mattie to think his excursion had lasted such a short time, so he walked to Shave Cross, where he sat on a milestone. Redvers' indecision had damaged his confidence. Shall I return and declare no further interest? I should hate to let him down. And Mattie? What will be her intention when the baby is born? All is unknown, uncertain.

Then, in the golden-pink glow of the evening, he thought about Hepsy: whether she was safe, had done something rash. She had once driven him away, and now she had separated herself from him. If he could only be sure she had come to no harm, he would be satisfied. And yet he would not look for her; she would, no doubt, scorn him for what she would see as his weakness.

As he walked up his lane to his cottage, he thought he could hear a strange sound. So used to the myriad calls of birds and animals was he that he stopped, listened more intently. Now he was sure it was a human cry of distress: a woman's scream, piercing, desperate.

"Mattie?" he wondered, breaking into a run.

His cottage was not far, and he hastened as the screaming rent the air, made sheep stand and bleat. Ditches rustled as creatures bustled at the sound of his heavy breathing, his exertion.

His door was open, and he ran inside. Mattie's chair was empty, and she cried, "No! Lord, help me!" She stretched each word, strained her voice to new notes of agony.

He took the steep steps two at a time.

"Mattie, I'm coming!" he called.

"Help me, Toller!"

Her bedroom door was open. Since he had returned, he had not been in that room. Once, he had stolen a peep, curious to know how a woman lived in private, where she put her clothes, what powders and potions she kept, what she wore underneath her dress. All these existed in his imagination, but he wanted to know for sure, unpick the timeless mystery that women embroidered for men. Now, without hesitation, he went into Mattie's secret chamber.

But he could not see her. Kneeling in front of her, hiding her, was a man. What is he doing, rummaging between her short, splayed, white legs, mumbling incoherently like a mad man?

Toller smelt him before he saw his face, recognised the tangled crown of briars. You take her, monster, so close to her time? Old Sojer not had enough in Bridport? In a single leap, Toller was upon him.

When Mattie saw Toller's wild eyes, she cried, "No, Toller, no!" But it was too late. Toller had grabbed the intruder's head, pulled him off her, and was about to strike Sampford dead when he saw the baby's head smeared with bright red blood.

Trembling, Sampford looked up at Toller's fist hovering over him as an eagle about to end the life of a field mouse.

"Go on, Toller Burstock, even as your own baby is born!" cried Sampford.

Then the baby came fully into the world, heralded by a scream that seemed to reverberate throughout the vale.

Sampford picked up the knife, brought up from the kitchen, he had dropped on the floor. All those years had not erased the memory of having done it once before, when he had obeyed a woman's cry. It was instinct in him.

Instead of using it as a weapon on Toller, Sampford said, "Here, you do it instead. Cut the cord. Do it for your daughter, as a father should."

Chapter twenty-one.

Hepsy scurried like a field mouse down the lane till she felt a safe distance from the cottage. The fear that she might change her mind, and return to cry over peeled onions for the pot, made her break occasionally into running for a few yards, and soon she was panting. She clutched a small bag embroidered with the red letters *HV* to her breast, expecting to come across a tramper, who might try to relieve her of the money she kept in it. There, too, was her father's sharp knife he used for whittling. And I will use it if my life be in danger, she vowed. Slit the throat of a pig or two, in my time, so a man's baint a bother.

Disturbed birds fluttered invisibly in the hedgerows, startling her. She thought she saw hideous faces, assailants, and her heart stuttered. She knew this road intimately; it had been, indeed, her daily escape route from her father's grumbling and the unlit corners of the house. Now, however, it seemed a stranger, leading her into unwanted exile. And she tried to explain it to herself. I must take my punishment, for I deserve no less. I had it all, including the love and promise of a good man, whom I would now gladly accept. But he hates me, I see, and as I have no choice, I shall leave, and let Fate lead me whither it will.

Soon, she realised that she must adopt a steadier pace or collapse, and she was glad when she reached the road that would take her into Bridport. The sun had gone down, and there was a sense that the long days had burnt themselves out, as a stubble fire in a blackened and barely smoking field. Twenty more minutes, she guessed, and she must find a room. She squeezed the bag, felt the hardness of the coins in her purse, the sharp blade. How I would unpick these two hated letters in red! she cried within.

Her plan was to seek help from Miles Yondover at his farm, but she was too weak to go further than Bucky Doo. He had not visited her in recent days, and she blamed herself. He had tried to kiss her, and she had relented just once, and had resisted his persistence so convincingly that he had put his hat back on and ridden off, calling, "A man don't know whether he be coming or going with such a one as 'ee!" She had tried to call him back, saying that it was just the ways of courting – that rationing of more kisses would lead to greater enjoyment of a few – and that he must not be greedy, but her words had been lost in the thud-thud of his horse's hooves. Still, he was her only hope, and might take pity on her, unlike Toller.

She remembered an inn in which Miles had mentioned he drank, and she hoped that if she found it, he would be there, so she might apologise and place herself at his mercy, or if he were not, she would beg directions so that she could begin her search, in the morning.

She looked up dizzily at the clock on the dome, where pigeons were squabbling, flapping in a great, grey cloud. She leaned, clutching her chest, breathing heavily, against a wall, and looked to see if anyone had witnessed her anxiety.

Then, from the other side of the road, came a gruff voice: "You lost, girl? Not seen you, these parts before. You want a bit of company?"

The unkempt man, who had lived more days than he had left and ought to have known better, slipped a small bottle, at the second attempt, into his jacket pocket, and tried to stand upright.

"I'm looking for a room for tonight. Do you know anywhere that'd have one?"

The man tried to cross the street in a straight line, and stopped, once or twice, to check his course by looking over his shoulder. Hepsy saw his bloodshot eyes, his bulbous, red nose, smelt his fiery breath. For a moment, she thought he was Forston Sampford, whom she had often seen stagger past the farmhouse after a day out in Bridport.

"I knows one, if you don't object to the mess it's in. There be a pile of this and that, and the whiff of a fish or two from West Bay, but you won't mind that, will you? Nobody's ever died from the smell of a fried mackerel."

As he leered, she saw that he had lost his front teeth, and the remaining ones were like the rotting groynes on the beach at West Bay. He reeked of foul sweat and urine, and she realised her mistake.

She turned and hastened away, and saw a possible refuge, lit up, through a window. The yellow faces were puffing like dragons into the air, as they laughed silently behind the glass. There be safety in numbers, she told herself.

Yet the sot followed her, was calling, "Don't you play hard to get with me, girl! Got you a room as good as any!"

Hepsy entered the inn. The man's words were muffled, just the other side of the door. He called that her bed would be as soft as a straw mattress, and that she was not to mind the mackerel, "As most folk, these parts, don't smell when they sleep, though I was hoping you'd stay awake a while, keep me company."

The men were sitting around a table, swapping tales of ghosts in Bridport, and fell silent.

The inn-keeper's wife saw distress in Hepsy's eyes, and called, "Come 'ee into the light, girl. You look like you seen one of the ghosts these fellows been telling tales of."

"A man!" gasped Hepsy. "Outside. He's following me."

Barnabus strode to the door, peered into the darkening street. A cart creaked past, its lamp already lit and casting a weak, waxy light into the face of Wynford Eagle, the undertaker. The horse plodded solemnly, head bowed respectfully.

"You seen a man round here? A suspicious-looking one?" called Barnabus.

Glad of an exchange not prompted by a request to take away a dead relative, the undertaker slowed his horse, and theatrically doffed his hat, as if greeting a mourner.

"No, but got one in the coffin behind me, though he baint alive, and, therefore, not in the least worthy of suspicion. At least, I hope he baint, or 'twill cause a barrel of consternation. The lid be laid on and not yet nailed, the corpse being without its powders and balm. Just fetched him from a house in which I was surprised he survived so long. Even with winter not yet fighting with autumn, the house was as cold as Dorset's worst. His widow sobbed for all she was worth. 'Save your tears and turn your hand to burning his things in the grate, or soon you, too, will have *rigor mortis* a-clamping your joints,' I advised. But her husband behind me baint your suspicious-seeming type, and the only others I seen be my grave-diggers, who dug their last a while ago."

"Woman, see, been followed."

"That be the way of the world. 'Tis how mankind survives, be how most folk see it. Move on, Gethsemene. Need to get this man into the back room. Don't want anyone afeart."

When Barnabus returned, Hepsy was sipping cider the inn-keeper's wife had drawn.

"And there be a room for 'ee, as the times demand. Such a coming and going of women, as well as men! Why, only a few months ago, we have a young woman comes here, and I wonder what a world it be when such a lonely one seeks refuge in an inn full of men clogging it with thick baccy smoke hanging like a Dorset fog."

On the verge of crying, Hepsy was conscious that the men were listening, expecting the tale of what had brought her there.

"And whither are you bound tomorrow?" asked Jude Broadwindsor.

"To find Miles Yondover, a friend of mine. He comes here occasionally, I believe."

The men glanced furtively at each other, withdrew their pipes from their mouths, avoided Hepsy's eyes.

"He do," said Barnabus, "though he aint been in for a night or two."

"He is unwell? Do you know why he has not come?"

"I do."

"Then please tell me, as this is a matter of some importance."

"'Tis because he be now engaged, and 'tis widely believed – though we aint had it from the horse's mouth, so to speak – that she hab put a stop to all his gadding about. No, I doubts he won't be in till the bells be rung at their wedding, till the shine be scuffed, and he remembers his friends here."

They nearly all understood, especially the inn-keeper's wife, who said, "'Tis a rushed thing, be my judgement, and one a friend, as I think he hab been to you, though seems not no more, will harvest in his own time and way."

Hepsy saw by their demeanour that they had guessed the nature of her association with Miles, and their averted eyes were a sign that he had let her down, as they knew handsome, young men were wont to do. Jude Broadwindsor, however, did not notice Hepsy's increased pallor, or jaw drop in astonishment and hurt. Instead, his praise of Miles' fiancee's many qualities only increased Hepsy's suffering.

"Rushed or no, they make a fine couple, and the match will see Miles the owner of the farm, one day, as his lovely bride-to-be, the daughter of Farmer Bradpole, be an only child, and Miles will surely take over the acres when his future father-in-law be plucked by the Lord. And who is to say whether slow be better than quick, in these matters? The world be full of quick and slow, and it seem to me that what matters is that they stick to each other like seeds to a collie's coat."

The inn-keeper saw that Jude's defence of Miles' decision to marry his employer's beautiful daughter was a further cause of distress to Hepsy, and intervened with, "Thank 'ee, Jude, though it be rightly a matter for them and not ourselves. You have had a bit of a shock, Miss."

Hepsy did not wait to give her last name, walked to the door, and said, "Your offer of a room be kind, but I must go to Dorchester instead, having heard that my quest ends here and now."

Her hand fumbled the latch; Barnabus had slid the bolt across, in case the man who had been following her tried to enter.

The inn-keeper's wife went to assist her, and said, in a low voice, "Mind not Jude, who don't see like the others. He meant no harm. Will you really go?" Hepsy nodded, swallowing hard. "Then be there anything you want me to say to Miles, next time he comes here?"

"No. I have said more than enough to him. Thank 'ee for your kindness."

And Hepsy slipped into the darkness.

"She gone?" asked the inn-keeper of his wife.

"Let's hope she aint in trouble, or Miles got a spickle of answering to do!"

Soon, the men restored their conversation to matters supernatural, but remained aware of Hepsy's lingering, invisible presence.

Their first opportunity to question Miles came the next day, when Farmer Lytchett Bradpole sent him to ask the inn-keeper if he would be kind enough to supply the refreshments for the Harvest Festival in the bottom meadow. The Reverend Stourton Caundle had assumed that he himself would bless, as usual, God's bounty in his church and the field, where the annual fair took place. Farmer Bradpole had told him that his assumption was correct, and that as long as Bridport was not over-run by Quakers sitting there waiting for the Lord to tap them on their shoulder, then the Reverend Caundle would officiate.

Miles entered the inn sheepishly, conscious that his long absence from their company might provoke some little criticism. He was hoping they might remember he had been one of them for ages, and that he had been good company. The inn-keeper's indifferent greeting puzzled him. Miles had always been a favourite, and had brought a youthful perspective to their discussions. Somehow, he had been an antidote to the cynicism that beset them, from time to time, and was still happy to take his place at the table with them. "Why, they be like uncles," he had once explained to the inn-keeper's wife, who had casually remarked that he was turning into one of them, when he should be mixing with men of his own age.

"Look what blowed in," muttered the inn-keeper.

The regulars puffed storm clouds into the air, and said nothing to Miles.

"The nights are cooler," remarked Barnabus.

"'Tis certain," agreed Jude, nodding exaggeratedly.

"The berries on the hawthorn betoke a wild and snowy winter," added the inn-keeper.

"Then a true Dorset! Shepherds best gather their flock from far fields. We all remember what happened to that poor farmer, Pilsdon way. The cold froze his eyelids open, so that he stared into the distance, not blinking, the stranger said, if memory serves me correctly," reminded the inn-keeper's wife.

Miles took off his hat, did not react to her reference to the mistake that might have contributed to Ebenezer Valence's death, and said, "The fire dances well enough, and no man here wears his hat, coat and gloves. Yet the air pinches, as if my presence draws the warmth from it. Your welcome be white and nipped as hoar. As one who understands not this unexpected weather, I ask for an explanation. I come with a message from Farmer Bradpole, who wants to know if you will provide the victuals and ale for the Harvest Festival, as usual. He asked me not to leave without an answer."

"'Tis certain. Tell him that."

"And will I take a drink with you all, as has been my pleasure for many a year?"

No one stirred or looked at him. Then Barnabus broke the tense silence with, "Woman come looking for you. Seem she knowed you."

Hepsy, it must be. She has said things about me, he reckoned. Her words hab been deadly nightshade, 'tis certain. My friends' faces are masks, as lifeless as any on flat tombstones.

"What woman? She has a name?"

"No name she told us, but she has a heart, nevertheless, and her hopes, be my guess, been left on her doorstep like a lover's posy: red roses, to show love, which we know rot to brown petals."

"She has a face I might know her by?"

"A pretty, and white as snowdrops; whiter still when she learned that you be almost a stranger here, now that you be a fiancé and 'trothed to marry another."

"And so be I 'trothed, not being promised to any other. But stated not this woman her business with me? Baint there a feature to know her by? My hair be long and yellow as straw, which folk use to mark me. Autumn's portrait be shades of red: a robin's breast, West Bay's blushing glow at sunset. What be her colours to note? Her eyes, hair? Have done with this now, this saying more by what you leave out of your words."

The men left it to the inn-keeper's wife to administer the rest of the censure. In truth, they were glad to see him again, but his changed circumstances changed theirs. Soon, thought Barnabus, we will be one less, if not so already – that is, till he tires of his wife's nagging, and the cost of her.

"Her hair be as black as a raven, and shines like its feathers when the sun varnishes them. And her eyes, too, are as dark as midnight when the moon and stars are smothered in clouds."

"She sounds a pretty. I be almost angry with myself for missing her."

But Miles' feeble attempt at humour drew no laugh.

"'Twas certain she knew you, and she reeled at the news of your wedding. All I knows is what I see, and I baint your mother or a stranger to you, and what I see don't fit with your circumstances, so to speak. There, now whether I got the right or no, you know my feelings on the matter, and I shall say nothing more but that we shall provide the victuals, ale and cider, as is the custom at the Harvest Festival."

Miles looked around him. Somewhere in that room, Hepsy had stood, heard about his imminent wedding. He recalled her early kisses, coaxed slowly, out of view; and as soft as raspberries her lips had been, when they had given way to his. Then she had unexpectedly pricked him with her thorny refusals. Begging did not sit easily with Miles, and he had chided her. And there was still the memory of sleepless nights spent in the bedroom next to hers, when the snow had prevented him returning to Bridport.

"As you wish. Good day to 'ee all, and though your greeting has been as chilly as a gale roaring down Marshwood Vale, I hope you will all come to my wedding, as friends, which I consider you still."

He left in silence. The inn-keeper's wife started to polish tables, to take her mind off the scene in which she had taken the lead role in warning Miles about his conduct. Her husband, unable to bear the awkward atmosphere for long, said, "Maybe you were a bit harsh on him. Times a-been when you've called him a son."

"No son of ours would have left a woman to come looking for him like that."

Jude interrupted with, "Let it all be, now. 'Tis none of our business, and he don't need our approval, one way or another, for something we can't sit in judgement on, on account of us not knowing the truth, which will, one day, be as clear as the night sky over Chesil."

"Well said," agreed Barnabus.

"Come," demanded the inn-keeper. "'Twill pass, and 'tis to be hoped it be nothing, as a wedding and a Harvest Festibal be times to rejoice and not condemn. Will 'ee drink to that, gentlemen?"

And, of course, their raised, empty glasses said that they would.

When the inn-keeper bolted the door after they had left, he was smiling. His wife was behind him, her arms round his waist, her head between his shoulder blades.

Then, after a few moments, their mood changed. Quickly, the inn-keeper opened the door again, and his wife fetched a lamp. Barnabus' shout for help was sudden, fearful.

"He looks gone," said Jude, crouching at the body lying on his front, twenty paces from the door.

The inn-keeper's wife screamed.

"Who be he?" asked the inn-keeper.

In the faint, yellow light, they all stared at the knife stuck in the part of the corpse where, a few seconds ago, the inn-keeper's wife had kissed her husband.

Chapter twenty-two.

The Harvest Festival required Reverend Caundle to deliver the usual thanksgiving, which he did with a strong emphasis on words associated with fertility, meals, and crops: "And we thank Him for *swelling* the *grain*, and the *seeds* we have *sown* will be ground to make our *bread*, which we break before *eating*, as did the Lord at his last *supper*." This he did to ensure that the simple country folk fully understood him, and to keep them all awake, but had he taken a quick glance at the faces before him, he would have soon noticed that he was failing on both counts.

He kept his congregation packed in the pews longer than was necessary, and released them, as if they were sheep jostling for freedom from their pen, only when the fidgeting became too vexatious to the religious swoon into which he had flung himself.

The citizens of Bridport and West Bay made their way to the flat meadow, where a white tent stood, its sides tied back, allowing merry-makers easy access to the cold rabbit pies and potent ale and cider. Soon, jolly fiddlers struck up a tune, and laughter could be heard. Children chased each other, and apples, pears, plums and damsons were on sale at various tables. The church choristers, a line of ghosts, arrived in their white gowns, which were a little inflated by the breeze. It seemed as if no one wanted to miss the celebration.

Jessie Bradpole was wearing her best, blue dress and a wide-brimmed straw hat decorated with a yellow ribbon. Her long, blond hair, treated only that morning with egg yolk to give it a special sheen, fell between her shoulder blades in a pony-tail. She scanned the field self-consciously, believing everyone was looking at her, the bride-to-be. In a few weeks, I shall be Jessie Yondover, she reflected.

She looked for Miles in the tent, but he was not there. The innkeeper had enlisted Barnabus and Jude to help him, as his wife had told him that she felt too unwell to attend. Her head was filled with drums, she had said: "'Tis as if the Dorset regiment be a-marching off to war." The effort of baking so many pies had worn her to the thinness of a shepherd's crook, and she would take to her bed when the inn was again quiet, and the barrels and food safely roped to the cart. "You remembered the mustard?" she had called. "The Mayor do like a bit of mustard. And pickle. 'Twill put him in a bad mood if he aint got his spreading of plum pickle."

"'Ee have never been known to miss the festibal," had remarked her husband. "Still, 'tis the way of things when you get older. Mustard be safely stowed. Don't want his Mayorship to go beout."

And his wife had retorted, "And don't 'ee come back all soused in ale. Sick as a dog 'ee were, last harbest day!"

Farmer Bradpole had ordered Miles to roast the hog, which meant that, as he had to start the fire early, he was excused from the church service. He had lit the wood at the correct time, and his face was now smudged by smoke, and his eyes were bloodshot and streaming, the tears washing lines like scratches down his blackened face. Alone, that morning, he had sat, turning mechanically the spit handle, watching fat drip from the pig, and hiss when it landed on the flaming logs beneath it, and puzzling over the woman who had come looking for him at the inn. And if she has changed her mind about me, then I am a doomed man, whicheber way I look at it, for I would never have chose Jessie if Hepsy had not rationed her kisses, which be ten times as soft and sweet as Jessie's. And the Master will send me a-packing if I jilt his daughter. No, I be like a rabbit, trapped by a terrier, down a dark, dark hole.

"Will you not stroll with me?" Jessie asked. "I have not seen much of 'ee, and the day be fine. This pig be yours all afternoon?"

"'Tis the wish of your father."

"Then I shall ask him to lend you to me, a while."

"I am all hot and bloody from the pig. My shirt be stained where fat hab spat at me. 'Twould shame you to be seen with me so."

"Suit yourself, then," she snapped, "though Sundays will be *ours* when we're married. You mark my words."

He watched her walk away, imagined again what it would be like to make love to her, and returned to the spit again.

Jessie spoke to friends, the Reverend Caundle, who was looking forward to a slice of salty pork, and even her father. He was busy telling a group of farmers how his new bull had lived up to expectations in the field.

"And, one by one, he jumps the whole herd, quick as 'ee likes, till they all been served. Never seen one like him before."

He embellished the bull's abilities, but though in a good mood, would not release Miles from the roasting hog, despite Jessie's pleas.

"Then 'tis a shame!" she cried. "Your future son-in-law, too!"

"Today be a working day," her father reminded her. "A farmer works seven days a week. Besides, Miles seem happy enough. A good worker, 'tis certain."

He raised his tankard to his lips.

"Fifty-two weeks, a year," added Barnabus.

Bored, Jessie drifted to the edge of the field, where through the gate hobbled a woman, a hood over her head, so that her face was obscured. In her gloved hand, she carried a posy of flowers she had plucked from the dusty side of the road.

"A pennyworth?" she asked, offering them, most of which had begun to lose their colour.

"I think not, when they are free to all, in the lane."

"Then a penny for your fortune to be told? Most say 'tis worth ten times that to know what will befall them."

Jessie was tempted. The dancing was yet a good hour away, and as she knew she could not have Miles as a partner, she thought this might be a suitable diversion.

"You are a gypsy? If so, I must warn you that my father will have none on his land. If he finds you, he will –"

"No gypsy, but a woman poor enough to come here, this day, to earn a few pennies for food."

"I have not seen you here before. You are a stranger? From Eype, or further afield? Charmouth? Or Abbotsbury?"

The woman did not reveal her home town, but said, "A penny be a spickle for your fortune. Have it told, then take your flowers for free. And, if my telling prove false, these next twelve months, meet me here, on this day, on this spot, where I shall pay my dues, according to your wishes. If I be true, then you must grant me one wish, whatever it be."

Out of the corner of her eye, Jessie saw a youth leading a girl, by the hand, behind a tree. They go to kiss, no doubt. And will this be my only entertainment: to wish that I were that maid? No, it shall not, she decided.

"A penny, and no more," said Jessie.

The woman rubbed the coin, and slipped it into her pocket.

"Then 'tis paid for."

"Will you not show your face? It is strange you should hide it."

"Hold my hands," said the woman, offering them.

The gloves were made of leather of good quality. Worth more than a penny, Jessie thought, hesitating, tempted but wary.

"Is it necessary? I cannot see any part of you. It is as if you are a spectre and not a woman, as you sound."

The hands stayed where they were.

"You wish to have your penny back?"

Jessie slowly took the woman's fingertips, and the woman firmly seized Jessie's hands.

"You are too rough!" protested Jessie.

But the grip remained constant, and the woman stayed silent, as if awaiting some knowledge to flow from Jessie's hands to her own. Jessie was transfixed, desperate now to know her fortune.

"You are not married."

"Pah!" laughed Jessie. "There baint no ring on my finger, so 'tis plain for you to see. 'Tis all a walk to the beach and back with you!"

"But hope to be."

"'Tis true. In a week or two, I shall be wed, and there be my fiancé, a-turning the pig over the fire." Jessie looked over her shoulder, only to see he was no longer there. "Perhaps, he hab gone to buy himself a drink."

Jessie was seething: and so he hab a-upped and gone his own way. 'Tis the way with all men, she mused.

"But measure not a wedding dress on the back of a hope, as 'twill be money wasted."

Jessie's hands began to tremble, and she tried to withdraw them, but the woman held fast, resulting in a momentary tug-of-war.

"Why so? We are 'trothed, and Miles will come to make me a wife in the church. Speak plain and tell me why money will not buy me a wedding."

"He loves another, and your wedding will come to nothing."

"How can you know, simply by touching my hands? 'Tis terrible trickery. Shame on you! Tell me how you know."

"Because you yourself just told me, Jessie."

"Jessie? I have not told you my name."

But the woman turned, and retraced her steps, back towards Bridport, leaving Jessie on her knees, crying, and rubbing her hands on dry grass.

The fiddlers began to make their way to an area unlikely to be affected by smoke coming from the unattended hog, whose skin had darkened, and acquired a natural glaze from being roasted in its own fat. Its ears and cheeks had become crisp, and its belly was in danger of burning, now that Miles had absented himself.

Farmer Bradpole took a stroll, and one or two people asked him when the hog would be sliced. Seeing no sign of Miles, he scanned the meadow like a buzzard, but could see him nowhere, so he went to the pig, and turned it himself.

"Your man not been here, these last twenty minutes," complained the Mayor, whose hunger had increased after two pots of ale in the tent. "My stomach rumbles, and the good folk of Bridport and West Bay will die of starvation soon."

Jessie composed herself, and refused to accept the strange woman's prediction that she would not marry Miles. Her father was irritated with her; he considered her guilty, by association, of neglecting the fire.

"You seen anything of that feckless man of yourn? He been gone ages, and this hog needs finishing off."

"I have not, though he might have been caught out by the call of nature. Judge him not yet. He can't have gone far. Or maybe it be the heat. It's a wonder he baint as basted as the pig, seeing he been a-turning since this morning. 'Tis too much, crouching like a pixie, with no respite."

Unexpectedly, the claim by the hooded soothsayer that Miles loved another kindled her love for him, and she wanted to protect him from her father, who spoke to *all* his labourers in a gruff manner.

"You all right, girl? You look not yourself. Go over yonder for the dancing, and choose a willow wand from the pile. 'Tis said the willow bring fertility, and maybe 'twill help you get with child. There, now that be better, eh?"

"A father no right to talk to his daughter that way. Such things be private between a man and his wife."

"And God, who has the biggest say!"

Jessie had no quarrel with God's omnipotence, and took her father's advice. The other girls had chosen their wands, and were waving them in the air, making patterns. Those who knew their letters were secretly spelling the name of the boy they loved, and guessing each other's inscription in the pale blue sky.

The dance began with a bow to all in the circle. Rising and falling like maids curtseying to their mistress, the girls made the circle turn, symbolising the rotation of Earth. They touched sticks, drew arcs in the sky: the rising and setting of the sun. And constructed a long, vaulting arch, like a rustic cathedral, through which they skipped.

But even as she moved – when the dance almost erased the memory of the woman's warning – Jessie could never share the enjoyment of the others. Indeed, the Mayor remarked upon it to an onlooker:

"Yonder maid, Bradpole's daughter, if I baint mistaken, looks as if the crops failed rather than growed better than ever before."

"'Tis certain. They say her banns be read, and that she be pledged to one of Bradpole's workers," replied the other.

"Then 'twon't work. There be plenty of land-owners and farmers able and willing to make her an offer. Why, 'tis just between you and me, this, but she be a comely and a pretty, and maybe if I set my cap at her before she goes down the aisle, then her father will be happier. Why, a corn merchant and a Mayor for a husband baint to be sniffed at."

The other looked at the Mayor's chain, and decided not to refer to the obvious difference in age, but to agree.

"'Tis a powerful, 'tis certain. And lucky be she who accepts you, sir. And Farmer Bradpole would prefer such a match, I be sure."

"I can't dance, though. The chain, you see. It be heavy, and I be not naturally as light of foot as I used."

"Then rest. Dancing be for maids, and we be spectators, and that suits all, for the maids be on show, and the men sort the wheat from the chaff, so to speak. 'Tis the way of the world."

With that, the other left, and the more the Mayor looked at the dancers, flowers woven into their hair and hung in chains around their necks, the less he was able to tell which pleased him most. Somehow, the fumes of the ale made him drowsy, endowed each maid with an irresistible beauty, so that Jessie Bradpole's charms became unexceptional.

Meanwhile, Miles and his horse were passing though a seemingly deserted Broadoak, the curtains in the cottage windows drawn to keep out the still strong autumnal sunshine. He had known the moment had come to mend matters with Hepsy. A life of obedience to Jessie and her father had been all that he could see before him. Why, Lytchett Bradpole might live till he be ninety! he had thought in the meadow, and I shall inherit the farm when my joints be too stiff to bend to shoe a horse or deliver a lamb. And Jessie loves the idea of marriage more than me. No, 'tis Hepsy I want. I shall lay myself before her, though 'taint what a man likes to do, beg forgiveness, and pledge myself to her. So he had abandoned the hog, caring not if it burnt and the folk were not fed, mounted his horse, and made for Pilsdon, vowing never to return to the farm.

Yet as he neared his destination, he remembered that he reeked of smoke, and was sure that his face must be as black as the pig's belly. On his left, he remembered that there was a water trough in the yard at Dugdale Farm. There he would wash his face, and make himself more presentable.

He dipped his head in the water, held his breath so that his hair would stay under longer, and be cleaner. When his lungs were near to bursting, he stood upright and shook his hair as a dog when it has been frolicking in a stream. Then Miles saw a long shadow stretching over the trough, had not heard the man approaching.

"'Tis a hot afternoon," remarked the man.

"The fire," Miles tried to explain, still gasping.

"Your hair was on fire?"

"No, I was roasting a pig."

"And the pig caught fire?"

"No, sir. 'Twas the Harbest pig, and my job was to –"

"I jest. I am Redvers Holditch. We have met before, I believe."

"And I be Miles Yondover. Why, I gave you a ride here. You told me that you were the new owner."

Miles wiped his hand on his shirt, but it still felt damp in Redvers'. Both men were now smiling, Redvers satisfied that his visitor meant no harm, but curious how he knew there was water behind the house.

"You stumbled upon my trough by accident?"

"I have not dipped my head in it recently!"

The water ran down the back of Miles' neck. Redvers noticed Miles' muscular frame, guessed him to be a labourer, used to long hours, lifting carts, saddles, dragging dead pigs to be beheaded and hung.

"You have been a regular visitor here?"

"Yes. Once got snowed in here with Miss. Valence, that bad winter, when her father got trapped in the snow, and died."

"Then you must know Miss. Valence."

"I do, and be on my way to see her now, to put right a wrong I did her."

Miles hung his head, made no mention of his terrible mistake: his engagement to Jessie Bradpole.

Redvers asked, "Farmer Valence died in the snow?"

"He did, sir, and 'twas I who misunderstood my left from my right, and he perished, his heart stopped, frozen."

Redvers suppressed a smile at this chance encounter, which was revealing the finer details of his father's death.

"I don't rightly follow, Miles. Left from right?"

"It be a shame that will blight me for the rest of my days. He was supposed to be in a field on the left – or was it the right? – from one direction, but, as you know, that depends which way you going, if you understands. Anyway, I did not rightly recall which way the man who raised the alarm told me, and Farmer Valence perished."

Redvers understood the gist of this explanation: that Miles felt partly responsible for the death.

"Come inside and take some refreshment, won't you?" offered Redvers.

"'Tis kind, but I must hasten to the cottage where Hepsy lives now."

"But the least I can do for the man who helped me is to offer a drink."

"You talk in riddles, sir, if you don't mind me saying."

"Then follow me, and let me elucidate with a glass of cool cordial in my hand, for though you know it not, you have inadvertently contributed to the changes in my fortune."

"But Miss. Valence –"

"Miss. Valence will not see you, Miles, even if you spurred your horse into a lather."

"And why is that, sir?"

"Because she has gone I know not where."

And that blow put Miles into a spin. Well, well, well! reflected Redvers. After such a misunderstanding of left and right, our paths have truly crossed, and I wager there's more to know about all this.

Chapter twenty-three.

Toller looked down at Mattie's baby, at her flecks and badges of blood, and at Sampford, who had assumed Toller was the father. Mattie wanted to hold her baby, had not expected this confrontation between two squabbling men. There should have been only a midwife there, not even the baby's father.

"Will you not cut the cord?" repeated Sampford, thrusting the knife at him. Toller froze. This scene of blood-smeared, snow-white thighs, between which he now knew Sampford had been kneeling to assist in the birth, horrified him. All those lambs, that gentle pulling into the world, counted for nothing. "The cord must be cut *now*!"

"Do it! One of you must do it," ordered Mattie.

Sampford turned away from Toller in disgust. Mattie sank, too weak to argue or to decide herself.

"The candle," pointed Sampford.

Obediently, Toller fetched it, guarding its flame with a cupped hand.

"What will you do with it?" he asked.

Sampford cut the flame four times, tested the blade. In a few seconds, when it had cooled, he took the slippery cord between his fingers, and, in one swift, upward cut, he separated the baby from its mother.

Toller watched him scoop up the girl, and place it on Mattie's breast. When she kissed it, blood rouged her lips and cheeks, robbing her face of its ghastly pallor.

"Feed her. Try when I'm gone," instructed Sampford.

You have done this before, thought Toller. You knew what to do, had no fear, unlike me. Your own? You happed, by chance, upon another like Mattie?

Sampford stood up unsteadily, as a newly born calf, and slumped to the door.

"Wait," called Toller.

Outside, Sampford waited, his back to the cottage.

"I'm sorry. I heard screaming. I thought Mattie in danger."

"You thought Ol' Sojer up to his tricks again? That be it?"

Sampford's disdainful look made Toller ashamed.

"I acted hastily, but now I be sorry – truly."

"You have never liked me."

Toller hung his head, then set the record straight: "I baint the father. Mattie be my sister, come to stay with me."

"'Tis a bastard child?"

"It has a father."

Sampford took a deep breath.

"And so do we all," he said. "And 'tis often so, that the absent father be the blamed. A father plants the seed, but he sometimes don't get to harvest."

With that, Sampford left.

Back inside, Toller turned away when he saw the baby at the breast.

"I did not know," stammered Toller.

"Stay. Fetch me a bowl, water, a blanket. No time for shyness."

Toller did as he was told, but kept his eyes averted, did not want her to think he was taking advantage of her.

"You ever seen a woman's breast before?" Toller stayed silent. "Well, now you seen mine, it baint worth a blush, your part. 'Tis nature. Why, you seen lots of lambs ramming their mouths onto the ewes' teats!"

"Baint the same. You be a woman."

"'Tis new to 'ee, that's all. Now, provoke that fire, so we don't freeze to death!"

Toller crouched, nimbly built a tor of kindling, to which he applied the candle's flame. Soon, the wood cracked and spat, and Toller withdrew from the hearth.

"She got a name?"

"Yes."

"And what be it?"

"Nightingale. She be Nightingale."

Toller went outside. A good name: a bird with a sweet voice. Forston Sampford: cut it like a surgeon, done it before. But to whose cord? Which woman had allowed him close enough to free a baby from her?

Toller made straight for his axe. His coarse fingertips tested the blade, as a blind man. His neglect was there: a bluntness, an uneven edge which would bite with only a wide, arcing swing and the downward stroke of a zealous executioner. Spitting on his whetstone, he sharpened the axe-head. With a long-forgotten determination to be a perfectionist, he was again able to chop wood for the fire.

This time, however, after faggots enough to keep the cottage warm for weeks, he carefully measured lengths to make what he wanted. With a chisel, he stripped the wood of its bark, and set about sawing a trunk into the necessary, short planks. It was all in his head, what it would look like.

While he was working, wiping stinging sweat from his eyes, Sampford kept interrupting, the image of him squatting before Mattie reminding Toller that he had wronged him, had believed him to be a predator instead of a helpful neighbour. He will not accept my words of apology, thought Toller, but he shall have them, or, if they don't join up clearly enough, I shall repay him by other means: not a gift or money, but by an act he will understand. I shall bide my time, and will recognise the moment.

Occasionally, Toller heard Nightingale's feline cry for food, and imagined Mattie baring her breast to pacify her. I am no brother, he concluded, for a brother would not entertain such hot, dangerous thoughts.

When he returned to the cottage, Mattie was rocking Nightingale. He hesitated, but Mattie said, "She has finished. And think nothing of it. You must not tiptoe on account of my feeding her."

"I have brought logs."

"You have been chopping for a long time."

Toller thought of the planks he had hidden in an outbuilding; the key was safe in his pocket.

"It clears my head, reminds me that I am still a young man."

In truth, he had tried to cut out his rejection by Redvers Holditch. With each thud of the axe in the wood, Toller tried to ease the pain, the shock of failure.

"It's your lack of experience in matters of commerce. Buying and selling cows will be important. I've no doubt you are a good shepherd, but I intend to grow wheat, and I need a man who knows his way around a field with a plough, and can tell good seed from bad," Redvers had explained. "I will hire you as a shepherd, but I'm looking for someone who can manage labourers, too. I'm sorry to disappoint you, Toller. What say you be my shepherd?"

Toller had shaken his head, had intended to start a new flock for himself, anyway.

"No, thank 'ee, but I could not. A farm manager be what I wanted."

"Then you will consider another proposition? You have three fields, I believe."

"'Tis so."

"Will you sell me the two on the other side of the lane? They are sloping, and would make ideal grazing. I'll pay you a fair price. What say you?"

"Was going to build a flock again. Need them myself. That's my intention: to start being a shepherd again, a good one."

Redvers was used to haggling, and had made a further suggestion.

"What say you sell me the fields, and you rent one for your flock? Makes good sense."

Toller had hesitated, and emphatically shaken his head.

"Always been Burstock land, always will be."

He had wanted to say, "Till the day I die," but if he ever had a son or daughter, the fields would remain in the family.

"Then I am sorry. I wish you well."

Without offering his hand, Redvers had left him, muttering to himself.

Soon, Toller overcame his shyness at Nightingale feeding. He did not stare, but stayed in the room. Indeed, he marvelled that her birth had taken place under his roof. Anything that needed doing – washing clothes and pots – he did without prompting. Mattie slept between Nightingale's demands, which were in step with the clock's eerie chimes. Sometimes, Toller pretended he was asleep, so that he would not be thought to be fussing, of which she lightheartedly accused him.

"'Taint becoming a man," she pointed out.

"Jobs need doing. I be a practical man," he reminded her. "I do what is necessary."

Privately, she was glad of his attentions; they made her feel secure. And she wondered if that was how she would have felt if she had married.

Toller chose his moment carefully. Mattie had gone to bed early, had placed Nightingale to her left, next to the wall, so that she would not fall out.

Quietly, Toller went to the outbuilding. The night was moonless, so he lit his path with a lamp. There it was, what he had lovingly made.

"'Tis wondrous," he muttered, "though I say it myself."

It was an unusual shape, not light, and he had tried to work out which grips were best, as he had carried it from the clearing to the outbuilding.

Where shall I put it? he wondered. She must find it as soon as she steps into the room.

So there it was, all ready to be discovered at the first sight of a grey dawn. Toller rose early, determined to see Mattie's reaction, but he had barely slept, and he began to doze in his chair. When he heard the stairs creaking, he started.

"She be a madam, this one," were Mattie's first words, distorted by yawning.

Then she saw it.

After what seemed too long a wait, Toller said, "Hope I spelt her name right."

And he had.

Mattie had Nightingale lying across her shoulder.

Speechless, at first, Mattie circled, like a ballerina, what Toller had made, to admire it from all angles. There was her daughter's name, carved into it; no more children can use it now it bears her name, Mattie mused, sliding her fingertips over the varnish.

"So that where you've been," she said quietly.

At length, anxious to elicit a response, Toller said, "'Tis a cot."

"And so it is!" replied Mattie. "'Tis beautiful."

"For Nightingale."

"Too small for me."

"And it rocks. To calm her so she sleeps."

With a gentle push, Toller demonstrated, and they both watched its motion, till it became still again.

"Wondrous."

"Will you try her in it?"

Mattie offered Nightingale, and Toller received her awkwardly, never having held a baby before. The blanket was still warm; Mattie arranged it so that Nightingale would not feel the hard wood. Nightingale looked up into Toller's face while Mattie was upstairs, and stretched her arms, as if wanting to touch his face. Toller felt her flutter in his arms, and held her more closely, so that he would not drop her.

When Nightingale was in the cot, Mattie began to rock it gently.

"Needs a rug underneath, stop the noise," Toller remarked.

"And all the time, you were making this?"

"I was. Need to pass my time somehow."

"Then thank you, dear." She reached up and kissed him on the cheek. "She be lucky to have such a cot."

Toller said, "Baby needs its own bed."

"I must dress. Will you watch her?"

Toller knelt, listened to her gurgling and snuffling. Mattie's eyes, 'tis certain, he thought. But that was all. The rest be her father, he presumed. Yet is not what I am doing being a father, now I am no farm manager? Maybe, one day, when she has grown, she will work the flock with me, till she marries.

Mattie saw, over time, that Toller was taking a real interest. He asked how Nightingale had been, when he returned to the house, and began to talk to her. She did not cry when he held her, in her mother's presence, rather held her alert eyes on his face, and blinked when he kissed her.

Then, one day, he burst through the door, and cried, "Come see what we have!"

We. Something in his recently habitual use of that word unsettled Mattie, who, though glad of the security of his world at Pilsdon, could not commit to any permanent arrangement. She feared that his growing love for Nightingale might compromise her, restrict the choices she felt were her right.

“Sheep,” she said flatly, when he had guided her to one of the fields Redvers Holditch had wanted to buy.

Toller was too excited to notice her indifference.

“Ram and four ewes. Got to start somewhere. Cost me money, but got to do what I know. ’Tis for the best now we have another mouth to feed.”

There it was again, that collective we. She had not asked him to be responsible for Nightingale.

Already the ram had pressed its red dye onto two of the ewes.

“See. The ram has made its mark,” pointed out Toller.

“But the ewe has no choice, poor thing.”

“’Tis nature and the way of the world.”

“Don’t make it right.”

“I be a shepherd, Mattie. In my blood. Nothing wrong with that. What I know is that I tried something else, to turn myself into something I could never be, but I was a fool. Ambition’s a fine thing, but it brings misery.”

Try as she might, Mattie could not get excited about the sheep, though she felt obliged to admire their fleeces, which she was sure she could spin into something warm for the bitterly cold days of winter.

“And I shall sit by the fire, if you have time to make a fine wheel, and tease out the strands, as my mother used to. ’Tis a dying art, I believe.”

“Then I had better increase the size of my flock, as these few won’t add up to anything but a shawl.”

Slowly, Mattie led him back to the cottage, and Toller said he would see if he could buy a spinning wheel from Bridport. He had seen a couple of them, recently, at Bridport market, and expressed the view that she would make a pretty picture by firelight.

Mattie said, “’Taint right you talking about me like I be a painting. You my brother, remember.”

"I don't fit words well together, I admit, though 'twas 'ee who sketched the scene first."

"Will 'ee take me to Bridport? Tomorrow, if it suits."

"You don't mind Briddy gossiping?"

"Toller, I need to register Nightingale's birth. She got a name now, a pretty one, and she needs a birth certificate. Everyone got one."

Toller had never seen his own. He had his father's somewhere, and his mother's, in a box. No one had ever doubted his name; no one had ever asked to see his certificate.

"Tomorrow morning, then."

"Thank 'ee."

All night, Toller thought about Nightingale, sat up when he heard her yell for food. What should he say to Mattie, the next morning? Why should he not follow his instinct?

When they were halfway to Bridport, Toller said, "She can take my name – Burstock. 'Taint the best, nor the worst. Solid, though. Not a gossamer, like some. A baby needs a strong name."

Mattie had prepared herself for the offer, knowing it would come as gently as a warm breeze. But it was not what she wanted, not what Nightingale needed.

"I have been dreading this moment, and an honest offer deserves an honest answer. I don't know what I would have done without you. You have been kind and generous, but she cannot take your name. She must not grow up believing you are her real father. These things hidden return unexpectedly, and rip up lives."

Toller stared straight ahead, not daring to look at Mattie, knowing her face would look like Hepsy's the day he trudged away from her into the banks of snow.

"But she has no other father."

"But you and I . . . well, we baint married, nor are we lovers, and 'twould confuse her – me, even. And we would pass our lives as brother and sister, yet we are young enough to learn to love again."

How he had tried to love Hepsy! And could he grow to love Mattie? Did it not take years for a tree to grow and bear fruit? There had been times when he had suppressed desire for her, and when she had become a mother, that changed things.

"Or we could live as man and wife, bring up Nightingale as our own."

"But she is mine already, Toller! We cannot be married! Don't you see that I can never be married again? I have sinned, and I must suffer the consequences. You are a good man, a true, but I cannot love you because I can never bring myself to love a man again. No man will touch me ever again, as a husband."

"You will give her the name Venn?"

Toller pulled the horse to a halt at the top of the hill in Bridport.

"'Tis a worthy, but she will take her father's. I am determined that, one day, she will know who he is."

Toller shook his head.

"You would give her the name of the man who forsook you in church?"

"I would."

She got down from the cart, and said, "Meet me here when the clock strikes twelve, mid-day, by which time she will be called Nightingale Cattistock."

Numb, Toller went to look for a spinning wheel, in the hope that one might keep her by the fireside. This changes everything, he acknowledged. She talks now like a stranger, and, in a way, is crueller than Hepsy.

Twelve became one. When Toller enquired at the registry, the clerk confirmed that Mattie had left in a hurry, birth certificate safe in her hand.

What, gone without a goodbye? Is there anywhere a woman who is not fickle? he wondered. He asked if anyone had seen a woman and a baby, but no one had, so he returned to his cottage, where the empty cot served as a reminder that good intentions are never enough.

Cattistock! he cursed, ignorant of the fact that Nightingale was the name Mattie and Roddy had, under a polished moon, promised they would call their first child, if God blessed them. The day of her disappearance from Bridport, she renewed her vow that Roddy would never be allowed to forget the part he had played in bringing their daughter into the world.

Chapter twenty-four.

Mattie's departure from Maidenhampton was described by the domestic staff as an acute embarrassment for her. Who would show their face again after being jilted at the altar? But Milborne, the butler, who had delivered to Cattistock the letter that had seemingly prompted his disappearance, was much troubled by the part he felt he had played. Fate's go-between: that's what I was, he mused.

Lady Intrinseca Dewlish gave much thought to the letter, and discussed its possible content with Lord Hector Dewlish, who had returned triumphantly from a day's shooting. Tired, and with the yet strong odour of wet grass and dogs on his clothes, and brandy on his breath, he listened with little sympathy to his wife's speculation.

"It is of little consequence to us, my dear. These things happen. They always will. Cattistock got cold feet, and fled. That is all there is to it."

"But the letter Milborne gave him seemed to change everything. Is it possible that he was called away on an urgent matter? Dulcie and Dora both say that the couple looked glad to be in each other's company. There had been no obvious sign of a rift, of a change of heart."

Tired of his wife's search for a happy ending, Lord Dewlish sighed wearily, and sat up to deliver what he hoped would be a decisive blow to her hopes.

"The fact that he left, my dear, without a word, and has not written, is indisputable. What can be more important than one's wedding day? What detains him elsewhere? And if you are not yet aware of it, let me apprise you of his unsavoury reputation, which followed him like a shadow. He was, and, I suspect, still is, a lady's man. Did you ever notice the little courtesies he paid to the kitchen staff? Only Mrs. Canford escaped his lavish compliments, and that was, I suspect, by virtue of her seniority. He was only too ready to place his hand in the small of Dora's back, to whisper in Dulcie's ear. Have you ever seen the blushes on her cheeks? And the girls encouraged him with their frivolous giggling. I need hardly insult your intelligence by connecting this reputation with his disappearance!"

"I did not know. I never saw him acting as you describe. Call it male vanity, selfishness. But it is Mattie about whom I worry. I do wonder what has become of her."

Milborne shook his head when asked if he could remember anything about the letter. The style of the handwriting, perhaps.

"No, Lady Dewlish. I don't think so. But, then again, there was a hint of it being written in haste, though I could not swear to it. The letters leaned forward in an exaggerated manner, as if trying to grasp something or someone, in desperation."

"And were you not tempted to remark upon it to him? To question him in a lighthearted way?"

Milborne looked down, then up, and Lady Dewlish could see that she had insulted him.

"Lady Dewlish, I had no cause to enquire about the purpose of the letter. Roddy Cattistock has – had, I should say – a right to privacy. I need hardly point out that as butler to this household, I must be the font of discretion."

"Of course, Milborne. I consider myself well and truly admonished. I shall seek no further information from you, but if you come by way of any, do let me know. And now, would you be so good as to pack a few things for Lord Dewlish? He will be going to London, in a couple of days."

"I will ask Pymore, my lady. His valeting skills are most invaluable in these circumstances."

"On this occasion, I would like *you* to do it."

When he had gone, Lady Dewlish smiled.

"Even a butler has to be put in his place, occasionally."

Lady Dewlish had been unable to persuade Mattie to stay, and to convince her that the humiliation of being made a public spectacle would fade, just as snow makes us shiver but eventually melts. There had been something about her that had drawn others to her, and her loss would be felt more than Cattistock's.

There had been no hasty explanation from him because what had compelled him to leave Maidenhampton was a matter so secret that no other human being should know or discover it. And had he lived in a hut a life of solitude, of self-sacrifice, instead of proposing to Mattie, the letter would still have come and dragged him away.

It was, fortunately, Mrs. Canford who opened the door to weary Mattie and Nightingale. Earlier, Mrs. Canford had set Dulcie and Dora to making pastry, into which they would later put rabbit and pheasant, his Lordship's favourite, and they must stay by their mixing bowls. Their faces glowed red from their efforts and heat from the ovens.

"Why, look who has blowed in!" Mrs. Canford exclaimed. "'Tis our Mattie, and with a tiddy one in her arms, too. Come in, girl. Don't stand out there. Come in and let's see who you've brought us."

Shyly, Mattie entered, and proudly adjusted the baby's shawl, so that they could see her. Dulcie and Dora were excused from their stations for a moment or two, and examined the baby's face.

"Go on, say it, for 'tis true, but I'm more ashamed of myself than little Nightingale here," said Mattie, predicting a relentless barrage of questions she would answer honestly.

"Here, sit down, girl," said Mrs. Canford, pulling up a chair. "You look as if you come a long way."

"Bridport, though there been kind Dorset folk a-willing to lend a silly girl a hand."

Dulcie and Dora began to make various noises to distract Nightingale, who was ready to be fed. Dulcie was a blackbird, and Dora a cat. Then they sang a lullabye together, though Dulcie mixed up her words, and Dora rearranged the notes slightly.

"'Tis more likely she be scared by all these wild animal impressions. Come, you two. Back to the pastry, while I catches up. And no listening, mind. I'm sure Mattie hab one or two things to say in private."

"I must feed the mite," said Mattie.

Dulcie and Dora giggled, and Nightingale latched on to her mother.

"She be you in the mouth, but Rod –"

Mattie said, "Yes, she be his. No one else's."

"He hab not set foot in here since . . . well, since that terrible day, and he bill get a piece of my mind if he ever does. And her Ladyship will, no doubt, have her two penn'orth, too."

"That's not why I'm back. My job gone?"

"Been filled and emptied, time after time, these months, but 'tas been as if only you can fill it, as if her Ladyship been keeping it open for you, like she knowed you were coming back here, one day."

At that moment, when Nightingale was murmuring contentedly as she was sucking, Milborne entered, and said, "His Lordship has asked us –"

But when he saw the scene before him, he turned round and walked out, and all the women laughed so loudly that they startled Nightingale, who clenched her gums rather too tightly for Mattie's liking.

"His face!" cried Mrs. Canford. "Oh, but it was a picture, though for just a second! Worthy of hanging in the gallery, without any doubt!"

As Nightingale fed, Mattie surveyed the kitchen. It had not been as difficult to return as she imagined. There was a familiarity about the place, yet she questioned whether the pots were in the same place on the dresser. Dulcie was taller, more willowy from bending over mixing bowls and plates; and Dora, the more shy of the two, had filled out. Mattie remembered her as the one who finished people's sentences. And in the air, the smell of roasting meat, and freshly chopped cabbage. Small changes gave Mattie the impression that, though they had not forgotten her completely, they had gone on living as Providence dictated.

After Milborne had fled, he had made straight to Lady Dewlish, and informed her of Mattie's return, and it was not long before she arrived in the kitchen. Mattie tried to stand, but her former mistress bade her to remain seated.

"You have a baby who is all but asleep. Do not disturb her. Tell me, Mattie, of this last year. A big part of your history is plain enough, but where have you been since you left us?"

Mrs. Canford shooed Dulcie and Dora back to the table, as if they had been chickens that had escaped from their coop.

"'Tis private between her Ladyship and Mattie."

"I mind neither the telling nor the listening," said Mattie. "The sharing is a relief. I wish it had been different in one particular way, but I be glad to have Nightingale."

"And did you hear a nightingale when you had her?" asked Lady Dewlish.

"No. 'Twas a name Roddy and I chose when we were planning our life together."

Lady Dewlish frowned.

"And she was his parting gift?"

Mattie winced.

"My anger and hurt were like a bolting horse, at first, but they are nothing now."

"Still, he is a scoundrel and deserves to be whipped."

"No, my Ladyship. That's not it at all. This little girl keeps him near, and I believe there be more to what happened than we know about."

"But come, Mattie. Your story."

Mattie left out not a detail. Dulcie dabbed at her eyes occasionally, and Dora clasped her arm to comfort her, for although they kneaded, they did so quietly, so they could just hear Mattie's story.

"And now you are here," said Lady Dewlish.

Mattie felt uncomfortable. There was a tone of disapproval in Lady Dewlish's words.

"I was hoping that I might have my old job back, or, if it be filled, some other employment on the estate."

"But what about the baby?" intervened Mrs. Canford. "I don't think Mr. Milborne will take kindly to having a baby downstairs."

"But it is *my* house," reminded Lady Dewlish, "and what I and my husband say goes. However, we must arrange things so we do not antagonise Mr. Milborne. As for Lord Dewlish, I remember he had a high opinion of you, Mattie, though he has no good word for Roddy Cattistock. It seems you would have been better off with this Mr. Burstock. Mrs. Canford, show Mattie to the room next to Dulcie's and Dora's. Have a maid light the fire, and I shall ensure that a cot is procured. After all, we have dear, little Nightingale to think of now."

Mattie's eyes were suddenly swamped with tears. Though tired, she thought clearly. She bears no resentment, has not turned me away, despite what has happened, and I should repay her loyalty with as much dedication as I will apply to finding Roddy, and yet she . . . I loved him, still do, always will, and now that my heart be as soothed as a moonlit night, I will discover the reason he came not to church, for I believe Nightingale be a sign that he did not stop loving me, and not the opposite.

Meanwhile, Toller went straight to Redvers Holditch to offer him all his land, the cottage, and his sheep. Imagine Toller's surprise, therefore, when he found Miles Yondover, pitchfork in hand, prodding a muddy patch of the farmyard. Toller watched him raking rills, firstly one way, and then at an angle, so that the water drained more quickly. Blond hair tied in a ponytail, Miles scraped and prodded quickly, as if there were many other tasks to complete by the end of the day.

Eventually, Redvers Holditch appeared, gave him money, and sent him away. Toller hid as Miles emerged, on the cart, into the lane, and singing:

"Come, my girl, come
to the fair with your love,
and kiss, my lass, kiss
these lips waiting above."

A pretty tune sung by a pretty boy, thought Toller. And that be the man come in vain to save Ebenezer. How Chance does play cruel tricks! Why, 'tis like someone or thing hab tip-toed round the lanes, and turned the fingerposts, so none of us knows for sure where our destination be.

"A moment of your time, Redvers, if I may," called Toller.

Redvers turned. Toller approached him, had surprised himself that he had sounded so friendly.

"Toller," said Redvers.

"I've come to say I am prepared to sell you everything I possess. That is, if you still want to buy."

"And what brings about this change of heart? I thought you were going to breed a flock."

"That was my intention, yes, but I must go elsewhere. No good can come of me staying here."

Redvers hesitated.

"You a price in mind?"

"Make me a decent offer, and 'tis yours."

Used to negotiating a good price, Redvers said, "I will have it valued. You in a rush?"

"Aren't we all, one way or another? The cottage and land be a heavy weight strapped to my back. There is a place where there are friendly faces, where I might find me a job, see folk again."

"You and I are not too different. The farm is an asset but not a home, and now that I have a new farm manager, I can return to the factory. This is no place to bring a wife who is used to the town. Oh, there is solitude when one wants it, I'll grant you, but I have missed working."

"He is the right man for the farm, you believe?"

"Yes, but he is on trial, and if he is not suitable, he will go. There is no room for sentiment in business. But I will buy your land at a fair price."

You did not give me a trial, thought Toller. But all that is passed. Dead.

Redvers' outstretched hand did not tremble as Toller's. Burstock land – sold, gone, in a brief clasp of hands.

The weight began to fall from his shoulders almost immediately, and when Redvers called at the cottage to make an offer, it disappeared completely.

"You will take the sheep, too?"

"I have no need of them."

"Then today I will slit their throats."

One by one, he seized them, turned their eyes away, so that he would not see the terror in them. The sheep twitched, squirmed, as blood pumped from their necks. He killed them where he caught them, and crows flapped and settled on them quickly, pecking, pulling. On the cart, the sheep were stretched out, side by side.

"These are for you," said Toller.

Sampford stared at the cart.

"All of 'em?"

"All."

"Why?"

"I am leaving – for good."

"But there are too many sheep. My appetite is not what it was. Why give them to me when you have never given me anything?"

"You know why. Shall you have them?"

"Help me."

The last of the blood dripped as the sheep were hung in Sampford's outbuilding.

"They must hang for a few days."

"For good, then, you go from Pilsdon?"

"Yes, so let us part on these terms."

Sampford hung his head.

"It should never have been like this, over the years."

"No, but what's done is done."

"'Tis certain."

Sampford trudged to the chest of drawers. On his shaking hands was the sheep's blood. He thought: blood at birth, blood at death.

He opened the top drawer. There it was, as it had always been, lying there, ready.

"I will go now," said Toller.

"Yes. Go if you must."

Sampford did not turn as Toller left.

When the moment had gone, Sampford slowly closed the drawer.

With money enough to come, Toller set off on foot, a curious sense of freedom consuming him.

"Come home," Miranda called to him. "You once saved me, soothed my horse, then you went. Now come back to me, and I will save you." The voice was all around him. Toller looked over his shoulder, at the hedges, up to the sky, and her voice was everywhere, in the air itself. "It is time."

Chapter twenty-five.

Mattie had been so used to the quiet and open spaces of Pilsdon that she felt oppressed by the long, echoing, windowless corridors, and was fearful that she would not be able to cope with a return to rules and taking orders. Then, of course, there was Nightingale, who needed feeding regularly. A crying baby would become tiresome to others, and should not be left on its own. Mattie knew there would be a conflict of interest. There are too many people here, she reflected. I baint used to them no more; only the crows and butterflies. No birds singing here now. At Pilsdon, I could tell the hour by the owl's screech, which used to scare me, but then I got to thinking it was calling to me, letting me know it was awake.

So she stopped in the corridor, and Mrs. Canford said, "Further down, dear, be yours."

"I'm so sorry, Mrs. Canford, but I've made a mistake coming back. Lady Dewlish has been kind, but it won't work, what with Nightingale a-mewing like a cat, all the time. I wasn't thinking straight," Mattie explained.

"You're tired, child. Sleep on it. Things feel bad now because you've had a long journey. In the morning, they'll look different."

The night's events only confirmed Mattie's worst fear: that her daughter would prevent her working normally. Mattie needed an income, and had saved a little of the money Toller had sent her, over the months. But she would not be a burden on others, had not come for charity, and if she could not do a day's work without interruption, she would leave. Soon Dulcie and Dora were woken by Nightingale's bawling, and Dulcie went to Mattie's room.

"I'm sorry. She doesn't seem to want any milk. I don't know what it is. She might be sickening for something," apologised Mattie.

"'Tis late," commented Dulcie matter-of-factly, holding the weak flame of the candle to the clock.

"I'll walk her."

Dulcie returned to her room, snuffed her candle, and groaned as she slumped onto her bed.

At first light, Dora knocked on Dulcie's door.

"We be late. Dress quickly, or Mrs. Canford will be after us."

"Is Mattie yet roused? The baby was crying, on and off, all night."

"She must be up already, for her room be empty."

Dulcie rose, and made straight for Mattie's room.

"Go down to the kitchen while I dress. See if she is there, and, if not, tell Mrs. Canford, for my heart thumps against my ribs at the thought that she and her baby have gone."

Mrs. Canford made straight to Lady Dewlish's room. Though it was too early to knock, Mrs. Canford did so, knowing it was important.

"Gone?" gasped Lady Dewlish. "Then we must have changed her mind for her. Go to Milborne and ask him to send Curry Rivell, the groom, to ride after her and bring her back. There is the baby to think of, even if she has little regard for her own welfare."

But Curry Rivell found no sign of them. No one had seen a woman and a baby.

"Then let us hope she finds what she is looking for," said Lady Dewlish, "though I suspect that if she cannot find it here, she is unlikely to find it elsewhere."

When he discovered what had happened, Lord Dewlish said, "Let the matter rest, Intrinseca. She has her own life to lead, and decisions to make. We must not get too close to the staff or we shall discover things about them we should not, despite their attempts to hide them from us."

Elsewhere in the house, news of Mattie's disappearance was being discussed.

"'Taint no place for a baby, a hot kitchen, and 'twon't do much for the reputation of Maidenhampton to have a mother and baby living here beout a husband and a father," opined Dulcie to Dora.

"Far too hot for a baby," agreed Dora, "and Maidenhampton got enough for folk to talk about, beout Mattie's troubles."

Meanwhile, Toller employed Hugo Lockington to oversee the sale of his house and land to Redvers Holditch. Lockington did not reveal that he himself was acting on behalf of Redvers, too. Indeed, there was no conflict of interest, as the price had been amicably agreed between the vendor and purchaser.

"And will you leave me an address?" Lockington enquired of Toller. "In case there is some urgent necessity to contact you."

"I'm not certain where I shall be, and it be unlikely we shall need to talk again on any matter."

Lockington moved awkwardly in his seat. His meeting, the day before, with Forston Sampford was still fresh in his memory, though professional integrity forbade him revealing its purpose.

"As you wish. However, it is always helpful to both notary and client to keep their records accurate. I find that the silent passing of years does not mean that there will not be one which makes a lot of noise requiring attention."

"Then you shall find me, unless Providence sends me down a track elsewhere, at Misterton Manor, near Dorchester. There do I hope to find the human companionship I have recently lacked, these parts."

"Then good luck to you, Mr. Burstock. I shall be in touch with you, should the need arise."

Toller was mildly troubled by the possibility of a need to

communicate further, and Lockington made a note of Toller's destination.

"Goodbye to 'ee, Mr. Lockington," said Toller.

"And goodbye to you, too, Mr. Burstock."

Hugo Lockington sighed. I have sacrificed my own life, helping others to manage theirs, and the burden of their secrets are as heavy as an anchor. My lips must be sealed, yet if they could be opened before their time, they would leave men howling in anguish.

Misterton Manor had to wait. Toller had counted the days, nicked with his knife each one on a wooden fence. The same time, each day, he sliced so that he would not forget the promised rendez-vous. Once, Mattie had asked him what all those marks meant, and he had answered, "Soon, there will be no more, and I will know whether one man's word to another be as strong as oak or as weak as straw." But Mattie had not lasted the year, and would not know the answer. I have kept the counting, and must know, now that Christmas is almost upon us, Toller reminded himself.

I stood here, he said to himself in Dorchester, and there he was, a stranger on the other side of the road. In his uniform, he lit his cigarette. By chance, we met, I a man intent on changing himself, he a soldier with a tobacco tin in his hand, bound for Southampton. And now 'tis Christmas Day.

Toller felt the coins in his pocket.

"I have kept my word, come to repay you. Let no man say that Toller Burstock does not repay his debts," he said aloud, as if the saying was likely to make their reunion more likely.

The feeling that he had kept his side of the pact was good. The hour was roughly the same. The windows of The King's Arms were flickering, and framed alternating shadows and light.

"Give a girl a nice Christmas present?" he heard in the darkness.

Toller pretended he had not heard. Only if the soldier did not return would he spend the money, but not on a common voice, a malodorous whore, as much as he wanted to.

Then, as he was about to leave the spot on which he had stood for an hour, he heard irregular footsteps, saw an outline in the half-light of the entrance to The King's Arms. Toller had already conceded that his benefactor might be buried in some arid, distant land, unable to claim what he was owed, but it was worth the effort, this testing of goodness, decency.

"'Tis cold, this Christmas Day," called Toller, "though not as sharp as last year's, when I stood here and borrowed from a man who fought for Queen and country. There were daggers in the air, that day."

The man limped across the street, glancing up and down it, checking to see that he was safe, for the moment, and was not being followed.

"I knew 'ee'd come," said the man.

Toller thought the man's hand shook in his. There was no uniform, no drooping, black moustache. The man knew Toller was staring at him, trying to remember him as he had been, when he had not been tormented by fear and guilt.

"Likewise. Look, 'tis here what I borrowed. I be a man of my word."

The man chuckled, shook his head as if he was working out a persistent ache in the neck.

"'Taint the money I come for tonight, but 'ee, just to see a friendly face."

"You knew I would, or you would not have wasted your time. 'Twas a feeling, like mine."

"Some of us just know."

"I know."

"I saw you looking: my moustache."

"The uniform's gone, too."

"Gone, yes. Like so many things."

"You limp."

"A bullet saved my life."

Toller offered the coins, a sum more symbolic than accurate, but the man refused it.

"Nearly killed you be closer to the truth."

"Saved me. A burden I was, then. Stretchered and shipped back. No use to the army with a leg goes its own way."

"I'm sorry."

"No, 'taint like that."

"You want a drink?"

The man followed Toller's eyeline to The King's Arms.

"Need to keep a clear head."

"On Christmas Day?"

"A young lady," the man lied.

"Sweetheart?"

"Was."

Toller was unsure how their meeting would end. The air was cold enough to discourage lingering in the street. What is it, this connection between us? wondered Toller. He remembers our last meeting, the invitation to repeat it in a year's time, but refuses what I owe him. I know why I came, but does he, really?

"Then let me not keep you from your intended visit."

"I must go."

Yes, felt Toller: your hand shakes even in a firm grasp.

"'Tis strange, this. Let us not leave it, brief though it be, a year till the next one."

"There will be no next one. In a year's time, I will be rotting in a silent grave."

"But your wound . . . your limp be slight, to my eye. The enemy was not a good shot. You have yet your life to live."

"'Twas not the enemy who shot me."

"Then was it a mistake of one of your own? These things be unintended, but happen, I imagine."

"No mistake. My aim was true."

Just then, they heard footsteps, soon drowned by ringing bells. Down and up the street came those the man had arranged to meet. They walked cautiously, in small steps, preventing an escape. Toller wondered why so many, on such a Christian day. No former sweetheart, then. That had been for me, to encourage me to leave, not see the worst. So, he shot himself, and now he will be arrested.

The truth shocked Toller like the near miss of a bullet.

"You shot yourself? Why?"

"No more running. I killed one man too many. But you? I wanted to see if there was a man I could trust, one with good intentions."

The police officers stopped, a few paces away, waited, unsure for whom they had come. All six had pulled themselves up to their full height, their truncheons drawn.

"Now, then," called the Sergeant, stepping forward. "We don't want any trouble, no tricks, just like you said in your letter. More of us, if need be."

"You'd better go," said the man.

"But what have you done?"

Toller edged away, raised both hands to the officers as a sign that he was not their man.

The Sergeant, with a gesture the others understood, marched slowly towards the man, widening their line, their feet in step.

"A year ago, I shot the man who took my girl. The ship sailed before they could catch me, but you can't run for ever. Better to hang here than be slaughtered in some dusty, foreign land, thousands of miles from home. He was a drayman, but he was here for her, whereas I wasn't. A drayman, I ask you!"

The Sergeant said, "Titus Chettle, I am arresting you on suspicion of murdering Arthur Abbott," but the rest of the words were swallowed by the night.

Toller moved quickly away, not wishing to be caught up in the event.

Then the truth hit him as hard as a truncheon, brought him to standstill.

"Ezra's partner!" he exclaimed. "I took his place. And to think that my chance at the brewery was the result of a murder committed by a man I would gladly pass an evening with in any inn in Dorchester! 'Tis passing strange."

He quickly made his way to The Raddleman. Would Durnovaria Brewery still be supplying ale to it? Ezra had nearly killed him with one punch. And I gave him the excuse: not the order to the landlord to stop serving, but because I had taken the place of his dead friend. My visit was the trigger, but the fuse was lit when I began to work with Ezra. A room for one night is all I ask, but if the inn is full, I shall go to The King's Arms. A shepherd I was when I took Mattie there, and one man looked down upon us, which I have not forgotten. But I now have money, which will buy goodwill.

The Raddleman was shut, and no one answered to his knocks. What has happened to John Trevelyan? he wondered.

At The King's Arms, the warmth of the fires hugged him. I never knew so many souls preferred the inn to their own hearth, he thought, as he made his way to the only unoccupied seat in the room, which had been filled, a moment or two ago, with the romp of fiddles. His entrance had coincided with the applause of the customers, some of whom had returned to chewing on their chicken bones, and others who were contributing to the hum of conversation.

Toller hid his embarrassment under the hat he had not yet removed. He looked for where he had sat with Mattie, the table at which they had agreed to become brother and sister, for appearance's sake at Pilsdon. And I would have grown into a good husband and father if she had let me, and the same I would have been to Hepsy, my first love, but now both are gone, like all the years past.

"You want something?" asked the woman with a tray in her hand.

Hat now on the table, Toller ignored her wink.

"I be hungry and thirsty, so whatever you got. And be there a room?"

"I'll ask. I be Sally."

Toller smiled at her second wink, gave in. Don't be a fool, he chided himself. 'Tis a merry gathering. I've long since forgotten what it is to belong to one. This be a good omen.

"And I be Toller."

"A handsome, 'tis certain," she said, turning, and winking again, over her shoulder.

While she was gone, a man at the next table leaned over to him, and said, "I don't recognise 'ee. You passing through Dorchester?"

The man had a red nose and cheeks, and his eyes had shrunk to a pin's head, so much had he drunk, and so close had he been sitting to the fire. Toller saw his grey hair as a sign that he had lived many years, and was skilled in the art of conversation.

"I hope for a room here tonight. I be after work. Shepherd I was, Bridport way, but am now after farm labouring."

"Then try up on the Misterton estate. She be a good mistress, and a pretty, too."

Toller smiled. Am I really close to my home? he wondered. Her reputation has spread, and soothes like balm.

"Then there shall I go, more than likely, though drink and food must I have tonight, and I will raise my pot to 'ee, sir, when it comes, for you have welcomed me more than the last time I was here with my –"

Then Sally returned with his food.

"Pies and tatties, Toller!"

Toller rummaged in his pocket for money.

"Let me see."

"No need. You can settle your debt in the morning, for the inn-keeper says there be a room to spare."

"For you," he insisted, offering a coin.

"'Tis kind, Toller, but the last man who offered me money got more than he bargained for!"

"Her wink settle everything," said the man who had moved his chair closer to Toller. "Famous, it be. Means she got the measure of 'ee, says you be one of us."

Toller raised his pot, fought back the surge of emotion that came when told he belonged to someone again.

The man touched Toller's pot.

"Your health . . . but I don't know your name. I be Toller Burstock."

"'Tis a name like a bell, and hab a certain ring about it!"

Toller laughed, too.

"A jolly man, 'ee be."

"Not always. I been a widower, see, and for years I locked myself away from folk, never joining their song or merriment, but my wife, now a ghost, said to me – from beyond the grave – 'stop your blubbering, and pick up life again as if it were a new-born lamb. You'll see me again, soon enough.' And so I casted off my mask of misery, and am happy again to live in Stinsford, and to go to church, Sundays."

"But your name, sir. What be it? Come, tell me, for I like it already, whatever it be."

"Many a name I be called, though I answers to one only."

"Which be?"

"Jonas. *Old* Jonas, in fact, though I've a few years left yet. Yes, Toller, I be Old Jonas, Stinsford born, and in Stinsford shall I be buried. But 'ee shall like the Mistress, though her brother, Seth, blow with the wind, as is the case with young men. And Master Nicholas."

"And what of him?"

Toller recalled him: a wiry man, grey, wavy hair, staring into the distance, looking for a place, people he would never see again, straining to hear words he regretted saying.

"'Tis Christmas, and I doubt if he'll see another, Easter, even. Only the Lord knows. No, Toller, he not got long. Not long at all."

Chapter twenty-six.

The ghostly lamp, swinging slightly to the rhythm of its carrier's stride, floated through the darkness.

"Father, you there? 'Tis late to be out, this season." No moon, no stars, just lamplight suspended on an invisible pole was all she had to help her look. "Father," called Miranda, more loudly. "You got your coat on? Your hat?"

Nicholas Misterton made his way towards his daughter, his face pale, gaunt, and framed by his now grey hair grown too long for Miranda's liking.

"Ruth?" he asked, shielding his eyes from the glare.

"Miranda, father. Come. It's late. You must rest, or the pain will get worse."

He took her arm, leaned on her, just as he used to do on the cottage door, on the heath, when it stuck in hot weather. She felt him wince as the pain stabbed him, and pull up, as if he had come face to face with an adder.

"You be your mother: dark, beautiful, so special. A sorceress she was, and had me under her spell with a glance and a dance."

"Miranda, your daughter, father. The air is cold and damp; the night is a dark cave. Come inside. Will you eat? You took only a bite, earlier."

She followed his pace, knew that he had been beyond the paling she had brought closer to the house, to remind him of what he used to lean on, in the early evening, when they lived in the cottage on the heath. But not beyond in a physical sense: elsewhere, to a time when she lived with the Chideocks, before she discovered that Nicholas was her real father, by birth.

Miranda knew his day, the one we all dread or embrace with gratitude, even knew what it would be like. Snow would fall silently on already high drifts sculpted by the spent wind. Winter would not howl or lament at the windows. But it was not here yet, was not even in the far distance into which he stared daily, despite his limp, his increasing forgetfulness, and the private speculation of one or two workers.

"What day is it?" he asked suddenly, as if he might have neglected to do something important.

"Why, it's Christmas Day night! Come, eat something, and then I shall be satisfied. Afterwards, I want you to tell how it was when you met my mother in Bucky Doo. That is my favourite, and though I have heard it many times, again must I hear it, as it brings her to life again."

"Will you join us, one day, Miranda, when your time come? Only you can make us a family again, a whole that never was – because of me."

"I will, father, but only if you promise to take a slice of lean meat, or a wedge of apple pie with a bonnet of cream on."

Nicholas shivered; the warmth he had felt at the prospect of being with Ruth again had quickly vanished.

"We will see," he said, his teeth chattering. "We will see." They took a few more steps. "Tomorrow I will go see . . . "

Sadly, he had forgotten the name of the young man who had first given him a pen and ink, but he remembered that that gesture had begun the search for Miranda. Without Tom Hardy – for it was the same whose name was evading capture – she would have been lost for ever.

The book she had bought for her father, as a present, was still unopened on the arm of his leather, winged chair. He had slept, that afternoon, his right foot up on a stool to lessen the pain, his hand still on the novel's cover, as if he were declaring an oath to a higher authority.

"Will you read a little of your book, before dinner? Miss. Godmanstone recommended it herself. One of Mr. Hardy's best, she thinks. You know how you like to read. I must go to the kitchen. We shall have Charlotte and Michael at the table, as usual. They seem almost part of the family, at Christmas. It would not be the same without them. I'm afraid we have had no reply from Aunt Emily. 'Tis strange. I suppose, though, she makes her own plans, and has a household to keep."

"Sherborne be not the other side of the world," grumbled Nicholas. "Not Australia."

"A reply would have been polite," admitted Miranda. "Still, we must manage as we are: a father and his daughter. And, later, if I am not too tired, I shall wander over to the barn, where there will be a reel or two among the workers. Charlotte has prepared them a bite to eat. 'Twill rescue the end of the day. Will you come and sit, father, or will you stay with your book, when the time comes?"

Nicholas picked up his copy of Far from the Madding Crowd, and carefully opened it at the first page. He breathed in deeply the heady scent of leather and paper, and fixed his eyes on the first few lines. Miranda hoped that he would stay, rest his swollen right foot. He would take none of her potions, especially the whortleberry, which he swore made his inflamed big toe even worse.

"I shall read, first, and though I shall not prance and dance like a devil on Hell's coals, 'ee should not find me as disagreeable as usual, and I shall watch from the edge, and take a pot of ale. But first, I shall read, for there baint anything written by Tom Hardy that do not deserve the best of attention. I've tried others – Mr. Charles Dickens himself, even – but I always come home to young Tom, as I shall always remember him."

At that moment, there was a knock at the door.

"Come in, Michael," called Miranda, for she knew it was time to be called to the table for their dinner.

"Evening again to 'ee both," said Michael, when he was inside the room, his initial reluctance to enter the consequence of him having been compelled to wear some items of dress his good wife Charlotte had bought him, and of which he had feigned approval, when shock and embarrassment at their bright tones and gay cut were his true feelings. "Charlotte calls 'ee to the table. I knows there be a plate of her best soup: chicken and all the vegetables we can name, which be tatties and onions and –"

But Miranda knew exactly what the ingredients were, as they were a regular feature of Charlotte's soups, so interrupted his list with, "We are on our way, Michael, if you would let Charlotte know."

Michael retreated, but, at the door, turned and said, "Don't feel right, though, Miss. Miranda, if I may say, not to have Miss. Emily at the table. Though it seems an age ago, I remembers her nuptials – and 'twas a wedding as merry and full of music to charm the birds from the trees and sky, and the dancing went on till sunrise, if I remembers rightly –"

"She will be missed, Michael, 'tis certain, though we shall be merry enough with four, and then we shall go to the barn, where, as is the tradition, we shall sing, and clap, and dance till we can do no more."

Michael nodded, and left with a suitably wistful mien, which a man in his privileged position felt obliged to wear as much as the new clothes.

"Come, father, for Charlotte is ready for us. Mr. Hardy will not mind you deserting his book for a little while. There will be time later to make some progress into it."

Nicholas took her arm, and gritted his teeth to suppress the raging gout with which he had been afflicted for six months. 'Tis my punishment yet, he was always thinking, and no conjuror daughter of mine will ease it with a special potion, for unless I feel it, I shall scarce be shriven.

The dining table had initially been set by Michael, after tuition he found difficult to absorb. He had polished the cutlery till he could recognise his distorted face on the back of the spoon, yet being a man who had eaten with a fork only till he met Charlotte, he could not remember what went on the right and left of the plate. Indeed, knowing he often confused his left and right, Charlotte had privately predicted mistakes, and had herself rearranged things. The candles were lit, and sprigs of holly the season had endowed with lots of berries were hung around the hearth.

"The table looks a picture," said Miranda.

"Thank 'ee, and I hab placed you, Master Nicholas, at the head of the table, as usual."

Charlotte glanced at Miranda to see if she had not offended her, and Miranda reassured her with, "As father is still the head of the house –"

Nicholas said, "Pah! The house be yourn. 'Twas left in my care by Miss. Palfreyman, when she passed, till you were twenty-one, which be . . . "

The number of years which had slipped by since the title passed to Miranda eluded him. Miranda had begun to anticipate those moments when her father clutched at facts and past events as if he were trying to catch an annoying fly, which eventually jumps out of reach and frustrates.

"Come, father, sit now, and we shall drink to Florence Palfreyman, my benefactor, shortly. Michael, you sit facing Charlotte, and I shall sit here. Now, I believe we have soup."

Charlotte smiled. How she loved the season's rituals!

"Come, Michael, and carry the pot, as 'tis too heavy for a woman with twigs for wrists."

Michael dutifully followed her to the kitchen, and Nicholas

could not help but share Miranda's snigger at the sight of Michael's unusual garb.

"We have a footman now?" Nicholas said.

"Father, 'taint our place to laugh. They don't suit him, 'tis certain, but Charlotte chose them, and we shall upset her if she sees us ridiculing him!"

"But he looks more like a footman in Queen Victoria's house than a horse breeder!"

"Do nothing to spoil this dinner, or I shall never forgive you."

Then he spied it, the extra place at the table. Too early, thought Miranda. Besides, Charlotte does not know, as do I, when he will come. Yet if I conspicuously remove the glass and cutlery, I cannot say nothing. And next to father are they, and so it can only mean that we should not forget, at this time of year. 'Tis born of love for us, but we would require, years hence, a bigger table for those who choose not to come or have passed away.

The soup arrived, and when the lid was removed from the pot, a mushroom of steam bloomed, and Nicholas sniffed the air appreciatively. For the first few spoonfuls, there was silence, then Charlotte said, "I hope there be not too many onions. Michael, see, believes you can't have too many."

"The soup be your best yet, Charlotte. What you say, father?"

"'Tis wondrous, though, next year, a leg or a rib or two of rabbit would set it off."

"'Tis what I told her, Master Nicholas. 'Taint as if we don't have any, what with 'em hanging up by their legs in the pantry. Whole line of them, eyes a-staring in their sockets," said Michael.

"Enough now!" insisted Miranda.

The more they discussed soup with or without rabbit, the more conspicuous became the spare plate at the table.

The goose came, and Charlotte offered the knife to Miranda, and said, "Perhaps you would like to do the honours, Miss?" Miranda glanced at her father, who usually carved, and Charlotte explained.

"What I mean is, if Master Nicholas be in pain if he stands, he might prefer to sit."

Nicholas held out his hand for the knife, and Charlotte passed it to him. They all watched him stand uncomfortably, but his hand was steady, his slicing precise and smooth. When he had cut enough, he sat, and pushed the plate towards Charlotte.

"You first. Cook's privilege."

He recalled all those pigs and lambs, his refusal to see them as anything but nourishment, as he had been taught by his father, the gushing of pulsing blood, the convulsion, and, finally, the stillness of black eyes.

"She baint coming. No need to keep a place for her. Emily be her own woman. Always scared of nothing. Slit me open, she did, a few times, with her sharp words. Cutthroats, they were. Now, let us eat," he said.

The bales of straw in the barn formed a rectangle. A barrel of ale and one of cider, paid for by Miranda, were far away from the doors. She had deemed it too dangerous to light coals in the old drinking trough; and, besides, though it was cold, it was not snowing or icy.

"Once Sydling Chilfrome's fingers start running up and down his fiddle, and everyone starts skipping to and fro, we shall all be warm, as if it were a summer's day," reassured Miranda, who knew that, once she left the merry throng, as was her habit, the ale would make them insensible to the low temperature.

Charlotte had baked a cake or two, and she asked Toby Wanderwell to keep an eye on them, so that everyone had their fair share. Tranter Cogden had groomed himself as well as any of his horses, and Lizzie Loscombe, who had set her heart on him, a long time ago, had had Fancy Laverstock heat her hair into ringlets, so that Tranter might have a better look at her face, which Fancy described as 'tolerable pretty'. But Fancy had nearly set poor Lizzie's hair on fire, so long had she left the tongs over the flames. The first sign of Fancy's misjudgement had been the acrid smell of singed hair. "Oh,

Lizzie!" had cried Fancy. "But your hair has melted a little!" Lizzie had burst into tears, but Fancy had saved the day by some judicious pruning of the half-burnt strands. "There!" Fancy had pronounced. "Neither Tranter nor the cows shall recognise you!" Lizzie had declared herself more than satisfied, and was confident that her changed appearance would win his heart.

Then arrived Wynford Chedynton and Huish Peverell, who made straight for the barrels.

"No use asking these legs to win a maiden beout a pot or two. They can follow a plough well enough, but 'tis the ale which leads them off the straight and narrow, and casts a spell over women!" confessed Wynford.

"Remember me, last year, when I trod on Olive Thorncombe's toes so hard she had to be carried to her bale? Her looks were pitchforks to me, from then on," said Huish.

When the dancing began, Miranda joined in. She had persuaded Nicholas to stay but an hour, and even then to remain on a bale, his feet up on another. He took a pot or two of ale, remembered how he used to enjoy dancing, as a young man, but as he studied the movements, some sure-footed, others clumsy, he reflected how absurd dancing was. "'Tis as if there be a bee trapped in their clothes!" he laughed. "All this flinging around, and whooping – why, men and women be locked in an asylum for less!"

When exhaustion set in, the women went to their beds, and the drowsy men lounged on bales, recalling Christmases past.

Wynford Chedynton, as confirmed a bachelor as Dorset has ever seen, told of how, the year before, he had seen a pale figure of a woman, dressed in a fine gown, pass across the doorway. She had smiled at him when she saw him looking.

"Pretty as a picture. A smiling face as kind as ever I seed."

"Why, it be Miss. Florence Palfreyman, I expect!" said Huish.

"No doubt she came to see our merriment. 'Twas she who left the manor to our Mistress. I don't myself speckilate why, though I heard it said that Miss. Miranda be her daughter, and 'tis true that she baint a mirror to Mistress Maisie, Master Nicholas' wife, when she was alive."

A groom, who could barely keep his eyes open, added, "There be more going on than we think. Mistress said to me that I might be having someone else work with me in the stables, and that when Michael retires, which, from his own mouth, be soon, on account of Charlotte wanting him to pay her more attention, the man bill be in charge of the stables, even over me!"

So they talked into the night, and fell asleep in the barn, which sounded like a pigsty, so loud was their collective snoring.

Sydling Chilfrome awoke with his bow still in his hand, and his fiddle on the floor. The barn door had been opened earlier by Miranda, to allow cold air in, so that they might wake up sooner rather than later. There were jobs to do, animals to feed and care for. It was not yet light, but not completely dark. Sydling rubbed his eyes, groaned, held his head, licked his dry lips with a furred tongue. He was cold, and his head ached. Around him, bodies were in unusual positions. It was like a battlefield, when there has just been a massacre, and the corpses have not yet been retrieved.

It was then that he looked towards the door. The ghost was in the opening, looking in. Sydling raised the bow still in his hand, and wafted it threateningly.

"Come no nearer, ghost," he croaked, "or 'ee'll feel the sharp end of this 'ere bow, and horsehair can cut as well as a sabre on a downward stroke!" he warned. The ghost raised its hand in acknowledgement, and walked out of sight. "Too much talk of ghosts, last night. Must have been so, or I baint Sydling Chilfrome!"

Chapter twenty-seven.

Miles Yondover tried to forget that he had left behind him a young woman, who now drenched her pillow, every night. Jessie refused, at first, to believe his sudden disappearance was anything to do with her own and her father's conduct towards him. But as days became weeks, she concluded there was no other explanation.

Of course, her spirits rose when she heard that he had been seen in this place and that. He had even, made up one particularly spiteful rumour-monger, acquired a family – a boy, a girl, and a pretty, blonde wife with a complexion as smooth as Dorset cream – and that he had been deceiving Jessie for ages.

"Dead. That's what he must be to you, girl," her father told her. "Dead as any in Briddy graveyard, and if, by some whim of fate, he be resurrected, then 'twon't be for long, as I shall take my gun to him, and blow his head off, and hanging won't bother me none. No, girl, not at my age. They can tie the thickest Bridport rope round my neck, and I would laugh, I would, for that Miles Yondover bill have got what he asked for!"

Jessie Bradpole opened her eyes so widely that her father thought she had seen Miles' ghost already. It was distressing enough to lose her prospective husband, but the thought of her own dear father swinging by his neck, eyes bulging, leaving her as well, was unbearable.

"Don't speak like that, father, as I fear we must bear the blame for Miles' going. 'Tis clear to me now, in the silence of his absence. A good man, he was, and I have turned him against me biv all my wifely ways, before he was even a husband."

"Nonsense, girl. 'Tis well he has gone now, before the vows be made, and the bells ring out in their finest mockery. No, girl. If Miles Yondover comes back here, then he shall feel a bullet or two of mine!"

When Miles had to go to Bridport, to buy provisions, he swathed himself in scarves, hiding his face, and wore a hat with a brim so wide that he could barely see his way in the cart. He took to handing over a list of items he wanted so that no one could recognise his voice, which he tried to make gruffer, to give the impression that he was older than he was.

Always relieved when he was on his way back to the farm, Miles could not, however, rid himself of the guilt he felt at leaving Jessie in such a cowardly manner. He had tried, once or twice, to write to her, make plain his reasons, but he came to the conclusion that somehow, no matter how carefully he constructed his sentences, his explanation was as flimsy as a cobweb.

And where is Hepsy now? he wondered. He had come back to find her, and as the world was so big, he felt it best if he stayed where he could imagine her living, looking after her father, spreading butter on bread, boiling eggs from their own coop. She might drift back to the farm when her quest – if that is what drew her from Marshwood Vale – ends.

Miles could never have guessed what had happened to her, following her discovery that he had been soon to marry Jessie Bradpole. Hepsy had been embarrassed to have been ignorant of his engagement, and her anger had been a swollen, turbulent river as she had left the inn.

She had heard grunting, muffled sounds behind her. And how had the knife she carried in her bag found its way into her stinking assailant, who had lurched out from a doorway? He had grabbed her wrists, pulled her this way and that in a macabre dance that resulted in him gasping and falling to the ground. One final, futile groan later, and the sot was dead.

What words she then exchanged with the man who was passing in his cart she will never recall, but she remembered that he had hauled her up into his cart, and covered her with a tarpaulin. By the time the others had emerged from the inn, and had discovered the body, he had borne her safely out of sight.

"And have I killed him?" she muttered. "All those times I have slit the throat of a pig or sheep have given me the instinct, and I fear his neck gapes."

"Don't 'ee talk so, Miss. He be soused in cider, and lecherous be his ways. I smelt it on him, as I undid his grip on 'ee. A strong drinker he be, make no mistake. No point staying. Best to come away. Seem he had it coming to him."

Miles did not know that the girl he really loved was well out of his reach, hiding from police officers, who were convinced that the woman who had been in the inn, a minute or two before a disturbance was heard, was the murderer. But she must not be found in Bridport, and Dorchester would be the best place to hide, had said her saviour. Melt in the throng, take a new name, cut your long hair, and she took his advice, on the verge of despair, having no other plan. As I have killed a man, most likely, I must pay for this sin, one day, with my own life.

"Come, let me do it," said the old woman with whom the man had left her. "Got a blade as sharp as the one that let that fiend's blood."

She knows, then, saw Hepsy. This woman, too, holds my fate in the other hand to that which grips a knife every bit as sharp as mine.

The woman stayed silent as she hacked Hepsy's hair. Hepsy closed her eyes, as she had done with her first muddy pig, and felt the blade brought downwards. Some locks fell onto her hands. No man will look at me now with my head so ugly, she thought.

"A new girl!" declared the woman.

"'Twon't make my heart look or feel different. Short hair don't stop a heart painting a face fit for the gallows. All 'twill do will be to help make the rope fit my neck more snug."

"Do as he says. 'Tis too late for all this caterwauling. What's done's done, and 'tis lucky he was there to save you. Now, tell me your name."

For the first time since the attack, Hepsy wept.

"My name be like a stickleback that slips through my fingers in the stream, and yet, if I caught it in the net, I would not recognise it, so disgracefully it now fits me."

"Then you must take the name Maude, which rhyme biv Lord, of whom you have the greatest need."

Maude, contemplated Hepsy. There be worse. Better Maude alive than Hepsy dead.

"And who be the man who saved me?"

"One who will not let anyone hang on account of such a vile man as lies with *rigum ortis* in his bones."

"And has he a name, that I might thank him?"

"He hab not told you?"

"His eyes were on the horse and road. He snuffed his lantern, and relied on starlight and glow-worms, when they came."

"Then his name be best known to you. He be John Trevelyan, of Dorchester."

"Then 'twas lucky his business was in Bridport!"

"'Tis certain."

Toller peered into the barn through its open door. The thunderous snoring had caught his attention. Bodies were slumped over bales of straw as if they had been slaughtered on the spot, in a surprise military attack. And the individual snores had come together, taken on such a common rhythm and volume that Toller thought it was a giant who lived within.

Other signs of the previous night's revels were visible: empty barrels still giving off the fragrance of cider; fiddles and bows lying carelessly by the sides of open-mouthed musicians; and tables bearing empty plates and overturned pots.

A wondrous sight to behold! thought Toller. A night of much merriment is suggested by their stillness and grunting. A celebration now spent will stay for hours in their thudding heads, when they are awake, and Miss. Misterton will have organised it, no doubt.

Then he saw one of the bodies stir: Sydling Chilfrome, hair sticking out at all angles like straw in a scarecrow's head. Toller could not have known that the tales of ghosts, swapped only a few hours ago, were still fresh in Sydling's memory. How ghastly Sydling's face looked in the barn's gloom! I have surprised him, thought Toller, who waved to him, and continued on his way to the manor.

Miranda had risen at her usual hour, though had gone to bed later than usual. Charlotte was up, and had lit the fires before heating a big pan of porridge on the range. After Miranda had looked in on her father, and found him breathing, she set about writing a letter to Emily, who had not come for Christmas. A sister should not neglect her brother, no matter what her domestic circumstances, thought Miranda. Yet she could not be satisfied with her expression and handwriting, could not physically settle in her chair, and was glad to be disturbed by Charlotte, who said, "You hab a visitor. You seed him before. Michael and I took him under our wing, so to speak, till he left. Wants to see 'ee, and sends the season's compliments."

So that was it! Miranda concluded: the restlessness of my pen, the vagueness of how I must shape my day, and the stirring in my head, once again, of a vision. All these distractions were but signs that he was on his way.

Charlotte fetched him, and left them alone.

"So, you are back," Miranda stated.

"You would have me?"

Miranda did not yet smile, was saving it for a better, less nerve-jangling moment.

"You still stop horses running wild? You calm them with a touch of your hand? Find and return dropped books?"

Toller shrugged, put on the spot.

"Might."

"Such modesty! Will you try – for me?"

"I will."

Then it came, the smile, the warmth, which he could not help but mirror when he felt it.

"But there is something else, I sense. This coming and going: have you done now? Are your quests over?"

"So many questions, all at once. But yes. One thing more I must do, but cannot without your help."

"And what is that?"

"I must find a man."

"Will any do?"

"Roddy Cattistock, and a woman – Mattie Venn."

"I will help you," promised Miranda. "And then you will stay?"

"'Tis certain."

Forston Sampford sat in his chair, and eyed the clock. He had not wound it for a day or two, and though it still chimed confidently, the hands moved grudgingly, as if the mechanism inside had become as arthritic as its owner. Sampford had no idea what day it was; he had long since stopped wondering. Only the distant peal of church bells, drifting across the vale like the smoke of a dying bonfire, marked the day as Sunday.

"'Tis almost time, I know. 'Tas been a while since Ol' Sojer obeyed an order, so there be no point in marching him to Bridport no more. And he was a raw recruit in my young days, and stood to attention whenever ordered. And if it be so, that he don't have the energy any more, then he shall be demobbed and never more go into battle, though not in disgrace," he said resignedly, "for he has never, till recently, let me down."

The room showed signs of neglect: cobwebs spanned window-frames and ceiling beams; dead leaves he had brought in on his boots had decayed, dried, and crumbled into dust; and the hearth was covered in grey ash blown from the grate.

Sampford breathed heavily. No longer did he stride through the lanes; his legs would not carry him. So he stayed in his chair, going out only to collect a rabbit or two from traps in the garden. For some time, he had not ventured beyond the rotting paling.

He tapped the sealed document on his knee. Many times he had read it, often by candlelight, and once, when his grip faltered, he nearly set fire to it, and the pain ran again through his chest and arm. Sleep, he told himself. Then the ache will go, and I will feel better, well enough to make sure this and Ebenezer Valence's pocket-watch go to Hugo Lockington. I have kept my will too long, imagining that the longer it stays here, the more likely it is that I will stave off the inevitable. 'Tas been a false hope, as all men pass when 'tis their time. But my life has not been in vain, though to me it has been a dinner without meat, a summer without the warmth to sit in the garden, and wait for bats to come out and dash this way and that.

When Miles Yondover knocked on Sampford's door, two weeks later, not having seen him pass at the usual time, Sampford stayed in his chair. No footprints were visible in the grass. Maybe he has left, thought Miles, shading his eyes from the light, as he peered through the window. He could see Sampford, head back, in his chair, mouth open. Asleep, by the looks of it. Yet I will rouse him to see if there is a reason why he does not walk abroad any more. So he tapped on the window, but Sampford did not stir.

Miles opened the door quietly, and a terrible smell greeted him. Sampford's eyes were turned up into their sockets, and plagued by flies buzzing frenziedly as they gorged. Covering his nose and mouth with his forearm, Miles quickly picked up the letter and pocket-watch on the floor, and leapt backwards when his movement disturbed the flies.

In the garden, he gasped, breathed in deeply, to quell the nausea, to rid himself of the stench of putrefying flesh, and to read the letter.

"And 'tis so? And knows the man of this? There be a meaning to me coming here today. All men should be warned that secrets hide beyond hills, in the nooks and crannies of time, and sooner or later, they will be made known, as sure as day and night follow each other. This be a sign to me, a reminder that the secret I kept from Hepsy hab removed her so far from me that I am unable to beg her forgiveness. This man, dead though he be, has passed his secret to me by chance, and so must I reveal it, as is proper and requested, whatever the consequences.

When Mattie left Maidenhampton, in the night, she realised that it had been a vain hope to be accepted with a baby. There would have been, too, the memory of her time with Roddy Cattistock in every corridor and those secluded places they had made their own. Her baby was his responsibility, too, and she was determined that he should know about her, but there were too many others to interfere, to remind her that things had changed since she had left. Even Lady Dewlish had seemed different, more remote.

Mattie calculated that the money she had saved would buy food and accommodation for a week or two. Tolpuddle, she was sure, would now be a stranger to her, and there was no one who could look after her baby while she earned money. No, she must find work where she could keep her child with her. A milkmaid I have been, and one I shall be again if a farmer's wife be willing to keep an eye on her when I be milking. Though there is always the workhouse, we shall not enter, for if we do, we shall never come out alive.

The first two farmers to whom she spoke at the Hiring Fair in Dorchester were looking for labourers, and did not think she was strong enough to stand in all weathers, and top and tail turnips. 'Tis the child, suspected Mattie, and they don't want me running back, all the time, to feed her.

But Farmer Evershot needed a milkmaid, on account of one of his regulars taking herself off to the 'bright lights of Weymouth', as he described it.

"The child won't cause no upset. Nightingale be her name, and when she cries, she sounds like that very bird," said Mattie, pre-empting the question she knew would come.

"And so there be a baby who sings?" said Mrs. Evershot. "A sweet face she has, and no mistake, and 'tis her smile which has won the day."

Mattie passed Nightingale to her, knowing that Mrs. Evershot would want to hold her, and she did, rocked her gently, whispering to her all the time.

"I be ready to work," announced Mattie, lest they all forget why she was there.

"You run along with the master, girl, and I'll see to Nightingale. Reminds me of my own daughter, who be a farmer's wife, Beaminster way."

Mattie was introduced to the other maids in the barn. One was holding her favourite chicken, named Victoria, after the Queen. The others were waiting for the master to bring the pails.

"And this be Mattie," he said. "And let's hope that she don't have her head turned by the bright lights of Weymouth, like one I could mention."

They made her welcome in a reserved way, until they discovered that she had a baby. Then they asked questions excitedly, pecked at her for details: what colour eyes and hair she had; how old she was.

And, finally, there were questions, as innocent as they could make them, about Nightingale's father.

"He's gone away for a while, but he'll come soon and see his little daughter."

It all went quiet for a minute. Mattie had put on a brave face, but the others eventually saw the pain in her eyes, knew the truth, had seen other Matties.

In the night, Nightingale did little to disturb the others, who all came to look at her, and kiss her by candlelight.

"Mind the wax!" warned Mattie, as they stooped to the cot, a box Farmer Evershot had found and cleaned.

This ritual is a joy to behold! marvelled Mattie, glad of the whispered jests in the dark, the hushed expressions of ambition, the dreaming of a better life. And when one of them yearned for a handsome man to marry, the others scolded her, and changed the subject.

Usually, Nightingale awoke to the rhythm of the maids dressing for the parlour, but, one morning, there was no gurgling or snuffling, no prelude to the cry to be fed. Mattie sat up, swung her legs off the bed, and looked in the box-cot. The others were yawning, stretching, grumbling that the rain on the barn roof had kept them awake.

Heart pounding, Mattie discovered Nightingale gone. She looked round the room; everything seemed normal.

"Nightingale!" Mattie cried. "Where is she?"

The others turned to her, her eyes as wild as the night had been, and came to see for themselves.

"You sure she's not in your bed? You take her in during the night?" said Cissie.

Mattie threw off her bed covers, to check.

"Lord, where be my baby?"

Mattie wanted to cry, but the need to act quickly quelled her rising grief.

Cissie put her arm round her.

"She can't walk yet, so she can't be far."

Then Esme said, "Let us hope so, for there be one of us not here."

They scanned the dormitory, and Cissie said, "One up and gone before breakfast?"

Esme put her hand to her mouth: "'Tis Gertie. Lost one child herself, and the Lord hab denied her another. Quick, fetch the master. This sends me cold, and I do not like my thoughts, which tend to mischief when I think of Gertie, who be as deep as the farmyard well, betimes."

Mattie quickly put on her clothes, and ran out into the cold farmyard, where she saw Gertie with Nightingale.

"Give me my baby! Why have you taken her?" screamed Mattie.

Gertie, puzzled, passed her back willingly. The others gathered, and Cissie said, "We have been worried sick where she'd gone. What you up to, girl, taking the baby so?"

Mattie kissed her baby's forehead, and said, "A baby in just her shawl will catch her death of cold, you foolish girl!"

"Why, dear, I whispered to you when she began to cry, and you were dead to the world. Thought I'd settle her, so she wouldn't wake everyone, what with you needing your rest from all that bending in the fields. And you says thank 'ee, and turns over, so don't accuse me of doing her any mischief."

Esme said, "Well, baint any harm done, but what's a mother to think when she finds her baby gone?"

Mattie made her way indoors. Used to sleeping fitfully at the behest of Nightingale, she tried to remember if she had heard Gertie in the dark, and Gertie followed her, muttering, "Only wanted to help. Way she goes on, you'd think I wanted to do the baby some harm."

Farmer Evershot usually kept his maids happy in the milking parlour.

"Sing, my girls, then the cows squirt more, see!"

Mattie joined in, and the singing took her mind off worrying about Nightingale:

"He promised that he'd marry her
when jonquils yellow came,
but summer bloomed, and he still made
excuses plenty, lame."

She refused to be saddened by these wistful songs, when they arose spontaneously, as she hoped that her notice to Roddy Cattistock, in The Western Gazette, of her whereabouts would bring him back to her, make her daughter less vulnerable as she grew up. Initially, Mattie feared that the notice might damage her reputation more widely, and drive him further away, but she calculated that the risk was worth taking.

Weeks passed, and she tortured herself again with the thought that he might have had a good reason to disappear, but when Farmer Evershot, who had himself seen the notice, said that there was little chance of Cattistock contacting her, she decided it was Providence, and, therefore, she must accept it as her lot.

Then, one day, Mrs. Evershot sought her in the field. Mattie was convinced, as her mistress approached, that there was something wrong with Nightingale.

"Tidy your hair, girl, though this wind pulls it all the ways of the weather-vane, for you have a visitor at the house."

"Who can that be?"

"A man who asks for a moment or two of your time. All he would say is that he will not leave till he has seen you. So, girl, tidy yourself, as he be a handsome man and a smart."

As she followed Mrs. Evershot, Mattie's heart galloped. It had been ages since such a man had shown an interest of any kind. The sun warmed her face, and the wind burnt it. Whoever he be, let him see me as I am, she decided, for my beauty, if such I ever had, is as faded as my hopes, which once had the colours of a rainbow over Lyme Bay.

Chapter twenty-eight.

Redvers Holditch wrote to Miles, announcing the date of his visit. His fiancée, Miss. Theresa Marshwood, a young woman who admired the income he derived from selling sails to boat and ship owners, declined his offer to accompany him to his farm. It would not be proper for her to be under the same roof as him. Marriage, she reminded him, was not to be taken lightly, and, besides, her mother would forbid it. This refusal was at odds with the idea he had of making love to her, an urge, as a man in his prime, he had been at pains to subdue since their engagement.

"As you wish," he shrugged, "but it is heavenly there, full of quiet, secluded places giving the soul the balm it needs after the trials of commerce. There are white, purple, and orange butterflies, and the hills wrap their arms around one comfortingly. Birds fill the vale with their songs, and always there is the deep silence of the night, broken occasionally by the high barking of the fox cubs, and the air-splitting cry of the owls."

Theresa Marshwood replied, "Poetical, indeed, Redvers, but I fear I would die of boredom, living in such a place. There is so little to do in the countryside. A young woman needs to pay visits to drawing rooms to connect with others, not wander in fields and lanes."

And you have such little poetry in your soul that I feel to inflict you on such a pleasant spot would be to insult it, he decided.

"Very well, Theresa," he sighed. "I shall go on my own."

"But how long will you be gone?" she asked, expecting him to change his mind.

"I imagine I shall not be long. After all, if you are, indeed, correct, there will be nothing to detain me!"

His last few words, however, she did not hear very well; he had turned his back, and was through the door before they could be deciphered.

Hugo Lockington, to whom Redvers made haste after his unfortunate scene with Theresa Marshwood, listened carefully to what his client had to say, which took ten minutes. Saunter through your gist as long as you like, thought Lockington; you are paying good money for my rapt attention. Once, Lockington had tried to calculate what he earned by the second, in his office, whose wood was so polished he could see his face in it, and he had rubbed his hands with glee at the sum.

During Redvers' peroration, Lockington had formed a church spire with his two forefingers, his remaining fingers, interlocked, forming a church roof. This gave him the air of a man taking his client seriously, and, the more money the client paid, the more seriously he took him.

"And so you see," concluded Redvers, "my position. I suppose you will tell me all is lost?"

"Not at all!" Lockington convulsed into life, and the church and its steeple fell apart. "No. No, indeed. I must admit that, though your position seems quite difficult, it is more common than you think."

"Then your words are succour to me, sir. Will you do all that is necessary? I, of course, will play my part. Some things are unavoidable, I suppose, and part of the rich tapestry of life."

"They are, indeed, Mr. Holditch. They most certainly are."

When his client had left, Lockington went over to a chest of drawers in which various legal documents were stored in alphabetical order. Opening the first drawer, marked A-F, he took out the first of a special collection, and put it onto his desk. Then he crouched to the bottom drawer, labelled V-Z, causing his knees to creak, and himself to make a complaint that he was not getting any younger, took out a second paper, and placed it next to the first. The drawer labelled G-M was next, and the paper extracted from it joined the other two. Finally, the fourth document was taken from the drawer marked N-U.

In a playful mood brewed with the intoxicating ingredients of power, Lockington moved the papers into a different order, then into another, till he tired of the game. He undid the ribbons binding them loosely, and read them carefully. Yes, they were as he remembered them.

His reflections were solemn. Only a man who is without a family, relatives living or unknown, can manage the fates of men and women, as they are decided by these wills. For if such a man could know, feel the hurt and surprise they inflict, then he would wash his hands of them, and become a clergyman, or an inoffensive journeyman. And such a man of solitude am I, knowing of no one who would admit to acknowledging me as their own flesh and blood, that, like the Almighty, I determine who gains and who loses, and reveal secrets – hoarded in these drawers – which change people's histories and identities, deprive them of what they see as rightfully theirs. It is all my responsibility, and it weighs heavily upon me, knowing what I do, more than on those whom the secrets damage or elevate. Yet I am paid well for the curse, for the sins of others, to lock the truth in such a chest till it emerges like some creature from the underworld.

Before Redvers left for the farm, and after his consultation with Hugo Lockington, he called upon Theresa Marshwood, who persisted with her dismissive attitude towards his 'rural infatuation', as she called his growing love for the countryside. Redvers said what he intended, and left her immediately, she in tears of anger, he relieved that he had been able to withdraw his offer of marriage, and his confidence bolstered by Lockington's judgement that his decision was triggered by an unshakeable belief that they were incompatible, and that to marry would be an act of folly.

Meanwhile, Toller set about helping Michael with the horses. Had I accepted Miranda's original offer, then I would know all the horses' names Michael now lovingly tells me, as if the horses were members of his family. Instead, patience must seep through my veins like a flagon of potent cider, and make me smile when he introduces them to me. He has done a good job with the breeding; the stables have fine mares and stallions.

"And which be Miss. Miranda's favourite?" Toller asked, winking.

"She rides several, though her favourite be Albert here, who jumps well. Soars over hedges, and mistress gives him his head, so that my heart be in my mouth when I sees her galloping away," said Michael.

For a day or two, Miranda avoided Toller, allowing him to settle, meet the others, forge relationships. Yet she was careful not to neglect him, and asked Charlotte if Michael had said how Toller was doing.

"Michael said that Toller got the hang of it, so much so that you might get to thinking that there bill soon be no need of my Michael. I says, 'Michael, you bend like your joints glued, these days.' 'Tis true,' he says, 'my riding at full tilt days be over, but I still help around the barn.' If you ask me, mistress, I be glad Toller come back to help. I got my bit of money coming in, and if you was considering sliding Toller into Michael's seat, then you shan't find me a-argumenting over it. We shall not starve," said Charlotte.

"Indeed, you shall not. You and Michael must stay here, as 'tas become more a home, and you be almost family to me and father. With a spickle of guidance, Toller will make a good one with the horses. When Michael says 'tis enough, then I shall pay him off properly, as befits a loyal worker."

"But he won't say. 'Tis his pride gets in the way like a Darset fog. No, mistress. *You* must tell him, so that no shame shall fall on him. And I sees 'tis almost time. Tell him when you will, but I do not want to see him so faded."

"Then I shall tell him tomorrow," said Miranda, hugging Charlotte. "And thank you. You have spoken wisely."

Charlotte wiped her eyes, and said, "A good mistress and true, 'tis certain."

When Miranda saw Toller, later, that day, he waited for her to speak first.

"At twilight, look for my lamp at the paling, and from there will we walk to your questions and answers."

"By the light of your lamp I will find you, and so will I seek to put right a wrong. That is my intention."

"And a good."

Miranda turned back to the house, and prepared for the evening by replenishing the oil lamp, and sealing a flask of a liquid she kept under lock and key.

"The moment is near," said Toller.

"And now to Michael. Like Toller in his quest, I visit him with the best intentions," said Miranda to the lamp.

The expectation of a strange experience which might release him from the past strangled Toller's voice, so that others thought him unwell or in a dark mood. He worked hard, trying to resist the inevitable speculation to which imagination gave birth. When Charlotte brought bread and cheese out to keep them going, he looked at them as if it would take too much effort to lift them to his mouth, let alone eat.

"You need food, Toller," said Michael gently. "All got to eat, 'less we sickening for something."

"I'll save it. I be fine, Michael. It be one of those times when my mind be crammed with other things jostling for my attention. 'Tis nothing, and 'twill pass."

"Then save it, as the blue vinney be moist yet crumbly, blue yet creamy, all which make a perfect, and only come along when the light be equal to the dark. 'Tis something I have noticed yet can't explain. Perhaps, 'tis God's decision, which most things be."

"But not all."

Michael looked up from his plate.

"Not all?"

"Humans, Michael. 'Tis humans who go against him sometimes."

"Oh, 'tis certain, Toller. Humans be contrary. Now, too much heavy thinking don't let the food go down proper, so let's to another subject which don't hurt the brain so. Now then, 'tis the horse fair soon, and you and I need ourselves another mare, says mistress. What say you?"

But Toller could only shrug. Horses were the last thing on his mind, that day.

When twilight came, and the pink sky had faded to dark blue, Toller began to look for the light by which Miranda said she would make her presence known. Soon he saw it, and it illuminated her face. Around her she wore a cloak, under which, in her left hand, she carried the flask she had prepared earlier.

At the paling, she stopped, looked beyond it onto the heath, her back to him. Toller wondered if he should call, but he did not want to alert others. He approached from a wide angle, so he would not surprise her by his sudden appearance.

"You are come," she said, maintaining her gaze ahead.

"I am, as you said."

She turned to him. In the amber glow of the lantern, her face acquired a beauty beyond that he had hitherto seen in her. Passing the lamp to him, and taking his other hand, she led him through the paling's gate. Her grip was firm, and a frisson, half-fear, half-arousal, rippled through him like the vibration in the air of a sudden clap of thunder.

"How far?" he asked.

"To the copse, where the badgers have built their setts. There in the natural bowl in the middle of the trees must we stop."

She knew every clump of grass, every entanglement of broom and thistle. When he stumbled, her grip tightened, steadied him.

It was too early for the badgers to be at play or feeding, but their holes were visible, like entrances into the bowels of the earth. When they stopped, Miranda released his hand, and showed him the flask in the other.

"You have done this before?" Toller asked nervously. "'Tis a form of magic or art I do not understand but must trust in."

"Nor do I understand why I am a conjuror, and if I do not have children, then the intuition dies with me. It is something I neither fear nor understand, but father once knew such a one, and 'twas Conjuror Sayer, an uncle I knew not I had, when I was all but lost to father. 'Tis part of my family, which, knowing none of my dead mother's, must survive, or the conjuring dies with them."

Then, if this works for me, so that I may carry out my plan drawn up with the best intentions, so will I love 'ee, and be a father to our children, for in your hand I felt a power beyond a human's, one no other woman could possess.

She took off her cloak, and laid it on the ground, careful not to drop the flask. Kneeling, she gestured to him to do likewise.

"I am scared.

"The names?"

"Roddy Cattistock."

"And the woman?"

"Mattie Venn."

"Drink," she ordered, after she had drunk some of the liquid.

He sniffed it; she had put it to his lips, and he had caught the mould of the soil, heaven and hell.

"I dare not," he said.

Miranda's black eyes had widened, and when he, at last, drank, they became badger setts indistinguishable from those beneath the roots of the trees. They became even wider, till out of them ran badgers, which began snapping at him. Miranda's voice melted in his ears, and he could not stop the badgers biting him.

"I shall be eaten alive!" he cried, but no sound came from his mouth. He closed his eyes, and, mouthful by mouthful, they devoured him, though he felt no pain, only the soft sensation of them moving up to his head. "A few more bites and I am dead, gone for ever!" He opened his eyes to see badgers trying to chew his neck, and then they set about his head. "Miranda, save me!" was his final plea, as he tried to stay alive. "They are eating me!" His final word stretched into minutes, as if to end it would acknowledge his death. Then nothing. Nothing.

The lantern's oil was all but spent when he became conscious again. He felt cool air on his skin, and the tickling of fluttering moths. Miranda had already put on her clothes, and was looking at his naked body. Toller had drunk more than her; she knew the correct amount for a woman of her size and strength. Her father had shown her what Conjuror Sayer had taught him. The first three times, Miranda had been sick, and then it had worked, and she had answered all her father's questions without hesitation, and he had been pleased with her, and knew that she really had the intuition.

When Toller saw her sitting there, he quickly covered himself up. Even in the weak light of the lantern, he knew that she could see all of him, and that she had lain with him.

"Roddy Cattistock," she said matter-of-factly.

"Help me," he pleaded, and she passed his clothes to him.

"Go to the man as naked as you and as big as the hillside. There his phallus stands tall, and he cannot be missed. You have heard of him?"

When Toller had his trousers on again, he asked, "Cerne Abbas?"

She laughed, remembered what had passed between them.

"Cerne Abbas."

"And?"

"There you will find him – and a woman."

So, he did betray her, thought Toller. Ah well! At last she will know the truth.

"And Mattie Venn?"

"Go to Evershot Farm, and there you will find her whispering to cows."

"And all is well with her? The baby? Little Nightingale?"

"To Evershot, Toller, and there you will find Mattie. Do what you must, once and for all."

This night, Miranda said to herself, you have given yourself to me, and I to you. And if my intuition proves correct, then I will not be the last of the Misterton conjurors, for I see a daughter, just like me, who will have her natural mother. This I know will come to pass.

Chapter twenty-nine.

"And what will you tell the others why I am gone again, so soon after coming?" asked Toller.

"There is no denying that you blow in and out of these parts like a Dorset gale, but the truth will shield you from rumour. Tell them that you must see friends, and that you will return and stay," advised Miranda.

"But what if they cannot be found?"

"You do not trust me?"

Toller drew her to him, smelt her hair, sighed, and said, "I do. Of all people, it is you I trust."

"Then go," she said, easing herself free from his tight embrace, "for the sooner you are gone, the sooner we shall be together again. And I must prepare myself for a visit from Zenobia Godmanstone, who has sent a scribbled note to say that she must speak to me on an urgent matter. Within seven days, you will return. Then you and I will talk about what must be, in the future."

He kissed her lips, saw her close her eyes, felt that a love between them was beginning to froth like cherry blossom.

The prospect of seeing his former employer hastened his departure. For a moment, a flush of embarrassment appeared on his cheeks at the memory of his failure to manage Durnovaria Brewery's debts. I tried my best, he remembered, but my efforts came to nothing.

He set off for Evershot Farm, where he would find Mattie,

pushing, nudging, sweet-talking, and milking cows. Yet Miranda had said nothing about Nightingale, had left doubt that began to burrow into him like an insect a windfall plum. If anything had happened to Mattie's baby, then there would be no visit to Cerne Abbas to find Roddy Cattistock. And the woman Miranda had seen in their fumes-induced writhing: who was she? The insect grew bigger, gorged on a fruity flesh both sweet and sour.

As he walked, he thought about Michael, who had asked, "And you're coming back? Got used to you again." There had been a fear, in his eyes, that the retirement Charlotte had been encouraging him to take might recede with Toller, till it disappeared.

Then, as if an adder had slithered across his path from the grass, Toller suddenly stopped. The mistake he had made in going firstly to Evershot Farm was all too obvious now. Mattie needed to know about the other woman before going to see Cattistock. It might change matters entirely if he had been married already. Turning up with a child might be such a shock that Cattistock might refuse to acknowledge any responsibility. No, Toller would go to Cerne Abbas, to the priapic man as big as a hillside.

When he saw the potent hunter-warrior, club raised threateningly or in celebration, he was reminded of Miranda, and what had happened in the copse. Who had done this, all those years ago? he wondered. Who had dared to outline in white this proud display of manhood for all to see?

Following the river, he went down into the streets, heard choirboys in the church. I must ask at the inn, he decided. Cerne Abbas be a size for all to know each other. If Miranda be right, Roddy Cattistock will be a neighbour to some one.

The candles' flames trembled when he opened the inn door. A fire cracked, cleared its throat. I hate what feels like an intrusion, the stares, the quiet that settles till I am welcomed warily by the innkeeper or his wife.

"You from these parts?"

"Dorchester."

"You sound more Bridport," observed a woman.

"Yes and no."

"Then you don't know whether you're coming or going!" laughed the woman. "A man needs to know where he's heading."

"And so will I once I find the man I'm looking for."

The others were reluctant to look Toller in the eye, fidgeted.

"Which might be soon, might not, depending on who's asking for him. You don't come this way. Least, I don't recognise you, and 'twould take a good reason for any one of us to tell a stranger where he abides."

Toller sat down, his legs aching. This place, he felt, sits alone, on a road to Dorchester, but cautiously, its people vigilant to strangers, protective of their own.

"I bring him news as good as any to be heard in the normal way of things. I ask nothing of him but that he listens to it. Roddy Cattistock lives by himself?"

"'Tis a sad story, his, though one for *him* to tell and not any of us, for each one of us has his own, a happy or sad, and no one tells his tale like himself, knowing it best, and therefore be unlikely to drape it with garlands or gargoyles."

"Then, good lady, please to bring me whatever food you can spare, and as much as a plate can hold, for if I do not eat, having followed the road from Misterton Manor, I shall die. Then, if you will be kind enough to direct me to Roddy Cattistock, I will deliver my news."

The inn-keeper's wife said, "Sir, our harshness should not offend you, but 'tis a natural thing when strangers come. Stay tonight, as 'tis dark, and the paths turn upon themselves betimes, and there be a marsh or two to swallow you, if you baint careful. A room we have that, when the fire has been made up, will suit your purposes, for a modest sum."

This acceptance of him as a *bona fide* guest reignited conversation, and soon Toller settled near the hearth, where he could avoid further questions, yet absorb the pleasant atmosphere as well as the food, and warmth from the fire.

His meal consisted of lamb chops and potatoes, and he sensed the others watching him out of the corner of their eyes. Such a strange feeling overcame him that, after the last potato had gone, he bade goodnight to those who nodded as he passed.

"'Tis a small but tidy," said the woman.

Only her face was visible in the eerie candlelight, on the landing, outside Toller's room.

"Perfect," said Toller.

"In the morning, we will point you in the direction of Mr. and Mrs. Cattistock's cottage."

She made to descend, but Toller called, "He is married, then?"

The inn-keeper's wife turned and said, "No, sir. Mrs. Cattistock be a widow, though a sprightly, and 'tis said that her son will never marry, but heed me not, sir, as 'tis speckilation, the worst of which be mere prattling, for which we women get all the blame!"

Toller heard her chuckling to herself, all the way to the bottom of the stairs.

"Goodnight, dear lady. You have held your candle to more than my door, this night."

The next day, the inn-keeper's wife gave him directions to Cattistock's cottage, to which he set off with a long, purposeful stride. At the end of my visit, he will know of Nightingale, and then I must to Evershot Farm, for if what I intend is to be realised, then it must be so quickly, for the freshness of their reacquaintance reunites them as lovers, or separates them as strangers for eternity.

When he knocked on Cattistock's door, there was no reply. Peering through the window, he saw the dull embers of that morning's fire. Not too long gone, he murmured, and he cannot be far, as I have seen no one on my way. I passed this house yesterday, so towards the naked warrior must he have gone. But such a sight a mother should not endure, he thought, except it be considered a chalky jest of some ancient fellow keen to leave his mark on Time's earthy canvas.

The land rose. He did not doubt Miranda. The slope seemed an unusual place to confront Cattistock with the news that he had a daughter. And yet not, for as the symbol of fertility came into view, it was the most appropriate of rendez-vous.

There, beneath the giant's feet, were Cattistock and his mother. Her arm was linked to his, and they were looking up the hill. Toller did not wish to surprise them, disturb what he assumed to be a daily walk. Even from his spot, he could see extensively the countryside, had views that had already imbued him with peaceful thoughts.

When they edged across, not up, the hill, to make their stroll less taxing, Toller increased his pace, till he came within calling distance. Cattistock sensed someone following, and glanced over his shoulder. Just another visitor come to view a landmark well known to local folk, he supposed.

Yet the follower was coming ever closer, as if intent on catching them up. Toller's pace had made him breathe more heavily, and Cattistock turned, while his mother continued to face forward.

"Roddy Cattistock?" gasped Toller.

"Who asks?"

"Toller Burstock, who brings you news you may or may not wish to hear in your mother's presence."

Cattistock's brow tightened. How does he know she is my mother? he wondered.

Without turning, Mrs. Cattistock asked, "Why do you bring such news that may not be fit for my ears?"

"I bring it in good faith."

"Then speak, stranger," said Cattistock.

But as Toller began, his voice became strangled. Mrs. Cattistock had turned, and her eyes were yellow, without irises, and covered by a thick, ulcerated film. Toller gasped, took a step backwards, and nearly lost his footing.

"I am listening," said Mrs. Cattistock. "My hearing is excellent, and in Roddy I have good eyes."

Toller was mindful that Miranda expected his return within seven days, so made his way to Evershot Farm, after he had given Cattistock the news that after he had left Mattie alone at the altar, she had given birth to his daughter.

"And how do you know that I live in Cerne Abbas?" had asked Cattistock. "I told no one."

"There are not enough creases in the hills to hide us all."

"I hide from no one."

Toller had ended the conversation with, "Do what you will with the news I have brought you. I come in good faith: to let a father know he has a daughter who lives with her mother at Evershot Farm."

Cattistock had watched Toller go, had begun to answer the questions his mother asked.

Farmer Evershot was wiping his brow when Toller arrived in the farmyard. Loading the hay for the cows was tiring. He had imagined the bales to be a foreign foe, and had thrust the pitchfork into them to ensure their death.

"Come for day labouring?" he asked. "Might have some tomorrow, but all's taken today."

Somehow, he guessed the stranger was there for another reason. Toller's clothes were not worn at the knees, frayed at the bottoms, and he carried a bag over his shoulder.

"Come to see Mattie Venn and her child, Nightingale."

Farmer Evershot scratched his head, and asked, "Now who says there be a such here?"

"I be Toller Burstock, her brother. Tell her that I be here with some important news for her."

"She say she was here?"

"No, but . . ."

"You got the wrong place, Toller Burstock. Baint no one of that name here."

Two weeks passed, and the farmer's wife showed her husband a letter, and he said, "There always be a way with things. Always a way, as sure as lambs be born to ewes."

It was a Friday when Roddy Cattistock rode his cart into the farmyard. He had taken care with his appearance, had put on his best clothes, and trimmed his beard. As Farmer Evershot strode into view, the chickens gathered round him to be fed.

"Can I help you?" he asked.

"I've come to see Mattie Venn. I believe she is one of your milkmaids."

"Then you are wrong."

"But I was told reliably that –"

"Reliable don't come near the truth, which be that she baint with us no more."

"So I've missed her?"

"Death has a step quicker than most. We buried her a week or two ago. A good worker, too."

"Dead?" Roddy gasped. "Mattie gone?"

"The feber did for her till she could scarce breathe. She never recovered, and hab left her daughter without a parent to her name. In decent time, we will hand her over to the parish, for though we be farming folk, used to rough, hard ways, we aint young any more, and have never been blessed with children of our own."

"The parish? Oh, poor child! No mother. 'Tis a cruel world. May I see the mite? You see, I am her true father, though she has never seen me before."

Farmer Evershot looked at his wife, as if seeking a decision.

"'Twon't do any harm, I suppose, though if you have come to

claim kin, then you best go to the parish, and fill in all the proper papers."

"She be my daughter, and I will fill in anything put in front of me."

Nightingale was awake in her cot in a room in the farmhouse. On the verge of crying, she wanted attention. Cattistock lifted her up, and said, "There, my pretty chick. And have I found you, at last? I shall never let you out of my sight. If only I had not had to leave your mother! And my mother, who has gone blind, could not have known that her infection would cause such separation between us. But I will never leave you again, my sweet, and if your dear mother is listening in her cold, cold grave, may she forgive me going to my mother's side. Such a life I could not have inflicted on a young wife, whom I have not stopped loving for a second."

The tears ran down his cheeks, and he held Nightingale closely, so that he could smell Mattie on her.

He turned to take his child into daylight so that he could see her more clearly, and waiting for him were Farmer Evershot and his wife.

"She the look of you around the mouth," observed the farmer.

"And dear Mattie around the eyes," added his wife.

"And, oh, I will always take care of her. I must do it not only for Nightingale but for the memory of dear Mattie, who be chosen by God."

At that moment, a figure stepped into the corridor from one of the rooms. Cattistock blinked, gasped.

"What? Come to haunt me so soon?" he cried.

"No, Roddy. Not to haunt but forgive."

"You are her spirit, escaped from the grave? My eyes deceive me, surely."

"No grave have I yet, Roddy, nor expect to have for many years, if the Lord be willing. But now that I see and hear your commitment to our daughter, so am I risen to forgive you, and to ask you to play a part in her life, so that she does not have to face a future without the love of her father."

Mattie stepped forward and held out her hand.

Roddy hesitated, then took it.

"Real and warm."

"Tis certain."

"And now we must leave you in peace," said the farmer's wife, "for 'tis wondrous that under this humble and mossy thatch such a couple, once blown apart like straw in a gale, be back together again. There must be words to pass, one to the other, till Nightingale's future be agreed."

Alone, Mattie, Roddy, and Nightingale took one word at a time, till it was mutually understood that they all had a life together. Mattie told Roddy about her honorary brother, the man who had told him of her whereabouts, and how she had planned to test Roddy's feelings. Farmer Evershot and his wife had taken Roddy's letter to her. When she had decided on her plan, she had enlisted their help. They had listened carefully, and Farmer Evershot had said, "'Taint the usual thing to be going on, on a farm, but we all grip, at one time in life, to something or other." In turn, Roddy told her of the letter, written by Doctor Hinton, and bearing the news of his mother's sudden blindness, that had torn him away from his wedding day.

"But why did you not send word to me? I would have understood," asked Mattie.

"She had, *has*, no one. I am her eyes. She has no one else."

"Then I must be another pair for her. I thought you disliked me, even loved another."

The tears flowed from Roddy's eyes again.

"I did not know you were with child. I would surely have –"

But Mattie put her finger to his lips.

"Only look forward now, Roddy. That is all that matters now." Nightingale started to cry. "There is time to make up."

Chapter thirty.

Miranda took Zenobia's green felt hat and black coat, and avoided the lifeless eyes of the fox fur. The short journey from Dorchester in the trap had taken less time than usual. Zenobia's haste had been caused by two things, the first a package in her hand.

"There. For you. A present, but not from me. Undo it. It has been a while in the making, but I wanted you to read it before me."

"A book?"

She ran her fingertips over its cover, and read the title: **Jude the Obscure**. Had Hardy really listened to her when she had given him the idea of the ambition of a young man who wanted to improve himself? Something, some instinct, had driven her to share Toller's overwhelming urge to make something of himself. That, it had seemed to her, was worthy of recording, as a celebration of the human spirit.

"All yours."

"Thank you. And am I to be pleased with the story?"

"I don't know, but he has signed your copy. He asked me to tell you that your idea had so much to recommend it that he took it up, and, like a blacksmith at his forge, wrought the shape of the story into the one you now possess. You must forgive him, he said, if you feel the ending too sad, but it is how he sometimes feels all such good ideas end up. It appeared, last year, in instalments. And you are not to feel guilty that your idea is the one to put an end to his story-telling, which he suspects to be the case. Personally, I think we shall see more of his work; he suffers, I am sure, from post-publication fatigue. But think, Miranda: Thomas Hardy's literary career might be brought indirectly to a full stop by you!"

Miranda sighed, and thought: I shall read it, but will keep my ideas to myself from now on. This sits uneasily with me. He has many years to live, and will surely discover the will to write again.

"I shall look forward to reading it. We should all make the most of our talents."

"I agree, but we are human, all with our own particular limits. I come also with the news that the soldier who shot Arthur Abbott, one of my draymen, a long time ago, will be sentenced, next week. Apparently, he has confessed to the crime, and has offered no motive for it. Of course, you can already feel some of the good folk of Dorchester bristling with morbid excitement at the prospect of a public execution. There has been none for years, but this seems a particularly unusual case. What is to be done, Miranda? He appears unwilling to appeal against his conviction. In the name of civilization, we must not return to the barbaric practice of hanging. How many more folk will swing and sway in the name of justice? What can be done?"

"But if he has done it, then the law of the land must prevail. To take the life of someone so young is to invite the wrath of the people."

"Arthur worked hard as a drayman, I don't doubt, but he was sly, a bit of a ladies' man, the word is. There is talk that his death was revenge for meddling with the soldier's fiancée."

Puzzled, Miranda screwed up her face.

"I don't follow you one little bit, Zenobia. He has killed another man, and he may hang. That seems a strong possibility."

"But what if he were provoked beyond endurance? We are all capable of extreme anger when wronged in some terrible way."

"Do you believe it was revenge? Surely, he would have made that point in his defence, in court."

"Oh, Miranda, do you know anything about the passion of men? Where their pride is concerned, they will do anything to hide their vulnerability."

"I know little, it is true, but it seems that it is too late to save him."

"No, Miranda, it is never too late until the trapdoor opens. There is time yet to persuade the judge to save him."

"But what can we do?"

"Firstly, we must await the judge's decision. A life of imprisonment may well seem unbearable, but it is infinitely better than having your neck broken in the full glare of the public."

Nicholas Misterton sat at the table, and peered intently at the newspaper, whose words moved as if they were a recently disturbed colony of ants. Gradually, the tumult subsided, and he was able to make sentences, which combined to inform him of events in Dorset. Turning the pages, slowly, he scanned the headlines, to see which article appealed to him.

Miranda was sitting in her favourite chair, reading the story Thomas Hardy had sent as an informal acknowledgement of the idea she had offered for it. Endowed with a conjuror's instinct, she had felt that such an eminent writer would be able to make something of the history of a man who had struggled to overcome setbacks, to lead a life of which he could be proud.

Such moments of peace, when father and daughter were reading silently, were enjoyed by both, but, on this particular occasion, the atmosphere changed when Nicholas said, "Eyes not getting any better, but baint this the Toller Burstock who be here, one minute, and gone the next? If so, he be on his way again, before long."

Miranda looked up from her book.

"You speak in riddles, father."

“’Tis the way with the Mistertons, whose patterns be in you, though it baint plain in your speaking yet, on account that you be your mother’s girl, too. Her words used to glitter like dew in the early morning sun.” Nicholas looked back through time, smelt her again, knew that while he could do that, he was alive, that *she* was alive, too. “Your mother was a rainbow: reached over Dorset, from Devon, with all her colours, and some I aint seen since. And then she disappeared, and all I could see were the things behind where she had been.”

“Come, father. No tears. Tell me what you have seen.”

“Come see for yourself, as I have smudged my eyes, and though I can read and write tolerable – thanks to Master Tom – I fear I won’t do him justice.”

Miranda went to her father, keeping her page with her forefinger of her right hand.

“What am I looking for?”

“The words *Toller Burstock*, who be summoned to Lyme Regis, if I baint mistaken.”

Miranda found and read the article. There be twists and turns in this man, she thought, but the sooner he finds out from this Hugo Lockington what be to his advantage, the better.

She put down her book; though reluctant to do so, she felt there was no time to lose in letting Toller see the article.

“And will you go?” she asked him in his stable.

Toller offered her the newspaper, but she gestured to keep it.

“I will, my dear, and while I am gone, you will go to St. Michael’s, and there speak to the vicar.”

“And why so?”

“To fix the date of our wedding.”

Against his chest, she sobbed.

“Then there be things to sort out, so, go on your way, my husband-to-be, and when you return, there be one more thing for you to do, and then ’tis done.”

John Trevelyan was hurrying back to the house where Maude, as Hepsy was now called, was a prisoner, for her own safety, argued John. He had thought a period of two months long enough to let the news of the stabbing in Bridport blow in and out of Dorchester. And he always returned to the same words: "I have been a fool, I have."

"John Trevelyan?" said a man, standing in John's way. "If 'tis 'ee, then 'ee be not dead, as some hab cast abroad. 'Tas been the season for those who drink with us to scatter rumours as a farmer his seed, but as you be resurrected, I say to 'ee 'tis good to see 'ee alive and well. Will 'ee be returning to your seat at the inn? We have kept it empty since you were last in, though some be claiming all sorts: that you be fled to Australia to make your fortune; that you be wedded to a comely maid from Wareham way; and that you be the murderer going around leaving daggers between men's shoulder blades, in Bridport."

"Why, 'tis my good friend Allington Sherborne. Dead I am not – though I feel almost a corpse with blood all dried to powder – and 'tas been only a sickness which has robbed me of a man's strength and determination to drink with his friends."

"Then I am satisfied, and will buy 'ee your first drink, on your return to that vacant seat. Many a time, one of us hab said, 'Why, I am sure that be the ghost of John Trevelyan, who –'"

"'Tis kind, but I must hurry."

John bowed his head, and continued his journey, conscious that he must not allow his ghostly pallor, and thinness of face, to give rise to further speculation.

His house was tucked up a side-street, squashed between two others in a shy row people passed on their way to the top of the town. One window upstairs, one next to the door, John's house looked part of the other two. By the dead grate, his mother, who had not been out of the house since it had become Hepsy's refuge, was darning a sock, and Maude watched her, planning her escape from her gaolers. In Mrs. Trevelyan's pocket was the key to the front door.

"Don't let her go outside, mother. 'Tis for her own good," John had instructed, fearful that she would fall into the hands of the police.

"Don't 'ee worry, John. She be safe with me, but you aint answered my question yet. At least, not so's I understand the answer. You says you saw the drunkard grab her, and that she had a knife in her hand. You tried to drag him off, and then –"

"Mother, enough of this. It was dark. We struggled, and then he fell to the ground."

"And there was blood on you and Maude when you got here late, that night. She scrubbed at it as if it were a badge of guilt."

"Stop, mother. Enough. Soon, she shall leave here, and must make a life for herself elsewhere."

Slow, heavy footsteps could be heard above. Mother and son looked at the door that gave onto a narrow, creaking staircase.

Maude opened the door, and entered.

"It is time for me to confess. This burden weighs on me like a tombstone. I cannot endure this confinement any more. I have fallen a great way from being the daughter of a prosperous farmer to a murderer on the run. Let me go, John, I beg you. You have acted in my best interest, scooped me up into your cart, as you were passing, but 'tis time for me to face justice. Perhaps, if I confessed to the police, the judge will be lenient with me when he hears that the man was drunk, and tried to take advantage of me. John, help me. If you could only know how I long for the punishment, whatever it is, that awaits."

"Punishment is reserved for those that are guilty."

Mrs. Trevelyan put down her sock, which was now mended.

"But I *am* guilty, John. I took a man's life."

"But he tried to have a man's way with you!" reminded Mrs. Trevelyan. "Don't throw your life away for such a vile one as him!"

“You cannot go,” said John. “To confess to murder in court would be wrong.”

“How so?” said Maude.

John’s eyes bulged white in the gloom.

“Because you did not kill him. ’Twas *I* who held the knife as it went into his back.”

“You? How so? I took the knife from my bag, just to warn him. It was in my hand. We grappled, and I told him that I had slit pigs’ throats before, and that another wouldn’t make any difference. You tried to pull him off me, but he would not let go. I tried to help you, but we all fell over. Then I heard a sharp cry, and he choked. He looked up at me from the floor, and I saw the knife in his back. You lifted me onto your cart, and we rode out of Bridport. My hands had his blood on them, and I scrubbed them, in your bucket, till my skin was almost raw. So why do you say that *you* killed him?”

“She must stay here, or *you* will hang, John. Why did you tell her? Now you are doomed, one way or another!” cried Mrs. Trevelyan, wringing her hands.

“What you say, Hepsy, be not as clear as you think,” said John, “and I have wrongly let you believe that you killed him, but the fact is it was not *your* knife which ended his life but mine.”

John went over to the mantelpiece, on which stood a clock, and leaned on it, in a casual manner strangely at odds with the situation.

“You stabbed him to save my life? Or was it your own for which you feared? Oh, why did we not just stand our ground and report what really happened? The truth will always come to light. It hounds the guilty, shakes them from their shallow sleep. Why did we rush from the scene?”

“So many questions, Hepsy, that I must answer, and I will do so honestly, as honesty has been my watchword, all my life, but my only concern was to avoid arrest for what was not of our making. Whose judgement has failed when thrown into such a panic?

Reason flees when all is chaos. Flight has been man's reaction to danger since the dawn of time."

"Say no more!" advised his mother. "You have said enough to hang yourself, and she will walk away. I wish you had not stopped to help her, that night."

Hepsy said, "He is a good man, and came to my rescue. Do not blame him for that."

"Though the knife was in my hand when it killed him, I did not strike a blow. 'Tis true I drew my blade, but when we fell, his frame was so big that I had no time to throw it away. I tried to protect myself with my right arm, fearing he would crush me. It is a knife with the sharpest point in Dorset. Its blade I whet daily. 'Tas been my companion since my father gave it to me, and now 'tas gone."

"And my knife?" said Hepsy.

"I expect the police have it."

Hepsy's thoughts were as sharp as Mrs. Trevelyan's needle, and she said, "'Tis our word against a dead man's. Only moments before, I was at the inn, and they will vouch for my mood. I had no inkling I was about to be attacked. Only the fleeing of the scene is against us."

"But don't you see?" said Mrs. Trevelyan, fearful that honesty would see her son jailed. "They will see your flight as a sign of guilt. You must not go to the police."

"I beg you to let me go. Maude, too, is now dead, but I am reborn," pleaded Hepsy.

"I must think," said John. "I shall wait and then decide. Remain just one more hour, and let me think of a way for each of us to part from the other without destroying us both."

He left, and the door remained unlocked. Hepsy could walk away, even overpower John's frail, willowy mother if she tried to prevent her. But if John bore false witness, to save himself, despite his confession of what really happened, she might hang, she thought.

Yet an hour was not required by John to help him think straight. A newspaper vendor was shouting the headlines to anyone who cared to listen. John asked him to repeat himself, which he did. Without hesitation, John bought a copy, and held it up to the weak light of a streetlamp. He read the front page twice before he began to hasten home to share the news.

Out of breath and agitated, he ordered Hepsy and his mother to pay attention. The oil in the lamp on the table was low, and John squinted as he read from the newspaper held closely to his face.

"But is it possible?" said Hepsy.

"It cannot be," mumbled Mrs. Trevelyan.

"But it is," insisted John. "Not only have they arrested an associate of the man, but the suspect has confessed!"

Hepsy began to tremble.

"How can a man confess to a murder he did not commit?" she said.

"'Tis passing strange," remarked Mrs. Trevelyan. "Does the report talk of a different man, a different murder?"

John scratched his chin, and said, "No. It refers to the night I was passing. I'd been to Bridport market, sold a pot or two, bits and bobs. It describes the dead man. It's him, all right."

Hepsy walked unsteadily to the door, the other two oblivious of her.

"And a man who knows him has been charged? Why, then you are both in the clear! Do it say that the associate hab confessed? Why, 'tis all settled, then!" said Mrs. Trevelyan.

"It says that the two men had quarreled, that very day, in Chideock. Though it was, no doubt, the cider talking, the accused was heard to say that he'd kill him just as soon as look at him. Seems he was drunk as a lord, early evening. Folk a-plenty heard him say it, and I guess he was too fuddled with the fumes to remember anything he'd done or said, that day."

"But it don't serve you two to go and get yourselves all trapped like lobsters in a pot, do it, Maude?"

But Hepsy had run quickly out of sight, out of Dorchester, under a moonless, starless night, knowing that the knife with which she had been warning the man was not the one that had killed him. Yet I cannot betray the man who stopped to rescue me, she thought. In good faith, he helped me, and, sometimes, strange events conspire to save a good man at the expense of a bad one. It be Providence, one way or another.

Chapter thirty-one.

Toller chose to take the coach to Lyme. Michael had suggested a boat from Weymouth, but Toller had laughed, and said, “And what if a storm a-stirs, and dashes us all on rocks we can’t see? Besides, the very sight of rolling waves a-clattering the cliffs makes me giddy.”

“A man chooses his own way to travel in this world, so go on the coach if you must, though you’ll all be a-squash with folk, and maybe they’ll be coughing and sneezing all over you!”

“The coach it be, Michael, and I am grateful to you for helping out while I be gone.”

“’Tis nothing.”

“’Tis something.”

The coach was full, though without the slightest hint of a cough or cold among the passengers, who all stretched their legs at Bridport, where Toller ate the bread and blue vinney Miranda had put in his bag. A man and a woman looked at him strangely, at last concluded that it must have been Toller’s cheese and not his personal hygiene that had been responsible for the unpleasant smell coming from him.

At Lyme, Toller bought a meal at an inn on Broad Street. Through one of its windows, he could see the indigo sea below him. The sun was smiling, and the waves glittered. That view, combined with a delicious dish of crab and buttered potatoes, induced a feeling of well-being so strong that he felt a keen anticipation of what advantage his meeting with Hugo Lockington would bring.

The office in which the lawyer would see him was, in fact, further up the street, and had an even better view than Toller had earlier enjoyed. Toller arrived but had not sent word that he was coming, so Lockington stared at him over round spectacles, as if deciding whether to admit him fully.

"I be Toller Burstock come about the notice. By all accounts in the newspaper, there be something to my advantage," said Toller.

"Then you'd better come in, so I can take down some particulars. I must be certain you are the person to whom I must convey wishes made by a deceased client."

Toller sat in the chair Lockington indicated. Lockington peeped under papers, opened various drawers until he found what he was looking for. The clock's ticking grew louder, till Toller could bear the tension no more, and said, "I have some connection with a dead person?"

"Indeed, you have, Mr. Burstock. A connection on the likes of which my profession feeds. I come across many such, and some have not yet seen the light of day. Am I to be blamed, Mr. Burstock, if my notices receive no response? Am I the one to be held responsible for people never claiming what is lawfully theirs? No, sir, I am not, I tell you, though the knowledge of it all is a weighty burden on me. I search high and low, some people escape me, and in the searching, so do I lose the time and chance to make a life others enjoy: a home, a good woman, the delights of the fireside."

"Then please tell me, before your clock explodes, what my connection with the dead person is. This is a complete mystery to me."

"All in good time, Mr. Burstock, all in good time. One's history cannot be rushed where the law is concerned."

"History? Whose? I do not follow."

"Patience, Mr. Burstock, for I have on my desk all that I require to satisfy your natural curiosity."

"Then please begin, as the sooner it is over, the sooner I will know what advantage awaits me."

Lockington removed the ribbon from the document that had been brought to his office by a young man, who had refused to give his name. All that Lockington could remember about him was that he had long blond hair, and said he had read it, judged it to be a matter for a learned man of the law.

"And your name, sir?" Lockington had asked. "'Taint important who I be, but 'tis vital that it be delivered to the man it is addressed to,' the young man said. It is to his credit that he took the trouble to find me. Had he thrown it onto the fire, out of jealousy or spite, then you would have spent the rest of your life in ignorance of circumstances, which, in my own view, ought to find the light of day."

Toller fidgeted, sensing that the reference to circumstances insinuated information he had not expected. Lockington again looked over the rim of his glasses, seemed to extract a curious enjoyment of the power he held over his visitor.

"Whatever be writ on whatever paper, I am ready for. Delay no further the heart of the matter."

"Many a man has declared himself ready but has found that it was not so. Nevertheless, as you are here, you must be satisfied, according to the law. Firstly, you say you are Toller Burstock. Can you give me some particulars of your life, which would persuade me to accept you are whom you say you are?"

"Indeed. I be Toller Burstock, and a shepherd I was on a small scrap of land, a field or two left by my father, who passed soon after my mother had been taken. The cottage was a small, just up from Dugdale Farm, and in the shadow of Pilsdon Pen."

"And can you name any of your neighbours?"

"'Tis passing strange, this question, as I could make up a name and you would be no wiser."

"But you are wrong, Mr. Burstock, as I know them all. I ask this question so you can prove you are the Toller Burstock for whom this letter was intended."

Lockington pulled the letter in question from under a book, and held it out of reach, as an inducement to Toller to answer.

"There be an old man, a cantankerous, a wizened, a vile, whose habits I care not for, and who went out of his way to annoy me."

Lockington placed the letter on the polished mahogany writing desk top, and slid it towards Toller, who picked it. The handwriting was spidery, but he was able to decipher his own name. He opened it with trembling hand, as if fearful that he might unleash some unexpected terror, and as he read, Lockington studied him closely for signs that he understood what its contents meant.

"And now you know," said Lockington matter-of-factly.

"All those years," whispered Toller. "And not a sign."

"It is more common than you think."

"I imagine so, and yet . . ."

"At least you are remembered. Others like you die in ignorance, in squalor, deprived of what is due, at least in the eyes of the law."

"Father never said."

"Fathers sometimes don't. It's the ignominy, more often than not, the need to protect people, loved ones."

Toller stood up, sighed.

"I don't know what to say. Does anyone else know?"

Lockington shrugged.

"Legally, the money is yours. I have seen many such cases, and I have found that it is best not to question those who have passed into the other world. Your father, God rest his soul, has said all he wanted."

Toller nodded.

"Do what you must. It is a considerable sum."

"You are, indeed, wise, Mr. Burstock. Not every father does as Forston Sampford has."

Outside, Toller looked up to the sky.

Oh, mother! he cried inside. Of all men!

The thought of returning home to Dugdale Farm was very much affected by Hepsy's acknowledgement that it was not home at all, as she had known it. It was only a property now owned by Redvers Holditch, to whom her father had bequeathed it.

Am I pretending that the house in which I was born is still mine, with all its memories of father and his high hopes for me? How he would despise me if he saw my hesitant, fearful footsteps, as I make my way through Broadoak, with its tiny church and a few thatched cottages grown along the wayside! Yet I admit that I feel a stranger in what was *my* country lane, with heady views towards Pilsdon Pen, in the distance. And the reason I decided to return – why anyone who has suffered as much as me would – seems trivial, she thought.

Yet though she occasionally talked to herself, stooped to examine the rose hips entwined in the hedgerow, she continued to Dugdale Farm, intent on seeing it again, and asking Redvers Holditch if he might, despite her father's wishes, bestow some of his good fortune on her, not in a monetary sense, but in the form of some menial employment, such as housekeeper or milkmaid. And what has become of dear Mattie and her child? Forston Sampford: does he still lurch drunkenly down the lane, and rant at the world, till he is once again indoors?

As she neared her former home, she heard the distant thud of an axe biting into wood. She guessed the sound was coming from the back of the farmhouse. If 'tis Redvers, then I am timely come, and the peace of the early evening, which he is sure to have come to value, will not be disturbed. I come in all humility, and wish to spend my days in the one place I truly love.

And was that the path with its straight edges I used to walk up? I cannot be sure, for the garden looks the same yet somehow different. Time blunts my memory: the house seems bigger, and the vegetable garden is new. 'Tis the work of a dedicated man, for the rows are as a regiment of soldiers, and the shoots are strong, have all been fed by manure, she noticed.

The chopping stopped. Blackbirds trilled. Hepsy walked round the back of the house.

"'Tis you, Redvers?" she called, anxious not to allow him, a stranger, to be alarmed by her sudden appearance.

There was no reply, so she called again, more loudly. So, my brother has tended the garden, which has lost much of its wildness. I will knock, make him aware that I am here.

No one answered, so she looked through the window, but the light played tricks, and she could see nothing but her own image. My beauty has faded, she lamented. Father, whose presence I yet feel in the air, used to call me his rose, but my petals have fallen, and I am a stem of thorns.

When the words came from behind, she started, flattened herself against the warm cottage wall.

The man before her bent to the ground, plucked a harebell, and gave it to her.

"What do *you* here?" she asked.

"Redvers Holditch be my master now. What do *you* here?"

"I come for work, a roof over my head from him."

Miles look puzzled, tipped back his hat.

"A roof? Then you are in luck, Hepsy, as the farm be my responsibility now, and, as you once took me in during a snow blizzard that snatched your father, so now will I repay your kindness."

Hepsy looked down at her harebell, a reminder of his liking of her, of his earnest kisses, his passionate promises in the lane.

"Let me think, Miles, and tell you what has brought me here, for there are things that have happened to me that have drained me of the looks I had when you knew me, and kissed me till the stars swirled and made me dizzy."

"Save that history for later, Hepsy, and let me give you refreshment in the house that should be yours. Though Master Holditch has put me in charge, so must I acknowledge your authority here as its mistress."

"'Tis kind."

"'Tis just."

The following morning, when Miles and Hepsy awoke to the warm, accidental touch of each other, fresh words were picked carefully, each lover unsure what their reunion meant, where it was leading. Miles had fed her, let her luxuriate in his attempt to reassure her that she was safe, that whatever had happened to her to paint that careworn mask on her beautiful face, as he remembered it, was now a distant memory. Exhausted, yet still recalling their secret kisses in the lane, their tender words smothered by the need to ensure that Mattie did not hear them in Toller's cottage, Hepsy rested her lips against his back.

"Eggs," he muttered. "Earn your keep, girl?"

"No," she replied. "Not yet. Not till you have convinced me that this is no dream, that I am in my home again."

Miles eased away from her ticklish breath, and turned to her.

"You are home, Hepsy."

"There is Redvers."

"I will tell him."

"And you will let me stay, knowing what I told you, last night?"

Miles could tell by the height of the sun that he had awoken later than usual. Already he should have taken his collie he had heard scratching at the front door into the fields to check the sheep were all there, that none had been snatched by a fox. Then he should have collected the eggs.

"Stay, and never leave. Tonight, I will tell you the rest of my story, which I must not conceal."

"It sounds as if you have saved this chapter till the end for a reason. 'Tis something that troubles you, your furrowed brow suggests."

Hepsy smoothed the lines with her fingertips, and he closed his eyes.

"Will you fetch the eggs, dear?" he asked when she stopped. "If the Master comes, neither of us will have a home."

Hepsy did not move; still tired from her journey, the day before, it was physical weakness rather than a battle of wills that kept her in the warm bed.

"But Miles, all that I have told you has made me a rag doll."

He swung his legs over the edge of the bed, scratched his head, and, looking over his shoulder at her, said, "Not a rag doll, last night."

The pillow, when it struck him, exploded, and the down and feathers floated and fell like the snow that had bound them together, a long time ago.

Hepsy laughed for the first time in ages, then cried.

"I'll go," said Miles, when he had cuddled her.

After he had gone to the fields, burping, Hepsy went into the garden, sought out the clump of chives growing against one of the farmhouse walls, and cut the shoots close to the ground.

"A tasty dinner he shall have, as did father. I shall chop these finely, fry them for the pot."

Meanwhile, Miles knelt to examine the collapsed and panting lamb, by the hedgerow. The shadows of the passing cart flashed through the gaps: shade, light, shade, light, slowly. He paid no attention to the voices, intent instead on saving what he suspected was a dying animal. He lifted it, but after a bout of futile writhing in his arms, the lamb became limp, twitched, and died. By Miles' side, the ewe stood still.

"One last smell?" said Miles, but the sheep turned away, went to find the other lamb with a similar marking.

After she had fried the chives, Hepsy returned to the garden, rummaged in the long grass for mushrooms. Knowing all the best places, she began to fill her basket, was comforted by the familiar way they gave in to her pinches as she plucked and popped them into the pile.

The snort of a horse startled her, and she looked towards the lane, shielding her eyes from the sun. The man stepped down.

What do they want? she wondered. Miles, no doubt.

The man saw Hepsy, and came to the gate.

"Miles Yondover be in, if 'tis Dugdale Farm?" he called.

"Yes and no. He be working in the fields somewhere. Who asks for him?"

Then the woman stepped forward, appraised Hepsy, and saw that, though her looks suggested a recent trouble, her beauty had not totally faded.

"I be Jessie Bradpole."

"And I be Hepsy Valence."

"And what be you here?" asked the man. "I must be blunt, and say we have come to see him over a grave matter, and will not leave till he has heard what we have to say."

His tone was as threatening as his facial expression.

"Then will you come in?" offered Hepsy.

"We will wait here," snapped the man, "and shall hear, from his own mouth, why he left my poor daughter, his fiancée, without a word. One minute, he be roasting a pig, the next, he disappears. 'Twas only the slip of a merchant's tongue in Bridport led me here."

"Fiancée?" gasped Hepsy.

"Yes," confirmed Jessie, "though 'tis plain he has told you nothing of our plans. And he hab run away like a coward, and must pay his dues."

It was then that Hepsy fainted, and the mushrooms spilled out of the basket, and into the overgrown grass.

Jessie leaned over her, saw the ghastly face as white as monumental alabaster.

"Why, father!" Jessie cried. "We have killed her with our words, which had too sharp a blade for one who merely picks mushrooms."

Chapter thirty-two.

The numbness gripping Toller on his return to Misterton Manor froze his face into a death mask. Several times, he had touched it, searched for those features he now assumed he had inherited from Forston Sampford, who had claimed him, in his dying hours, as a son. They are there, he said to himself, and so he must be right. Why else would a man breathing his last reveal himself to me, a humble farmer, and pass on all that he possesses?

Miranda noticed Toller's changed appearance, and ushered him into a chair in front of the fire.

"Whatever is to your advantage has robbed you of the smile I had succeeded in coaxing from you prior to your departure. Come, Toller, share the misery moulding your face so," she urged. "I had expected good news."

"I am not the man you think me," croaked Toller.

"Then who are you, dear? For you be about the same height as when I last saw you, and hab the same colour hair and eyes. Your voice, though, lacks life. 'Tis perhaps the long journey?"

"Tease me not, Miranda. Though I be Burstock by name, I be Sampford by a father who left me, on his death-bed, all his worldly goods and property. A pretty penny, says Mr. Lockington, who oversees the will."

Miranda held his head to her breast, and he felt its warmth bringing him back to life.

"You never knew this Sampford?"

"Yes, and he was the worst of men that ever lived. My mother never hinted, and my father, the one who looked after me, all those years, treated me as a true son. Never a moment passed when I thought them not my real parents."

"Dearest Toller," said Miranda, kneeling by his side, "all of us come from a past, or a slice of one, we know little or nothing about, including me. You and I have much in common. I, too, have two fathers. My first adopted me, believing me left all alone in the world when my mother died, but he felt that I should know who my true father was. He be Nicholas, who never gave up his search for me. Your Forston Sampford hab kept a watchful eye on you, all these years, and never gave up on you, either. 'Tis passing strange, dear, but we are bound together by those men, and I shall be here for you – always. It may seem odd now, but, in time, you will accept what has happened, just as I did. Let me fetch you some tea and cake, and then I will tell you what Zenobia Godmanstone has been up to, and how, literally, a matter of life and death compels us to act urgently."

Then the door opened.

"Why, 'tis Toller!" cried Charlotte, entering with a tray, and saving Miranda the effort to go to the kitchen herself.

"Well, blow me down as if I were a flimsy stook!" followed Michael. "'Tis good to see 'ee, though 'ee hab the face of a man who took the boat from Weymouth and not the coach from Dorchester, after all!"

When pleasant words had been exchanged between Toller and Charlotte and Michael, Miranda sat and listened to Toller as he tried to describe, between mouthfuls of sweet apple cake, his feelings about the letter he had read in Lockington's office.

"And was he sincere, or did he merely acknowledge you were his son out of a sense of duty?" asked Miranda.

"Though I detested the very sight of him, as he lurched along the lane, I admit that the words in the letter were full of genuine regret, though there were no details about his relationship with my mother."

"'Tis so delicate a matter that 'twould be harmful to you both if your dying memory reeked of hatred."

"You are wise as well as beautiful."

"And are you now rich?"

"He had money, according to Lockington, though where it came from I have no idea. But let us change the subject, which hangs like a leaden sky over my soul. Come, tell me what matter requires our immediate action. I had not thought to see Miss. Godmanstone ever again."

"She does much work to help the unfortunate, particularly women, but the case in question relates to a man whom she has visited, and who has confessed to shooting dead the drayman whose place you took at Durnovaria Brewery. He refuses to say why he did it, claiming it matters not. This silence condemns him to the gallows, when there be a public feeling that Dorchester should be humane, and confine him instead to a lifetime in prison."

"He will say nothing?"

"No. He hab a wish to die rather than explain. Tomorrow the baying mob will pack around him to hear the bang of the trapdoor, the crack of his neck, and his gasps. 'Twill be a late Christmas present that will send him to the Lord."

"Christmas present?"

"He shot him, one Christmas, before he went overseas, and when he returned, his conscience weighed so heavily that he arranged for his own funeral."

Toller bit his lip, and his blood ran cold.

"He was a soldier?"

"Yes. Will you say to the Judge what he will not? You see, I know you met him, being a conjuror."

"Titus Chettle is the man?"

"'Tis certain."

"The dead man took Titus' sweetheart while Titus was away, fighting for Queen and country. But tell me, dearest, is there anything you do not know about me? As a conjuror, have you looked into all the grimy corners of my life? If so, say. I understand what true shame is."

This time, Miranda bit her lip, and nodded.

"You would save him?" she asked, at length.

"I will say what he told me."

"Then, come. We must go now. Zenobia's march and protest will be doused by the police. Once you tell the Judge the real reason Chettle shot the man, he may commute his sentence."

"They will not believe me. It is a long time ago. They will think it a ruse, wonder why I only come now with what I know."

"'Tis a chance we must take, for the gallows are erected and guarded, and only a noose and the guilty man are missing."

"He kept his word, and I kept mine, one year exactly after our first meeting. That be worth something, in this world: a promise made and kept. This be the one thing I will do, with the best intentions, that may have a worthwhile ending!"

"Except marrying me!" added Miranda.

Around the gallows, the crowd – *my army*, as Zenobia liked to think of them – maintained a silent vigil broken only by muttered prayers. She wandered amongst them, the curious, the bloodthirsty, the homeless, the compassionate, placing a comforting hand on the shoulders of the most distressed, whispering brave words of encouragement, of hope that all was not yet lost. And the police looked down on them imperiously for a sign that they were about to storm the gallows.

Inside the police station, Miranda and Toller asked the Sergeant if they might see the Judge, who had sentenced Titus Chettle, on a most important matter.

"He don't live here, or at the court, for he travels far and wide, pronouncing on life and death. Such is his work," he told them.

Miranda was undaunted by this news, and said, "I have brought this man, Toller Burstock, who was with Titus Chettle only moments before Chettle shot Arthur Abbott."

The Sergeant eyed Toller suspiciously, and asked, "And did you see Chettle pull the trigger?"

"No, but we promised to meet up again, in one year's time."

"But why?"

"He was on his way to a troop ship, to fight. We were two strangers who exchanged a few words at a lonely time, had already parted and were out of sight of each other when the shots rang out."

The Sergeant scratched his head, and said, "I fail to see why you have come. Your evidence, which seems to me as flimsy as a cobweb, can have little relevance *after* the trial."

"Tell him!" begged Miranda. "Tell him about the girl."

"Always a girl," sighed the Sergeant. "But the fact remains that he has admitted to shooting the man. There's no arguing with that."

"But Chettle told me that he had shot Abbott, as Abbott had stolen the woman he wanted to marry."

"In a rage of jealousy, he took revenge. Surely, we are all capable of crimes of passion if the circumstances conspire. This man was pushed beyond endurance. We must find the Judge. He might, even at this late hour, commute the sentence if he has new evidence. Chettle fought for his country, and should not hang for an offence committed under unbearable duress. Do you know what war does to a man? Lock him up for the rest of his natural life, but, for his sake, do not hang him," begged Miranda.

"Can you send someone to fetch the Judge? Does he not stay to see his dirty work done?" added Toller.

After some moments of silent reflection, the Sergeant said, "I will send word to The King's Arms, but if he has left, I have no power to delay the hanging. Now, give me some peace, or your news can have no sway with him."

Miranda and Toller joined the others at Gallows Hill, where the stage had been built to a height to permit all to see the proceedings. Zenobia grabbed Toller by his shoulders, and said, "Did you tell him?"

Toller explained what had happened, that the Judge in whom the power to stop the hanging resided was being looked for, that very moment.

Langton brought two lamps for his sister, and candles, which he distributed to the others. In the darkness, the flames of the candles swayed in the light breeze, and the lamplight throbbed.

"They are ghastly," he said, looking up at the policemen, who maintained their position.

Zenobia shuddered, and said, "They would, no doubt, say they are merely following orders, but in this weak light, I see that they, too, suffer a kind of death, a discarding of their humanity at the part they play in securing Titus Chettle's fate."

"I fear this delay means that the Judge has already left his lodgings, and that they are searching for him," Toller whispered to Miranda. "Can you look into his heart, and see if there is a chance of a reprieve?"

Miranda sighed, and said, "The Knowledge comes only when it is ready. Do not burden me, dearest, with an expectation I will sometimes not meet."

Then there was movement on the steps leading to the gallows.

"'Tis the hangman. I hab seen him before, could never forget the spring in his step as he climbs to do his duty," a woman cried. "He has the gait of a soulless executioner."

"Then it is surely time," said Langton. "There is no reprieve, and we are helpless."

The policeman to whom the hangman had spoken watched him retreat down the steps, and disappear. The others guarding the gallows gathered to listen to what had been said, relaxed their aggressive posture, and descended, too.

"I am sure they have gone to fetch Titus Chettle!" cried Zenobia. "His life will soon be snuffed as easily as these candles."

There then arose a wailing from the crowd, and a man was heard to shout, "Get on with it! I want to get home to my bed!"

It was an hour before anyone else appeared at the gallows. Their arrival was heralded by the church bells chiming midnight. The onlookers pressed more closely to the stage, as if trying to obstruct the six men pushing through the human barrier.

"Shame on you all!" cried Zenobia. "No human being should be put to death in this way!"

She stood defiantly in the front man's way. In his hands, he held a box of tools, which Zenobia failed to see in the crush.

"Get out of my way, and let me do my job," the man said, pushing her.

Langton immediately sprang at the man, and shouted into his face, "Keep your hands to yourself, or you shall have me to deal with."

"The law must take its course. We all have to live by the rule of law."

"But hanging this man will not bring back his victim," argued Langton.

"I agree," said the man, "but my job baint to hang a man but to put up and take down these gallows, which me and my men 'ere are being prevented from doing. We have instructions, and there baint going to be no hanging, be what I'm told. So if all you good volk got homes to go to, I suggest you let us pass so we can take down the scaffolding."

Miranda grasped Toller's hand, and squeezed it nervously.

"The Judge has been found?" whispered Toller, not daring to think that his evidence had changed the Judge's mind.

"It appears so," said Miranda.

"Then let these men pass!" commanded Zenobia. "Titus Chettle is saved. These men have come to remove the scaffolding."

The crowd was too baffled to rejoice as they would have liked, but parted miraculously as the biblical Red Sea, and the men set about dismantling the gallows.

Zenobia hugged Miranda, then Toller.

To the latter, she said, "If you had been in any other place, in any other time, you would not have heard the truth. At the brewery, we parted in a most unfortunate way, Toller, but you are a good man. I have no doubt of that."

"And will make an even better husband," added Miranda.

Zenobia did not, at first, understand what Miranda was saying, but in the weak lamplight saw a smile, which explained matters.

"Then you are to marry?" said Zenobia. "This is truly a night to remember!"

And as the workmen's noise increased, the vigil dissolved, and all went to their beds, most not quite comprehending how they had helped to save Titus Chettle from the noose.

The following morning, Miranda awoke early, considering that it had been in the early hours that she and Toller had arrived home in the trap. It was not, however, the events in Dorchester that preoccupied her, but the realisation that she had to tell her father that she and Toller were going to be married. She was sure he would not judge her; in fact, he had once remarked that, though Toller sometimes left Misterton Manor on matters more than was usual, he always came back relatively quickly, which was more than he himself had done when he had left Ruth, Miranda's mother.

The best time of day was early morning, when his mind was at its sharpest. In the afternoon and evening, it would be elsewhere: in the hidden vales of the past, down wriggling country lanes, righting wrongs.

Once, Miranda had asked him, "Father, where do you go when

you look out towards the hills? You stand there so still I think you must have locked your bones, betimes."

"Go?" he had replied. "Why, I go to faraway places, where my legs will never carry me again, where your mother and I went, or intended to go."

"And do you wish me to take you there?"

Nicholas had shaken his head.

"No need, for I am there all the time, and she is alive as ever again. Our time was too short together."

So Miranda decided to tell him straight after breakfast. She joined him on his little walk – more a stuttering limp – to the copse.

"Father, Toller and I will be married in Stinsford, within the month, and you will be by my side, all the way down the aisle, if your legs agree," she said, after she had linked her arm with his. "What say you?"

"What say I? I say 'tis but a short aisle."

"To our wedding!"

Miranda squeezed his arm.

"I say the aisle be short, as be marriage if one or both of 'ee don't take care. Marriage be like riding a willful horse: you don't grip the reins tight, you fall off. And 'tis my belief that a trot be safer than a gallop!"

"Wise words we would be wise to heed. But you do not object to Toller as a son-in-law?"

Nicholas said, "'Taint I who be marrying him."

"But I love him dearly, as I do you, and we shall live here together, for ever and a day."

"'Twill be different when you are married. You won't want your bent and clackety father around, slurping at the dinner table, or falling asleep, a-snoring like a pig, all the time."

"So that is it: you're worried about how it will affect you?"

Nicholas bowed his head.

"Don't want to be a burden, that's all."

"Stay," ordered Miranda, "and I shall fetch Toller himself, who will make the matter as plain as can be."

Miranda hastened to the house, but had to delay her business when she saw Langton and Zenobia Godmanstone stepping down from their trap.

"Oh, Miranda!" cried Zenobia, rushing to her friend, and hugging her desperately. "It has all come to nothing."

Miranda wiped the tears from Zenobia's cheeks, and said, "Come inside, and you, too, Langton, where you can tell me what distresses you so."

Zenobia tried to control her sobbing, but it was impossible, and so it was Langton who told Miranda the bad news.

"Our interpretation of the taking down of the gallows was wrong, I'm afraid. They were removing that infernal machine because it would not be needed on account . . ."

But Miranda was listening to Toller talking to her father in the very spot she had left him. She heard him say, "And you and I will come out here, when Miranda and I are married, and we will watch the bats circle that tree as if they were attached to it by an invisible thread."

"'Tis certain," said Nicholas, fighting back the tears.

Langton noticed her remoteness, and said, "Are you listening, Miranda? I said it would not be needed because Chettle has hanged himself with his belt from the bars of his cell window."

Miranda felt faint, and had to sit down.

"And now must I tell Toller," she said wearily. "And the Judge was found?"

"Yes," said Langton.

"And he would have saved him from hanging?"

Langton shook his head, and said, "We called to visit Chettle, this morning. 'Twas then we learned of his suicide."

"And he knew of a possible reprieve?"

"No. As far as he was concerned, he was going to swing from a noose, one way or another."

Outside, Nicholas took Toller's hand, and said, "You have my blessing, as long as you promise to take better care of her than me."

"That is my intention, Nicholas, my very best intention."

Chapter thirty-three.

Redvers Holditch thought seriously about the ultimatum Theresa Marshwood had given him. Both had once considered themselves promised to each other, but Theresa could never live in such rural isolation at Dugdale Farm, and feared that all the marauding, biting insects she imagined lived there would make her life a misery. Yet when Redvers reflected on their time together, he recalled neither a moment when he had actually proposed to her, nor an acceptance, real or otherwise. Somehow, their initial introduction to each other had sparked mutual attraction, which had been encouraged by friends and associates, and had changed into a belief that they were committed to each other. However, the absence of visible proof, such as a ring or a date written in the vicar's diary, emboldened him to call upon her, and release her from the delusion from which they had both been suffering.

He surprised himself. Words flowed easily. He sensed she knew they had been fermenting like strong cider, and her pretence of being shocked and devastated hastened his parting from her.

Yet his acquisition of the farm, after an early blooming of shock and excitement, eventually made him realise that he would never make a farmer. As for a sister he never knew he had, he had resigned himself to being out of her life for ever, until, one day, he paid a visit to Dugdale Farm, at the written request of Miles Yondover, who had risen to the challenges of being a farm manager well, and had grown herds of cattle and flocks of sheep. The letter Miles had sent had been a request to discuss taking lambs to market, yet its real purpose, Redvers discovered, was somewhat different.

Miles began their conversation after he had provided cider and blue vinney, and Redvers listened, and eventually said, "So you wish to know if your marrying Hepsy would affect your position here?" summarised Redvers. "Not at all. As you know, my business is the manufacture of sails for boats and ships. Oh, I would be quite happy to take what profit you can make for me here, but I'm now inclined to choose a different path. I think I shall now return the farm to Hepsy, as a sort of wedding present. She should have inherited this place. I imagine she has told you all, by now?" Miles nodded, slightly embarrassed. "Ebenezer decided he ought to do right by me, and not the daughter who had looked after him. But where is Hepsy? I know her only as someone I have felt I have wronged through no fault of my own. It was avarice born of leading a life of business that clouded my judgment when I accepted the farm, but it must be hers again."

"There be one thing, sir, and that be that Hepsy don't know I asked you to come so's I could explain the wedding in person. On top of that, your gift of the farm might tilt her, her never imagining, I suppose, that it would be hers again."

But Miles did not know that Hepsy had returned from her errands in Beaminster, and had spotted Redvers' trap. She had listened to their conversation behind the door, and her heart began to beat so loudly she feared it might alert them to her presence.

"I see," said Redvers.

"There be one thing, sir, that makes me ask you to be kind in manner to her, and that be that she was set upon in Bridport – oh, 'twas quite a while ago now – and that her drunken attacker died in the struggle. A man passing through saved her, but 'twas *his* knife that finished him off. 'Tas taken its toll on her, 'tis certain. She came back here when they arrested someone who admitted to the stabbing, and I took her in."

"And were you already acquainted with her?"

Miles blushed, and said, "In a manner of speaking. 'Tis a long time ago, and it won't do for either of us to go upsetting her."

"And you knew our father?"

"I tried to save him in a great snow storm, but I could not find him, and 'twas too late."

"I'm sure you did your best."

Miles stayed silent, had never rid himself of his feeling of guilt at his mistaking his left from his right.

Hepsy then opened the door. For a fleeting moment, she thought she saw her father's lines in Redvers' face, his upright bearing, and wide shoulders. 'Tis true he is my brother, she instinctively acknowledged to herself.

As they looked at each other, they both saw what connected them, recognised that moment as defining, as the one where the past becomes indisputable, and would paradoxically and necessarily end their short association.

"Miles has told me your good news, and I can now say – though I did not know it till now – that I have learned more about myself than that I have two fathers. Dugdale Farm will be made over to you again. It should never have come to me. And you can have Toller Burstock's fields, too."

Hepsy did, indeed, tilt, but recovered to accept his offer, and to picture herself again as the undeniable mistress of what she had always believed was hers.

One day, when the light was so pure that it appeared that the landscape had been washed thoroughly in the night, Toller rose early, and took the trap to Cerne Abbas. On the way, he rehearsed what he would say, trying different inflections to avoid the wrong impression.

There he found the cramped, thatched cottage in which Mattie now lived with Roddy, Nightingale, and Mrs. Cattistock. Mattie had left her job at Evershot Farm; Roddy had promised that they would be married, and had persuaded her that his mother, too, wanted her to come, so that she would have some female company, and, of course, her very own granddaughter to cherish.

"Will her eyes frighten me?" Mattie had asked, as they neared the cottage.

"She is blind, that's all. But tell me, Mattie, are you sure this is what you want? She has only me. It will be a big sacrifice for you, living with her," Roddy had said.

"I am sure. Give us all time to get to know each other."

From a distance, Toller saw Roddy chopping wood. There, too, was Mattie with him, taking advantage of the chance to be out of the gloomy house.

"'Tis dark inside," she complained. "Maybe 'tis the lack of light which made your mother blind. I would like, one day, to live in a bigger house, where Nightingale can run about freely."

Roddy stopped the rhythmic swinging of the axe, and piled the logs against the side of the cottage.

"I, too, would like to move, but 'tis this I feared all along: that a life here with mother would not be good enough for you. I don't want you feeling like a chicken trapped in a wire coop, looking at an outside world that would be forever denied you. We are never going to be Lord and Lady Dewlish."

Then Roddy saw Toller approaching.

"Why, 'tis Toller Burstock!" said Roddy.

"You know him?"

"I do. 'Tis he who told me where to find you again."

"And how did he know I was at Evershot Farm?"

"I've no idea."

As Toller neared, he noticed changes in Mattie: a fuller face but fewer lines in it, an ease of movement as she picked up Nightingale, and gently swung her through the air as if she were, indeed, a bird.

"My sister," said Toller, taking her shoulders, at arm's length.

"Brother Toller, this be Nightingale."

"You have forgotten that I have already seen her?"

Mattie reddened.

Roddy looked questioningly at Mattie.

"Toller looked after me, after our . . . wedding day."

"Looked after you?"

Toller came to her rescue.

"Mattie be my adopted sister. She lived in my cottage for a year, while I was searching for someone."

Puzzled, Roddy shook his head.

"'Tis passing strange."

Just then, Mrs. Cattistock emerged from the cottage, breathed in deeply the fresh air.

"We have a visitor whose voice I have heard before," she said.

"A man who brings Nightingale a present," said Toller.

"A present?"

"A cottage, a farm, fields on which you, Roddy, might graze sheep and cows till Nightingale is old enough to decide if she wants to manage the farm herself."

Mattie asked, "And who's be this farm?"

"Mine now, though it belonged to a man who helped to bring Nightingale into the world."

"Mattie?" said Roddy, when he saw a shadow darken her face.

"Forston Sampford?"

"The very same, the man who has left me all he possessed."

"But why?"

"Because I am his son."

It was Miles who told Hepsy that the man who had admitted to murdering her assailant had been freed. There had been a violent altercation, witnessed by several people, but the confessor, a well known, habitual drinker, had confused his intention to kill him with *actually* killing him. He supposed, when police arrived, after witnesses had reported their drunken struggle, that he must have done it. Indeed, he was quietly pleased that he had won the day in such a definitive way. He signed his statement, and the law assumed that he must know whether or not he had done the deed.

His release, however, came when it was noticed that there were no signs of a struggle on his body: bruises, cuts, scratches, swellings. Nor was there blood on his clothes. After several days of incarceration, no clear memory of the murder began to undermine his initial conviction that he was the murderer. It was only when he remembered the names of several drinking companions, with whom he was safely ensconced in an inn on the night in question, was he able to provide an alibi for the police. Yes, he had cursed the dead man, had roared that he would see him in his grave, but he had not actually killed him.

And poor John Trevelyan must live in fear and hiding, all because of me, and I, too, must live expecting a knock at the door, when it is known that I have returned to Marshwood Vale, reflected Hepsy.

"Why, you hab become a ghost!" remarked Miles. "A bad man is dead. It could have been you breathing your last. And the story be, in the Western Mail, that a man has owned up to what really happened. No action is being taken. Seems the man was scared to show his face, at first, but the police accepted his version: that in the struggle, the dead man fell on a blade."

"Thank God!" Hepsy cried. "I don't mean to take the Lord's name in vain, but my and poor John's suffering has ended."

"Think no more of it, Hepsy. We have both had narrow escapes: you from a drunken sot, and me from a woman I never loved."

"Remember the Harbest Festival? I was there, too, my face obscured by a hood. A fortune-teller, I was, and Jessie learned from me that you loved another, that she and her fiancé would never marry. There you were, turning the hog over the fire. I passed within a few feet of you."

"But why did you not speak to me? It was you I was thinking of."

"I decided that if I could not have you, at least I could try and make her doubt you."

"A fortune-teller!" laughed Miles. "So tell me, gypsy girl, what our fortune be now."

"Cross my palm with silver," teased Hepsy.

Miles did so, and she whispered in his ear.

Hugo Lockington paid the woman who had cleaned his house thoroughly from top to bottom.

"Why, 'tis passing generous of you, sir," she said, as she put the money into her purse.

"You've done a fine job. Now, come back in two weeks' time, when I shall have need of you again."

The woman curtseyed and left, and was careful to look around her warily for anyone who might steal her wages.

Lockington watched her from behind a curtain, then sat down in his scroll-winged chair, pleased that he had ended his neglect of the house.

I have all this, he mused: fine furniture, a library, and a good income, yet my life is somehow incomplete. I put into order the lives of others, spend each day, come drizzle or shine, doing so, but all I have to show are material possessions. So my search for a more fulfilled life begins today.

His thoughts were interrupted by knocking at the door. From behind the curtain, he could see the well dressed, young man he had invited.

"Rupert Forde," the man said, removing his hat. Then he consulted his pocket watch, and added, with a generous smile, "Fifty seconds early!"

Lockington ushered him in, took his visitor's coat, and showed him into his study.

"I shall call you Forde, but think me not too formal. Our business is of a professional nature, and these things matter."

"Indeed, they do. They do, indeed."

"Then let us address immediately the purpose of you coming. As you know, I am looking for a partner to relieve me of some of my case workload, which has been so considerable that I have had little time to enjoy life as I would wish. You understand, I am sure."

"Indeed, I do. I do, indeed."

"I have read your references, which are exemplary. If you don't mind my saying, I wonder you have not secured a similar position before now, perhaps in London, where the law is everywhere."

"I have been waiting for the best opportunity, which is what I consider this to be."

"You see, my salary is entirely dependent upon the sharpness of the grim reaper's scythe. You are fully conversant with the law regarding wills and codicils?"

"I am, indeed, sir. Indeed, I am. You can rely on me to manage a caseload which will permit you to enjoy those aspects of life which have hitherto escaped you."

"Then, I shall welcome you as my partner just as soon as I have drawn up a contract. If we find that we are not suited to each other, we shall part with severance terms agreeable to us both."

"Then I accept your offer, and ask only that you confirm my starting date as soon as you are able. Forde and Lockington. We shall be a splendid partnership."

"Lockington and Forde," corrected Lockington. "I will, of course, remain the senior partner."

"Indeed, you will, sir. You will, indeed."

Forde's propensity to reverse the first parts of sentences in the second began to cause Lockington a little annoyance, but Lockington had a bigger reason to usher Forde out quickly. A client would soon be arriving at his office, and it was quite a brisk walk there.

"Then await the contract," said Lockington, shaking Forde's hand, and guiding him off the premises.

Slightly out of breath, Lockington welcomed his client into his office, where the client explained the reason for the visit. Matrimonial matters were not his forte, Lockington explained, but the law was everything, and what he did not know, he could learn.

After a moment or two of profound consideration, he said, "I have never been married, or engaged, and would advise you not to seek revenge for what appears to be a natural human response to a change in affections."

"I am most grateful for your advice, but there must be justice," said his client.

"Where there is genuine incompatibility, it is rarely worth pursuing the matter in court. The courts are slow and costly, and you are by no means certain to be compensated."

"So what do you suggest now?" asked Theresa Marshwood. "I wanted to take the wind out of Redvers' Holditch's sails, in more ways than one, but I shall sleep on it."

"An admirable idea. There is, of course, no charge for this initial consultation."

His client half-insisted on paying, smiled, and left.

Lockington said to himself, when he was once again alone, I wonder Holditch did not marry her. She has a pretty face, but is scornful of him. Though I am married to the law, I, like the rest of men, have been lured from my senses by a pretty face, only to be discarded. Occasionally, I hear her voice from the summer which brought us honeyed happiness, and then I hear her talking to me as if I were a child, explaining that our love had soured like cream left too long unused. And so I chose a more compliant wife. The law puts dinner on the table, a roof over my head, and only occasionally answers back. Damn it all, I shall write to Forde and revoke my decision. In a moment of weakness, Hugo Lockington, Notary, nearly threw away his practice.

He picked up his pen, and wrote to Rupert Forde.

"I am Hugo Lockington, Notary," he said brightly, when he had signed his letter. "I make and break lives, and in doing so, block out the hurt."

Chapter thirty-four.

Nicholas had wrapped himself up in the scarf Maisie had knitted for him when they had been living in his mother's cottage on the heath. Strangely, in the air cold enough to turn his breath white, he could smell Ruth on it, especially her hair and skin. She used to wash, when it was the time of year, in bowls of water and crushed honeysuckle and rose petals, and continued to do so long after he had gone, in the hope that his nose would find her again, by some curious power of memory or imagination.

Sent out by Miranda to keep an eye on him, Michael watched him from a distance.

"Don't want him getting lost or falling over on today of all days," she had said.

"Don't 'ee fret, Miss. Miranda. I shall make sure he be ready for two o'clock, though the sky be that grey white that carries snow in it," Michael had pointed out.

"Then 'tis just as well my brother Seth and Aunt Emily came yesterday."

"'Tis always a risk, a winter wedding, though a pretty if there be just a coating."

Nicholas muttered to himself, "Too cold to shave, even if my daughter wish it. 'Taint me she be marrying."

He examined spiders' webs made visible by frost, and enjoyed the crisp crunch of the grass underfoot. Whenever he moved, Michael followed, at a safe distance, as a collie a sheep that needs bringing down from the top field.

Toller was tending to a horse in the stables, running the flat of his hand down between the horse's ears to the nose.

"And 'twas 'ee got me into this little scrape!" laughed Toller. "If you hadn't bolted, your mistress would never have dropped the book I then returned."

It was important to him to keep the day normal, until the time when he must take a bath, and put on his wedding suit. Miranda had given him instructions. Somewhere in his head, he was re-running the conversation he had had, the day before, in the estate workers' dormitory.

"And 'ee have made your bed up, just as you always do, even though 'tis for the last time," had said Sydling Chilfrome.

"I baint leaving the country!" Toller had said. "Will still come to work in these stables."

"*Master* Burstock soon," had said Toby Wanderwell, and Wynton Chedynton and Huish Peverell had looked at each other as if Toller's new position threatened the established order of things.

"Come Harbest, I shall drink you all under the table!"

And though he had meant every word, he sounded less certain on this cold wedding day, as if he, too, knew things could not stay the same. Even the horse looked at him distantly.

Miranda, Emily and Charlotte were busy laying out their dresses. Michael would take Toller and Seth in the trap, and return the short distance to fetch the bride and her entourage.

"Time we be going in, Master Nicholas," Michael said softly.

"You go in. Two more minutes. Got a daughter to give away if I remember rightly."

"Miss. Miranda said – "

"Two minutes," insisted Nicholas.

When Michael had gone, Nicholas breathed in deeply and, as he sobbed, said, "Our girl be wed today, Ruth. I know you be here somewhere. Can't change what been, dear. 'Twas too short a summer 'twixt us, and too soon a deathly winter. But I put things as right as I could. Do you hear me? I done things as well as I could. And you, Maisie: tekken from me, too. Both my wives been good ones, more than I deserved. But gone. There baint no more suffering left in me. My lamp is nearly spent, and soon all this will mean nothing. But Nicholas Misterton has one more job to do afore the flame be snuffed, and Miranda be a-waiting. Come, snow, if you be an uninvited guest, and do your worst, but you shall not have this day to yourself."

Later, when Toller looked at himself in the mirror, he was reminded of his appearance when Zenobia Godmanstone had dressed him up, at the tailor's, as what was meant to pass for a respectable debt collector.

"I cannot believe now that this is what I was prepared to do. 'Twas no improvement on shepherding," he said regretfully.

Nicholas, too, shook his head when he had put on his new attire.

"A new suit don't make me look any younger," he concluded. "Wavy hair, once coal black, still be frosty no matter what the cut and cost."

Langton Godmanstone helped his sister into the trap. Each had taken care to put on hats, scarves, and gloves, as well as their warmest coats.

"The sky can't hold the snow much longer. We may well find ourselves stranded in Stinsford church, where we shall perish," warned Langton.

"Always the optimist!" mocked Zenobia. "Come. We must not let Miranda down."

So Langton drove his horse urgently, so they would not be stuck in a lane, and miss the wedding.

All the workers gathered to see their master and mistress off. Toller had already said there would be food and drink for everyone, after the wedding, and so fiddles had been tuned, ready for the dancing. Fancy Laverstock and Lizzie Loscombe began to discuss what dress they would wear, and Fancy said, "Hark at we both, as if we had the pick of our mistress' wardrobe!" and Lizzie said, "I got a nice blue one, and I be saving it for this day, so's I can catch Sydling's eye, and I'll be flogged if 'twon't get me down the aisle with him." They both laughed, and Fancy thought that she herself would wed Toby, though Lizzie said she should avoid a man with a name like Wanderwell.

"And why be that?" asked Fancy.

"Why, he be likely to wander!" pointed out Lizzie. "Women want a man to chop wood, and say sweet things at the end of the day."

"And be that likely with any man on the estate? I think not."

They both collapsed into laughter, and said they would make do with the first they could put their hands on. However, neither knew that it was poor Wynton Chedynton who would have had either girl as a wife, and that he had as many sweet whisperings in his heart as they would like to hear.

Emily wrapped a cloak around Miranda. Feeling the cold herself, she then put on her own. Miranda shivered when she went outside to the trap. 'Tis my stubbornness for winter nuptials to blame, she reflected.

"And don't 'ee bump us out like sacks of turnips falling off!" said Charlotte to Michael.

"'Twill be here any minute, the snow, and we don't want Miss. Miranda to be all wet for the groom."

Nicholas was waiting in the graveyard. He had said a few words to his father and uncle, both buried there.

"And 'tis 'ee and not me who got the Knowledge passed down the family," had said Nicholas to his uncle, "and 'tis to be hoped that Miranda continues to use it wisely, as 'tis a help and not a hindrance."

Then Miranda arrived. Inside the church, Toller was waiting

patiently, and Reverend Mitchell was reassuring him that his bride-to-be would turn up. Toller explained that he had no doubt she would, that no one should be anxious about that.

Nicholas walked up the path to welcome his daughter at the gate.

"Father, your coat! You will catch a chill!" Miranda warned.

"Then come take your father's arm. Inside be a good man who waits to make 'ee a wife."

As she walked down the aisle, she smiled at Zenobia. A few rows behind those gathered – one or two from Stinsford had braved the plummeting temperature – sat a man on his own, his moustache hanging limply, but his eyes still bright under the brim of his hat, which he removed when Miranda drew level.

"Why, 'tis Mr. Hardy!" she whispered to her father.

"The writer," remembered Nicholas.

"The very same, though I wonder why his wife is not with him."

The service began, and Charlotte and Emily shed enough tears for the whole congregation. Even Michael gulped, once or twice. I have lived to see her married, he said to himself. She be the closest I'll ever come to a daughter of my own. One or two from Stinsford wondered why there was no one present from the groom's family, but one said, after Reverend Mitchell had declared them man and wife, "'Tis the way of things betimes, and 'taint for the likes as such as us to go asking questions."

During the ceremony, something had happened outside the church that all who were there would never forget. Snow began to fall, each flake trembling, rocking, fluttering, creating a haze, and distorting the true shape of the rectory and other cottages. The air was silent and still, and all the villagers came out to marvel at the slowly descending flakes the size of the palms of their hands. And when Sydling Chilfrome had suggested surprising Master Toller and Mistress Miranda by cheering them as they came out of church, the others, especially Lizzie and Fancy, had agreed, and put on their coats and set off at a brisk pace. Toby and Huish had taken their fiddles, and Sydling had passed to them a small bottle of brandy to make their fingers more nimble.

"'Tis to make sure your knuckles don't freeze!" he had explained.

The horse's blanket was now stiffening, and Lizzie stroked the horse, and said, "Not much longer to wait, then we can all go home."

Indeed, almost at the end of her last word, Toller and Miranda appeared.

"Why, Toller, look: snow!" cried Miranda.

Even through the snow, which blurred his vision, Toller was able to recognise who had come to see them.

"And a few from the estate," pointed out Toller.

Then the fiddles began, and Thomas Hardy recalled moments, many years before, when his father and the choir had played and danced on the flagstones by a warm hearth, at their cottage at Higher Bockhampton.

"Why, 'tis a wonderful sight!" exclaimed Charlotte. "And it don't seem a wink of an eye since you and me were meant to look after Master Toller in these very pews."

"It don't, indeed, girl. It don't, indeed."

"Come, Miranda. Let us get your father home, as though it be a sight to behold, he baint as young as we."

"First, let us thank those who have come to see us."

Lizzie began to clap her cold hands to the rhythm of the fiddlers' tune, and Fancy joined her, as did the others, till the churchyard was filled with such merry sounds that Mr. Hardy remarked that he would not be surprised if any one of those buried rose from their coffin and reappeared as a ghost to see why their eternal sleep had been disturbed.

"Thank you, one and all," cried Miranda, "but do not let this snow catch you out. Go home. There will be no work outdoors today."

Recalling how such a snowfall had taken the life of Ebenezer

Valence, and how he associated it with the beginning of a quest to start a new life, Toller said to them, "None of you must perish in this. Do as Miss. – or should I say Mrs.? – Miranda asks. This snow has the feel of *Dorset* snow, which buries the land and folk as if they were both the same. And back there, you can pick up your instruments again and dance away your numbness, and we will serve you food and drink till you sleep as if drowsed by a conjuror's potion."

They took little further persuasion, and saw that they should follow the sensible advice they had been given.

When Mr. Hardy bade the couple goodbye, Miranda enquired if Mrs. Hardy was well.

"Today she is indisposed. An ailment confines her to her room," Hardy explained.

"Thank you," said Toller.

"In a providential way, it is *I* who should thank *you*, whom I feel I know already," replied Hardy, before disappearing into the whiteness, as if he had become one of the ghosts he had imagined inviting themselves to the impromptu musical interlude.

The flakes settled on eyelashes as the well-wishers stooped into them. The snow had begun blowing at an acute angle, and, where the lane was exposed by a gate or a widening, in skittish eddies. No one talked, just looked to see if anyone was in difficulty, and took an arm when necessary. Soon, it was difficult to tell where they were, and it was only due to Michael making return journeys in the trap that they got back safely.

The fire in the hall blazed, and Miranda beckoned to them to approach it, but Toller warned, "Mind you don't get too close, or you'll get hot aches."

Great puddles formed on the stone floor, and only gradually did they realise how lucky they had been. Miranda, Emily, and Charlotte brought towels, and dry dresses for Lizzie and Fancy.

"And what were we talking about, earlier? Why, the pick of Mistress' wardrobe, no less!" whispered Fancy.

Toller took Miranda aside, and said, "They cannot eat alone in the barn in this cruel weather."

"But our table is not big enough for us all."

"We must not be heartless. They will get wet and cold again. They must not be miserable on a day when we should all be happy."

Miranda agreed.

So Toller announced that they could hold their celebration in the hall or kitchen, where there was a fire, and logs to keep them warm till the next day. But there was no immediate response. Then Huish Peverell broke the silence when enough knowing glances had been exchanged.

"'Tis kind of 'ee, Master, but we set out the tables in the barn earlier, this morning, and 'twon't take Sydling here long to spark some kindling for the logs. All that be wanting then be a barrel of cider and a pie or two, which Mistress hab already promised. And it be kind of 'ee, Mistress."

Huish looked at the others, and they muttered their support.

"Then so be it, though do not think you will get away with a pie or two!" said Miranda. "For there be suet pudding, tatties, and chicken, which will be golden in an hour. And then there will be apple cake and blue vinney, for 'tis our wedding day, and none shall go hungry or cold."

Sydling then spoke up.

"Thank 'ee, though what Huish forgot to add was that you and Master Toller be welcome to join us, once the bows and strings be acquainted right, so to speak, and the barn be smoky and warm."

"'Tis kind, Sydling, and when the time be right, we shall visit 'ee, and show 'ee that we reel as well as the best!" said Toller.

All went their various ways: the men to the barn, and Lizzie and Fancy to fetch the food from the kitchen. Charlotte organised everyone, and joined the wedding couple, Emily, Seth, Nicholas and Michael for their meal.

"Will 'ee make a speech?" asked Nicholas.

Seth looked at his father, then down at the table. Somewhere in the room, he sensed his mother, the font of tact, probably in a corner of the room, allowing others to have private conversations, as she always used to, when she knew she had not been there for that part of their life.

"Be words necessary, father?" said Miranda.

Toller looked at her.

"Things sometimes need saying," pressed Nicholas.

"Say them, then, Nicholas," encouraged Toller.

Seth looked at his sister.

"All I'm saying is that 'tis the custom," said Nicholas.

"'Tis certain, though we all know what we be to each other. Don't fit to say the obvious," concluded Toller, wanting to draw a line under the embarrassment.

Nicholas said, to alleviate the tension, "Legs be awake now. Time was when there was a queue to dance with me."

And they all laughed, relieved.

Later, when Emily had fallen asleep, and Seth had accompanied his father to the barn, where all had eaten and drunk so well that they had to rest before moving the tables and chairs to make room for dancing, Toller and Miranda found themselves alone.

"So, 'tis done," said Toller. "Married."

"Married. All your stuff in the house now?"

"My stuff be a small bag. Why so glum?"

"Not glum: tired."

"Then no dancing? No a-skipping and a-ducking, and a-weaving? No red cheeks? Come, dear. Even your father be over at the barn."

She smiled weakly.

"In a minute, though we must come back before we see things we ought not."

"We must not disappoint them. A dance or two, a toast to them, and then back to our bed."

"'Tis certain."

Outside, they walked in the snow falling like confetti from the night.

"No moon," said Toller.

"Snow," said Miranda.

Then, overcome by the realisation that, at last, he had found happiness, Toller pulled Miranda to him. And during those next few moments he had once thought he would never experience, a sequence of images and voices, of people he had met from Pilsdon to Misterton Manor, passed by, nodded, smiled or waved, and disappeared.

"Goodnight," said Nicholas, not stopping. "Mind you keep an eye on Seth, who hab drunk too much. He laughs like a crow."

"Goodnight, and mind your step."

"And you mind yours."

Toller kissed Miranda, and said, "I love you."

"And I love you."

The snow had thickened on the ground. Toller had waded through such depths before. There will always be a struggle to go forward, he now knew, when the lifting of one foot after another in pursuit of a dream seems almost impossible. But, he thought, I did what I could, and here I am: Master Toller Burstock of Misterton Manor. *Someone.*

Miranda squeezed his hand, knowing what he was thinking, loving him for those best intentions that had delayed their wedding day.

Toller opened the barn door. All the lamps and the fire were lit. The music and laughter ceased suddenly when they were spotted. They walked into the middle, where marks on the ground showed there had been dancing. They looked around at the revellers now silent and still.

Then Toby Wanderwell stepped forward, and said, "Why, 'tis Master Toller and Mistress Miranda!" Then he began to clap, slowly, at first, but then more quickly, and others joined in till Toller and

Miranda were lost in valleys and mountains of noise that could be heard at Pilsdon, and its ripples felt in all the fields and lanes of Dorset. The applause grew to a crescendo, then slowly died away, and in the silence of contentment and knowledge of what the future held for them, Miranda squeezed Toller's hand.